Everyone is talking about Maxym M. Martineau's

KINGDOM OF EXILES

"Keep an eye on Maxym M. Martineau. If I'm not mistaken, we have a bona fide genius in our midst."

—**Darynda Jones**, *New York Times* bestselling author

"Original, breathtaking, absolutely fabulous."

—**C. L. Wilson**, *New York Times* & *USA Today* bestselling author

"A fresh new fantasy. Left me with a happy sigh and a fervent wish for a beast of my own. Highly recommend!"

—**Jeffe Kennedy**, RITA award-winning author

"Maxym Martineau weaves an irresistible blend of adventure, magic, and romance. A unique world full of danger and intrigue and a delightful ensemble of characters will leave fans of fantasy romance breathlessly awaiting more. Prepare to be charmed!"

—**Amanda Bouchet**, *USA Today* bestselling author of The Kingmaker Chronicles

"*Kingdom of Exiles* captivated me with its distinctive fantasy world of exiled Charmers, enchanted beasts, and alluring assassins. A fantastic tale of magic, romance, and adventure—I can't wait to read more."

—**L. Penelope**, award-winning author of *Song of Blood & Stone*

"A strong female lead and a band of lovable assassins? Count me in! I cannot wait to see what more Maxym has to offer."

—**Alexa Martin**, author of *Intercepted*

ALSO BY MAXYM M. MARTINEAU

The Beast Charmer
Kingdom of Exiles
The Frozen Prince
The Shattered Crown

THE
SHATTERED
CROWN

MAXYM M. MARTINEAU

sourcebooks
fire

Published by Sourcebooks Fire, an imprint of Sourcebooks
P.O. Box 4410, Naperville, Illinois 60567-4410
(630) 961-3900
sourcebooks.com

Library of Congress Cataloging-in-Publication Data is on file with the publisher.

Printed and bound in the United States of America.
SB 10 9 8 7 6 5 4 3 2 1

For my children, Remmy and Ronin. May your lives be full of adventure, wonder, and love.

A PROPHECY OF FLAMES

*"Awoken of ruin and blood, to command
the skies and scorch the earth,*
Peace will return on the breath of his wing,
When a loving hand with the gift to break,
Offers their heart."

ONE

LEENA

Fragrant, charcoal-gray smoke curled toward the midmorning sky, twisting away from the crackling flames devouring the ceremonial white oak pyre. A tribute to those who'd passed in the wake of Yazmin's unexpected attack. Their individual funeral pyres had burned to ash days ago, but this? This would remain until the Crown of the Council called for the flames to be doused. Until *I* called for them to be doused.

Crown of the Council. It still didn't seem real.

Letting out a quiet sigh, I tore my gaze away from the flames to scan the open clearing. Crystalized dew clung to the dormant grass beneath my feet, and glimmering icicles dripped from the trees encircling Hireath. Winter was here, but it wouldn't stay for long. I'd missed the first frost of the season and the customary celebrations that came with it. We all had, in a way.

Had it only been a week since Yazmin unleashed fury on her own people? Ordered beasts to kill Charmers for the sake of some plan we didn't understand? Those who had died that day might have already moved on to the gods' realm, but the aftermath remained. There were no happy bestial calls competing with the crashing waterfall. No lull of conversation from Charmers wandering about their once peaceful city. It was all too...quiet.

Boots crunched against the grass behind me, and I turned toward the keep and the lone man approaching. "Gaige."

"Crown." He tipped his chin in a polite bow.

A smile touched my lips. "Not yet."

"In a matter of hours, you will be." His steel-blue eyes twinkled with a hint of mischief. Steady hands brushed along the signature liquid-mercury robes of the Council. He was polished and prepared to present himself—rather, present the new Crown—to his people. "Are you ready?"

"Yes."

A week ago, I'd balked at the idea of ruling. But now... I stared at the trees laden with houses and the keep standing tall against the mountain. Something warm, heady, and true brewed in my gut. Determination. This had been my home, and I'd do anything to protect it.

"Good." Gaige offered a knowing grin before turning away. "The others are already waiting. Let's get our affairs in order before the ceremony begins."

I fell into step beside him. "They're back?"

"Arrived just a few minutes ago." He nodded toward the monstrous tree just a short distance away. An arched opening large enough for six people to pass through shoulder to shoulder marked the entrance to our communal library. Stained-glass windows were fitted between knots in the bark, allowing sunlight to bathe the hollowed-out interior.

I'd never been to a Council meeting before. Aside from my inauguration into their ranks, I'd never gotten the chance. Even so, something told me this particular meeting would be unlike any they'd had previously.

The grass beneath our feet turned to moss as we passed through the threshold into the library. Heavy wooden tables littered the first floor, and shelves were arranged in a circular pattern, pressed firm against the trunk, and all packed full of books. A spiral staircase crawled upward, and muted conversation carried from an open landing a few stories up. My heart tightened as one voice, calm and collected, threaded through the rest.

Noc.

He, along with Calem, Kost, and Oz, had departed shortly after I'd recovered from Yazmin's attack. They'd left Cruor in the capable hands of Emelia, one of Noc's most trusted sentries, but with Yazmin on the loose, there was no telling whether the guild was safe. She just as easily could've attacked them, like she had her own people, while fleeing through the Kitska Forest. Not to mention, there was still the matter of Darrien.

My hands clenched into tight fists as I climbed the stairs a few steps behind Gaige. *Darrien.* He was no better than Yazmin, betraying his own family to get what he wanted. He'd failed to kidnap me and force Noc to relinquish his title as guild master—and the power to raise the dead that came with it—but I highly doubted he was done trying to exact his revenge.

When I hit the final stair and stepped onto the landing, a barking laugh from Calem shook me from my thoughts. He leaned against a bookshelf, lazy smirk on full display as he tilted his chin in silent hello. Kaori stood quietly beside him. Her lustrous black hair was done in an artful knot, and she traced the leaf pin holding it all together. The same pin she'd used to skewer her hand and offer Calem her blood, effectively saving his life.

Gaige had already seated himself at the round table beside Kost. Felicks, Kost's fox-like beast, had been dutifully sitting by his master's side. But at the sight of Gaige's open lap—and the folds of his mercury cloak that made for fantastic snuggling—he launched onto Gaige's thighs and turned in a series of circles before plopping down and closing his eyes. Gaige chuckled as Kost raised a brow at his beast, but he reached forward and scratched him beneath the chin just the same. Inaudible words passed between Gaige and Kost, and a foreign smile—relaxed and warm—claimed Kost's face. Gaige seemed to notice, too, and he tilted his head closer. When he was only a breath away from Kost's ear, he adjusted the fold of his collar and whispered something that turned Kost's cheeks red.

Kost pulled back with a visible swallow, and then made a show of clearing his throat before turning to Oz and Raven on his free side. He immediately engaged in a conversation with Oz, but my focus remained on Gaige's satisfied smirk. He met my eyes then, and his grin deepened.

Oz and Kost chatted quietly as Kost's embarrassment abated. Raven, on the other hand... The lightness I'd felt upon seeing my family dimmed. She was practiced in appearing bored—shoulders loose, one arm draped over the back of her chair, lips pursed. But a maelstrom of rage and pain brewed in her eyes. She'd just begun her courtship with Eilan, only for Yazmin to murder him during the attack on Hireath. We'd hardly spoken in the past few days, as she'd chosen to remain in her chambers and grieve privately.

Oz looked up and followed my gaze to Raven. His expression warmed, and he shifted in his seat, angling his broad shoulders Raven's direction. Voice low, he asked her something I couldn't hear. She blinked, some of the anger in her eyes fading, and then responded slowly. Kost nodded as he took in her words, and Oz shot me a knowing look before returning to their conversation.

My chest tightened at the sight. Oz. Always looking out for others. As I made a move to approach them, a gentle hand draped in wispy shadows gripped my waist. "Miss me?"

A tingling warmth surged through my limbs, and I turned, throwing my arms around my *anam-cara*. The last of those dark tendrils disappeared with his surprise greeting, and I nuzzled against his sternum before tilting my chin up to meet his gaze. My breath caught in my chest. His new appearance still startled me, but in the best kind of way. Shock-white hair. Intense, crystalline-blue eyes that tore right through me. Even the glass cut of his jaw. Everything about him was sharper, more defined, since the glamour that'd obscured his identity had been removed.

"Of course I did. What kind of question is that?" I rolled my lower lip into my mouth, biting back a laugh.

Lightly, he ran his knuckles along my cheek. "A silly one." He cupped my chin and pulled me in for a kiss that made my toes curl.

Beside us, Gaige cleared his throat. "Shall we get started, then?" Felicks perked up at his words and abandoned his lap, once again taking his place by Kost's side.

Unwillingly, I broke away from Noc's embrace, but lingered in his arms. "I suppose."

Noc's grin turned sinful before he dipped his head toward my ear, lips ghosting along my skin. "You can properly welcome me back later, in the privacy of your bedroom."

My stomach clenched as a burn crawled up the back of my neck. We'd only been apart for a handful of days, yet I ached to end this meeting before it even began just so I could take him up on his suggestion.

Before my body could betray me, I approached the table. We had important things to discuss, like my coronation as Crown. And the plans I had for our people. Plans I wasn't sure the Council would agree with.

We all took our seats, and for a moment I stilled. Charmers and assassins together at a Council meeting, eager and willing to ensure our people were protected. There was no hesitation, despite our different backgrounds. Which was good, because uniting was the only way we'd have a chance of taking down Yazmin. Hope, steady and warm, filled me as I sat beside Noc.

Maybe my plans would work. Maybe the Charmers would agree, if they saw Cruor was on our side.

Gaige shuffled the loose papers before him. "I hereby call to order the first Council meeting under our new Crown, Leena Edenfrell."

I raised a brow. "Almost-new Crown."

"Semantics." He waved his hand loosely before reclining in his chair, targeting me with his steely gaze. "First order of business—modifying our Council to include Noc, Kost, Ozias, and Calem. At least temporarily, while we deal with the current threat."

Everyone straightened in their chairs, curious glances darting from one person to the next.

Calem found his voice first. "Wait, what?"

"Is that really for the best? I don't want to cause an upset," Oz added, bracing his forearms on the table.

I shook my head. "Right now, our people need to see they're not alone. We've been told since the beginning of time that it's us against the rest of Lendria. We need to show them that's not the case."

"I see no problems with this arrangement," Kaori said, her soft voice full of quiet authority.

"Me neither." Raven drilled her fingers along the table, tension seeping out of her frame with every definitive tap.

"If Leena thinks this is the best way forward," Noc said, pulling my focus, "then we'll do it." He dropped his hand to my leg, giving it a tight squeeze of reassurance.

"Then it's done." Gaige dipped his quill into a nearby inkwell and jotted something down on a stray piece of parchment. A soft hoot sounded from the ceiling, but Gaige continued to write unperturbed. Between the leaves and branches that knit together like rafters, an owl with bark-like horns perched on a low-hanging limb. Actarius. The Whet had been trapped outside the beast realm when Celeste, the goddess of beasts, died.

Even though he'd use his powers to commemorate this moment, Gaige hadn't been the same since he discovered his memory had been wiped. He took notes all the time now, carrying spare scraps of paper in his pockets in case he needed to write something down on the go. It was as if he didn't trust his own memory anymore. As if writing somehow solidified the moment and eased the stiffness in his shoulders.

"What does this mean for Cruor?" Kost braided his fingers together, first looking at Noc before slowly allowing his gaze to drift back to Gaige.

"We're all equal in the eyes of the Council. Our threats are your threats and vice versa. Which means," Gaige said, quill tapping against parchment, "the Council won't hesitate to come to your aid, and you'll be expected to do the same."

"Our people, however, are another story," Kaori said.

"So we fight for them, but they don't fight for us?" Calem asked.

"Charmers haven't participated in any type of large-scale conflict since the First War," I said. "Give them time to see you're trustworthy, that you're part of our community now, and they'll come around."

"I'll fight whenever you need me." Raven's words were sharp. "I don't care who it is."

My stomach dropped at the same time Oz winced. The amount of pain Raven must've been in. I wasn't sure if succumbing to rage was the right path, but I needed her fearlessness. *We* needed it. If the Charmers saw how passionately she was willing to fight and confront injustice, then maybe they'd follow suit.

Gently, I placed a hand on her shoulder. "Raven…"

She shrugged it off. "What about Yazmin?"

My hand fell to the table, but I didn't pull away. I'd wronged her in my pursuit of the truth behind the bounty. She hadn't sent us on a fruitless beast hunt. It wasn't her Fabric Spinner that had captured Noc and spirited him away, allowing Cruor's Oath to take hold and drive him insane. But at the time, I couldn't fathom that Yazmin, our former Crown, could do anything so…wrong. And in my anger and confusion, I'd turned on Raven. Accused a broken woman of something she'd had no part in.

I'd never wanted to rectify something so badly in my life.

Gaige let out a long sigh, extracting a piece of parchment from his pile that looked more like stretched-out, decades-old leather. "I'm getting close to deciphering her notes. This bit right here," he said, pointing to ancient glyphs etched in darkened red ink, "is a spell for taming. I think. I've translated two of the ingredients—bones of a tainted Charmer and blood of an undead prince—but the third piece still eludes me."

A dull ringing sounded in my ears as the hair on the back of my neck stood on end. "Bones of a tainted Charmer?"

He nodded once, locking gazes with me. "I think that's what started this whole mess. She placed a bounty on you because she needed your bones. But when the Myad deemed you worthy and purified you with his magic, she had to look elsewhere. To Wynn."

A chill swept over my skin. "Wynn?"

"Yes." He swallowed thickly. "He successfully charmed you, which tainted him. After Noc killed him, all Yazmin had to do was collect his remains."

"You know this for a fact?" Kost asked.

Kaori rested her chin in her hands. "Yes. She was the one who disposed of Wynn's body while you all were recovering." Her eyes darted to Calem. We'd certainly been preoccupied, both with my injuries and his near-death experience.

Kost frowned. "The bounty called for bones to be delivered within six hours of death. There's no way they'd still be usable for a spell after all this time."

"Yazmin's beast collection far surpasses all of ours," Raven said as a tremor feathered through her jaw. "I'm certain she has a Visavem. They produce a dust that preserves the essence of any item. She can bide her time while collecting whatever else she needs."

"Fuck all." Calem slid lower into his chair.

"And we know she already has Noc's blood," Oz said as he ran a hand over his head.

Noc barely suppressed his growl. "That's why she sent us on that outlandish beast hunt." He let out a long breath and shook his head. "Blood alone didn't make me a prince—I had to be recognized as one by the gods. She sent us to the two ruins so I would meet the criteria for her spell."

Calem cursed again, and Oz formed tight fists on the table.

"Which leaves that third item," Kost said.

"And a date." Gaige's soft declaration silenced us all.

My throat tightened as I searched for words. We needed time. So much time. Time to convince the Charmers to fight, if it came down to it. Time to decipher Yazmin's notes so we could stop her. Time to find out if her claims were true.

The royal family's Sentinels have been capturing Charmers on beast hunts and locking them away.

Noc and his family are responsible for the death of your parents.

Yazmin's words rattled through my mind, shaking me to my very core. I still hadn't confronted Noc about her accusations. He wouldn't have allowed something so horrific to occur. But he was only a prince when he died. How much power did he wield? How much did he know? My gaze slanted to him. He met my stare without hesitation, concern bright in his eyes, and reached for my hand. When his fingers intertwined with mine, he gave them a gentle squeeze before turning back to Gaige. "How much time do we have?"

"The spell to awaken Ocnolog will only work on the anniversary of Celeste's death."

I squeezed my eyes shut. We only had a few weeks. Panic clawed at my insides, but I forced it down, counted to three, and opened my eyes. "Gaige. Kost. Double your efforts to decipher her notes. We need to know if we can stop her."

"And if we can't?" Oz asked.

I gripped Noc's hand tight, trying to pull whatever support I could from our connection. This was the plan that would be hardest for my people to swallow. "Then we go to war, because it will take an army to bring down the king of beasts."

No one moved. After a beat of silence that felt like an eternity, Kaori spoke. "How will you convince the Charmers to fight?"

"I'm not sure. But I have to try. Maybe…" I tilted my head, holding Noc's gaze. "If they see Cruor is with us, they'll join our cause."

Noc frowned, running a tight hand through his hair. "We're forgetting about King Varek. He wants me dead. We'll fight with you against Yazmin because she's a threat to us all. But subjecting Charmers to Varek's wrath, for people they hardly know and certainly don't trust…"

"Like I said, I'll fight whenever you need me," Raven declared.

Gaige shook his head, eyes cast downward. "So long as you're part of the Council, we'll provide aid. That said, Yazmin is the more imminent threat. We don't know how long it will take Varek to make his move, but we do know when Yazmin will strike. Let's deal with her first."

"Agreed," Kost said. "In the meantime, we should move everyone from Cruor here."

"What?" Calem straightened in his chair. "Why?"

Kost removed his glasses and began polishing them. "Because it's the most prudent thing to do. Both as a show of unity and to make it easier to protect our own. We've been running ourselves ragged trying to cover both locations. With everyone in Hireath, we'll be able to fortify our defenses more efficiently, in case Yazmin returns."

"But Cruor is our *home*." Something akin to anxiety flickered in Calem's normally playful gaze, and the mercury thread around his irises seemed to glow. He glanced between Noc and Kost as his fingers drilled against the table. "We can't abandon it."

A deep, familiar ache invaded my chest. None of my assassins ever spoke about their past, where they came from or what their lives were like before they died. But I remembered watching Calem as he helped orphans in the streets of Ortega Key. And I remembered the strange mixture of pain and gratitude in his eyes when I gifted him Effie.

I wasn't sure if Calem ever had a home—not until Cruor. And I knew exactly how painful it was to have something like that stripped away.

"It's only temporary. I promise," I said. He nodded, but his fingers continued to rap against the wood.

Oz studied his brother for a long moment before shifting his focus to Noc. "And what of Darrien? All he's ever wanted is to run Cruor. If he finds out our home is unguarded, he'll attack."

"I'll lock it down." Noc's voice was low. "No one in, no one out."

"You can do that?" I asked.

He nodded once, expression hard. "Yes. It's only been done a handful of times. The spell is draining and not really feasible unless Cruor is under siege and everyone is safely inside. Or in this case, everyone has evacuated."

"This way, both Cruor and our brethren will remain protected. It's the best path forward," Kost said. "We'll make the journey immediately."

"Perhaps I should join you," Gaige said as he straightened his papers and laid down his quill. "I want to take another look at your library to see if there's anything that can help us with Yazmin's spell."

"Good idea," I said.

"Take whatever you need. Once I lock down Cruor, it will be a while before I can open it again." Noc looked first at Calem, then Oz and Kost. "We *will* come back."

Calem's shoulders slumped, but he nodded wordlessly along with Oz.

The safety of our people was more important than Cruor, but I wouldn't brush aside their concern. Not now, not ever. "Cruor and Hireath will stand together."

Kaori tipped her head. "Together it is."

"Agreed." Raven stood, shoulders rigid. "Shall we?"

All gazes focused in my direction. We didn't have much in the ways of concrete plans—not yet. But we had hope. Family. As I looked back at my new Council, warmth brewed in my chest. We had an uphill battle before us, but I had faith in my friends, new and old. I glanced at Raven, the harsh glint in her eyes feeding my determination. At Gaige and Kost, their quick minds strategizing outcomes I hadn't begun to fathom. Calem and Oz's unflinching loyalty. Kaori's quiet authority. Her presence alone would sway many Charmers to our side.

And Noc.

He'd once told me we were each other's greatest weakness. But we were also each other's greatest strength.

Squeezing his hand, I stood. "Let's go change history."

He smiled, genuine and true, and placed a soft kiss on my forehead. "Whatever you say, Crown."

TWO

NOC

The throne room had seen better days, but Leena had insisted the ceremony be held here, where everyone could bear witness to the damage Yazmin had caused. And inevitably, the damage *I'd* caused. I pressed my lips together as I tried in vain to replay the events of that day. But Yazmin's control had been strong, and the memories of what I'd done were hazy. The aftermath, however, was not. Bile soured my tongue as I glanced around the space. Attendants had done their best to clean it, but there were still charred marks from the Vrees's lightning scorched into the floors. Deep gouges from his claws. Crumbled columns and broken branches from the makeshift ceiling moved off to the sides. At least they'd managed to remove the blood.

Yet, in spite of it all, there was an air of beauty that couldn't be dampened.

The midday sun peeked through the barren tree limbs above our heads, and birds with snowy feathers and emerald breasts chirped softly from their perches. Frostbitten leaves had tumbled to the earth and covered the floors in patterns of umber and gold. The Charmers stood in quiet rows, much like they had the day Yazmin summoned them to spew lies about the Council. They stared at us with a similar sense of apprehension, too. Never before had non-Charmers stood at the front of the congregation, on the raised dais meant for their leaders.

Gaige, Raven, and Kaori were positioned in front of us, leading the ceremony we knew nothing about. In their mercury robes, they were something familiar their people could hold onto in the wake of Yazmin's attack.

"There are no words that can soothe the pain we've been dealt," Gaige began, deep voice rumbling over the crowd and silencing the quiet murmurs. "In fact, in times of great agony, I find that speeches do little, but action gives us purpose. *Action* gives us an avenue to heal." He paused for a moment, letting his words sink in. I'd half expected an immediate outcry from the Charmers. A denial for the need to act, especially if that meant going to war. But the room remained silent. Still. For now, that was a win.

"And so we must press on. Together, under a new Crown, we will find a way to rise above the tragedy." With a sweeping gesture, he commanded everyone's attention to the end of the room where Leena stood. It was as if nature herself bowed in recognition. A breeze rushed over the frost-kissed fields, their sparkling blades ablaze in the sun, and carried with it a mist from the crashing falls. It wreathed Leena's form before settling over us all. "I present to you Leena Edenfrell, Crown of the Charmers Council."

She held her chin high but kept her smile soft, warm. With her mercury cloak open, her cream-colored floor-length dress was on full display. It trailed behind her as she walked toward us. She was more than stunning—she was regal. When she stopped before Gaige, her gaze swept my direction and held for a beat. Her resolve was palpable, and I nearly dropped to my knees in a display of loyalty.

Raven scooped up a violet pillow made of velvet from one of the nearby thrones. Resting in the center was a delicate rose-gold diadem with hundreds of twisting branches and countless leaves dotted with diamonds. It wasn't the crown Yazmin had taken with her, and somehow, that made it all the more special. This was the diadem that signified a new beginning. Leena's crown.

Leena kneeled before her, and Raven cleared her throat. "Will you protect us against threats both near and far?"

"Yes," Leena said without hesitation. Even with her chin tucked to her chest and eyes cast downward, her voice rang out loud and clear.

"Will you guide us in times of doubt? Offer wisdom when you have it, and lean on your Council when you need it?"

"Yes."

Raven's eyes bored into her. "Will you keep Celeste in your heart and cherish the lives of all beasts?"

For a brief moment, Leena tilted her head up to look past Raven. I followed her gaze to the statue of Celeste and Ocnolog carved into the wall behind the thrones. She seemed to track the ancient symbols etched beside them, as if reading the words she must've known by heart. After a beat, she closed her eyes in reverence and dropped her chin once again before answering Raven.

"Always."

Gaige took over, gently lifting the diadem high into the air before placing it on Leena's head. "In the name of our goddess, we accept you as our Crown. You may now address your people."

Rising to her feet, Leena faced her congregation. "It is an honor to stand before you now. Though I didn't ask for this role, I will serve you." She clasped her hands before her and inhaled deeply. "As Gaige said, there are no words to alleviate the pain of this tragedy. Yazmin cannot take back the damage she's done. She has scarred us in ways we never thought possible. But she also sparked something I don't think she intended to: Courage. Strength. Independence.

"I know war is something we never want to live through again." She stepped off the dais and began walking down the aisle. "But this isn't something we can run from. We can't allow Yazmin to threaten our home. If she wants a war, we have to give it to her."

Silence filled the throne room, until one young woman spoke out. "You sound like her. How do we know we can trust you?"

Sharp gasps followed the woman's question. An elder gentleman, possibly her father, gripped her arm tight and begged her to be quiet with a stern look.

Leena paused halfway down the aisle. With a furrowed brow, she glanced between the pair. "Are you afraid of me?"

"No." His denial was too quick. "Please, forgive my daughter. She didn't mean to offend."

The woman pursed her lips but said nothing.

Leena gripped the bestiary dangling around her neck. I longed to join her side, to offer her comfort in the face of uncertainty. But a different part of me, the prince I used to be, recognized she had to do this on her own and instill confidence in her people without my aid. She glanced my direction, and I nodded once. Ruling was so incredibly new to her. And even though it was old to me, something from a distant memory, it was as if my father were beside me in that very moment.

"Look your people in the eyes when they speak. Acknowledge their concerns. Be a pillar of strength when they need it."

His words rattled through my brain, and I willed her to hear them. She couldn't have, but she straightened her spine just the same, shifting her gaze back to the woman. And then, she gently extended her hand outward. Rosewood light sparked through the air, and the heavy groan of the beast realm door opening rolled over us. Startled gasps were quickly drowned out by the deep yowl of a legendary feline beast. Onyx appeared beside her. Lithe muscles bunched and stretched beneath his glossy, black fur. With a look of pure motherly love, Leena turned and ran her fingers through his feathered mane before bringing her gaze back around.

"May I?" She held her out her hand to the woman.

Hesitantly, the woman nodded.

With the woman's hands cupped in hers, Leena kneeled. "Please, don't fear me. Hear my truth—I will protect our home. Our beasts. Our people. And I won't force anyone to join me if they don't want to."

The sincerity in Leena's words was unmistakable, but she knew just how important a beast's approval was to her people. Onyx ignited his power, and while I couldn't see the invisible flames surrounding Leena, I could feel their soothing, reassuring warmth. He'd pried into her thoughts with his magic and deemed her worthy once again. Had she been lying or untrustworthy, Onyx would've burned her mind to ash. But she remained unharmed, determination shining in her eyes, and we all knew that she wouldn't betray anyone like Yazmin had. Not now, not ever.

The woman's gaze turned glassy with unshed tears, and she pulled Leena to her feet. "I will follow you," she said, voice rough but full of promise. When she kneeled before Leena in turn, before the Crown of the Charmers Council, the rest of the room followed suit.

Leena blinked and pressed a hand to her chest. She turned in place, a smile building with every breath, as she took in her people. I glanced at my brothers, and we all sank to our knees. As did Gaige, Kaori, and Raven.

Not a single person in the throne room remained standing.

"Find someone worthy of standing beside you. Someone who inspires you, but more importantly, inspires your people."

My chest tightened. My father had wanted so much for me. So much for our *kingdom*. He would've liked Leena, I had no doubt of that. He would've seen her potential to rule, the depth of her kindness, and handed over his throne just to put her in charge.

That can still happen.

The errant thought nearly upended me. Not because it was entirely new. While I'd been under the influence of the oath, driven mad by Yazmin's wishes, I'd fallen prey to visions of an inky-black snake. Of Zane. He'd been known as the Viper of Wilheim and was the heir to the throne before becoming the first undead assassin. His presence had pushed me toward the ruins, toward reclaiming my title. But when the oath had been fulfilled, the haze of Yazmin's control had faded along with him.

So thinking about taking the throne now, even for the sole purpose of making sure Leena was on it... That thought was wholly mine. And one I didn't want to acknowledge.

Clenching my jaw, I buried that notion deep inside. I didn't want to rule. The only crown I wanted to abide by was Leena's, here in Hireath.

"I promise to be transparent with you, always," Leena said. Her steady voice reverberated through the room, once again capturing my attention. "Yazmin is planning to raise Ocnolog. She has two out of the three ingredients needed to do so. My goal is to stop her before that happens. I don't want a war. But if she succeeds..." She looked past all of us to study the statue at my back. "Ocnolog cannot be controlled, and we will be forced to fight."

"How will we stand up to Yazmin?" the same woman from before asked.

"Raven will organize our forces." Leena gave a deep nod to her fellow Council member. "It's not a question of strength—we have our beasts—but she will help orchestrate our defenses."

Raven's brows climbed toward her hairline, but she didn't refuse. "I can begin training anyone who is interested immediately."

"Me too," Ozias said, clearing his throat. Every pair of eyes rounded on him. Some thankful, some uncertain, most fearful. "I've been training new recruits for decades at Cruor."

"Thank you, Oz." Leena gave him a warm smile, then addressed her people again. "Cruor will join us in this fight. For the first time in centuries, we are not alone." Reaching for her beast, she placed a steady hand against Onyx's hide. "My beast trusts them, and so do I. Together, we are stronger. Together, we will protect you."

A resounding roar from Onyx punctuated Leena's promise, and the birds above abandoned their perches in a startled flurry. A litany of calls slipped from their beaks, and I stilled when I noticed one sparrowlike beast that hadn't moved. Its steel-gray feathers and violet breast were different from the rest of the flock. It cocked its head in Leena's direction, targeting her with three black eyes. A yellow film slid over them.

Time came to an immediate halt. I *knew* that beast. I'd first seen its kind in Midnight Jester, the black market tavern near Cruor, when I'd met with Wynn to discuss Leena's bounty. He'd summoned that creature and promised to watch our every move. And he made good on it, too.

Until I'd summoned a blood blade and put an end to his spying.

Thin, near-invisible shadows festered around my fingers. Someone was watching us. No doubt it was Yazmin. One icy tendril took shape, floating above my hand in the form of a small needle. To end the beast's life now, right here, before all these Charmers? Battle strategy told me it was the right thing to do. We couldn't have our enemy spying on us. And yet... My gaze flitted over the captivated audience. They'd yet to notice my slender weapon. If they saw me take down a beast, right after Leena's promise of unity, we'd lose all the ground she'd just made.

My fingers twitched. Would capturing it cause the same

reaction? The blade dissolved, only for more shadows to intertwine in the shape of a small net.

"Noc?" Kost asked in a whisper, eyeing the tendrils. With their heightened senses, Calem and Ozias heard him, too. They tilted their chins in my direction, avoiding obvious movements so as not to draw attention.

Seconds ticked by. My gaze flicked first to Leena's smiling face, then to the crowd. The amount of trust she'd garnered was palpable, but it was also new. If we damaged it now, there was no telling if she'd be able to regain it.

As much as it pained me, I let the shadows disperse and nodded tightly in the direction of the beast. "Spy." As if it somehow heard my barely audible words, the bird jerked its head in my direction. And then it took off in an erratic flight pattern, escaping after the rest of the flock.

"Yazmin?" Calem asked. The mercury line around his muted-red irises flared. He'd gotten better at controlling the beast within, but there was no telling when he'd explode next.

"Likely." My eyes narrowed as I peered through the branches. Leena continued speaking, calling the ceremony to a close. Charmers rose from their kneeled positions and headed for the exit, some stopping before her to bow or whisper words of hope. Gaige and Raven joined her, milling about the crowd to offer reassurances.

Kaori strolled toward us. She stared at Calem, likely studying that dangerous thread of silver in his eyes. "Something happen?"

"Noc says we're being watched." A rogue muscle throbbed down Calem's neck. Kaori grazed the back of his arm, just the briefest of touches, and then clasped her hands before her. He exhaled slowly, rolled his neck from side to side, and then let out a sheepish smile.

Kaori looked back at me. "Tell me what you saw."

"A bird beast. The one with three eyes and a yellow film covering them. Wynn had one."

She turned without speaking and signaled to Gaige, Raven, and Leena. They excused themselves and walked over to us, and we waited in silence for several minutes until the last of the Charmers left the room. Leena sidled in next to me, eyes alight and cheeks rosy. She was beaming. I hated that we'd have to bring her back down to reality so soon. But this was war. Celebrations were always cut short.

"Noc spotted a Femsy. We have to be more careful," Kaori said.

Leena's smile fell away. "Yazmin."

Gaige let out a frustrated groan, rubbing a hand along his jaw. "We have no way of keeping beasts out of Hireath. This place is a sanctuary for them as much as it is for us."

"We'll figure out a way to strategize in secret when we return from Cruor." Kost adjusted his glasses before folding his arms across his chest. "Any more advantages and we won't be facing a war. We'll be facing certain death."

"He's right." I sighed, glancing down at Leena. I'd only just got back. Spending my nights away from her had been hard. Not as bad as those nights where the line between reality and fantasy had blurred, and the ghosts of those my curse had killed haunted my dreams. But unpleasant nonetheless. Still, time was not on our side. We had to decipher the last of Yazmin's spell in order to stop it, and we had to move Cruor here. Delicately, I brushed a stray lock of hair behind Leena's ear. "Looks like that welcome you promised will have to wait."

"I'm coming with you." She tipped her head to plant a kiss on my fingers. "I can help Gaige and Kost search for information while you and Oz prepare the assassins to move to Hireath."

"What about me? I'm not entirely useless." Calem let out an indignant huff.

"Only mostly." Oz chuckled. "You can carry our bags."

"I'm not a damn pack mule."

A bemused smile tugged at my lips. "It's either that or you stay here. Take your pick."

"You can't be serious." Murder flashed through his eyes. "If you think I'm hauling anyone else's belongings, you're out of your mind."

"That so?" I asked.

Low curses slipped through his bared teeth, and he balled his fists.

"Enough." Kaori swatted the back of his head so fast I barely caught it. Calem jerked forward and swung his bewildered gaze toward her. "They're baiting you."

He blinked. "I know that."

"Besides," she folded her arms across her chest, "your inner beast *would* make a good pack mule. If you could control yourself for a change."

Calem's jaw dropped at the same time Oz let out a rumbling laugh. Leena inhaled sharply, barely muffling her own giggle with her hand.

"Now that everyone has a role..." Gaige muttered as he turned to Leena. His hand absently traced his citrine Charmer's symbol. "Have Reine's powers been restored yet?"

Leena frowned. "We drained her when she had to carry three of us from Silvis's Ruins to Cruor. It'll be a while yet before she can teleport more than a few feet. Why?"

He sighed. "I'm thinking in terms of transportation. We can use some of our beasts to move the assassins faster. We don't know when Yazmin will strike again."

Leena rubbed her chin, considering his words. "Even if Reine was fully recovered, she could only carry a few people at once. She'd expend her power before we moved even a quarter of the assassins."

My mind raced as I pictured the faces of my brethren back at Cruor. "Not all of us are fighters. If we can protect those who have little skill in battle, that would be best. The rest can travel through the Kitska Forest on foot."

"What about a flying beast?" Oz asked.

"I only have Onyx," Leena said as she peered at each one of her fellow Council members. They all shook their heads and grimaced. Leena had told me once just how rare flying beasts were. Hard to track, hard to tame. There just weren't that many of them. At least not in Lendria, and few Charmers ever ventured outside our country's borders.

"The alternative is a Telesávra," Raven said slowly, as if mulling over each word. She folded her arms across her chest. "You won't be able to move everyone, but it's better than nothing. I have an extra one that hasn't bonded to me yet that Leena can have."

"Raven..." Leena's voice was soft.

"It's necessary. We need to unite our forces." She didn't look at Leena, but there was something behind that hardened, faraway stare. Something beyond just blanket loyalty. "If you must, think of it as a show of gratitude for giving me something to do with the Charmers."

Leena smiled. "Of course. Training."

"Yes." Raven's stance softened. "I'm looking forward to it."

Ozias gave her a wide grin. "Tell the Charmers they're welcome to join our new recruits for drills when we get back. Your hand-to-hand combat is great, but mine is better."

She scowled before brushing him off. "In your dreams. But it might be helpful for Charmers to see how easy it is for me to hand you your ass."

My brows arched as Ozias let out a soft chuckle. He and Raven had spent time together while Leena recovered from Yazmin's attack, but the extent of their friendship was still a surprise. Ozias could barely talk to some of our brethren outside of training, let alone banter with them. Seeing him bond with Raven so quickly reminded me of when he'd met Leena. She'd been alone and he'd been there, and in a way, Raven had been, too.

"Whatever you say," Ozias said.

"That's the right attitude." She splayed out her hand, igniting the air in a faint, currant-colored glow. "I'll be back in a minute with the Telesávra."

"Thanks, Raven," Leena said.

"Don't mention it." And with that, she disappeared into the beast realm.

"Glad to see she's coming around," Gaige mused. Then, he called over his shoulder as he exited the throne room through a nearby corridor. "I'll rejoin you momentarily. I just need to collect a few things."

Kaori targeted Leena with a pointed look. "Please, be safe. I'll field any concerns that might occur while you're away." She tipped her head in a slight bow before following the same path Gaige had taken.

Calem's gaze lingered on her a fraction too long before he brought his attention back to us. "I don't care what she says, I'm still not carrying anyone's bags."

Ozias laughed, drowning out the sound of Kost's exaggerated sigh. Leena sidled closer to Calem and made a show of examining his back, as if assessing exactly how many bags he could carry. Her happy jests and his playful griping filled me with warmth, but as I glanced over their heads in the direction of Celeste's statue, a chill crept down my neck. The anniversary of her death wasn't far off. We'd been at it for a week, researching endlessly for a way to end this catastrophe before it began. And still, nothing. Yazmin had the upper hand already, and it was only a matter of time before she'd strike.

Three

KOST

The courtyard outside the keep was quiet. For the most part, the Charmers had cleared the area after Leena's coronation, and only a few milled about with their beasts. I watched closely as a young woman found a stick on the ground and tossed it for her wolf beast. The creature reacted without hesitation, bounding toward its mark and returning it with a joyful yip. A smile lit the woman's eyes, and she gave her beast an approving pat on the head. The love these Charmers held for their creatures was palpable, and that made it all the more inspiring to know they were willing to align themselves with our cause.

A few feet away, Leena barked out a curse and stumbled to the side as Raven laughed. She'd only just returned from the beast realm with the Telesávra, and the beast had the energy of a toddler. He'd darted around in erratic patterns before ramming his head into Leena's leg, only to take off again in a dead sprint. Leena chased after him, leaving behind Raven, Noc, Calem, and Ozias, all bemused.

Sinking to a nearby stone bench, I extracted a bronze key from my breast pocket and summoned Felicks. He appeared with ease, ears alert and eyes bright. I'd summoned him frequently to strengthen our bond, which meant he was able to spend even more time with me outside of the beast realm. I worked my fingers down his spine, and he let out a satisfied huff. As soon as Leena wrangled her ill-behaved beast, we'd be on our way.

"At least you're much more civilized," I muttered, stroking Felicks's fur. The amethyst orb atop his head clouded, and a series of pictures formed in my mind as my beast shared his vision. A thorough rubdown for Felicks, Leena finally controlling her Telesávra, Gaige approaching from the keep... A fluttery sensation overcame my stomach, and I tensed. It wasn't a surprise to find that Gaige was heading my way. It was the way he'd paused in Felicks's vision when his gaze landed on my back. A slow, genuine smile—devoid of its usual mischief but full of anticipation—had claimed his face. He'd run a hand through his hair and adjusted the cuffs of his mulberry-colored tunic. And instead of joining Raven, who'd waved for him the moment he'd appeared, he'd elected to sit beside me.

Felicks's orb cleared, and he gave me a knowing look.

"Hush." I adjusted my glasses, ignoring the thrum of excitement brewing in my chest. The crunch of boots against frozen grass sounded at my back, and I schooled my expression into nonchalance. Clamping my hands together, I focused instead on Leena as she corralled her Telesávra.

"I've seen a lot of Felicks lately," Gaige mused. Dropping to the bench, he reached over and scratched my beast beneath his chin. My legs tensed at his nearness, but I didn't jolt. Drawing attention to my body's involuntary reaction—something I certainly couldn't control—would only result in awkward embarrassment. "You've been training a lot?"

"Of course." I continued to watch the rogue Telesávra. "The last thing I want is, well, *that*."

Gaige tracked the rambunctious beast. He snorted. "Yes, well, Felicks is a bit more dignified."

"I should hope so," I said.

Gaige continued to run his hand down the length of Felicks's spine. "And his visions?"

I flinched, jerking my head slightly to the side and meeting Gaige's unnerving stare. His eyes crinkled at the corners, and his lips quirked up on one side. He couldn't possibly have known what Felicks had shown me not two minutes ago. But he looked at me just the same, as if he were in on some private joke and could barely contain his mirth.

"They're...informative."

"Good. They'll only get more detailed as time goes on." He folded his hands in his lap, and Felicks let out a disgruntled sigh before nudging his snout beneath my fingers. "I imagine learning to harness Felicks's power is a lot like learning to control your shadows."

The tension coiled tight between my shoulders loosened. Talking about the shadows was easy and far safer than examining the nature of Felicks's visions. Especially when they involved Gaige.

"To a degree, yes." I held out my palm and called on the dark tendrils lurking in my peripheral vision. They flew to me with ease and swirled about my wrist before wreathing my gloved fingers. Even through the fabric, I could feel their cool touch. "It's similar to the bond I have with Felicks, in that it's always there. I can sense it and call on it. But Felicks is a living being, unlike these." One tendril dripped from my hand and gently grazed the back of Gaige's arm, though I hadn't realized I'd meant to touch him. He stilled, eyes transfixed on the shadow, and a wave of gooseflesh rippled across the exposed part of his neck.

He cleared his throat. "Do you enjoy being an assassin? Commanding the shadows?"

"Those are two very different questions." I tilted my head

and called off the smoky tendrils. Gaige's eyes fell, as if disappointed, but he recovered quickly and offered a familiar grin. My stomach clenched in response. "Work as an assassin is tolerable. It doesn't bring me fulfillment or sadness, it just is. But the shadows…" I let my voice trail off, thinking about what Talmage had given me by raising me from the dead all those years ago. At first, I'd resented him for something that wasn't remotely his fault. My former lover, Jude, had abandoned me the moment I'd shown him those onyx wisps.

I hated the dark for a long time after that. But now… I glanced at my brothers a short distance away. To the untrained eye, the shadow realm was a dark and terrifying world. To me, it was a haven.

Gaige studied my expression as he waited for me to respond.

"I suppose I quite like controlling the shadows. They're familiar. Reliable. Not to mention, they're useful in times of war." In an instant I recalled the tendrils and fashioned them into a glittering rapier. Gently, I gripped it by the handle before turning it over to Gaige. He marveled at the creation, holding it up to the sun to examine the ink-black weapon.

After a moment, he handed it back to me. "You sure it won't dissipate upon contact?"

I scoffed. "I'm not a fresh recruit."

Gaige smirked. "Good. Wouldn't want you dying in this coming war." He hesitated, then added, "I'd really like to get to know you better, once we have the time."

Heat once again simmered beneath my skin, and I flicked my wrist, sending the shadows racing away. "I have no plans of dying."

"Good." Unexpectedly—or had I known this was coming all along?—Gaige's eyes fell to my lips, and an uneven breath escaped his chest. As much as I wanted to, I couldn't ignore the gentle tingle in my fingers begging me to reach out and touch him for real. He was close enough that I could do it if I dared. Time slowed, stretching that moment as I waited, wondering—

Calem clapped his hands loudly, the sound breaking Gaige's hold over me, and I jerked my head to him. Without my knowledge, he'd sauntered over and crouched before us. A dangerous teasing spark filled his eyes. "I thought you'd be interested in knowing we're all ready to go. That is, if it's okay by you two."

I launched to my feet. At some point, Leena must've calmed her Telesávra, because she was now idly standing beside Noc and pretending incredibly hard not to look our way. Ozias shuffled his feet and tipped his head to the sky, while Noc simply gave Calem a tired, disapproving look.

So wrapped up in my conversation with Gaige, I couldn't even pinpoint when Raven had left. I took a few harsh steps away, putting distance between me and the man who could derail my thoughts so easily. Certainly his Charmer's lure was to blame, but I should've been more alert.

"Let's go," I said, taking long strides toward our group.

The mirth in Gaige's voice was unmistakable. "To be continued."

Calem laughed at his comment, but as we made our way toward the Kitska Forest, I let my mind wander, just for a moment. Just long enough to picture a possible future where perhaps Gaige and I could continue down a path I hadn't truly entertained in years.

FOUR

YAZMIN

There was only one place in Wilheim's castle I enjoyed: the Queen's Respite.

At first, I hadn't been permitted to enter this hidden sanctuary. Each time I tried, the Sentinels stationed at the entrance turned me away. Their adamant refusal only confirmed my suspicions: something was here. And after days of futile searching for any leads on the missing Charmers—the ones my people foolishly presumed were dead—I knew I had to see what this chamber held. Even if it meant trading a beast to King Varek—a lowly one with minor abilities, though I may have exaggerated about its powers—in order to be granted entry. Of course, he obliged. Though his rule for me to be escorted at all times certainly soured the deal. Not like I could show anything but gratitude for his *magnanimous* agreement.

So here I stood, four Sentinels still as statues against the walls. Before me was a single tree with white bark and pale-pink leaves. A circular hole had been cut out of the ceiling, and sunlight poured through the opening. Columns of the same ivory that made up the castle surrounded the space. Rich soil and moss encircled the trunk, spanning outward until it met the edge of cool tile where I stood.

Magic ran deep here. I could feel it in my core. When Mavis, the princess during the First War, died, her mother planted this tree. The Queen's Heart. More had blossomed throughout the city, but this was the first. The original. Here, her mother had mourned the loss of her daughter.

And she'd never left. Her lifeblood, her bones, her *body*, had given sustenance to this tree. It was the only thing I wanted to protect when I brought Ocnolog's fires upon this wretched city. I wasn't sure why, but something about this place kept calling me back. A deep nagging in my gut I couldn't ignore. I'd been searching for the Charmers Wynn had said were being held in the capital. Every hour—every minute—not spent preparing for Ocnolog or planning against Leena was devoted to them. And yet, nothing. When my hours of sleuthing left me empty-handed and defeated, my feet carried me here. Always. Here, I could breathe. Think. Rest.

But rest was for the dead, and I had work to do.

Tracing a finger along the Charmer's symbol across the back of my hand, I found my Femsy's branch. I glanced at the Sentinels. They wouldn't be able to tell I was about to connect with my beast, but I made a note to be quick nonetheless. The world spun before me as I connected to her vision, taking in a sea of jagged treetops and snarling, purple vines. The Kitska Forest was just as ominous from above as it was from within. She'd been flying low over the branches, tracking Leena's moves since her inauguration. While I could only tap into my Femsy's sight three times before sending her back to the realm to recover, her presence in our world was barely a drain on my power. Keeping tabs on my enemies was necessary, and should they spot her and dispose of her... One beast was expendable.

If only that coward had struck. I bit back a hiss as I thought of Noc's shadows. He could've ended my Femsy's life in the throne room. I almost wished he had. If only to prove to my people just how dangerous he was.

Pushing that thought aside, I watched as they trekked through the woods. I'd waited for nearly two days to check in again to not waste my Femsy's power. Celeste be praised they'd left Hireath and were likely on their way to Cruor. And without a flying beast and their own creatures likely drained from the battle against the Vrees, now was a prime time to strike.

Cutting off the visual connection between me and my beast, I tucked my hand in the folds of my dress and focused on the beast realm door. Ruddy-red light seeped through the fabric, but it was faint enough not to pull the attention of the Sentinels. I doubted they'd believe I was merely sending my Femsy home rather than summoning a creature to attack. I'd earned Varek's attention, but certainly not his trust. Better to play it safe for now.

Turning on my heels, I stalked out of the hidden sanctuary and back into the main parts of the castle. The Sentinels followed for a short while, ensuring I stuck to approved hallways and corridors before finally peeling off and returning to whatever posts they'd been assigned. Varek would be preoccupied overseeing the defenses of Wilheim. He'd insisted on fortifying them in case the Charmers or Noc came calling. Unnecessary, but it kept him busy and out of my hair. I had things to do.

My heels clacked against the polished tile of the grand hall as I continued on, spying the very man I needed. He sat at a table with his brethren, feasting on roasted meats and fresh fruit. As he took a heavy swig from his jewel-encrusted goblet, his amber eyes met mine and the line of his jaw tightened. Varek might not have been able to see through my niceties, but Darrien was far less trusting. He sat his glass down and fiddled with the carving knife by his plate.

I fought the urge to laugh. If I wanted him dead, his severed head would already be on a pike outside. "Darrien, come with me. Your troops, too." I didn't even bother to stop and instead kept walking. He'd follow. People always did.

There was only a moment's pause before the scraping of wood against tile. Then, a sudden influx of cold and whoosh of shadows as he used his power to catch up to me, stride for stride. More shadows raced across the floor, and the rest of his assassins fell into line behind us.

"I'm not a soldier you can boss around."

"Aren't you?" I took the nearest corridor, ignoring the muffled gasp from one of his brethren.

Darrien's brow twitched, but he kept pace. "What is it?"

"I have a job for you."

"As I said, I'm not a soldier—"

"I know where Noc is going to be, and I can send you to him. Now."

He stutter-stepped beside me, all traces of disgust wiped from his face. "Go on."

We rounded the corner on a set of double doors, and I pushed them open. My quarters weren't nearly as appealing as what I'd grown used to in Hireath, but it didn't matter. I headed for the sitting area, sinking into a tufted, cerulean settee near the hearth. Warmth bled from the crackling fire. Darrien took the high-back armchair across from me and leaned forward, pressing his elbows to his knees. With a simple jerk of his chin, he commanded his troops to line the walls and wait. At least they were loyal, unlike my own people.

"Noc and his merry band of miscreants are on their way to Cruor as we speak."

Darrien didn't move. "You know this how?"

I scowled. "I've had a beast in place to spy on them since I left."

"Even so, it would be suicidal for me to attack him while he's at Cruor."

My fingers twitched. "You think too small."

His lips peeled back in an unattractive grimace. "I don't have to sit here and listen to your shit."

"Then stop jumping to conclusions, and I'll stop pointing out the obvious." I crossed one leg over the other, waiting. He swallowed thickly, but didn't open his mouth again. Thank the gods. "They're currently traveling through Kitska Forest. I want to attack them there. You're skilled with a bow and arrow, I believe? You can strike from the treetops and disappear before they even notice. Separate them, and then ambush them. We have the numbers."

A wicked smile toyed with his lips. "It's doable. We could pick them off one by one. Gods, the look on Noc's face when he sees his family go down..." He stroked his jaw as he peered into nothingness, smile stretching impossibly wider. After a few moments, he let his hand fall away and pinned me with a quizzical look. The eagerness in his eyes faltered. "But why now? They can't reach us here. And with Varek building his forces and you on the verge of raising Ocnolog... Is it necessary?"

Heat simmered through my veins. Of *course* I'd thought of all that. I knew that, tactically, there was no reason to attack, even if they were weak. Cruor and Hireath alone weren't strong enough to take on the capital of Wilheim, let alone Ocnolog. But the Charmers... My fist clenched. Why had they listened to her and not me? What was it about her that inspired their trust? The way they'd knelt before her in the throne room, even after admitting she'd lead them into war—the very thing I'd asked of them—was a sight I couldn't shake. It haunted me as I worked to unearth King Varek's secrets about the captive Charmers. I wanted to hurt Leena like my people had hurt me. I wanted to rip away her family, dispose of her allies, so she was just as alone as me. Then they'd see. I was the only one capable of leading our people. I would persevere.

I'll show them. I'll show them all.

"If we take Leena's allies off the board, she'll crumble. And the Charmers won't follow a weak leader—they'll fall quietly to the wayside. They don't *want* a war. As for Noc, well, if reclaiming Cruor for yourself isn't something you want, then so be it."

Darrien glowered. "I didn't say that."

"Glad we're aligned. We have to leave now if you want to get into a good position before they make it to Cruor." Flicking my wrist, I channeled my power into the emblem on my hand. The beast realm door swung open, and my Telesávra appeared. She cracked open her maw, summoning a sparking, white portal. "I changed my beast's hearth point to Midnight Jester as I was fleeing. Near enough to Hireath and Cruor, but not close enough to catch the eye of any patrolling guards."

Darrien regarded my beast. "How easy is it to change hearth points?"

"It's not terribly difficult," I said, studying my creature. "But both me and my Telesávra have to be present at the desired location in order to set the teleportation point. I can't simply point at a location on a map and make it so. Hence why I seized the opportunity outside Midnight Jester before coming here."

"And my brethren? How many of us can come?" He gestured to the assassins waiting silently about the room. A few had inched forward, showing obvious signs of interest in joining our mission.

I stood and extended my arms. "As many as we can fit without breaking contact. They'll need to be touching me in order to use the portal."

Darrien didn't hesitate, wrapping his fingers around mine and taking a step closer to my beast. He signaled to a handful of assassins, and they flocked to our side. They gripped my arms, my back, my waist. I would've transported the whole damn group if it were possible, but there was only so much space available. And if one of them accidentally let go during travel, we'd never see them again. Not that I particularly cared, but a body was a body and we needed the numbers to maintain our advantage.

Anticipation gleamed in Darrien's eyes. "This should be fun."

"Yes. But leave Leena to me." I didn't bother to keep the disgust from my response. She'd threatened far too much already. And now, as Crown of the Council, she had the power to move against me—and the support to do so. I could win my people back to my side, if only she were gone. And with Ocnolog under my command and the missing Charmers found, no one would be able to deny me anything. I couldn't, *wouldn't*, be stopped.

Darrien smirked. "As long as I get Noc, I don't care who you take down."

My smile turned feral. "Good. Shall we?"

Without a moment's hesitation, we stepped through the sparking portal and emerged moment's later on the fringe of Midnight Jester. The second the assassins released their grips, I flicked my wrist and opened the beast realm door, sending my Telesávra home. She wouldn't be able to transport us back to Wilheim, anyway. As we moved toward Kitska Forest, a low, bone-shattering roar rumbled from somewhere in the wood. Closer than expected. A wondrous idea bloomed in my mind.

I can use this.

Laughter bubbled from my chest, and Darrien shot me a glance. I waved him off and pressed on, veering toward the eerie call. These monsters had nothing on me.

FIVE

LEENA

My newly acquired Telesávra was a bit of a handful, and a small part of me wondered if that had something to do with Raven's willingness to give him to me. There was no mistaking the mirth in her eyes when he nipped my fingers, then rammed his dense skull into my leg. I could already feel a bruise coming on, but at least he'd bonded to me. With his hearth point set to Hireath, we were able to leave as soon as I'd received him. And since Gaige's Telesávra was set to the same location, we could transport a decent number of assassins safely to the keep in a matter of minutes once we arrived at Cruor. For now, though, we were forced to trek through the Kitska Forest on foot.

For the hundredth time, I brushed aside a spike-covered vine only to have it snag on my coat. A few threads gave way as I shoved through. Even in winter, the forest was dense and unrelenting. Not to mention, the monsters. One deadly call after another rolled through the air, as if they were on edge.

Or out hunting.

I shivered, pushing that thought away. Legend suggested the Kitska monsters were the trapped souls of deceased beasts from the First War. Their terrifying appearance and unconstrained rage were the exact reason Charmers hesitated to fight. Their existence was our punishment for letting ourselves be dragged into war. I wasn't sure if that was true or not. It didn't *feel* right. We'd only been defending ourselves from the Wilheimians. But something had happened to these beasts, that much was obvious. And while they rarely attacked Charmers—perhaps out of some fealty to us in their former lives—it wasn't unheard of. I'd only spied one of these creatures once before, and I wasn't in a hurry to repeat that encounter.

Calem let out an irritated grunt as he kicked away a fallen branch obscuring our path. "Remind me again why we aren't using our shadows?"

Noc's gaze swept over our surroundings. "We don't have any idea what Darrien is planning. But we do know he has his sights set on Cruor, and we're all familiar with how deadly he can be in the shadow realm."

"Prick," Calem muttered. Oz nodded his agreement.

"There's also the matter of Leena and Gaige," Kost said. "We could try to outrun Darrien in the shadows, but if we found ourselves cornered, neither of them could summon their beasts."

Suppressing a shiver, I dipped my chin in the direction of Quilla, my Asura, to ensure she was still nearby. Slow-moving but ever alert, she swiveled her cow-like head back and forth as she pushed aside vines and sauntered by my side. Gaige had summoned his Asura as well, along with a Femsy of his own. He'd sent the bird beast ahead to scout our trail and tapped into its sight twice already to ensure we were safe. To boot, Kost had called on Felicks, who was securely perched on his shoulder. Every few minutes, his amethyst orb would cloud and Kost would pause, reviewing the contents of our future, and then we'd press forward. We hadn't forgotten about Yazmin's spying. And since we had no real idea where she was hiding, we had to remain alert.

"We're almost to the winnow point." Noc jerked his chin, presumably in the direction of Cruor, though I couldn't be certain. The guild's secret entrance was near impossible to find without the aid of an undead assassin. "Once we reach it, we'll be at Cruor's doorstep."

A memory of the first time I'd traveled to Cruor surfaced in my mind. My Iksass, Iky, had trapped Kost with his barbed limbs and forced the assassin to escort us to the guild. The swirling, dark vortex—accessible only by a member of Cruor—had transported us instantly and safely without fault. It'd been nerve-racking to set foot in a manor full of assassins, but now it was one of my homes. And I desperately wanted to protect it.

"You okay?" Noc asked.

"Yeah, I'm good." I gave him a tense smile. I had little faith we'd find any additional information about Yazmin's spell at Cruor, but I had to do *something*. I wouldn't be a ruler who sat on her throne, commanding from afar and putting other people in jeopardy.

Noc held back a branch for me to pass by. "We'll find something, Leena."

I ducked under the tree's limb and stopped. "Am I doing the right thing?"

"What do you mean?"

"I mean declaring war. Is that the right thing to do?" I glanced around at our party. Kost and Gaige had shifted their conversation to spellwork ingredients, while Calem and Oz walked quietly behind them. I didn't want to jeopardize my family, or my people, by making the wrong decision.

"You're not declaring war. Yazmin is." Noc brushed a stray lock of hair off my face. "There's a key difference, there."

"Really?" I sighed. "It doesn't *feel* all that different. What that woman said..." I swallowed thickly, remembering how her words had rattled me to my core. Yazmin had asked her people to go to war, right before unleashing the Vrees on us all. And her reasons for doing so… Charmers captured at the hands of Wilheimians… It had sounded like a valid reason to fight.

Noc gripped my shoulders tight. "Don't doubt yourself. Think of Onyx."

I blinked. "What?"

His fingers tightened. "Onyx deemed *you* worthy. Not Yazmin. The Charmers saw that. Besides, what about Ocnolog? You said he couldn't be controlled. So even if Yazmin succeeds in summoning him, everyone will be in danger."

"Yazmin tamed the Vrees before I broke his bond with her." My words were low. Uncertain. I glanced at my Charmer's symbol. Even now, without channeling my magic, it seemed to throb with power. Since welcoming the Vrees, who I'd named Aeon, to my family, I'd felt stronger. More capable. As if the goddess herself had granted me a sliver of her power. Aeon, a giant teddy bear at heart, enjoyed roaming the endless fields of the beast realm, tongue lolling out the side of his maw. Celeste's magic was strongest there, and I think he felt that. Relished it. Just being connected to him was like being connected to her.

Yazmin had tamed Aeon alone, and she'd gone to extraordinary lengths to do so. She was stronger than me. Stronger than all of us; of that I had no doubt.

"You think that means she'll be able to control Ocnolog." Noc's words echoed my fear.

I nodded. "And I think she'll use him to destroy everything."

"Yazmin is power hungry. Even if her motives were sparked by something righteous, she's going about it the wrong way. War is…" Noc looked away, gaze tight. Everything about him stiffened, as if he were reliving some long-ago memory. He became a soldier, a warrior, in that moment. "It's not pretty, Leena."

"I know," I said. "But you were fighting for something you believed in, right?"

"Yes." He studied my face carefully. "I believe in our cause enough to go to war now, too."

"So does Yazmin. She's certain there are Charmers being held captive in Wilheim."

The tension riddling his frame fled. He placed one hand on my shoulder and looked me directly in the eyes. "You know I have no idea about these captive Charmers, right?"

"Of course, Noc." I let out a breath. "You wouldn't do something like that." We still hadn't talked about my parents. I wasn't sure if there was anything to talk about. Yazmin had insinuated they were dead, that Noc and his family were responsible. But how could she possibly know that? And if they weren't, did that mean...did that mean they were captive, too?

I shook my head. I couldn't grasp at straws. Couldn't feed the hope that they were alive somehow. They'd died on a beast hunt, and Yazmin was just using their lack of remains to her advantage.

Noc's voice was low, apologetic. "If I'd known, I—"

"We've got a problem," Kost interrupted, abandoning his conversation with Gaige to rush to our side. Felicks had dug his claws into Kost's shoulder, and his hackles were standing on end. Clouds brewed in his amethyst orb. "Something's coming our way. Fast."

My blood turned to ice. "A beast? Yazmin?"

Calem, Oz, and Gaige joined us, each of them picking apart the woods with tight glares. Kost pressed a finger to his temple, his gaze faraway as he connected with Felicks's vision, and his lips thinned. "I'm not entirely sure. I didn't recognize it, but it's heading right for us. There's something else, too." His brows drew together. "Another attack, something small and fast. But I can't decipher it from the creature."

Our Asura acted without prompting, settling into the ground and firmly planting their palms against the earth. Glistening domes covered us as we peered into the dark wood. Calem's jaw was clenched tight, and his gaze bounced frantically from one place to the next. Oz went completely still, save for a few shadows that trailed from his fingertips and curled around his wrist. Grazing the back of his hand, Gaige fingered a small branch on his Charmer's symbol. No doubt using the last bit of his Femsy's power to aid Kost and scout the area.

"Anything?" I asked, peering at Gaige.

He swallowed thickly. "My Femsy won't go near it, which could only mean one thing."

Monster.

As if answering my fear, a deep, bloodcurdling roar crashed through the air. My stomach plummeted to my feet. Why now? What had we done to attract the attention of a Kitska monster? The trees seemed to shiver in anticipation, pinesco pods dancing above our heads in a frenzy. Beside me, Noc cursed and slit open his palm. Blood dripped down his fingers before hovering about his hand.

"It's approaching from the north," Kost said. Beside him, Calem shuddered, and the mercury thread around his eyes widened.

"Gaige," I murmured, tilting my chin slightly in his direction. "What do we do?"

"Until I know what we're dealing with, I can't say. I'm sending my Femsy back and calling on Okean." He flexed his hand, and citrine light exploded from his symbol. The beast realm door groaned open, and while he sent one beast back to safety, he summoned another to his side. A threatening yowl preceded the Zystream's entrance as the liquid-blue legendary feline manifested beside his master. His claws sank into the soft earth, and wet mist gathered around him. Dew droplets welled along his slick hide before trailing the length of his body and splashing against the ground. I knew from my research that he was a formidable beast, able to summon and control water to take down his prey.

"What do we do?" Calem asked.

"Kitska monsters can't be tamed. We'll have to subdue it." Gaige glanced around, frowning slightly at our Asura's domes. "I have no idea if our shields will hold against a creature like this."

Thrusting out my hand, I channeled power to my symbol and wrenched open the beast realm door. Reine still needed to recover, but her ability to teleport in short bursts would come in handy while maneuvering through the trees. She emerged from the realm, indigo spots glowing and hackles on end as she stalked to Okean's side. Dominus followed a beat later. Despite the lack of light permeating the dense wood, his crystal-plated chest and the jagged, jewel-like wings along his legs glittered without fail.

On Kost's shoulder, Felicks's orb cleared and he peeled back his maw in a menacing growl. Kost eyed his beast before fashioning a rapier out of shadows. In a few minutes' time, we'd know more, thanks to Felicks. But until then...

"Are they normally this aggressive?" Oz asked while he formed a slew of blades and tucked them between his knuckles.

Gaige's fingers twitched. "Not typically, but—"

A sharp whistling, followed immediately by a loud crack, rang through the air. As one, we stared at an oily, slick arrow that'd burrowed into Quilla's dome right in front of where Noc was standing. Beside me, my beast shuddered and closed one of her ten milky-white eyes. A low, murderous hiss escaped Noc's lips.

My breath caught. "What the hell?"

Noc's gaze snapped to the treetops. "We're not alone."

"Darrien." Kost's voice was deadly, and the shadows around his frame spiked in erratic patterns. "That's the attack I couldn't place."

"What the hell is he doing here?" Oz asked. Like Noc, he jerked his head upward and scanned the thick network of branches.

Scales formed and receded along Calem's skin as his body shook. "I can't see him."

"Me neither. But I can sense his shadows." Noc rotated his wrist, and the blood droplets around his hand formed into blades, each one waiting to do his bidding. "He's using the forest to his advantage."

A terrifying bellow, much closer than before, rattled the leaves above us.

Before we could formulate a plan, a creature came crashing through the wood, splintering trees with the force of its attack. My blood went cold. Of course it'd be a Gigloam. Or what once was a Gigloam. The A-Class bear beast was the size of an elephant bull with stag-like antlers protruding from its head. A thick skull, separate from the one beneath its hide, grew from the base of its neck and protruded down over its snout. A bone helm to protect its face. Glowing red eyes—eyes that should've been green or brown—peered through the sockets. His fur, which was likely once a lustrous, mossy green, was now matted and gray.

Does it still have its powers? I spied the half-moon etching on its skull and cursed. At least the full moon had already passed; otherwise we'd be better off running than fighting.

Felicks's orb clouded again, and he let out a sharp yip. Kost's eyes went wide. "Brace yourselves!"

The monster roared, and moonlight gathered between its antlers. Not a moment later, it exploded in a wide beam, targeting our troupe with deadly accuracy. The powerful light slammed into our domes with the force of a battering ram, and splintering cracks spiderwebbed across the near-invisible surfaces. By the time the moonlight had faded, Quilla had closed all but one of her eyes.

And then a volley of three arrows sang through the air—one piercing my beast's dome and the other two sinking into Gaige's. Our creatures sighed, their powers fading as they closed their last eye. Our protection was gone.

"What the hell is happening?" Calem shouted as we scattered to avoid the charging Gigloam. Yowls scraped from the backs of our legendary felines' throats as they formed a circle around the aberrant monster. Howling in answer, the Gigloam stood tall on its hind legs. Okean and Dominus lunged in unison as Reine blipped out of existence. A moment later, she reappeared, teeth and claws deep in the thick hide of the Gigloam's neck. A gargled cry escaped the creature's maw, and he fell to all fours at the same time Okean and Dominus attacked.

More arrows pierced the air, pulling my focus away from the beasts. Noc dropped to the ground and rolled, narrowly avoiding one aimed at his head. Leaping before him, Oz extracted a bronze key from his trouser pocket. The beast realm door groaned open, and Jax, his young Laharock, appeared.

"Protect them," Oz growled as he launched into the trees and hurled blades in the direction of Darrien's attacks. His creature roared, and a deep rumbling shook the forest floor. Walls of near-impenetrable rock shot from the earth, their veins of lava a dangerous, glowing red, just as a volley of arrows whizzed through the trees. Most ricocheted off the newly erected barriers, but one slipped through and nicked my shoulder. Wincing, I slapped my hand over the shallow wound. A worried caterwaul rose above the volatile snarls of the Gigloam fight, and Reine released her hold on the monster to peer at me.

"Reine!" I shouted, but not quickly enough. The Gigloam capitalized on his relinquished neck and stood once again, tearing off the felines one by one with his massive paws. Each one went flying into the forest until they crashed into tree trunks.

"We have to stop it!" Gaige shouted. Flush against one of Jax's rock walls, he'd been avoiding the continued onslaught of Darrien's shadow arrows. Okean recovered first, and a torrent of water exploded from his maw and slammed into the creature's belly. It stumbled backward, slashing at the relentless stream to no avail.

"And Darrien," Kost hissed, his gaze darting from the beast fight to the endless, snarling expanse of woods before us. Above, Oz grunted his consent as he continued to sling blades into the dark. A sharp, distant curse answered in response, and a body wreathed in shadows darted from one tree to the next.

Mercury dominated Calem's eyes. "That wasn't Darrien."

"He brought backup," Kost seethed.

"Darrien!" Noc bellowed, crouching near me. "Show yourself!"

A dark laugh carried through the air, but he never appeared. Instead, he sent more arrows our way. We dodged them all, but Felicks leapt from Kost's shoulder and let out a guttural bark as he flattened himself against the earth.

Kost's frantic gaze swept the area, then he grabbed Gaige's wrist and dragged him to the forest floor. "Get down!"

We didn't hesitate, and a breath later, a rush of shadow blades soared through the trees from every direction. They sliced through leaves and cut into branches, showering us in debris. Dominus let out a gut-wrenching cry that rattled my bones. A blade had cut open his hide, and blood wept from the wound. Snarling, he faltered for only a moment before returning his focus to the Gigloam.

I pushed myself from the ground, desperate to get to my beast, but Noc wrapped his hand around my wrist. "Wait." Ire filled his ice-blue eyes, and he fired the blood blades hovering about his body deep into the woods.

A pained scream rose above the treetops as one of them found its target.

"Kost, Ozias, on me. Calem, stay with Leena and Gaige." Shadows flung to him, and he bolted around Jax's protective barriers and into the forest. Oz paused only for a moment, his gaze bouncing to his beast. Jax let out a reassuring growl before hunkering down behind a rock wall. Safe, for the moment. It was enough to spur Oz into motion. He launched from the trees, the groaning of branches beneath his feet clashing with the endless roars of the legendary felines and the Gigloam.

Kost sprinted after them with Felicks at his side, only for an enemy assassin to dart in front of them. Felicks let out a startling bark, and then weaved between the attacker's legs, sinking his pointed teeth into the man's calf. He buckled forward, and Kost lunged. His rapier slid cleanly through the assailant's chest, and they were gone before the body even hit the ground.

Darrien's eerie laugh once again filtered through the dense woodland, and the arrows and shadow blades stopped.

With the air clear, I leapt from the ground toward my beasts, eyes locked on Dominus's injury. He seemed undaunted, but the constant strain from fighting only made the bleeding worse.

Gaige rushed to my side. "Okean's attack is about to fade. Stay back!"

The sound of rushing water died as Okean's torrent gave out. Seizing the opportunity, the Gigloam let out a fierce battle cry and charged toward Okean. With its head angled down, the creature's antlers were poised to spear Gaige's beast. But Reine materialized before it could make contact, flanking the creature's side and sinking her teeth deep into its shoulder. Blood spilled from the wound and the Gigloam howled, peeling off course and ramming into a tree.

Gaige winced. "The only way to subdue it is to sever its skull helm. It won't fight without it."

My mind raced as I watched Dominus and Okean rejoin the

fray. None of them could come within striking distance of the helm, let alone get the needed leverage to physically sever it. Even with Reine's teleporting powers, the monster somehow was able to deflect every time. Why was this happening? Was this monster really that much stronger than our felines? Yes, Gigloams were powerful, A-class beasts, but this one had *died*, according to our legends. Then again... My gaze slanted to Calem and the shadows festering around his frame. The assassins became something else, something stronger, when they'd passed, too.

Moonlight once again gathered between the Gigloam's antlers. Charging time and power were dictated by the phase of the moon etched into its bone helm. Half moon, half power—but half the amount of time it took to summon a deadly attack.

"Run!" I screamed at our beasts. The felines scattered in response, barely dodging the disastrous beam of light. The Gigloam's face swiveled to me, and he let out a bone-chilling growl. Claws gouged the earth as the beast stalked our direction, crushing Jax's erected rock walls with its skull. A warning rumbled from the back of Jax's throat, and Calem shoved us back, putting himself between us and the approaching beast.

"Stay behind me," he commanded as he summoned a shadow blade and sent it flying through the forest. It sailed toward the beast with deadly accuracy, but right as it was about to slice into the soft spot behind its helm, the Gigloam jerked his head and caught the blade with its antlers. It careened off course and thudded into the trunk of a tree before disappearing.

The beast let out an enraged roar, but Calem didn't back down.

"Are you insane?" My gaze darted between him and the Kitska monster. Calem's form wavered, scales creeping up his neck and over his temples, and he crouched low to the ground. The Gigloam pressed forward as a glimmer of something gold peeked through the dense wood behind it. Before I could get another glimpse, it disappeared, and the Gigloam shuddered. It tossed its head back and frantically scoured the woods at its back.

Gaige narrowed his eyes. "Something drove it this way. That's why it's attacking."

"Darrien?" Calem growled.

Another flash of gold flickered in my peripheral vision, and unease stirred low in my gut. The Gigloam twitched in answer. Then, snapped his attention back to us. Something was out there. Something even this Kitska monster didn't dare face.

My mouth dried as I took a step back. "I don't think so."

In the distance, an angry shout, followed by a pained cry, echoed through the night. A chill swept through me. Oz. Calem's head jerked in the direction of the sound. Scales consumed the rest of his body as devastating claws erupted from his nail beds. Any minute now and he'd shift completely.

"We can't help them until we deal with the Gigloam," I said. The creature rammed into another one of Jax's walls, clearing the last barrier between us and him. Lava rock scattered before our feet, and the monster roared. Wild eyes targeted us with ferocious certainty.

Our felines slunk through the woods, soft chatters slipping from their maws. With the Gigloam's attention on us, they inched closer and flanked his rear. They moved like predators with gleaming, narrowed eyes transfixed on the creature's bone helm. We just needed to pin the monster, and then we could help our family.

Another sickening scream sounded in the distance, and my body thrummed with fear. We needed to act. Fast.

Pin the Gigloam, sever the helm... If only I could call on my Graveltot. My small, spherical beast could manipulate gravity and hold the Gigloam down, but there was no way to solely target the creature. We'd all be unable to move. My mind whirred. What else?

The Vrees? We'd only just formed a bond. He'd been so reluctant to fight while under Yazmin's command, and he was still recovering from the emotional toll of attacking his own kind. He needed his time in the beast realm, free from worry or concern.

The Gigloam roared and spittle flew from its yellowed teeth. And then it charged.

Jax moved first, and the ground rumbled beneath us as a rock wall exploded from the earth, right beneath the Gigloam's feet. It toppled backward, and Dominus lunged. His gleaming claws raked against the monster's hide, and blood coated the dirt beneath them. Okean went for the jugular, and Reine teleported to the base of the creature's neck. She sank her fangs at the juncture between the protruding bone helm and the Gigloam's skull, and the creature howled so deeply, so violently, that the very air seemed to shake. He tossed his head in an attempt to shake her off, skewering her with his antlers and cutting a wound deep into her belly.

"Reine!" I cried, tearing toward them. Gaige raced after me, but neither of us were as fast as Calem. A hound-shaped blur barreled ahead, crashing into the thick hide of the monster. Dominus and Okean scattered to avoid the collision, and Reine teleported to me before collapsing at my feet.

"Shh, you're okay," I said, running my hands over her fur. My fingers came away sticky and bright-red. Panic clawed at my throat. Where Dominus's wound had been shallow, Reine's was much deeper. Tendons and muscle were ripped to shreds, and I pressed shaky fingers over the laceration.

"Let's get you home." I sent her back to the beast realm to recover as Calem and the Gigloam slammed into a tree, splinters erupting around them. Snarling, Calem leapt a few feet away. Kaori's Ossilix, with her healing saliva, had saved his life, but also changed him forever. The dominating hound that was once my friend stood tall before us with thick, stone-like scales covering the entirety of his body. His mercury eyes were feral, and yet...

He turned his head a fraction, gaze softening for an instant. As if to assure us he was fine. In control. But when the Gigloam lumbered to its feet, Calem crouched and peeled back his maw, revealing razor-sharp teeth.

It was beast against monster, and after seeing just how deadly the Gigloam could be, I wasn't sure if Calem's newfound power would be enough.

SIX

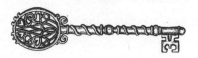

LEENA

Calem and the Gigloam crashed into each other, neither one buckling, and they pushed onto their hind legs in a lethal wrestling match. Violent snarls barreled from their chests as their teeth gnashed together. Quaking beneath the weight of the Gigloam, Calem took a step back as his paws skidded in the dirt.

"Okean, help him," Gaige urged.

"Keep the monster distracted," I said to Dominus, and both legendary felines yowled in answer before lunging. Taking advantage of the monster's stance, they attacked its heels from behind.

"How do we get to the helm?" I asked.

A low, citrine glow bloomed from the back of Gaige's hand. "I don't know. I don't know what beast to summon, either."

Again, gold flashed from the trees behind the beasts. I blinked, but it was gone in an instant. My heart hammered against my rib cage. Even if we managed to deal with the Gigloam, there was still another predator out there lying in wait. A pained whine brought my attention back to Calem. "Why won't it go down?" Adrenaline raced through to my fingers as I watched him and our beasts struggle to keep their footing.

The citrine light around Gaige's hand sharpened as his voice faltered. "I don't know!"

Subdue the beast. Subdue... I let out a scream as the Gigloam pushed forward and scraped his claws along Calem's belly. But Calem's scales held, the soft flesh beneath unscathed, and he roared in the face of the Kitska monster. The only thing I'd seen pierce Calem's hide had been my Naughtbird.

"Naughtbird!" I shouted. Thrusting my hand forward, I pulled open the beast realm door and Kels, my small, finch-like creature came flying out. She zipped through the air, her iridescent feathers shimmering even in the dimmed light of the woods, and cocked her head in the direction of the beast fight.

"The Gigloam," I said, pointing toward the lumbering creature. "Hurry!"

Kels darted through the trees and hovered above the beast's head. Her tail feathers twitched from left to right as she tried to pinpoint an opening. Before she could strike, the Gigloam overpowered Calem, shoving him to the ground with his massive claws. Moonlight burst from its skull, and beams lanced the felines still tearing into its hind legs. They darted away, leaving the Gigloam to turn all its terrifying fury on Calem. Saliva dripped from its teeth as it pulled back its maw and roared.

"Now!" I shrieked. Kels dove, and her thin, needle-shaped beak drove into the one of the Gigloam's hindquarters. For a moment, nothing happened. Then, the beast let out a long, low groan, and it swayed over Calem.

"Okean! Dominus! Help him," Gaige called. Both felines lunged. They dug their paws into the back of the Gigloam and clawed up its spine. A pained roar rattled from the back of its throat, and it shook violently in an attempt to throw them. Pressing flat to its hide, they held on as the beast released its hold on Calem and began ramming into trees.

"It should be sleeping by now." I desperately looked between the Gigloam and Kels. "Her saliva should've put it under."

Gaige tracked our yowling felines still clinging to its back. "Our beast's powers aren't as effective against Kitska monsters. But the Gigloam is slowing. It can't hold out forever." The creature stumbled, barely catching its footing before crashing face-first into the earth. Abruptly, Gaige straightened. "Calem, now while the Gigloam is weakened. Remove the helm!"

Calem hesitated just long enough to glance my way and judge my reaction. The Gigloam would immediately stop fighting once the helm was removed. It would take days for it to regrow, but there'd be no lasting damage.

I nodded, and Calem howled before charging the beast. He leapt over our felines and targeted the creature's bone helm. The Gigloam roared and tossed its head, attempting to impale Calem with its antlers, but Kels's serum had made it sluggish. Dodging the sharpened points, Calem dug his elongated claws into the soft flesh where the protective skull protruded from the beast's head. A stomach-turning crack splintered through the air as Calem pried the helm free. It fell to the forest floor with a loud thud, and the creature went completely still. Okean and Dominus slumped to their haunches and began licking each other's wounds, while Calem sauntered over to Jax and gave him a gentle nudge with his snout. Kels landed on a nearby branch and let out a soft chirp. Everyone was safe.

Relief sang through me, and my shoulders sagged. "Thank the goddess."

Gaige nodded, then looked to the woods. "We should rejoin the others."

I scoured the scene, halting for a moment as I studied the immo-bilized Gigloam. "What about the Gigloam?"

Gaige frowned. "What about it? It's a top predator, so nothing will bother it. Any minute now and it will fall into a hibernation until its helm returns."

I chewed the inside of my cheek. Gaige wasn't wrong, but something about leaving the beast unprotected didn't sit right with me. Darrien's men were lingering in these woods. What if they hurt it? What if they tried to capture it?

"I have an idea. It'll only take a minute." Turning on my heels, I signaled to Jax. "Form a barrier around him. When he wakes, he can destroy it and have free rein again."

Jax swiveled his head in the direction of the beast, and the ground began to rumble. One by one, rock walls with veins of lava erupted from the earth and towered over the creature. They curved toward one another, forming a dome that would keep the Gigloam safe.

As the last wall was shifting into place, a far-off, heartrend-ing cry filled the now quiet woods. The agonizing sound seemed to linger around us far longer than it should have, and a dreadful sinking sensation tugged at my stomach.

Calem's ears shot toward the sky, and a worried whine trickled from the back of his throat.

"What's happening?" Gaige's eyes flashed between him and the woods.

Panic crested in my chest as I stared at Calem. "Noc? Oz? Kost? Who is it? What's wrong?"

Before he could react, a gold streak lunged from behind a thicket of trees toward Gaige and me.

I didn't have time to move. To think. Neither did Gaige. A gold and umber cloud engulfed us, blocking out our surroundings and muffling the worried cries of Calem and our beasts. Gaige whirled, realization donning quickly on his features. Mouth agape, he stared at me for one harrowing moment before tackling me to the ground. My head cracked against a trunk, and my vision blurred. Through the haze, I spied the reason for Gaige's reaction: a Cumulo Leo. Yazmin's legendary feline. I'd been too warped by Wynn's charm to truly notice its power the day Cruor attacked Hireath, but there was no escaping its might now.

With a mane that resembled billowing clouds and four curling horns, it emerged from the haze and struck. Fangs sank into Gaige's back, and he screamed. As quickly as it had attacked, the Cumulo Leo pulled back. Then let out a misty breath that glimmered with gold flecks. It settled over Gaige's wound, and he went limp. A torturous cry broke through the cocoon the beast had created, followed by a burst of raging water that tore apart the clouds and rammed into the Cumulo Leo. It howled as it flew backward into the woods, and the last of the mist and clouds disappeared with it.

A haughty laugh seemed to erupt from the forest itself.

Gaige was entirely too heavy, and my fingers went cold. "Gaige," I croaked, unwilling to look directly at his face. "Come on, Gaige. Get up."

He didn't move.

Okean made it to us first, and he fell beside me. Slowly, I moved out of Gaige's grasp, and his beast immediately occupied the space. He let out a soft mewl, like a question, before nuzzling Gaige's cheek. When Okean's nose met his skin, the beast's entire body stilled. He let out a deep, gut-wrenching yowl that would live in my memory for the rest of my days.

Calem and Dominus rushed to our sides, followed immediately by Jax and Kels. Okean dropped his head and curled tight against

Gaige's side. I kept waiting for him to console his beast. To run a hand down his finned mane. But nothing happened. He stayed limp. Unmoving.

Tears pricked at my eyes as my breathing turned shallow. Slowly, I forced myself to look at Gaige's slackened face.

Dead.

My throat dried. *Gaige.* I reached for him, and then let my hand fall away. He'd protected me from the Cumulo Leo. He'd *known*. He had to. I knew the beast was fast and hard to target, but I didn't know about the breadth of its magic. Of the mist that could kill in an instant. But it hadn't affected me. Why?

Okean's body trembled. Dominus nudged him with his snout, whining softly. Blood puddled beneath Gaige's motionless form. The Cumulo Leo had pierced his skin and provided an open avenue for the mist to travel into his system, extinguishing his life.

A sharp cry escaped my lips, and I dug my fingers through the earth to keep the world from spinning. Why? Why had this happened? Why was Yazmin with Darrien? Suddenly, there was a frantic crashing from the woods. With Felicks glued to his side, Kost raced toward us. Blood dripped from a shallow cut on his cheek, and his clothes were torn and stained. Wild shadows spiked about his frame as he skidded to his knees, and his trembling hands hovered over Gaige.

"I saw..." He choked on his words, tears lining his eyes. "Felicks saw..."

A heavy ringing sounded in my ears. That wail. That gods-awful wail. Kost had seen Gaige's death while battling Darrien's forces. But two minutes hadn't been enough time for him to get to us. Instead...

"Heal him," Kost turned to his beast. "Heal him!"

Felicks darted forward and gave Gaige's wound a gentle lick.

When nothing happened, he sniffed the air before trying again. His ears drooped. Slowly, he looked at Kost with heavy eyes and ducked his head. His orb clouded, then cleared.

Kost blinked rapidly, as if trying to digest Felicks's vision as quickly as possible. Then, he blanched. "No." His voice rose an octave. "No!"

More crashing came from the woods as Noc and Oz emerged. Countless wounds in the process of healing lined Oz's arms, and he stumbled forward, barely putting any weigh on his left leg. Noc, too, had thin lines of blood tracking his arms and face, and a deep gash on his thigh.

"Darrien is gone. Injured, but he'll recover." He scowled at his words.

"Managed to take out a few of his followers, though," Oz grumbled, stretching his ankle. He looked up then and paused, thick brows crawling together. "Kost?"

Noc's gaze followed Oz's, and he stilled. "What happened?"

Slowly, I craned my neck upward. Words escaped me as I stared at Noc, and I swallowed several times as I released my grip on the earth. Blood and muck coated my fingers. "It's my fault."

Noc didn't move. "What?"

Shaking my head, I closed my eyes to try to stop the sudden rush of tears. "We took too long. We should've left the moment we took down the Gigloam..." Guilt ravaged my stomach, and the sharp taste of acid flooded my tongue. We should've left. Gaige wanted to. There was no reason to stay behind and protect the Gigloam. He would've been fine. But Gaige? Slowly, I peeled open my eyes.

We'd never see his mischievous smile again.

"He's dead." My voice was quiet, but Kost flinched just the same. Unconstrained shadows lashed around him, and Calem inched forward, unperturbed by their wild slashes. He inhaled deeply, as if he needed to check for the scent of death to believe it himself—or maybe to confirm if summoning his beast, Effie, would help revive our friend—and then whimpered. Noc and Oz stared at Gaige's lifeless body in horror. Only after Calem fell to his haunches did they finally jolt forward to join Kost's side.

Time stretched as we waited for Kost to say something. Anything other than the quiet "no" he'd been muttering on repeat since Felicks's vision. Unbridled agony filled his green eyes, and his whole body trembled. Okean glanced up at him and let out a soft, heart-wrenching bellow. The low, somber note was an unbearable weight we couldn't escape, even after Okean had tucked his head back against his master. That horrifying sound shook Kost from his reverie, and the maelstrom of shadows surrounding him exploded outward. They slashed into trees, severing limbs from trunks and tearing into underbrush. And yet he remained still.

Noc waded through the dark tendrils and gripped his brother's shoulder. "Kostya."

The shadows spiraled in response.

"I'm sorry." I fisted the fabric of my breeches and averted my gaze. I couldn't look at Kost. Couldn't stand his pain and fury. All those emotions he never spoke of were on display, and it was too much to bear. Especially when Gaige had reacted to save my life. Especially when it was my fault we'd lingered. "I should have protected him."

"Raise him." Kost's voice was soft but cut like a blade.

Noc didn't flinch. "Are you sure that's what's best?"

Kost whirled on him, turning all his ire on the brother he'd known the longest. "Gods help me, Noc. Raise. Him."

Noc glanced at me, silently asking for help. Shakily, I brought myself to my feet, feeling Kost's eyes on me, waiting. "Kost... I'm not sure Gaige would want that. I didn't." Images of my death filled my mind. Of Noc's crazed eyes and the way his hands had felt around my neck. I hadn't wanted to die. To live a life without him. But had he raised me... Had I been born again, unable to access the beast realm... The symbol on the back of my hand would've been a painful reminder of everything I'd lost, of everything I could never have again. Could I have lived with that? Could Gaige?

"Please." Soft. So soft. The shadows around Kost died, and he curled in on himself. "I never got the chance to... I..." He slipped his hands beneath his glasses and pressed his fingers against his eyes, choking back a sob.

Noc let out a slow breath. I knew how much he hated to raise the dead. Especially when he had a strong suspicion that the one being raised wouldn't want to live with the shadows. But for Kost... I doubted there was anything he wouldn't do.

And still, he looked to me. A fist wrenched my heart and twisted it violently. This had to be my decision. Gaige was a Charmer. I was his Crown. Even if Noc held the power to raise him from the dead, Gaige would look to me for answers. Slowly, I rounded my gaze on Kost. Who's wish was I supposed to honor? An ache simmered deep in my bones, and I took a steadying breath.

"Do it," I said. My quiet words tasted like ash. Kost snapped his head upward, spearing with emotion-filled, glassy eyes. I hated to say it. Hated to put Gaige in the position I would've never wanted to be in myself. But looking at Kost now... Maybe I'd do just about anything for my family, too. Or maybe I was being selfish. Maybe I wanted Gaige back because I couldn't stand the thought of him dying when I was partially to blame. "We can talk to Gaige after. He... He might feel differently than I do."

Noc stared at me for a long moment before letting out a sigh.

He shifted his focus to Kost. "Do you remember the rules? The ones I made you follow when I was raised?"

Kost nodded. "Of course. If he doesn't want this life, at any point, then I'll end it. Just like I promised you."

Noc seemed to consider each word before relenting. His shoulders loosened a touch. "Good. But not here." Noc gestured to the wood. "The transformation is jarring enough. He should be somewhere comfortable when it happens. Let's get him back to Cruor."

Calem, still in his beast form, sauntered toward Oz and knelt before him. With a belabored look, he nudged Oz's battered limbs. Oz grumbled, but didn't deny Calem's help. Instead, he climbed onto his back, extracted his bronze key to send Jax back to the beast realm, and collapsed in an exhausted heap. Yazmin had struck first and won. Both she and Darrien had escaped, and we were left a bloody mess. Opening the beast realm door, I sent Dominus and Kels home and moved to Noc's side.

"Thank you." Kost swallowed back his emotions, keeping his voice low and even, and then summoned a bed of shadows to lift Gaige off the ground. Okean stood and rubbed against Kost's leg, gaze still locked on his master. Something deep and painful flared in my chest, and I had to look away. Okean would remain in this world, unable to return to the beast realm, unless a Charmer took him in like I had for Dominus. And I would do it without question, if that's what Gaige wanted. But a Charmer had never been raised before. Maybe, just maybe, Gaige would still be able to open the door when he woke and send Okean home.

But as we hurried toward Cruor, a sinking feeling settled in the pit of my stomach. I feared the shadows would take over Gaige's life completely, barring the beast realm door shut for eternity. Countless beasts, simply...gone. He'd never be able to call on them again, or feel the warm bond that tethered them together. Or even enter the realm, the very world Celeste created solely for us and our beasts, without the aid of a Charmer. If I were faced with such an existence... I'd let the shadows swallow me whole, with no desire to ever claw my way back out.

SEVEN

NOC

We made it to Cruor's doorstep within an hour of the attack, just as the sun crested over the forest line and ushered in the morning. Wasting no time, we brought Gaige's body into the first available room and placed him on the bed. Calem had shifted back to his human form and snagged some clothes before helping Ozias to the infirmary. Which left Leena, Kost, and me to stare at Gaige's lifeless body. Even with the morning light slanting through the open curtains, his skin looked gray. Cold.

Leena gripped the hemline of her blouse and cast a glance at Okean. He paced along the far wall, never settling. Occasionally a soft, pained yowl would slip from his throat. Leena's face fell. "Kost, are you sure about this? Are you prepared if he says no?"

"No." He'd never stopped looking at Gaige. "But I need to hear it from him. I need him to decide that it's over. Not Yazmin. Not anyone else."

I flexed my fingers, but didn't move. When I'd first been raised, I felt like I'd been robbed of my choice. And if what Leena said was true, that the beast realm door wasn't accessible to her when she was in the shadow realm, then I doubted this was a life he'd want to lead. He'd likely choose death. And Kost... My gaze flickered to him. I wasn't sure he could live with that. He'd always cared more about people than he ever admitted. If Gaige held a place in his heart, no matter how small, losing him would destroy Kost.

There was no other choice I could make.

I moved to the bedside and ripped open Gaige's shirt. Honing to fine points, my fingernails cut into his rib cage and exposed his quiet heart. Okean stilled, but he didn't move to defend his master. Instead, he pinned me with a stare so full of agony that I winced. Dominus had been lost after Wynn died. Okean would be the same.

Slitting open my palm, I drizzled blood over Gaige's wound. My cut healed swiftly—Gaige didn't. A few miserable minutes passed with nothing happening, and a flicker of fear sparked in me. What if the beast's magic prevented me from raising him? What if I couldn't give Kost what he wanted? What if my brother blamed me for this horrendous outcome? I glanced at Leena, and she edged closer, Okean by her side. Tension filled the air as we all waited for Gaige to react. Maybe it wasn't the beast, but *him*. Could Charmers even *be* raised?

Something unreadable flashed in Leena's hazel eyes. Concern? Despair? How conflicted she must have felt, both wanting Gaige to be okay and knowing he'd resent a life without his beasts. Or... I studied the way she worried her lip and gripped her bestiary. Maybe it was something more. Proof that, if she ever changed her mind, decided she wanted to stay by my side forever, she couldn't.

My breath stilled.

Please.

I needed to know if this would work. If I *could* raise Leena, if it came to it.

Kost kneeled at Gaige's side and gripped his limp hand. "Gaige."

It was too much. Too many unspoken emotions were wrapped

up in that name. Something broke inside of Kost, that much I knew. I had to fix this.

Reopening my palm, I poured more blood over Gaige's heart. *Please, Zane. Don't fail me.* I needed his power, my power, to restore life to the fallen now more than ever before. Again, my wound healed. And again, I tore it open. Blood spilled outward until it filled Gaige's chest cavity completely. The room around me spun and darkened as my body tried to regenerate. I was depleting it faster than it had the chance to heal. Sweat broke out along my forehead and down the back of my neck, and my knees turned weak.

Leena cupped her hands around mine, ignoring the blood that ran between our fingers. "Noc."

Words raspy, I barely found my voice. "I can keep trying."

"No," Kost whispered. He gripped Gaige's hand tighter. "If this is how it has to be, then..."

Suddenly, Gaige's heart thumped. Not the slow, shuddering beat I'd always seen when raising the dead, but a resounding thud full of power and life. The heady cadence started in earnest, and I pressed my palm flat against his chest. As the last few droplets of my blood spilled out, I willed his wound to heal. And it did. Faster than I'd ever witnessed. Tendons, muscle and flesh all knitted back together until there was nothing but smooth skin.

Kost's brows creased. Clearly, he'd never seen such a reaction, either. "Perhaps it has something to do with the mix of Charmer and assassin magic?"

"Is everything okay?" Leena asked. She wrapped her arm around my waist, offering support, and I slumped into her. Fatigue was normal post raising, but never had I felt so drained. Breathing sparked pain in my chest, and my stomach roiled.

"Rise," I commanded, ignoring the way my voice wavered.

Gaige's eyes flew open. Steel-blue and so...*alive*. Color returned to his body, and he blinked several times before glancing down at the hand Kost had clutched in his fingers. An uncertain smile claimed his lips, and then he went completely still. He rounded his gaze on me.

"I can hear your heartbeat." His words were measured, cautious. As if he knew what that meant but wasn't ready to admit it.

My shoulders tensed. "Yes."

His brow twitched. "And Leena's. And Kost's."

"Yes."

No one spoke. No one moved. The only sound aside from our hitched breaths was the near-silent hum of the rycrim heater in the corner. Something Leena likely wouldn't have noticed, but Gaige, but *us*… Shadows slithered in my peripheral vision, snaking between the rafters and curling around the foot of the bed. They were always just a thought away from being summoned. He'd see them now, too. He jerked his head to the side, as if trying to study them head on. His breath came quickly then, and he sat up, tearing his hand away from Kost. Leena inhaled sharply.

The jeweled color to his emblem was gone. Instead, the tree looked as if it'd been etched with graphite, complete with smeared edges. Worse, it was barren. There were no leaves, no flowering vines. No life at all. Slowly, he lifted his hand and finally looked at the damage I'd caused by bringing him back.

"No." His voice cracked. He thrust his hand forward. Muscles bulged along his forearm, and a cry wrenched free of his chest. Tears gathered in his eyes. Try as he might, nothing happened. There was no rush of citrine light, no groaning hinges. The beast realm door remained shut.

Kost reached for him. "Gaige, I'm the one—"

"No!" His shriek rattled my bones. The shadows reacted to his sudden influx of emotions and flared to life around him. I dropped my gaze. I'd hoped he would've been able to access the realm, that Leena's inability to do so was simply because she hadn't been raised. But now, her fears were confirmed. Our shadows took over *everything*.

Gaige stared in horror at his own hand, fingers shaking uncontrollably. "What have you done?"

And then, as if nearly erasing his symbol wasn't cruel enough, a sharp sizzling sounded from the bestiary around his neck. An invisible flame seemed to eat away at the book, and the cover turned black before crumbling to ashes, leaving nothing more than a smear on his skin where it used to be. The chain fell into his lap.

The horrified cry that escaped Gaige nearly broke me in two. Silent tears bisected Leena's cheeks, and she burrowed her head into my chest. Her fingers dug into my sides as she gripped me tight. After witnessing this, there was no way she'd ever agree to be raised now. And I couldn't blame her.

"You died. I couldn't... I..." Kost failed to find words. He stood and took a small step back, face carefully blank but green eyes full of uncertainty. Of guilt.

"They're gone. I can't... I can't feel them anymore." Gaige sobbed. His hand fell into his lap. A slow finger traced his faded emblem. He halted on one of the branches that still had just a small sliver of life. A tiny flower, barely hanging on. With a gasp, he jumped out of bed and searched the room, stilling when his gaze landed on Okean.

The legendary feline hadn't moved since I'd started. Cautiously, he stepped toward his master. Then sniffed. His hackles stood on end as he inhaled a few errant shadows. Gaige sank to his knees and offered Okean the back of his hand.

"It's me," he whispered. "I'm still me." His voice cracked, as though even he couldn't believe it. His trembling fingers hung suspended before his beast. Seconds crawled by, and Gaige's hitched breaths came hard and fast.

Okean peeled back his maw, teeth glistening.

Squeezing his eyes shut, Gaige placed his hand on Okean's snout. I had no ties to Celeste, the goddess of beasts, but in that moment, I prayed to her. I begged her to let Gaige have this, at least. Let Okean remember him. Let him have just a piece of his former life. Because if he couldn't... If his beast rejected him...then I had no doubt he'd walk away from this life for good.

Okean inhaled deeply again, and slowly, the tightly coiled muscles beneath his hide loosened. Finally, he pushed past Gaige's hand and rammed his head into his chest. He let out a deep purr as he tried to climb into his master's lap.

"Thank Celeste," Gaige cried, wrapping Okean in a hug.

Leena broke away from me to take a few careful steps toward Gaige. She touched his shoulder, and he flinched. "I gave them permission. We wanted you to have a choice."

He swallowed thickly. Something fierce flashed through his eyes. "*You* made a choice for me. I had no say in the matter."

"But you have one now." She lowered her lashes. "Gaige, I...I'd understand if you didn't want to live this life. I'd support your decision, no matter what anyone else might say." She didn't look toward Kost, but he flinched just the same. Kneeling, she took Gaige's hands in hers. "And I'd take care of Okean. I promise."

He looked at her then. So much understanding flowed between them that it almost felt wrong for Kost and me to be there. Kost glanced my way, spine rigid. Since Gaige had brushed him off, he'd turned to ice. He was still waiting, still expecting Gaige to turn his back on this life. At any moment, Kost would crack. Unless we could convince Gaige to stay.

Leena ran light fingers over Okean's hide, pausing when she

grazed the shallow wounds left from the Gigloam. "If you choose to stay, I can give you a key. I'll take him like I did with Dominus. The beast realm will heal him, and then I'll return him to you. He'll be safe, and you can still see him since the magic is tied to the key and not...you."

His chest heaved. For a long moment, all he did was stare at his beast. Voice rough, he whispered, "Okay."

Rosewood light bloomed from her hand, and Okean looked between her and Gaige. A soft mewl, like a question, sounded from his throat.

Gaige nodded. "It's only for a little bit. I promise."

The rosewood light sharpened, and the groaning of the beast realm door rumbled through the air. Gaige winced at the sound and turned, letting his arms fall away from Okean. Leena bit her lip but continued to focus her power on the legendary feline. Finally, he sighed. And just like that, the last remaining flower bud on Gaige's emblem disappeared. A strangled sound escaped his throat, but he nodded anyway. A picture of strength so Okean would go with Leena.

Together, they disappeared into the beast realm, leaving Gaige alone with me and Kost. Silence stretched between us. Kost still refused to move. The weight of what we'd done, of the suffering we'd caused, settled heavily over us. Slowly, I crossed the room and offered Gaige my hand, just like Talmage had done after raising me. Gaige studied it a moment before standing, ignoring my gesture altogether.

"You should've let me die."

I let my hand fall to my side. "If that's what you want, then I can arrange for it to happen."

"What, and torment Okean all over again?" Gaige's face hardened. "Leena should've taken him from the start. Now..."

"At least you can still see him," Kost said, voice soft. Tentative.

Gaige tensed. "Do you know how many other beasts I have? Excuse me, *had*?"

Kost finally looked up, meeting Gaige's gaze. "I'm sure Leena can fashion more keys for you."

"That's not the point, nor is it feasible," Gaige hissed. Tight fists formed at his sides. "You expect me to carry around hundreds of keys just to have some semblance of the life I used to lead? What if I lost one? What if it fell into the wrong hands? Not to mention, I'm not even sure I could call on them like I used to. I feel...different."

Kost braved a step his direction. "The transition is rough on everyone. We all felt different, too."

Gaige glared at him. "It's not the same. You can never understand what I've lost."

"We made the decision to raise you so you could live, Gaige." I slipped my hands into the pockets of my trousers. "Like I said, if you don't want that, death is still a possibility."

"Live?" His laugh was brittle, broken. "What's living without my beasts?"

"What about us?" Kost asked.

"What *about* you?" Gaige's question cut like a blade. Kost stiffened. This wasn't the first time a newly raised assassin had turned their ire on us for being handed such a fate. But Gaige's anger was different because it was tinted with torment. We *knew* him before the change, and we knew just how devastating a life without his beasts would be. And to hear that we—that *Kost*—weren't reason enough for him to stay... Kost looked away and pinpointed an indistinct spot on the wall as he adjusted his glasses.

"I will take responsibility for what happened. Now, do you want to live or die? Is anything here worth it to you?"

Tension flickered between them, unseen yet palpable. My

stomach turned with unease. I longed to disappear into the shadows. To give them a moment alone. They'd barely spent any time together since Yazmin's attack, and Kost was always so close-lipped with his emotions.

Before Gaige could answer, the beast realm door groaned open and Leena reappeared in a flood of rosewood light. With flushed cheeks and mussed hair, she strode toward Gaige and handed him a bronze key. "Here you go. Okean's healing up nicely. You should be able to summon him in no time." She glanced between him, Kost, and me. "Everything okay?"

"Everything is perfect," Gaige said with a sharp bite to his words as he accepted the key. "Now if you all would kindly *leave*, I'd like to be alone with my thoughts."

"Oh. Of course." Leena drew back, tossing me a sidelong glance. "We should probably check on Oz, anyway."

"If you need anything, just ask. There's a bathroom through that door there." I pointed to a door on the other side of the room, nestled between an armoire and the rycrim heater. "Spare clothes can be found in the dresser."

Gaige didn't respond. Instead, he turned his back on us, making what he wanted—*needed*—abundantly clear: privacy. Without another word, I led Leena and Kost out of the room, hoping space would give him a chance to come to terms with his new life.

———◆———

The day came and went without Gaige emerging. And while he was newly raised and unable to fully control the shadows, the tendrils that spilled from this room were impossibly strong. It was as if the power he'd wielded as a Charmer had nourished the darkness in a way I'd never seen. Rather than waiting to be manipulated or called upon, the shadows clung to his sides like beasts. Alive. Thriving. I sensed them writhing around his room, creating a cocoon of sorts that blanketed out all noise and masked his presence even from us. It put Kost on edge, and he paced in front of the hearth in the foyer, occasionally glancing at the ceiling only to shake his head.

Fully recovered, Ozias sat on the couch with Calem, each of them tracking Kost's movements. In the armchair across from them, Leena pressed her elbows to her knees, cupping her chin in her hands and staring into the crackling fire. I stood beside her, silently wishing Gaige would come down and put my family at ease. A few other assassins milled about the residence. Some upstairs, some in the library playing games or reading books. A few were loitering in the kitchen, munching on food. One thing was clear: they were all waiting and eavesdropping without showing their faces. Since Yazmin's attack, I'd made it clear that changes were coming, and that we'd be working with the Charmers against our enemies. They just didn't know exactly what that meant.

"So," Calem said, finally breaking the silence, "how's he holding up?"

"I don't know," Kost replied, voice tight.

"Okkkaaay." He dragged out the word and glanced at me. I shook my head once. It was better to leave Gaige out of this conversation for now. Calem sighed, but didn't argue. "Now what?"

"We move forward with the plan," I replied. "Get everyone to Hireath so we only have to defend one location. Today proved just how vulnerable we are." Running a hand through my hair, I sighed. Yazmin and Darrien had attacked and escaped, despite how prepared we thought we were. The worst part? We were all familiar with battle. If they had struck against anyone else, Charmers or even assassins who weren't skilled in combat, the damages would have been far worse.

"We need to move faster," Leena said. "The anniversary of Celeste's death is only a few weeks away. As it stands right now, we'd never survive against Yazmin."

"Leena," Ozias said, voice hushed.

"She's right." I shook my head. "We're severely outnumbered. Even more so when you count the number of people who are actually willing to fight. We need an army, but all we have is a small force."

"Why?" Calem asked. "Who are we really up against? Yazmin, Darrien, a handful of traitorous assassins." He ticked off his fingers as he spoke. "It's not as many as you make it sound."

"There's also the obvious fact that Yazmin and Darrien attacked us *together*." Kost continued to pace despite his halting words. "I wasn't even aware they knew each other, which tells us a few things. First, Yazmin is likely in Wilheim, because that's where we last saw Darrien."

Leena's eyes widened. "Wilheim? But she detests the king and his people."

Kost grimaced. "I can't say why. But if she's there, then she's likely spoken with King Varek. She's no doubt gained his favor somehow, just as Darrien has. Which means it's not *just* Yazmin, Darrien, and a handful of assassins we're up against."

Ozias let out a quiet whistle. "It's the entirety of Wilheim. Their army. The Sentinels."

My hands curled into fists. "That's why she went there. She's safe from us behind those walls. There's no way we could attack her while she prepares to raise Ocnolog."

Calem slumped forward. "Fuck."

"That was our entire plan. Stop her *before* she can get to Ocnolog. How are we supposed to do that if she's hiding behind King Varek?" Leena turned in her chair so she could look up at me. Worry filled her eyes. I'd told her that trying to stop Yazmin might result in war. We'd hope it wouldn't come to that, but if we had to move against Wilheim to get to her, then a war is exactly what we'd get.

"We can send in some assassins to do reconnaissance. Once we determine her location, we can strike." Kost finally stopped and turned to us. "I'll go."

"Like hell you will," Ozias said. "Do you not remember what happened last time we tried to sneak through Wilheim?"

"We'll be better prepared this time." Kost clenched his jaw, his words harsher than normal. He yanked a cloth out of his breast pocket and began polishing his lenses with fervor.

Ozias raised his brows and folded his arms across his chest. "Don't be rash."

"Rash?" Kost replaced his spectacles. "I'd never act without considering every angle."

"Like fucking hell you wouldn't," Calem mumbled.

"Do you have something you'd like to say to me?"

Calem leaned into the couch, cradling the back of his head with his hands. "Relax. You're not the only one who wants Yazmin dead, all right?" His eyes flashed, and the mercury thread around his irises widened a fraction.

"Enough," I said. Moving to Kost's side, I placed a firm hand on his shoulder and gave it a squeeze. "We'll get her. We just have to be smart."

Kost didn't pull away, but he didn't acknowledge me, either. Instead, he turned his harsh glare to the snarling fire. Orange flames reflected across his lenses, and he flattened his lips into a thin line.

"So all of Wilheim..." Leena mused, voice soft. She stared at the coffee table before her, twisting her fingers in the chain of her bestiary. Her brow furrowed. After a beat, her hand stilled. "Is King Varek well liked?"

I shrugged. "No idea. It doesn't matter, though. Wilheimian

soldiers are known for being steadfastly loyal to the crown. The Sentinels even more so." My mind rewound back to the years we battled against Rhyne. Our soldiers never failed to pick up their swords when enemy forces approached, no matter how many of them often—and not so subtly—grumbled about the war. No matter how many of them didn't believe me when I claimed to have no part in Amira's death. They'd been right all along, just not in the way they assumed.

Leena stood suddenly, realization clear as day on her face. "So if the king tells them to stand down, they won't fight."

"King Varek wouldn't do that," Kost said.

"King *Varek* wouldn't." Slowly, she rounded her gaze on me.

A prickling sensation raced across my skin. "What are you getting at?"

"I know you never wanted it, but..." She waited, as if giving me the opportunity to interject. I blinked. She *couldn't* be asking this of me. Not after all these years. Not after I abandoned my title to save my country from ruin. A dull ringing started in my ears.

Beside me, Kost dragged his gaze away from the fire to glance my direction. "With the mage's glamour lifted, there's no doubt people would recognize you."

My throat tightened. "No."

"Noc." Leena took a careful step my direction. "You said it yourself. We need an army."

Ozias leaned forward, bracing his forearms on his knees. "Are you guys suggesting what I think you are?"

"Don't expect me to start addressing you as 'King,'" Calem said. The teasing lilt to his voice should've made me chuckle, but it only made me cringe.

"I'm not anyone's king."

"Not yet," Kost said. "You'd need to finish the rites by visiting the remaining mage burial sites. Only then would the Sentinels and Wilheim's army think of joining your side. There might still be some who remain loyal to Varek, as you technically *did* die, but..." He started to pace again, eyes tight as he gathered his thoughts. He nodded. "It just might work."

"It won't."

Kost waved away my response. "Certainly not all would join our cause, but every person who comes to our side is one less soldier on Varek's side."

"No." My hands fisted by my side. "I don't want to rule."

And that is why you must.

The ghost of Oslo's words rumbled through my mind. He'd said that very thing to me when I'd first rebelled against the thought of ruling. He'd judged me and deemed me worthy, all in the span of a breath. I still didn't understand how he came to that conclusion. How, after everything I'd done, the mages—the gods—believed I belonged on the throne.

You two can rewrite history.

My gaze snapped to Leena. Maybe it wasn't me after all. Maybe it was her they wanted.

She grabbed my hands. "I'm asking Charmers to risk everything to stand against Yazmin. I'm their leader now. And you, my *anamcara*, have a voice, too." With pleading eyes, she gave me a gentle squeeze. "Please. Please help them. Please do whatever you can."

Her words tugged at me. Choosing to rule after I'd willingly abandoned my title and my country... I didn't belong on the throne. But she did. Some of the tension that had gathered in my shoulders softened as I threaded my fingers with hers. She was strong. Determined. Caring. The compassion she showed for her people, the will she had to protect them... My former kingdom deserved a ruler like her. I needn't be anything more than a figurehead. All I had to do was support her, offer advice, and teach her Wilheimian customs.

Gently, I brushed a thumb along her jaw. "One condition."

Her smile stretched wide. "Anything."

"Take the throne with me." My chest tightened. Yes, she was my pair bond. My *anam-cara*. She would always be those things—and that was enough for me. But our country needed a queen. I wanted the people of Wilheim to hear her thoughts and her opinions, always. I wanted her to look at the capital and find ways to repair it, just like she was doing with the Charmers and Hireath. And I wanted Wilheimians to look to her with the same authority as they would to me.

Cupping my face in her hands, she laughed. "Did you think I'd let you marry someone else?"

Sweeping her into my arms, I slanted my lips across hers. I'd never thought much about proposing, not even when my father chastised me to find someone suitable. I wasn't sure how I would've asked for her hand if circumstances had been different, if we'd had more time. It hardly mattered when she'd already bestowed the title of *anam-cara* on me. But I knew I would've given her the world if that's what she wanted. I still would.

Calem coughed. "Now that *that's* out of the way..."

I broke my kiss with Leena to glance at him over the top of her head. "We need to get to Tyrus's and Yuna's burial sites. After that, I can address Wilheim as the rightful heir and ask them to produce Yazmin and avoid conflict altogether."

"And if they don't fall in line?" Ozias asked. "It's been years. And you said it yourself, you weren't exactly well liked before you died."

"Leena's right. I have to try."

Leena wrapped an arm around my waist and leaned into me. "We'll figure something out, but at least we can start with this."

Warmth filled my limbs, and I hugged Leena tighter. There was no telling if her plan would pan out. But I believed in Leena, in the good she could offer. And it wasn't just me. My family—Kost, Calem, Ozias—believed in her. The Charmers. The gods. She was already a pillar of strength, of security, for so many. If anyone could take down Varek and Yazmin, it was Leena.

And I'd be right there with her, every step of the way.

"But first," she said, "we need to move everyone to Hireath."

"I can help with that."

Gaige waited on the stairs, his arms draped over the wrought-iron railing. How long had he been there? The shadows typically masked our movements, but new recruits rarely wielded them well enough from the start to deafen their footsteps. Yet there he stood. He'd bathed and dressed in fresh clothes, but something about the ebony attire felt wrong on him. Stiff. He'd rolled the sleeves of his tunic up over his forearms, exposing a gray filigree pattern on the cuffs. Leather gloves hid his hands—and his mark.

Leena spied this, too, and she winced. "Gaige. I'm glad you're okay."

"'Okay' is a relative term, but I'm here."

Kost stilled and looked away. "Good."

Gaige remained impassive. "I'll escort the assassins to Hireath. It sounds like you have places to be."

"I'll assist you," Kost said.

"That's not necessary." A flicker of emotion raced through Gaige's expression, but it was gone in an instant.

"We've been looking into Yazmin's plans *together*." Kost's voice rose and trembled before he cleared his throat. His hands formed neat fists by his sides. "We cannot deviate from our strategy now. We must stop her."

Gaige said nothing.

"I agree," I hedged. It'd been ages since I'd struck out on a journey without my brother by my side, but Kost was right. We needed answers. Leena, Ozias, Calem, and I would travel to the ruins, and Kost and Gaige would lead the assassins back to Hireath. Hopefully there he could decipher the remaining parts of Yazmin's spell so we could stop it.

Gaige's lips thinned. "I suppose I can't stop you from coming. After all, it's your *choice*."

Kost bristled. "An obvious one to make." Despite his sharp response, there was an uncharacteristic restlessness to his stance. His fingers tapped against his pant leg, and he peered at me for a fleeting moment. Finally, he looked downward and murmured, "Even if it isn't easy."

"Sure." Gaige scoffed. "Tomorrow, then." Without another word, he turned and left, ascending the stairs as silently as he'd appeared.

Kost looked after him, but didn't move to follow. "I don't like the idea of not coming with you, Noc, but..."

"It's the smartest move." I tucked my hands into my trouser pockets and gave a tight nod. "We won't be gone long. Everything will work out."

His smile was weak. "I thought you weren't in the business of making false promises."

"I'm not."

But as he left to gather his things, leaving the rest of us to notify the members of Cruor of our plans and pack for our own journey, an undeniable weight settled in my gut. Gaige had *changed*. Already, things weren't going according to plan.

EIGHT

LEENA

The morning air was still, quiet, as we sat atop our Zeelahs and watched the assassins leave their home. For the most part, they were silent. Faces blank. As they reached the iron gate marking the edge of their land and the beginning of Kitska Forest, shadows swallowed them whole, carrying them a short distance away, where they'd continue to remain hidden in darkness, per Kost's orders. Since our plans had changed and we were no longer using beasts to help transport them, the shadows provided better protection from Yazmin's spies. And because Darrien's attack had failed, Noc believed it would be some time before he recovered and would attack again. The best time to move was now, even though it was difficult to leave Cruor behind. I couldn't imagine what it must have felt like to walk away from the only place that offered haven after their own people cast them out. When I'd been exiled from Hireath for crimes I didn't commit, I'd found a home in Midnight Jester. If Dez had forced me to leave, I would've been devastated.

I gripped the reins of my mare tight. The move was only temporary and for their own protection, but it chafed just the same. Beside me on his mount, Noc was a statue. Whatever emotions brewed inside him were unreadable in his expression. Oz and Calem weren't quite as skilled at burying their feelings. Or maybe they didn't care to. Calem's jaw was set tight, the mercury line around his irises flaring wide. Thick brows knitting together, Oz looked after his family with worry.

"They'll be fine, right?" I asked.

"Yazmin is after you and me. Not them," Noc said. "If anything, they're safer without us."

"I don't know about that." Kost manifested before us in a swirl of shadows. They disappeared as quickly as he'd appeared, and he ran an errant hand down his vest. "Iov and Gaige are leading the charge. Emelia, Astrid, and I will bring up the rear." He gestured to a pair of assassins lingering near the gate. It was weird to see Emelia without her twin brother, Iov, but Astrid was still newly raised. She was fearless, though, with her perpetual grin and fighting spirit. She bounced on her heels next to Emelia, who stood with quiet authority and directed the assassins into the forest.

"You'll make it to Hireath before we get to Tyrus's Ruins. Send word when you arrive so we know you've made it safely."

Kost nodded curtly. "Understood." He gave us all one last look before pausing when his gaze met mine. "I have something for you." He dove one hand into the satchel he'd draped across his body and extracted a thick book with archaic, bold font.

I took it from his extended hand and trailed my fingers over the title. "*A Brief History of Wilheim?*" I cracked the binding and thumbed through the pages. Gaige had used this very tome, along with one other, to unearth Noc's hidden identity as the Frozen Prince of Wilheim. "What am I going to do with this?"

"Study, of course." He frowned. "You're an outsider who's about to become the queen of Wilheim. A little knowledge of the capital's history wouldn't hurt."

Gently, I closed the book before tucking it into one of my

saddle bags. "The first act I'm going to do as queen is appoint you to be my adviser."

With a strained smile, Kost nodded. "I'd be honored." He gestured toward his brothers. "Look after them, will you?"

"Of course," I said.

"We can take care of ourselves, you know," Calem grumbled.

"I know." He looked away, back to the train of assassins, and then off into the forest where Gaige and Iov must have been. My stomach squirmed. It was unusual to see Kost so...frayed. His typical composure was gone, replaced by fidgety limbs and uneasy glances. No doubt he was questioning his decision, wondering if he should have stayed with Noc, with us. But if he'd done that and left Gaige behind just a day after being raised...

"Hey, Kost?" I shifted my mount closer to him. "Ask Gaige to show you the prophecy in the throne room when you get back. I know you've already talked about it at length, but...maybe revisiting it will help." Kost's mind was built for solving problems, and I got the feeling he needed to be reminded of that. I hoped giving him some kind of purpose, something to hold onto until we got back, would keep him grounded. Especially if Gaige wasn't himself anymore.

Kost met my gaze, eyes and voice soft. "I will." And with that, he stepped backward into shadows, disappearing from my view.

"I miss prick Kost." Calem frowned, his gaze tracking something I couldn't see. Probably Kost.

"He'll be fine." Noc's too-quick response spoke volumes, and for a moment, his stoic expression cracked. Eyes tight, he pressed his lips together before tugging on the reins of his Zeelah. Nudging my mount's sides, I guided her after him with Oz and Calem on my heels.

"He *will* be fine."

Noc let out a heavy sigh. "I hope so. I still don't know if I did the right thing. If I caused more harm than good."

I wrapped my fingers in my bestiary, savoring the flicker of power that warmed my fingers at its touch. Life without my beasts would've been unimaginable. And the look on Gaige's face when he saw his mark…when his bestiary turned to ash… A chill crawled down my spine, and I dropped my hand into my lap. Still, Gaige had chosen to live. Perhaps only because of Okean—trapped or saved by his beast, I couldn't say—but he was here just the same. He'd hung Okean's key around his neck where his bestiary used to be. It was almost too painful to look at it.

"You may have raised Gaige, but I encouraged you to do it, and he made the ultimate decision to live—just like you did when Talmage raised you. Give him time to figure it out."

Noc nodded and then fell silent, his gaze trained on the path before us. It would take nearly a week for us to reach Tyrus's Ruins. Not to mention, we'd be entirely exposed for the length of our travel. The rolling plains that stretched from the Kitska Forest to the Gaping Wound, the massive canyon where Tyrus's Ruins was located, was nearly devoid of trees. It made for easy travel, but even easier detection. And we had plenty of enemies who were all too eager to find us.

We didn't even bother to make camp that first night, instead choosing to move forward and put more distance between us and the capital. Its gleaming walls were a beacon in the night, competing with the moon for brilliance across the frostbitten landscape. We gave Wilheim a wide berth, adjusting our route to avoid the city's outskirts and the train. With Noc's shock-white hair and crystal-blue eyes, there'd be no mistaking him now. The last thing we needed was someone sounding the alarm.

But by the following evening, we'd pushed our Zeelahs to their limit and were forced to rest. Wilheim was still there, a harbinger we couldn't escape on these flat, endless plains. Noc stared at it, jaw tight. After a moment, he shook his head and then slid from his mount's saddle. His feet crunched against the grass.

Oz followed suit, craning his neck about as if searching for something. "Here? There's no cover."

"There's no cover anywhere." Calem dismounted and scowled. He made quick work of removing his Zeelah's saddle and our bags. She let out a soft whinny of relief and nudged her head into his shoulder.

"We don't have a choice." Noc unbuckled his mount's saddle and gave him a gentle pat on the neck. "Fortunately, that means we'll be able to see them coming, too."

Unless Yazmin had a beast we couldn't detect. I ignored the thought altogether, pushing it to the back of my brain. There was no use in speculating what creatures she did or didn't have. We simply didn't know. But Yazmin wasn't the only one with beasts.

With a deep inhale, I focused on the well of power in my core and thought of my bestiary. Mentally leafing through its pages, I found a creature who could help. I called to him in the beast realm and felt him answer, eager to cross through the door and be by my side. A deep groan rolled over the quiet expanse just as rosewood light doused my hand. The door swung open in my mind's eye, and Fig came soaring through, flapping his massive wings and chattering excitedly. I let the beast realm door shut and smiled.

Calem stilled, gaze tracking Fig's erratic flight pattern. "That looks like a monster from the forest."

"Oh hush. He's not that scary." My bat-like beast soared through the evening air, twisting this way and that. Soft gray fur covered his body, giving way to leathery wings that were almost see-through. Circular glass-blue eyes tracked insects as he flew, and he chomped at them with fervor. "Come here, Fig. Settle down."

He landed beside me, head reaching my waist. Calem still didn't move. "His name is Fig?"

I shrugged. "He likes figs."

Oz grinned, dropping his supplies and strolling over. "What does he do?"

"He's a Gulya." I ran my fingers over his scalp and gave him a good scratch between his radar-like ears. "Once I tell him to stand guard, his power activates. He uses soundwaves to detect disturbances from miles away. I used him once before when I was first exiled. I wasn't strong enough to keep him out for more than an hour, but now," I eyed his branch on my Charmer's symbol, "I think I can manage twelve hours, give or take. He doesn't have an immense well of power like some beasts, so he relies heavily on our bond to stay in this world."

Noc tilted his head to the side, studying Fig. "Can he sense shadows? What if Darrien comes instead of Varek's forces or Yazmin?"

I frowned. "Never tested it out before. Shall we?" Noc nodded, and I jutted my chin toward Fig. I didn't need to say anything—one look and he understood. I felt the flux of his power before he shifted. His gray skin gave way to an inky hide as soft fur transitioned to onyx flames that licked the sky. His eyes were fire-red pinpoints in the dark, and his ears stretched impossibly taller. Driving his claws into the ground, he rooted himself in place and became a protective statue on high alert.

Oz's lips parted. "So cool."

"Care to see if he can detect your magic?"

Oz obliged, calling forth shadows and masking his presence entirely from my view.

"Move somewhere. See if he can tell," Noc said. Oz didn't respond, but I assumed he listened. Calem and Noc didn't track his movements, as if waiting to see if Fig could detect him without any outside help.

"Fig. Find the intruder," I said.

It took less than a second. His head snapped around, red eyes glowing brighter, until his gaze snagged on a space a few feet to my left. His jaw cracked open and he emitted a bone-grating screech. Oz let his shadows fall away and clamped his hands over his ears.

A proud smile graced my lips. "Guess we can all sleep soundly, then."

"I don't know about that." Calem let out a weak, nervous laugh.

"Calem, are you scared?" I couldn't stop myself from grinning. Oz, too, regarded his brother with a wide, teasing smile. "He's not going to hurt you."

"He's still a bat," Calem mumbled. "Seriously, 'Fig'? You can't slap a cute name on it and think—"

Suddenly, Fig's head rotated to the right, and he let out another piercing scream. I jumped, whipping around to see what he'd spied. A plume of dark tendrils appeared out of thin air. They began to take shape until Kost manifested, shadows forming and disappearing with the faint breeze. Wincing, he covered his ears and took a halting step back. I'd never seen one of them shadow walk, but Noc had described it to me before. Apparently, all members of Cruor could separate their consciousness from their physical bodies and travel in the form of smoky projections. With a sigh of relief, I signaled for Fig to stop, and he went back to standing guard.

Kost frowned at my beast. "Not exactly a pleasant greeting."

Noc strode toward him, shoulders tight. "Is everyone safe?"

"Yes. We made it to Hireath a few hours ago. I wanted to get everyone settled before I contacted you."

"Good." Noc's muscles loosened.

"How did you find us?" I asked, joining Noc's side. He'd shadow walked to Midnight Jester once while dealing with my bounty, and he'd mentioned being able to do so because he knew the location. He'd simply *willed* himself there. But out here, there were no concrete landmarks. Just rolling plains that seemed to stretch on for eternity.

"I reviewed your travel plans before you left, so I had a faint notion of where you'd be. Plus, like calls to like. I could sense their shadows when I got close enough." He gestured to his brothers before letting his hand fall to his side. "You're farther along than I anticipated, though."

"We didn't camp last night. I wanted to put more distance between us and the capital."

"Smart," Kost replied.

"How's Gaige?" I almost didn't want to ask. But I had to know. Both out of concern for a fellow Council member and because he was my friend.

Kost stiffened subtly, but he managed to keep his voice level. "Not great. He hasn't stepped foot inside a single building. Convincing the Kestral to let him through the barrier was...tough."

My chest tightened. I hadn't even *thought* about the barrier. That invisible wall was meant to keep monsters out of Hireath and protect Charmers. Just knowing that the Kestral had to be convinced to let Gaige enter, even though he was a member of the Council... I hugged my stomach.

"How?"

"He summoned Okean." Kost's words were rigid. "Fortunately, that was enough."

Tension hung between us for a moment, none of us knowing exactly what to say. I wasn't even sure there was anything that *could* be said. Everything I thought of, every apology or promise of a better future, felt flat. All we could do was move forward and hope things got easier.

"I see."

Noc ran a tender finger down the back of my arm. Even through the layers of clothes I wore to protect myself from the chill, I still felt lingering warmth. "We'll stop Yazmin before anything else happens."

"Yes, well..." Kost hesitated, then shook his head. "I should get back. Raven promised to escort me to the throne room to inspect the prophecy."

Raven. Not Gaige. A rock formed in my throat, one that took several swallows to force down.

"How's she doing?" Oz asked.

Kost lifted a shoulder. "Fine. She trains in the morning with Emelia and Iov before running her Charmers through similar drills."

Oz grinned. "Good. Tell the twins to sweep her legs. She's not great on that recovery and needs the practice."

"Noted. If there's nothing else..." He stared at the horizon.

"Go," Noc said. "I'm sure you're needed."

With only the slightest nods, he disappeared. Oz's smile faltered as Calem sighed, and the two of them shared a long look before busying themselves with our bags. Rigid, Noc continued to stare at the space where Kost had been. My shoulders rolled forward. I wanted nothing more than to be there for Kost. For Gaige. For Raven. For all of them. But I couldn't. Not with Yazmin, Darrien, and King Varek plotting against us. Not with both the assassins of Cruor and the Charmers' lives at stake.

Charmers' lives... A chill raced over my skin. Every damn time I thought of my people, my mind inevitably raced back to Yazmin's words. What if there *were* Charmers trapped in the capital? It was my duty as the Crown to protect all Charmers, even those who might be held captive in Wilheim's walls.

Rubbing the back of my arm, I moved to Noc's side. He had barely blinked since Kost left. "Noc?"

"Yes?"

"Let's say Yazmin wasn't lying, that there are Charmers in the capital."

He cut me a glance. "I know nothing, I swear."

"I know." I pressed my palms flat against his chest, and he deflated, loosely draping his arms around my waist. "I believe you. It's just... Can I really blame her for wanting to save them?"

Noc's smile was sad. "No. But that's not the problem. The problem is her actions. Attacking her own kind in the name of saving them? Nothing justifies that."

Closing my eyes, I buried my nose in his tunic and breathed in his honeyed scent. It soothed my nerves and chased away the doubts brewing in my gut. I needed to be strong. A figure my people could trust. And if there were actually Charmers in the capital, I'd save them, too.

"We should get some rest." Noc lifted my chin up with his forefinger. "We still have a few days' ride ahead of us before we reach Tyrus's Ruins."

Standing on my toes, I wrapped my arms around his neck and kissed him. We had a fight on our hands, but at least we had each other. But as we walked back to our camp, the gleaming city of Wilheim still glowed in my peripheral vision, a distant fortress where our enemies safely waited for the right moment to strike.

NINE

YAZMIN

You went after Noc? Without my knowledge?"

King Varek sat before us, reclining on his golden throne and drumming his jeweled fingers along the armrest. Candlelit fixtures lined the pale, ocean-blue runner and cast the room in flickering orange light. Darrien and I remained kneeling before him, neither of us flinching at his obvious disgust. He wasn't a real threat. The Sentinels stationed along the brick walls, however... I glanced at the nearest one and pressed my lips together. A pair of cold, brown eyes stared back at me through a slitted helm. They'd never move against their king, which is why I needed Varek's favor. For now.

"My king," I said, voice low. "It was my mistake. I should have informed you of my plans, I just..." I tilted my chin upward and looked at him through my lashes. I needed to be subservient. Reverent. No matter that the sight of him made my stomach churn. He needed to believe I was on his side. "I wanted to do something for you, as a show of my devotion."

Beside me, Darrien coughed. He recovered quickly, clearing his throat and keeping his head bowed.

King Varek spared him a momentary glance before turning his attention to me. His salt-and-pepper hair was freshly oiled, and the air around him was heavy with the scent of rosemary. With a bela-bored sigh, he adjusted his platinum crown before steepling his fin-gers together. His hard glare softened.

"You are forgiven. I'm no stranger to those looking to seek my favor." After a moment, he relaxed and gestured to us. "Please, stand."

Both Darrien and I rose to our feet, but Varek only had eyes for me. His gaze roved from my collarbone to my feet, and though my long-sleeved gown obscured everything, there wasn't an inch of me that felt unseen. I suppressed a gag and waited for his gaze to return to my face. Moments later, it did.

He cleared his throat. "I take it he escaped. Again."

Darrien flinched beside me. Noc and his brethren had man-aged to kill a handful of our forces, while Darrien had been entirely unsuccessful. It certainly would've been advantageous to take Noc off the board so early, but it hardly mattered to me. I got what I wanted. I bit my lip to keep from smiling in satisfaction. Eliminating Gaige would shake the Council and make Leena weak.

Darrien finally found his voice. "We were able to take down one of his most trusted accomplices."

Most trusted accomplices? Gaige was powerful, yes, but one of Noc's brethren? Hardly. But Darrien knew as well as me that some syrupy words could go a long way.

"Better than nothing, I suppose." For a moment, Varek's brows scrunched together. He raised two fingers and gestured to his near-est Sentinel. Quiet words carried between them, much too soft to be audible. The soldier gave a curt nod, and then hurried off. Two more peeled off the wall, abandoning their stations and following their leader.

"Everything all right?" I asked. This figurehead king didn't strike me as a master strategist. He'd spent too many years locked in his castle, steeped in festering paranoia, to plan anything truly brilliant.

Varek smirked. "I know where Noc is heading. If you'd come to me in the first place, we could've formulated a stronger attack. Now..." He pursed his lips. Sighed. "We'll play the hand we have."

"Where's he going?" Darrien inched closer. Anger edged his words, and the hint of a shadow toyed with his fingers. Varek eyed it more out of curiosity than concern. With so many Sentinels nearby, all with the power to completely annihilate Darrien's shadows, he was hardly a threat.

Fool. If only he'd act like the assassin he was supposed to be. Slinking through shadows, unseen. Killing in an instant, without any warning. He could've had the world. Instead, his judgment was clouded by misguided rage. His conviction wasn't strong enough. Not like mine.

"The Gaping Wound. That's where Tyrus's Ruins is." King Varek stood, brushing his hands along his indigo tunic. His fingers paused over the silver griffin embroidered on his chest. "Assuming you're not mistaken and he has already visited Nepheste's, Oslo's, and Silvis's Ruins."

"I'm not mistaken." My words came out too harsh, and he raised a brow. I tilted my head in apology. "It's worth noting that exceptionally strong beasts reside in places of power. There's a creature in the Gaping Wound no Charmer has tamed. It can take them down."

"Interesting." King Varek walked toward the throne room's exit, simply waving over his shoulder and expecting us to follow. It vexed me to my core, but I did. As did Darrien. "That said, we've relied on beasts before and come up empty-handed." Darrien opened his mouth to speak, but Varek silenced him with a hard glare. "The same can be said for your...talents."

We stepped into the main hall of the castle and were met with an already assembled group of Sentinels. Clad in mercury-tinted armor, they stood a full foot taller than us and waited without moving. Even their breaths were hidden behind their chest plates. Varek came to a halt before them, a glint of pride in his stare.

"We'll combine our forces and send an ambush. Darrien, you and your assassins will join forces with my Sentinels. Yazmin…" He turned, arrogant smile on full display. "Tell me about this beast."

TEN

NOC

We rode our Zeelahs hard for days, only resting when absolutely necessary. At some point, the endless, frostbitten plains had given way to dusty-red, claylike earth. Large boulders and small mesas dotted the otherwise barren expanse. We were tired and stretched thin, so when the Gaping Wound came into view late last night, we elected to make camp and rest before attempting to reach Tyrus's Ruins. Now, in the early morning hours, it was easy to see why.

A thin fog hung over the ground, stretching all the way from our tents to the jagged, open canyon before us. It cut through the earth like a lightning bolt and stretched on as far as the eye could see. No one knew how deep the canyon ran. Those who ventured into its depths never returned. And smack-dab in the middle of that terrifying death trap was a lone butte. Its sheer face made it near impossible to scale, which meant the only way to access the ruins waiting on the center of the plateau was by a single bridge. A simple wood-plank structure with rope railings, no less.

With a quiet sigh, I brought my attention back to my family. We all sat around a dying campfire, tin mugs with rapidly cooling coffee in our hands. Ozias poked at the coals to keep the flame alive while Calem glanced between Fig and the horizon. So far, we'd gone undisturbed in our travels. But that didn't mean I was eager to have Leena send her Gulya back to the beast realm.

Leena let out a wordless hum as she worried her lip. *A Brief History of Wilheim* lay open in her lap, and she gently leafed through the pages as she devoured the book's contents. I couldn't help but smile. Her dedication to her people, *all* her people, was inspiring. She'd only just agreed to become queen, and here she was poring over Wilheim's history in order to better understand the people she'd soon govern.

Gently, I brushed a lock of hair off her cheek. "How's it coming?"

Her brows creased. "Fine."

"Can I clarify anything? Believe it or not, that book *is* brief. There are bound to be details missing."

"Like with the ruins?" She set her mug down and held her place with one finger, flipping to a different page toward the back of the book. "There's not much in here, only that there are five sacred sites—one for each mage. That, and the text explicitly states only royals are welcome here."

"Which we knew." I took a sip of my coffee. "You probably won't find anything else in there about it."

"Right." Leena's frown deepened as she scanned the lettering.

Ozias glanced up from the fire. "Something up?"

"No. I don't know. It's just..." She sighed and finally craned her neck upward, but her gaze was faraway as if she were still parsing together the text. "Charmers only know of these sites because of our beasts, and for the most part, we avoid them."

Calem cupped his chin. "Why?"

"Because of the beasts that linger there. Think about it." She closed the book only to touch her own bestiary. "At Nepheste's

Ruins, we found a Gyss. At Oslo's a Drevtok. And we found a Nix Ikari at Silvis's Ruins. They're all dangerous."

"Well, Reine, sure. But Tok and Winnow?" Calem shrugged.

My stomach hardened. "Winnow's magic is dangerous. The way she twists her words..." I shook my head, remembering how my Gyss had granted my wish. She'd successfully removed the decades-old curse plaguing my existence, but doing so had come at a great cost—Leena. Wynn, her former lover and Council member, had stolen her and charmed her, turning her into his puppet. Even now, the memory of her clouded eyes and somber, monotone voice still made my fists clench. "There are more powerful things than might."

"And Tok is young. In a few years' time, who knows how strong he'll be." Leena shook her head. "The point is, unless it's absolutely necessary, we don't visit these sites."

"You think there's something there?" Ozias looked over her head to the lone butte housing Tyrus's Ruins. A gust of wind rushed through the canyon, rattling the bridge and chasing away the last of the morning fog.

"Yes," she hedged. Clasping her hands together, she met my gaze. "Is there anything we need to know about Tyrus's Ruins? Anything about the ritual itself?"

A memory bubbled to the surface of my mind, the same one I'd experienced just before meeting Silvis's spirit at the last ruin site. My younger self, sitting upon my father's knee and recounting the singsong meant to teach young royals about ascension.

"The first Welcomes,
while the second Questions.
After the third Realizes,
the fourth Blesses,

and ascension is granted
when the fifth Bows."

I spoke the words aloud for them to hear, then set my cup on the ground. "Tyrus will bless my claim. It should be fairly straightforward, now that I'm not resisting the gods' wishes."

She picked at the hem of her sleeve. "That's it? Nothing about beasts?"

"No." I gripped the back of my neck. "But Wilheimians have never really known anything about beasts other than that they exist. Why? What are you getting at?"

"It's only a rumor, but there are whispers of a dangerous beast lurking in that canyon. And since we've encountered a dangerous beast at every site we've visited so far, I'm inclined to believe we'll find one here, too."

Calem shrugged. "Nothing we can't handle. Haven't we tamed an unexpected beast or two before?"

"This won't be like before." Gazing toward the damning crevice, she stood and folded her arms across her chest. "Again, it's just a rumor. But if it's true, if the Prentiss is real…"

"Can you tame it?" I asked.

"No."

"Aw, come on." Calem cracked his knuckles. "This beast sounds totally badass. We could use it against Yazmin."

She gave him a hard look. "I'm telling you, I can't tame it. No one ever has."

"But they weren't you." Calem's smile was strained.

"It eats people, Calem. I'm not sure being 'me' will make much of a difference."

My brows drew together, and I ran a tense hand through my hair.

"How come I've never heard of this before? Royals have been travel-ing to these burial sites for centuries to have their claims recognized by the gods. There would've been details about this somewhere."

"No one except your ancestors have ever crossed into its terri-tory. Maybe the royal line is protected." She eyed the book resting on the ground by her bag. "Between that explicit warning in the text and the rumors from my people...I don't know what to expect, but I don't have a good feeling about it." Shaking her head, she turned back toward us. "Maybe we should wait here while Noc goes alone. We can—"

A terrifying screech split the air. Fig had jerked his head around, targeting something in the distance opposite the direction of the canyon. A billowing cloud of red dust had bloomed on the horizon, and I narrowed my eyes. Something like metal glared in the sun. The frenzied cadence of Zeelahs' hooves smashing against the earth rever-berated in my ears. Too far away for Leena to hear, but clear enough for me.

"Sentinels." I rocketed to my feet and slit open my palm, letting blood blades form above my hand. Calem and Ozias cursed as they took up their stances, calling forth shadow blades and crouching low onto the balls of their feet. This was a first. Sentinels rarely left the castle gates and were only dispatched to battlefields as a last resort.

Or to protect a rebellious prince.

Just as I was about to bark orders, Fig again let out a bone-shattering screech. This time, his head riveted to our left, gleaming red eyes targeting another billowing cloud. Except this one wasn't red, but smoky and black. And through the snarling mess of shad-ows, I spied my former brethren barreling toward us. Including Darrien.

"I'll kill him!" Calem roared. His frame shook as his control splintered, and stone-like scales raced across his skin.

"Wait!" At the same time Leena screamed, Fig cried out yet again. To our right, a lone woman with platinum-blond hair stood wreathed in ruddy-red light. Foreign beast cries shook the very air around her, and she thrust her hand forward. It was a silent command I knew all too well.

Gripping Leena's wrist, I yanked her toward the only escape we had left: the bridge.

"Run!"

Calem practically screamed with frustration, but somehow managed to put a stop to his transformation and chase after us, Ozias right beside him. We abandoned everything. Our tents. Our belongings. Our mounts. There wasn't time. Leena only had a moment to send Fig back to the beast realm before I called on the shadows and swept her into my arms, racing through the onyx abyss to get us to the ruins faster. Calem and Ozias were on my heels, each one of them tossing glances behind us. We hit the bridge and the wood groaned beneath our feet. Even our shadows couldn't totally blanket our rushed escape, and every footfall caused the planks to tremble and sway. Beneath us, the endless depths of the Gaping Wound waited to swallow us whole. Leena's grip on me tightened as she looked down into the nothingness, then to the threat at our backs.

For a moment, I looked over my shoulder and my heart lodged in my throat. All three groups were nearly at the lip of the canyon. Yazmin didn't bother to rush. She didn't have to. Beasts I couldn't begin to name snarled and raced ahead of her, maws gnashing and claws gouging the earth. One of them I recognized from the Kitska Forest. The cloud-like legendary feline that'd killed Gaige. The Sentinels had launched off their Zeelahs and were racing toward the bridge on foot. Their blinding columns of light ate away at the tail end of our shadows, and a sharp hissing met my ears. Darrien and his men wielded ink-black weapons, blades hovering above their hands. He reached for his bow. Then, nocked a shadow arrow and smirked.

"Ozias! Calem! Heads up!" I shouted. Darrien's arrow whizzed through the realm, barely missing my cheek and embedding itself deep into the wood of one of the planks. His men followed suit, sending a volley of expertly thrown blades after us. We were easy marks. A lucky few missed us, a few more blocked by shadows we controlled, and the rest... Telltale grunts from Calem and Ozias. The sickening sound of something dastardly sinking into flesh. A red-hot pain in my shoulder, followed by the sticky heat of blood. Only Leena was protected.

My gaze snapped back to the path before us. We were almost at the butte. Just a few more feet. Another blade pierced the flesh between my shoulders, and pain sparked deep in my muscles. I bit back a curse and pushed forward. What would we even do when we got to the ruins? We could take cover behind the rock altar housing Tyrus's remains, but what then? They'd just follow us across the bridge. At least they'd be forced to travel one by one, narrowing their attack and making it easier for us to target them.

Again, I glanced back, only to find that they'd come to a halt at the bridge. The closest Sentinel unsheathed his sword. And then he swung it in a deadly arc, slicing through the bridge's railing and disconnecting it from the edge. Time slowed as I watched it fall. Gravity pulled at us as the tension gave out from beneath our feet.

Focusing only on the ledge ahead, I threw Leena toward the plateau. She sailed through the air, wild eyes frantic and damning as she realized what was happening. She bellowed my name as she was jettisoned from the shadow realm and tumbled to the earth in a plume of red dust. As she stretched her hand toward the canyon, I caught a glimpse of flickering rosewood light.

Ozias, Calem, and I gripped the railing just as the entire bridge went slack, and we careened into the sheer face of the butte. The force of the hit thrust us from the realm and shook Calem's grip. He let go of the rope railing with a frantic scream. Faster than I could blink, Ozias snared him about the wrist and then yelped as his shoulder gave a nasty *pop*. His eyes glazed over, and Calem dug his fingers into Ozias's forearm.

"Noc!" Leena's face peered over the ledge. Another volley of shadow blades from Darrien's army, and she pulled back as quickly as she'd appeared. Her cry echoed through the canyon and set fire to my veins. Across the way, Darrien laughed.

"You make this too easy." His haughty words carried effortlessly to us—as did the stretching of his bow as he nocked another arrow and aimed directly for me. Somewhere, the beast realm door opened, the deep rumbling shaking the mountain and covering us in a spray of dust and debris. I heard the twang of his bow as he let loose his arrow, but lost sight of the glistening blade in the shower of dirt. Covering my face with my arm, I braced for impact.

It never came. Just the resounding thud of an arrowhead burrowing into wood.

And then a strange tugging sensation around my waist.

I threw back my arm to see a wood plank before my eyes, complete with Darrien's arrow and wrapped in a peculiar, green vine. The same kind of vine that had now looped around my waist several times and was yanking me up. All at once, Ozias, Calem, and I were hauled into the air, each of us lassoed in vines and being pulled to the safety of the plateau. Leena stared up at us from the rock altar. Her Charmer's emblem throbbed with power, and beside her stood Tok. Two spheres covered in bark made up the Drevtok's body, and he produced endless vines as a means to safely secure his food. And in this case, safely rescue us. Tok's vines receded, and we landed on our feet behind the first rock pillar marking Tyrus's ruins—for a moment, out of our enemy's reach.

Calem's face was parchment pale. "I have never been happier in my life to be on solid ground." Reaching out, he gave Tok a gentle pat on his head. The beast responded with a happy call that was reticent of leaves scraping together.

"Me too." Ozias grunted as he slouched against the wall, cradling his arm.

Leena crashed into me and buried her face in my chest. "Thank the gods."

"Thank Tok." I glanced at her beast. If only we'd had time to pack our bags and store them in his lower, cagelike sphere. The bars could snap open on command to store both people and belongings in the beast realm without disappearing. Now, even if we made it out of this alive, we'd have to stop in town to resupply before we could move on to the next site.

"Him, too," Leena said warmly. She moved to touch him and then winced, her hand immediately going to her side. Blood had bloomed across her cornflower-blue blouse, and her fingers came away red.

I kneeled before her and peeled back her clothing. "You're hurt."

"So are you." She nodded to my shoulder before glancing at both Calem and Ozias. "We all are."

"Someone needs to set my shoulder." Voice raw, Ozias lumbered our direction. "Quickly. Before the muscles freeze up or they attack."

"Do it now," I said to Calem as I peeked around one of the rock pillars and spied Yazmin, Darrien, and the Sentinels. None of them moved. Certainly Yazmin had a beast that could cross the canyon to us, and Darrien and his men could send more blades our way. And while the Sentinels' magic weakened with time and distance away from the capital, they must've had enough power to call on their beams of light and teleport to us.

A deep, pained grunt from Ozias signaled that Calem had set his shoulder, and the two of them sidled up to a column a few feet away. "What are they doing?" Ozias asked.

"I don't know," I replied. Yazmin turned her head and said something inaudible to Darrien. A grin split his face, and he disappeared into the throng of assailants only to reappear with a limp, body-shaped sack.

Leena looked out from behind the same pillar as me. "What's that?"

My blood ran cold as Darrien undid the twine holding the burlap together. An unmoving form fell by his feet. With heightened senses thanks to my powers, I focused on the motionless body and listened for signs of life—a beating heart, a shaky breath—and found none. But there was an unmistakable pull, an energy of sorts, that radiated from his form and told me I still had the ability to raise him, if I wanted. Which meant he'd only recently passed. I was no stranger to the dead, but this was just...wrong. What was their angle? Had they killed someone just to bring them here? For what reason?

Beside me, Leena blanched. And then her eyes went impossibly wide. "Noc."

"Yes?"

"How long will it take you to receive your blessing from Tyrus?"

Across the way, Darrien placed a booted foot on the back of the lifeless body.

"A few minutes, maybe," I said.

"Do it. Do it now." Thrusting her hand outward, she called on her power and showered us in rosewood light. The beast realm door groaned open, and she sent Tok home while simultaneously summoning Onyx. Likely feeding off her energy, he appeared before us with hackles already raised and deadly yowls slipping from his maw.

"Leena? What's going on?" Calem asked.

"We're about to meet the Prentiss."

With a wide smirk, Darrien kicked the lifeless body over the edge of the canyon. Eons passed in the silence that followed. Adrenaline rushed through me, each minute more terrifying than the last. We never heard a thud. No indication that the body hit the ground. No sign of any danger at all. And just when I thought we'd finally be able to breathe, it happened. An unsettling, distorted howl—like that of a raging wind whipping through a confined space—bellowed from somewhere deep in the canyon.

Darrien, Yazmin, and the Sentinels bolted away from the ledge. Their unwillingness to stay, to be anywhere near the eerie sound that kept repeating on a loop, growing louder every second, told me everything we needed to know.

Death was here.

ELEVEN

LEENA

Fear flooded my limbs. That sound, that awful, terrible intonation, was a death knell I wasn't sure we could escape. Every fiber of my being screamed at me to run. To flee. Yazmin had tamed a Vrees. She was going to try and raise Ocnolog. And she *still* didn't want to be within striking distance of the Prentiss. And here we were, isolated on a butte with nowhere to run. Our enemies had played us well. Yazmin likely knew I didn't have a beast large enough or fast enough to fly us out of here all at once. They'd come at us from all sides, backing us into a corner they knew we couldn't avoid.

But not all of us had to die. I had to get my family *out*.

"Noc, now!" I pointed to the rock altar. He took off, sliding to a halt before the slab in the center and then kneeled on the ground. Pressing his chin to his chest, he closed his eyes. Again, the Prentiss howled, and this time, a gust of wind shot up from the deep. The stream cut through the sky and kicked up dirt. A red, dust-filled haze settled around us, obscuring our surroundings and turning the sun into a bloody orb.

I turned to Onyx and cradled his massive head between my hands. "Listen to me. I know you don't like to fly with people on your back, but I need you to work with me. Okay?" I ran a tender hand through his feathered mane and dragged my fingers under his chin. "Please?"

He must've sensed the building anxiety in my voice, because he didn't object. Instead he simply kneeled and tilted his wing to the ground. I would've used Reine, my other legendary feline beast. But her teleportation magic was still depleted, and the gap between the butte and the safe side of the canyon was too great. We'd never make it. It had to be Onyx. And we had to survive long enough for him to make multiple trips.

"Good boy." I gave him one last pat and then turned to Calem and Oz. "You two are up first. He'll carry you to the other side of the canyon."

"What about you? And Noc?" Oz asked. Another disastrous current of wind screamed through the air, and we jumped in place.

"It's already a risk for him to carry both of you at the same time. He's used to only transporting me, but he can do it." I glanced at my beast, and he huffed in anticipation. "He'll come back for Noc and me."

"Leena, no. This is—"

"Don't argue with me!" I snapped, cutting Calem off. "If you don't do it now, we'll all die."

Calem slammed his mouth shut and nodded, making a beeline for Onyx. Oz paused only for a moment, casting a worried glance toward Noc, then to me. He clambered onto Onyx's back behind Calem, and I gave my beast a pat on the haunches.

"Fly like hell."

Onyx let out a war cry and then sprinted toward the ledge, heavy paws thudding against the ground. Just as he reached the lip of the plateau, another monstrous channel of wind erupted right in front him. Followed immediately by the Prentiss.

My whole world stopped. A scaled, serpentine body large

enough to wrap itself around the butte emerged. Using the talons at the joint of its bat-like wings, it anchored itself on the edge of the cliff. Gleaming eyes targeted us with unparalleled ferocity. The Prentiss cracked open its maw, revealing monstrous fangs longer than elephant trunks and twice as thick, and inhaled. Air whirled in a vortex down its throat.

I threw myself to the ground and summoned my Graveltot. Grundy, my small, spherical beast covered in stone, rolled into place in front of me. The slate rocks hiding his feet shifted, and he thrust his hooves into the ground, activating his power. A dome of gravity formed above us and shoved me face-first into the ground. My lungs threatened to collapse with the weight, but I'd stopped sliding toward the Prentiss's gaping mouth. I barely had the strength to turn my head and look for Noc.

He was completely immobile, head still bent in a reverent pose. Whatever commune he was having with the gods, it left him in a trancelike state. The Prentiss's wind cut around him, doing nothing more than tousling his hair and confirming my fear—only royals were welcome here. And while I was his intended, I still wasn't yet one of them.

A sharp yowl rattled my ears. Onyx skidded wildly against the Prentiss's vacuum. His claws left deep wounds in the earth, but it wasn't enough. The beast reared back, pulling even more air into its once-deflated belly, and Onyx lost all control.

And tumbled right over the edge of the butte.

"Onyx!" Body trembling under Grundy's magic, I reached for Onyx. Black spots dotted my vision, and my chest heaved. Onyx. Calem. Oz. My *family*.

Tears filled my eyes. The Prentiss paused his attack and sniffed the air around me, as if trying to determine why I hadn't moved. A low growl simmered from his throat as he targeted my Graveltot.

From somewhere in the canyon, a triumphant caterwaul echoed through the air. And then Onyx exploded from the deep, wings furiously beating and chasing away the red dust. He climbed higher and higher with Oz and Calem still safely secured on his back.

"Thank the gods," I whispered.

But Onyx's call had pulled the Prentiss's attention, and it once again cracked open its maw. A dangerous vortex formed and Onyx slowed, fighting against the current with all his might. Calem and Oz desperately tried to help by throwing shadow blade after shadow blade toward the beast. Maybe if the Prentiss inhaled one, it'd damage its organs and halt the assault. The first one came hurtling toward its maw, and just before it could be sucked down into the beast's guts, the blade simply disappeared. The beast's wind magic was too strong for the shadows to hold their forms.

Think, Leena. I was painfully aware of how small, how insignificant, I was in comparison to this S-Class beast. *S-Class.* My mind whirred. The Prentiss had either sucked up or dispersed most of the dust with its whirlwinds, which meant the air was at least semi-clear and free enough for another substance to settle in. Say, mist.

I'd been waiting to call on Aeon, giving him room to adjust after his time with Yazmin, but I needed him now.

Inhaling deeply, I channeled all my power toward the symbol on my hand. The beast realm door rumbled open, and I sent Grundy home just as a wolf-sized creature manifested before me. My Vrees's usual, playful demeanor was nowhere to be found. Aeon's burning white eyes targeted the Prentiss with deadly accuracy, and his ears pinned to the base of his skull. With hackles raised to the heavens, he let out a threatening snarl. The ball of lightning in his center sparked with blue electricity, visible due to his sieve-like body composition. Mist gathered in the negative spaces, flooding outward around him, and he took a predatory step forward.

The Prentiss stopped inhaling, its once-deflated belly now swollen with air. Still focused on Onyx, it peeled back its maw with ferocious certainty.

"Protect Onyx." I backed up, nearly colliding with Noc, to give Aeon as much space as possible.

Immediately, Aeon grew, towering above us and shielding Noc and me with the underside of his belly. Mist fell in droves from his frame as a swell of static energy filled the air. The hairs along my arms stood on end. It'd take him a few more minutes yet to fully charge, meaning his lightning would have to wait.

Before that could happen, the Prentiss attacked.

The wind stored in its belly swirled outward from its open jaw like a tornado, aimed directly at Onyx, Calem, and Oz. Onyx cut hard to the left, barely avoiding the devastating torrent and nearly ousting Oz and Calem from his back. But the Prentiss followed them, jerking his head sharply to bring the violent stream of air their way.

Aeon lunged. With a loud snap, he gnashed his teeth around the Prentiss's neck, cutting off its wind supply and eliciting a bloodcurdling growl. A far less forceful gust eked through and hit its mark, knocking Onyx off course. But at least he was alive. At least Calem and Oz were still clinging to his back for dear life.

The Prentiss screeched and dislodged from the butte's edge. Wings flapping erratically, it tried in vain to break Aeon's grip. Each gust of wind threatened to chase away Aeon's mist, but he kept pouring more and more from his body. Soon, the air was thick with moisture. Breathing hard, I edged toward Noc.

"Noc." I gripped his shoulder.

Nothing happened.

Electricity surged through the air, and I shuddered. Aeon was ready. A crack of lightning erupted from the sky and struck the Prentiss with deadly precision. The current slammed into the beast, spiderwebbing over its scales. The force of the hit had me rattling in place, and I expected to see the Prentiss go limp. Instead, it simply shrieked and wriggled harder as it flailed its wings about. Dread crawled up my throat. Did its scales make it immune to lightning?

Above, Onyx yowled as he returned into view. Calem and Oz were nowhere to be seen, which hopefully meant they were safely on the other side. Onyx circled once before diving to the plateau and snaking between Aeon and the ground.

"Noc." This time, I shoved him. "C'mon. Snap out of it!"

Finally, he lifted his head. Blinked. Then went rigid as he took in the scene.

"Let's go!" I yanked him toward Onyx.

The Prentiss twisted and jerked in the air, and one fateful clawed wing slammed right into Aeon's eye—one of the only vulnerable spots on his body. He howled and released his hold on the Prentiss, backing up and bowing his head to the earth. Finally free, the serpentine creature took flight, wasting no time inhaling every ounce of mist while Aeon was distracted.

Noc and I leaped onto Onyx's back, and I dug my heels into his sides. He roared in answer and bolted toward the edge, jettisoning into the sky. We barely escaped the Prentiss's attack. Turning all of its fury onto Aeon, the beast unleashed a massive tornado directly at the ruins. The stone altar cracked, and a deep gouge splintered through the middle of the butte.

"Aeon!" I screamed. He'd hunkered down to endure the whirlwind, but the ground began to tremble beneath his feet. Snarling at the Prentiss, he launched into the air, snared the beast's wing, and slammed it into the rock formations. The force of his attack split the chasm wider.

Onyx continued to race toward safety. His muscles bunched and released, wings pounding the air. We were almost there. In the distance, I spied Calem and Oz looking on in horror, two S-Class beasts locked in battle as the very ground beneath their feet gave way. Rocks and debris tumbled around the butte. Red dust once again billowed up toward the morning sun. Time was up.

Thrusting my hand outward, I channeled every ounce of power I had into wrenching open the beast realm door. The deafening groan of hinges sounded at the same moment rosewood light ruptured from my emblem.

"Now, Aeon!"

I felt him release his hold on the Prentiss and step into the beast realm, into safety, just as the butte itself gave out. The Prentiss went down with it, a snarling, howling mess trapped by the debris. Its hide was tough, though, and even if it fell to the bottom of the canyon, there was no telling whether or not it'd come crawling back up. I didn't want to stick around to find out.

Onyx crashed into the earth beside Calem and Oz, his tired muscles giving out and making for a rugged landing. He dropped to his belly immediately, and we quickly slid off his back. Panting heavily, he glanced up at me and let out a weak yowl.

"You were perfect. Rest now." Stroking his head, I once again opened the beast realm door and then sent him home. A faint roar echoed from the canyon, and I shivered. "We need to move before the Prentiss comes back."

"We'll use the shadows. Let your beasts rest," Oz said as he helped me to my feet.

Noc nodded, and then glared across the Gaping Wound. "Quickly, before they catch up," Calem hissed. "Fucking brutes."

Craning my head over my shoulder, I spied our enemies lingering by the far side of the canyon. They were just miniature, indistinct statues at this distance, but one thing, one *person*, was discernable—Yazmin. Her rage was unmistakable as currant-colored light blossomed around her. We could call beasts back to the realm no matter where they were, but summoning them anywhere else but by our side was impossible. Not like that mattered—she could call on a flying beast and be on us in minutes.

"Let's go," Noc said. As one, he, Calem, and Oz summoned shadows and we disappeared into their hidden world, out of sight and out of reach from Yazmin's grasp.

For now.

TWELVE

KOST

My time in Hireath hadn't been as illuminating as I'd hoped. A few days had passed since I'd visited Noc, Leena, Ozias, and Calem, and the longing I felt to join them was…inescapable. It would still be some time yet before I heard from them again. Travel to Invere would require the utmost level of caution if they wished to remain hidden from Varek's forces. As much as I wished to be journeying with them, there was no denying the need for me to be present in Hireath.

First, I'd orchestrated temporary living arrangements for our brethren—tents for sleeping and one large canopy that acted as a common space for them to gather. Otherwise, they were encouraged to explore Hireath and get to know the Charmers. That hadn't really happened. For some, the memory of the open lawn where we camped—the battlefield where so many had lost their lives when we challenged Wynn to save Leena—was hard enough. Mingling with Charmers and integrating our lives with one another would take time.

Once we were settled, I put Emelia and Iov in charge of daily training. Our newer recruits had barely had a chance to get acquainted with their surroundings at Cruor, let alone actually master the shadows. Now, they were in foreign territory with an impending war on the horizon. Even the more seasoned assassins were on edge.

All of that was manageable. Expected. I'd planned for such reactions and a strenuous few days. What I hadn't anticipated was Gaige. Sighing, I ran a stiff hand over my vest and glanced around. Nighttime in Hireath was beautiful. The indigo sky was sprinkled with millions of stars, and they twinkled through the overhead network of branches that covered the buildings. Frost clung to the grass and sparkled in the moonlight, creating a vibrant enough light that many Charmers didn't even bother to ignite the floating rycrim orbs that hung about their city. Yet despite it all, there was a darkness here that couldn't be ignored. And for the first time in history, it wasn't the assassins of Cruor.

It was Gaige.

Sitting alone in front of one of the communal fires near the library, he stared into the hungry, orange flames. His own shadows festered around him, eating away at the soft light. He needed training but refused to participate in any lessons. One gloved finger repeatedly stroked the key dangling from his neck. Over and over again. Guilt ravaged my stomach. I'd felt an unbearable sense of responsibility when I convinced Talmage to raise Noc all those years ago. But this? I couldn't explain the way my hands shook. Feelings I hadn't begun to acknowledge were suddenly...there. It was too much. Chest heavy, I walked toward him. Paused for a moment to give him a chance to object when I reached the open bench across from him.

He didn't bother to meet my gaze. "Sit if you want."

"We should look into the prophecy tomorrow," I said, sinking to the stone bench.

"For gods' sake." His hand fell away from Okean's key. "Is that all you can think about right now?"

I frowned. "Should I be thinking about something else? We must stop Yazmin."

Gaige tossed his hands up to the sky. "Are you really that insensitive? Do you have any idea how difficult this is for me? Screw Yazmin. She can have her damn war for all I care."

"Don't say that." My fingers started to tremble, and I clasped my hands to keep them still. Steady. "I can't imagine what you're going through. It must be—"

"Don't." His steel-blue glare cut through the night, targeting me directly. "Don't you dare try to assume what it feels like."

"You're not the only one who's died here, Gaige."

The fire in his gaze was more intense than the crackling flames before us. "And that's supposed to make me feel better? What do you know about losing the very thing that made you who you are?"

"Everything!" I shot to my feet, surprised by my own visceral reaction. I blinked several times and tried to soothe the erratic rise and fall of my chest. Where were these emotions coming from? Why couldn't I control myself around him? No doubt it was the guilt for raising him, but it felt deeper, somehow. That realization only made me spiral further, and memories of my past flooded to the surface. Of the life I used to live before joining Cruor. Of Jude. Slowly, I brought my fingers to my chest. A raised scar long healed rubbed against the fabric of my tunic, and a phantom pang throbbed outward from my touch.

Gaige's shoulders tensed, but he said nothing. Only continued to glower at me.

Steeling my emotions, I cleared my throat. "In Cruor, it's customary to not share details about one's past."

"How lucky you don't have to relive your pain. I, on the other hand, am reminded of my choice every single moment." He stripped the glove off his hand and thrust it toward the fire, basking his faint symbol in the warm glow.

"I have scars, too." My hand formed a fist against my chest, and the pang deepened. "I died because I protected someone I loved. I did it willingly. And he *promised* to stay by my side, even after I became...this." Body shaking, I tried in vain to get a grip on the sudden, unexpected heat rising to the surface inside me. And failed. "He lied. I know it isn't the same, but I do know what it's like to lose something, *someone*, I love. That pain isn't foreign to me—I deal with it every day. But I keep going because I have to. Because my family depends on me."

For a long time, he said nothing. Shaking his head, he stood. A dark cloud obscured his gaze. "We're undead, Kost. We'll live forever. One love lost doesn't compare to the hundreds of loves that just vanished from my life. You'll have the chance to find someone again. I'll never get my beasts back."

"Don't belittle my pain."

"Then don't belittle mine!" Gaige bit back, a snarl escaping from his lips. Shoving his hand back into his leather glove, he scoffed. "I need some air."

I gestured stiffly to the space around us. "We're already outside." It felt childish, *wrong*, to fight with him like this. Why on earth was I letting him elicit such a reaction out of me?

Gaige turned away and stormed toward the forest line. "*Fresh air.* This space is full of bullshit."

Shadows swallowed him and he disappeared into the darkness. I didn't have the heart to follow. The burning ire I'd felt had immediately subsided with his retreat, and I was left with nothing but emptiness. Sinking back to the bench, I cradled my head in my hands. I knew better than to bait a newly raised assassin. I used to train them before Ozias came along. Their temperaments were wild and unpredictable, thanks to the influx of power that came with controlling the shadows. Gaige's reaction was normal. But mine… wasn't.

Slipping my fingers into my breast pocket, I extracted a bronze key. Holding it out before me, I opened the beast realm door. My Poi came bounding through the moment I called. Felicks's fox-like head tilted to the side, and the amethyst orb nestled between his ears clouded. Cleared. Images flashed through my mind, traveling down the bond between us, and I sighed. I'd hoped to see Gaige returning to the fire and us speaking in much more civilized, amicable manner. Instead, I just saw two minutes of me sitting with Felicks. No one else.

I scooped up my beast and settled him in my lap. "I really messed that up, didn't I?"

He let out a quiet whine and then shoved his snout beneath my palm. Minutes stretched into hours as I quietly sat in front of the fire, stroking the length of Felicks's spine. Every two minutes a new future would brew, and every two minutes my breath would catch. But nothing happened.

Eventually, Felicks drifted off to sleep and the visions stopped. The quiet hum of his snores soothed my frayed nerves. Even so, I couldn't convince myself to move. Returning to camp meant that this conversation was truly over. That Gaige wouldn't come back. All because of something I'd said. I hadn't meant to be callous, but the more I turned over our exchange in my mind, examined each word and winced at my choices, the more I realized my empathy hadn't been empathetic at all.

As dawn crested over the forest line, ushering in a new day and reminding me that we still had so much work to do, I couldn't shake the fear that my time with Gaige had come to a staggering end when it'd only just begun.

THIRTEEN

GAIGE

T he errant, bone-chilling howls rumbling through the dark woods weren't enough to keep me from venturing deeper into the Kitska Forest. Nothing was as terrifying as returning to Hireath and seeing Kost again. Not when he didn't understand. Not like he ever *did*. For someone so incredibly brilliant, he was also so terribly dense.

Scowling, I kicked aside a stray branch and kept going, ignoring the swirling, angry shadows that clung to my every move. I couldn't get them to disperse. They were relentless, flanking my arms and legs and wrapping around my fingers. I hated their cool touch.

You didn't before.

I bit back a wordless shriek of frustration. When Kost had summoned his shadows and sent one gently curling around my arm, my knees had gone weak. I'd longed to feel more. It'd felt so personal, as if I'd somehow been granted permission to see a private part of Kost's life. There was nothing frightening about those dark tendrils. If anything, they'd excited me. They whispered of hope and possibility and even something deeper. Something I dared not name, especially now.

Funny how much could change in no time at all.

Brushing back a curtain of thorny vines, I continued aimlessly through the forest. Another eerie call crested in the distance, and I winced. I knew the monsters here were different from the beasts I'd lost, but I couldn't stop myself from tracing my emblem. Even hidden from sight beneath my leather glove, the image of that lifeless, faded tree was burned into my mind. I'd never escape it.

Gone. They're all gone. My chest heaved as heat pricked at the backs of my eyes.

I wished he'd never convinced them to raise me. He destroyed something with that decision, something I'm not sure he even realized was there—a possible future. Never mind that Yazmin killed me. Rationally, I knew that we couldn't have had a future if I'd stayed dead. But logic couldn't keep the anger, the feeling of betrayal, from festering in my heart. Because now I was trapped in this gods-awful world with too many reminders of what could've been. Of the life I was supposed to have with my beasts. Maybe even with him.

The shadows around me spiraled out of control, snaking through trees and severing branches in a violent display of power.

Before, I could've loved him. Now...

The darkness around me was suffocating, but I didn't care. I couldn't decipher my shadows from the all-consuming suffering of the Kitska Forest. I'd never noticed it before. But as I waded through the thicket of trees and underbrush, there was a hopelessness that tugged at my senses. It beckoned to me, to my shadows, and guided my feet deeper into the heart of the woods.

A shiver raced down my spine as another chilling howl scraped through the air, much closer than before. Coming to a halt, I peered around tree trunks and tried to determine the source of the sound. I knew little about the monsters that inhabited this forest. If the rumors were true, that they were the trapped souls of deceased beasts from the First War, then maybe they weren't so different from me—undead and lost.

Undead. A dull ringing started in my ears as my breathing hitched, and I straightened my spine. *What if...*

When nothing revealed itself, I started up again. A strange sense of invigoration filled my limbs, and my pace quickened. There was no telling how many beasts had died that day. The loss was devastating enough for my kind to sequester themselves in Hireath. They never would've returned to a mass grave of beasts. They never would've thought that death didn't have to be the end.

Zane. My mind rewound to the time I'd read one of Cruor's more peculiar tomes, *Zane and the Fallen Leaders*. He'd become the first guild master of Cruor and established a home within the confines of the Kitska Forest. As the first of his kind, his power was unmatched—and no doubt as equally unsettling. I tracked the chaotic tendrils weaving around me. If he'd made his way through here with the power to raise the dead...

A desperate hope flickered to life in my chest. If the Kitska monsters were undead beasts, and I was an undead Charmer... Could I tame them? Did I want that?

Yes. Undoubtedly so. I wanted—no, *needed*—some connection to my former life. Some proof that there was a reason for me to endure.

Pulse climbing, I maneuvered around gnarled roots and vines until I came across a clearing. Moonlight bathed the grass in a pale glow, and I cautiously made my way to the center. The scent of moss and decay was heavy in the air. A breeze trickled through the pinesco pods, their unnerving pattern giving the impression of thousands of blinking eyes.

Gaze wary, I turned in place. My shadows furled outward, crawling across the forest floor without my command, and shooting off into the trees. They dispersed entirely after that, leaving me surprisingly vulnerable and bare. Gently, I rubbed my arms.

Following the sudden whoosh of my shadows, the woods fell silent. Minutes dragged by as I waited for, well, I wasn't entirely sure. But the urge to keep trekking forward had disappeared, and so I stood.

Please. I scanned the forest line, but nothing happened. *Please.*

My shoulders drooped, and I sank to the ground. With trembling fingers, I pulled off my gloves. A phantom pain, stronger than anything I'd ever experienced in my life, throbbed from my emblem. I wasn't sure if that ache would ever go away.

Pressing the symbol to my lips, I whispered, "I just need a reason to stay." All I wanted was a sliver of my life back. And if I couldn't have my beasts, and I couldn't bring myself to even look at the man I'd yearned for, then maybe, just maybe, these monsters could save me.

A horrendous roar shook the trees, and suddenly my shadows reappeared. They surrounded me in a brutal maelstrom of darkness, and I snapped my gaze upward. There, on the edge of the forest, was the outline of a beast shrouded by trees. Burning red eyes stared back at me. The creature let out another guttural roar, and the pinesco pods above its head danced in a panicked frenzy.

As if preparing to charge, the creature dipped its head low.

Slowly, I stood. A strange, almost manic smile claimed my lips. I didn't know if I would survive this encounter. This beast would end my life for the second time or I'd find a way to tame a Kitska monster—and either outcome suited me just fine.

FOURTEEN

NOC

Without our mounts or gear, we were forced to travel on foot to the port city of Invere, adding countless days to our journey. We had to hunt for food and stick to the shadows at all times. We did everything possible to reduce our tracks and stay out of the capital's eye. By the time we hit the quiet cobblestone streets, we were beyond exhausted. Constant use of the shadows ate away at our energy, and Calem, Ozias, and I were feeling the lack of rest in our bones. Leena, too, was ragged. We hadn't slept much. Hadn't really rested at all. We were too afraid to be caught off guard again.

Night fell over the slumbering town, and the wrought-iron light fixtures along the streets did little to illuminate the paths. Which meant we could use the buildings' shadows instead of our own, and we let our powers recede. The off-white structures were packed tightly together, and we snuck down alleyways to avoid the main roads. In the distance, a low horn bellowed, signifying a ship's arrival. Perhaps the very same ship we'd try to gain passage on come morning.

"There," Oz said as he pointed to a small inn up ahead. Tucked away in a neighborhood full of sleepy cottages, it saw far less traffic than the main lodge just off the port. "I've stayed here before while on a job. The owner doesn't ask questions, so we should be safe for the night."

With its beige brick, oak accents, and sloping roofline, it looked unassuming enough. A few unopened barrels of ale waited out front, illuminated by a lantern clinging to the building's wall. A plaque by the door read *The Slumbering Knoll.*

"Are you sure about this?" Leena asked. A drunken man swayed on his feet a few houses down, his babbling incoherent. Hardly a threat.

"We need to rest. Get some solid food and new clothes. The ship heading for Kings Isle won't depart until morning, anyway," I said.

Kings Isle. Yuna's Ruins. We were one step closer to my claim being fully recognized by the gods. One step closer to calling myself king—and more importantly, Leena queen. Things had gone smoothly at Tyrus's Ruins, at least for me. I hadn't even been aware of the beast fight that'd been occurring right over my head. Instead, I'd been floating in nothingness—the same, quiet expanse where I'd communed with Oslo. Tyrus had appeared, a ball of warm light, and spoke at length about what it meant to be a ruler. How important it was to possess a strength of spirit, a resilience, and a dedication to one's people. These values, he said, were reflected in the child, mother, and elder statues outside of Yuna's Ruins. And, they were reflected in me.

I wasn't entirely certain of his assessment, but I knew that Leena possessed those qualities and more. So I received his blessing without argument, because I knew that with her on the throne, we could begin to heal our divided world. There was an unshakable heat in my chest now, as if the mage himself was guiding me toward that last ruin site. Yuna and the gods were waiting.

We crossed the cobblestone street and pushed through the door.

An elderly woman with deeply tanned skin and wrinkles hooding her eyes stood behind a sturdy podium, scribbling notes onto parchment with her quill. She looked up at us through the tops of her glasses, then drew her gaze back to the paper before her.

"How many rooms?"

"Just one," I said.

She sat down her quill and yanked open a thick guest book. Dragging her finger down the page, she nodded. "I have one available that'll do, if you don't mind sharing beds. Two aurics for the night."

Slipping my hand into my coat, I dug a coin purse out of one of the inner pockets. Thank the gods I'd kept it on me instead of stowing it away in our bags. I pressed the bits into her open hand, and she stowed them in a locked drawer before leading us to a set of cramped stairs just off the tavern. Once at our room, she handed over the key.

"It's late, but you should be able to scrounge up some food from the bartender." She narrowed her eyes, taking in our disheveled appearance, and snorted. "There's a bath down the hall. I have some spare clothes left behind by travelers. I can't speak for where they've been, but they're a right lot cleaner than what you've got. I'll leave 'em outside your door."

"Thank you," I said. She left without another word, and we piled into our room. Cramped but surprisingly clean, it was more than sufficient. Leena collapsed on a bed big enough for two and let out an elongated sigh. Calem and Ozias made for the bunk beds, each of them sinking onto the lower mattress and kicking off their boots.

"I'm more muck than man," Calem said, running his hands along his dirt-covered coat. Dust sprinkled to the sheets around him.

Ozias shoved him gently. "You just officially claimed this bed. I'm not sleeping in your mess."

Calem let out an indignant huff. "You're too big for the top bunk. It'll come crashing down on me while I sleep."

Leena laughed—the sweetest sound I'd heard in days—and for a moment everything was fine. We were safe. We had a place to sleep. To eat. To recover. We knew where we were going and how we were going to get there. And even though we'd spent more time on our journey than anticipated, we still had some time before the anniversary of Celeste's death. With a tired smile, I sank onto the bed next to Leena. She leaned her head against my shoulder.

"I wonder how everyone is doing," she mused aloud.

A weight settled deep in me, and the temporary happiness that had filled my chest deflated. Gaige. Kost. All our brethren. "I'll shadow walk and find Kost. Once I inform him of our location, I'll come back and he can shadow walk here and fill us in. In the meantime, go freshen up. Relax a little."

Planting a kiss on the hollow of my neck, she said, "Okay. See you in a few." And with that, she, Ozias, and Calem all left, and I reclined on the bed. Giving way to the shadows, I felt my consciousness separate, and I sped through the night in the direction of Hireath, eager to see for myself that my family was okay.

Kost stood before us in a plume of shadows as his form wavered at the edges. There were only two candles in our room, one on each bedside table, and the flickering, low light of their flames made Kost appear even more ghostly—in part due to his shadow form, but more so because of his gaunt expression. Bags had formed beneath his eyes, as if he hadn't slept in days. His usually styled hair was lank and unkempt, and his shoulders were tight. Leena sat on our bed twirling the chain of her bestiary. Arms crossed, Ozias leaned against the wall and looked at Kost with as much concern as I felt. Even Calem was uncharacteristically still. He'd perched on the edge of his bed, forearms braced against his knees.

Standing by Leena, I slipped my hands into the pockets of my trousers. "Kost, what's going on?" I'd waited long enough. After shadow walking to Hireath, I'd found him quickly. He'd been standing outside the library looking at nothing at all. Simply staring. When I'd asked what was wrong, he said he'd prefer to tell us all at the same time.

"Gaige is gone." His words were soft. Broken.

Leena's hand froze against her collarbone. "What do you mean, 'gone'?"

"Gone. No longer in Hireath. We don't know exactly when he left. We don't know...why." He swallowed thickly, as if unsure of his own statement. "We don't even know where he went. He's just...gone."

"Shit." Calem dropped his head into his hands.

Leena squeezed her eyes shut. "Gaige..."

"Both assassins and Charmers have searched for him, but something's not right in the Kitska Forest. The monsters are more agitated than usual." Kost removed his glasses and stared at them for a long moment. "Our sentries returned for their own safety."

"We'll find him. He'll be okay," I said. But my words felt hollow when we were so far away and without a means to make good on them. "I doubt he's in any danger."

"Right now, the only danger he's facing is himself." Kost blinked at his spectacles, as if he'd forgotten why he'd removed them in the first place. After a beat, he slid them back on his nose without polishing them. "Unfortunately, we can't spend any more time searching for him. We need to focus on stopping Yazmin."

"True, but..." Leena peeled her eyes open, and a tear slid

down her cheek. She wiped it away with shaky fingers. "We *will* find him, Kost."

He gave a tight nod. "We will. But Yazmin comes first. To which, I have news." He cleared his throat. "I think I know what the final ingredient is for her spell."

I knew he was emotionally drained, thanks to Gaige's disappearance. But I expected *some* sort of positive reaction with that discovery. A slight smile. A look of hope. Instead, he remained as tense as ever. So much so that instead of joy, all I felt was a deep, unsettling weight in my gut.

"And?"

"And it's a heart."

Leena's face fell. "Any heart?"

"No." His brow furrowed. "I believe it's *her* heart. By giving it up, she'll become one with Ocnolog and be able to control him."

"You *believe?* Kost, we need to be absolutely sure." I hated that I sounded so harsh. He was going through way too much, and without Gaige there, without a partner to help him sift through old texts and decipher a centuries-old prophecy... The stress of his task was evident in his appearance. But we had to know. We had to stop her.

He leveled me with a tired look. "I know. I'm trying. I wish Raven could've traveled with me to fill you in. She's been an incredible help. It was after discussing the prophecy with her that I was able to deduce the final ingredient."

"Then where's the confusion?" Leena went back to tangling her fingers in her bestiary.

"The prophecy speaks of a Charmer who will soothe Ocnolog by offering their heart. But there's a line in the lyrics, something about 'a hand that breaks,' which is puzzling." He ran his fingers along his jaw. Scowled. "I don't know if that's right. The spell itself that Yazmin left behind doesn't mention anything about that prerequisite. Just a Charmer's heart."

"The prophecy is more of a children's lullaby, right?" Oz asked. "Could just be language to make it easier to remember."

"Maybe. Or it could be true," Leena murmured. "Yazmin *has* broken things. She's violated our way of life. Attacking Charmers, using blood magic… She's already met that requirement." Leena shook her head and dropped her gaze to the floor. "We've long believed that Celeste blesses those on the right path. Maybe she's been blessed. Think about it. She tamed a *Vrees*. No one has ever done that before. And, she's somehow managed to gather these near-impossible ingredients."

"That can't be true." I kneeled before her and placed my hands on her knees. "Don't lose faith now. Think of your beasts. Of Onyx's blessing."

Her smile was weak.

Calem stood and began to pace in what little room he had. "So, what do we do?"

"We have to get to her before the anniversary of Celeste's death and stop her from completing her spell. The problem is Varek," Kost said.

"But that's why we're visiting these ruins. So Noc can be recognized as king and sway his forces. If Varek is outnumbered, he'll be less inclined to fight us," Calem said.

Giving Leena's knee another squeeze, I stood up. "He'd never willingly give up the throne. Even if the entire kingdom of Lendria depended on it. One way or another, we're going to have to fight to get to Yazmin."

"Precisely." Kost ran his hands over his tunic, then moved to smoothing his hair. A glimmer of his old self. Nothing like a problem that needed solving to get some of my brother back. A flicker of hope ignited in my chest. "We need more soldiers," he said.

"How many Charmers have agreed to fight?" Leena asked.

"More than anticipated. But even with Cruor, it's still not enough to stand against the entirety of Wilheim."

"Where do we find more forces?" Ozias asked.

"I have an idea," Kost said as he tilted his chin my direction. "But you're not going to like it."

I let out a sigh. "I came around to the first idea I didn't like." Becoming the king of Wilheim didn't exactly top my list of wants, but I'd agreed to it because it meant Leena would be queen. Together, we'd be mending a centuries-old rift that'd split our country into three factions: Cruor, Hireath, and Wilheim. Once Leena became queen, once our union was solidified, we'd be uniting all Lendrians. No more wars among ourselves. No more exiles in a land we all belonged to. So if there was something else I could do to make that future real, then my like or dislike of the matter was irrelevant.

"We ask Rhyne to be our allies. We need forces, and they have the numbers."

Silence followed in the wake of his suggestion. My body froze, and a soft ringing started in my ears. We *couldn't* go to Rhyne. Amira's homeland had waged a war against Lendria because they thought I'd killed her. They only stopped attacking when I was presumed dead. To willingly walk back into their court... To show them that, after all these years I'd eluded their grasp... It'd be war all over again.

"You can't be serious."

"I am."

"When are you not?" Calem mumbled. I shot him a glare, and he shrugged.

Ozias cleared his throat. "I can't see how that would go over well, given Noc's history with them."

Kost pursed his lips. "It's Rhyne or Allamere, and we know how likely the mages are to help us."

"Not likely at all," Ozias groaned.

For a moment, we all sat in silence, sifting through Kost's words. Unease brewed in my gut. We *could* risk venturing to Allamere, Land of the Mages, but they'd deserted Lendria after the First War and showed no interest in returning. Aside from the handful of rogues here and there—like Eryx, the mage we'd met about removing Cruor's Oath from my wrist—they didn't give a damn about our country. Or who ruled it. Rhyne, on the other hand, was once a treasured ally. Maybe enough decades had passed for them to at least entertain the notion of reestablishing that relationship once again.

"Well," I finally said, carefully measuring my words, "if I were a member of Rhyne's royal family and learned of my existence—not just my existence, but my goal to retake the throne—I wouldn't be happy." I folded my arms across my chest. "No warning. Just a sudden reemergence of the person they thought they'd killed. Not only would they feel robbed of justice, but now they'd feel like fools for being tricked all these years. They'd attack Lendria on principle.

"But if we go to Rhyne, if we have a discussion with them and make an alliance, we have a better chance of keeping the peace, both now and in the future." As hard as it was for me to admit, I knew this was the right move. With so many threats in our own country, I hadn't even thought about what being crowned king would mean to the rest of the realm. To Rhyne. A tendril of guilt threaded through my stomach, but I steadied it with a long breath. Personal history aside, this was the best path forward. For the sake of my people.

Leena nodded her agreement and then paused, fingers halting along her jaw. "How do we know they won't attack us when we arrive?"

"I'll head for Rhyne now while you visit the last ruin," Kost said. "They don't know who I am, so they'll have no reason to harm me. It'll give us a chance to understand what kind of environment we'll be walking into."

"Prior to our war with Rhyne, we had an amicable relationship with their country. Both of our economies benefited from trade, but that has since ceased. Varek never made attempts to reestablish that relationship. Maybe if we do..." Frowning, I slipped my hands into the pockets of my trousers. "We'll try. Kost, dig up whatever information you can on their trade routes and how a relationship with Lendria would benefit them. They'll need something out of this alliance."

"And a reason not to execute you on the spot," Calem said.

"Right."

Kost nodded, a slight approving smile on his lips. "Rhyne's capital city, Veles, is a bit foreign to me. But I have heard of a tavern called the Polished Goblet. I'll meet you there."

"Travel safely." Leena stood and approached him, and even though her hands moved right through his wispy frame, she hugged him. Shadows licked her skin, but Kost didn't move. After one achingly deep breath, he dropped his face to her shoulder and closed his eyes. Let his hands hover over her back where they would've met had he been solid.

"Thank you," he whispered. And then he was gone. Back to Hireath. Back to problems he couldn't fix and a world without us or Gaige. A fist gripped my heart tight, and I moved to Leena's side. As many problems as we'd face in Rhyne, one thing was for certain: I was desperately eager to get there so I could see Kost again and embrace him myself.

FIFTEEN

LEENA

The *Sea Mare* was a sight to behold. Rich, dark wood made up the ship's body, accented by inlays the color of seafoam. Waves of the same shade were carved into the bow, and horses exploded from the crests and raced toward the front of the ship. A single mare, larger than the rest and with her mane flowing behind her, was the prow. Her giant hooves reared up in anticipation, and water crashed behind her. She was ready to take on the high seas, and we were fortunate enough to board her.

The ship's captain, Harlow "The Marauder" Saber, was even more impressive—and terrifying. Her mischievous grin was borderline devilish, and there was an unspoken, heated emotion clear in her gaze as she stared at Calem. She'd allowed us to board her vessel, in part because she knew him, but also because we'd offered up all the bits we had on us. She'd escorted us to a secluded room, accessible only through the captain's quarters. Beds occupied most of the space, save one small, ramshackle desk. Stacks of parchment, quills, and ink covered its surface. A single window was open to the sea, and the light of the morning sun reflecting across the ocean was near blinding.

Harlow stood before us, arms folded across her chest. Her

black corkscrew hair was held back by a gold bandanna, and she wore a long-sleeved magenta blouse that complemented her smooth brown skin. Dark trousers were tucked into leather boots, and she crossed one ankle over the other.

"Calem, Calem. I always wondered if you'd come crawling back." She jutted her chin toward the rest of us. "I just didn't expect you to bring company."

"Hey, Harlow." Calem's normally flirtatious grin was somewhat reserved. He finger-combed his hair, tying it up in a loose bun. "Look, about last time—"

Faster than I could blink, Harlow unsheathed a cutlass at her waist and poised it just before his neck. "If you ever try to cut me out of a bounty again, I'll kill you. Don't think that just because we had a romp in the sheets, I'd act any differently."

Beside me, Noc stiffened. He didn't make a move to intervene, though, only tossed his brother an irritated glance. Oz rolled his eyes.

Calem raised his hands in a show of submission. "Trust me, I know. But you got your share. Not to mention the bits we've just given you."

She let her sword fall, a broad smile on display. "Just reminding you. Out on another job? We could team up again." Her voice went syrupy at the end, and she gave him an eyebrow waggle that had me stifling a laugh.

Calem shot me a glare, then dropped his hands. "Not this time. We just need a ride to Kings Isle."

"My ship's charted for Ortega Key. Paying customers, and all." She made a loose gesture to the door behind her and the deck beyond. Her crew was currently boarding passengers—rich travelers out for a leisurely cruise along the coast of Lendria—who expected to spend the next few days sipping ales and enjoying the sights. All manner of sea life migrated closer to the coast during chilly weather, eager to find food in the tepid, shallow waters.

"Tell them you're extending the trip. Sailing around Kings and Queens Isles before docking in Ortega Key. I'm sure they wouldn't mind."

"That's a drain on my resources, love." She picked at her cuticles, somehow eyeing us and her nails at the same time. "I didn't charge my passengers nearly enough for that."

"I'm surprised to see you entertaining nobles. Is there no more money in raiding ships on the high seas?" Calem asked.

She lifted a shoulder. "Stealing from the rich is equally as lucrative during this time. Marauding is a summer gig."

"It baffles me that the capital lets you go unchecked," Noc said, voice level. No doubt wondering if he'd have to deal with the Marauder once he retook the throne.

"You'd be surprised what the king has me steal for him." Her grin turned wicked. "Of course, those terms might have to be renegotiated, Prince Aleksander."

Tension flooded the space. None of my assassins moved. Whatever amicable feelings Calem may have still held for this woman were gone now. The ring of mercury around his irises flared. We'd always known there was a chance Noc would be recognized without the glamour from his magic ring. To a degree, that was needed, especially when it came time for him to publicly reclaim the throne. But now, while running from the king, Yazmin, and Darrien, any acknowledgment of his heritage could be devastating.

Noc clenched his jaw. "You do realize it would only take seconds, if that, for us to kill you."

"Oh, certainly. But then who would sail this ship? How would you get to Kings Isle?" She let out a laugh that hung in the rafters, damning us to her will. "I'm harboring a fugitive. I'm taking all the risk. If you want to go to Kings Isle, a little compensation is in order."

"We already paid you." Noc's words were cool.

"You paid to board my boat."

"Fucking pirate," Calem muttered. "What do you want?"

"It's always about the bounty. I assumed someone in your line of work would appreciate that."

"We can pay you more once we return from our journey. You already took everything we have." Shadows began to fester around Noc's fingers. We might have been forced to play by Harlow's rules, but he wasn't about to let her forget just who she was dealing with.

She glanced at his hands, unperturbed, then dragged her eyes back up to his face. "You'll have to do better than that. Grant me something only a king could."

"Calem, I don't know who this woman is to you, but I'm just as happy to tie her up and lock her in the bowels of the ship. We can find someone else to sail the *Sea Mare*." Oz moved toward her with clenched fists. Veins bulged along his forearms and raced toward his corded neck.

"Good luck with that." She sneered. "My crew is loyal to the bone. I used to work the deck with them until the late captain met his untimely end." Her eyes flashed. "Pity, really."

Bile soured my tongue. Whether or not Harlow had orchestrated the death of the *Sea Mare's* previous captain was probably knowledge she'd take to her grave, but she wasn't above lording that threat over our heads. Minutes stretched by as she let us sit with that thought. None of us moved. Finally, Noc let out a *tsk* and his shadows dispersed.

"Trade routes."

"What?" She tilted her head his direction.

"I'll grant you access to the trade routes we plan to set up with Rhyne. They've already acknowledged my claim to the throne and are awaiting my announcement. Start your own fleet. Build an empire. As long as it's done *legally*, I'll give you sole rights to transport goods to Rhyne on behalf of Lendria."

I kept my face carefully blank, as did Calem and Oz. Harlow didn't need to know that we hadn't negotiated that deal yet. Truth be told, it was a safe thing to barter. If we got to Rhyne and couldn't come to such an agreement, we'd likely end up dead, anyway. No need to worry about the ramifications of deceiving one conniving pirate. Harlow studied Noc for a long time. Folding her arms, she tapped her pointed nails against her elbows and mumbled wordlessly to herself. Finally, she extended her hand.

"Shake on it, and you've got yourself a deal."

Noc shook her hand once. Harlow practically giggled, then turned on her heels and headed for the room's only exit. "I've got to alert my crew of the travel changes. Keep yourselves occupied 'til nightfall. You can get some fresh air on the deck once the passengers have turned in for the evening."

And with that, she waltzed out the door and shut it firmly behind her.

The white light of the moon bounced off the ink-black ocean waters, casting the *Sea Mare* in a pale glow. Harlow had alerted her workers to our presence—not who we were, just that we were onboard and not to be disturbed. The skeleton crew that tugged at the sails and kept the ship on course during the late hours of the night hardly paid us any mind, anyway. The air was thick with salt, and I breathed in deeply to steady myself against the perpetual rocking. Calem and Oz had pulled up a couple chairs and were feasting on bread and fish. Noc and I leaned against the rail, our hands draped over the side and fingers grazing each other's. We'd hardly had any time alone since we started this journey. And it was far from over.

Leaning my head on his shoulder, I sighed. "How are we going to get to Rhyne, anyway?"

He planted a kiss on the crown of my head. "By boat."

"Harlow's?"

"No. She only promised to drop anchor and allow us to use one of her rowboats to approach Kings Isle. I'm not bartering with her to stick around—or to take us to Rhyne, in case she finds out we were less than honest about our deal."

Oz grimaced. "That's a long way to row."

"Not to mention dangerous with all that open water," Calem added.

"We don't have another option if we want to stay hidden from Varek. He knows about our journey to the ruins, but not about this. It's best we keep it that way."

"At least we re-upped on some supplies," Calem said. Before we'd boarded the *Sea Mare*, we'd made a quick stop at the local market to pick up food, clothes, and means for shelter. All of which were now safely stored in a bag in Tok's belly, protected in the beast realm, just in case we had to run for our lives yet again.

While we only had one ruin to go, Kings Isle was almost as treacherous as the Gaping Wound. The rocky mound jutting out of the ocean was inhospitable to both beasts and humans alike. Somewhere along that smooth, slate surface was an opening to an underwater cave where Yuna's Ruins rested. Noc had assured us that we'd have no trouble holding our breath while swimming to it, but just the thought of being trapped underwater with immovable stone above my head made my stomach knot.

And, since Varek knew where we'd be going, it was the perfect opportunity for him to lay a trap.

"Do we have any beasts to worry about at this site?" Oz asked around a mouthful of bread.

"I'm less familiar with water beasts, but…" My mind whirred as I sifted through years of reading from Hireath's library. There wasn't much to go off. Charmers hardly left behind knowledge of beasts since our bestiaries recorded everything for us. Instead, we set out on beast hunts after sharing information via word of mouth. And not many of us had ever ventured into ocean waters.

Except your parents.

One memory bubbled to the surface, and I swallowed hard. Ever since Yazmin's threat, visions of them kept surfacing in my mind. I didn't even remember them, not really. But I remembered that day. The way my aunt had wailed and the deep, unbearable sense of agony that her voice carried. One I felt in my bones, but didn't fully understand. They'd journeyed to the southern coast to tame a beast that could safely transport us across the open seas. They wanted to travel the world with me at their side.

They never came back.

"We might run into a Revmandra."

Calem set his food down in his lap and scowled. "I can't take another run-in with an S-Class monster."

"Not S-Class. A-Class. Still dangerous, though. It's the beast my parents were after when they disappeared."

Disappeared. Not died. Pressing my eyes shut, I shook my head. I needed to stop doing that. Stop pretending, *hoping*, that they were among the missing Charmers Yazmin kept raving about. But her lies were tantalizing. A past I never had. A chance at something I'd long forgotten. If they were alive…

"Leena." Noc brushed a gentle finger along my cheek, startling me. I blinked up at him. "Are you okay?"

"Yes." Turning my face toward him, I sighed. "I promise."

His smile was sad. "Okay."

"So is this another cut-and-run type of deal?" Calem asked.

"Maybe. I know the ingredients necessary to charm one, and if we were successful, it would make traveling to Rhyne much safer. A rowboat across open waters sounds...awful." She grimaced. "But I'm not sure we have everything to tame the beast."

Oz polished off the last of his bread and brushed his hands along his loose work shirt. "What do you need?"

"Fish, seashells, pearls," I said, ticking off the items on my fingers as I began to pace. "The first two are easy enough to acquire on-site. Pearls are a bit more difficult. Manageable, but if we're pressed for time, then not so much."

"Does it matter what color they are?" Noc asked.

I frowned. "No. Why?"

"Yuna's Ruins is covered in pink pearls. But stealing them is considered sacrilegious. I suppose we could ask Yuna beforehand, but I can't promise she'll say yes." Noc turned so his back was to the sea, white hair framed by the moon and stars above.

Frowning, I peered out over the endless ocean. "We'll try that first. If she disagrees, then looks like we'll go oyster hunting and hope we find a pearl before Varek finds us."

"Great." Calem glanced between us. "Is that it?"

"Ah, well, no." I cleared my throat. "There's still the matter of the final taming ingredient: a pirate's treasure."

"What, like buried treasure? A chest of aurics?" Oz leaned forward, bracing his forearms on his knees.

"Not necessarily. The treasure just has to be something invaluable to said pirate."

Slowly, Noc turned his gaze on Calem. "Good thing we know a pirate."

Calem blanched and shook his head. "No. You've got to be

kidding me." He turned toward me with a pleading look as he wrung his hands together. "We don't need that, right? I changed my mind. Let's just flee. We can outswim a terrifying water beast. Totally. No need to involve Harlow."

Oz's laugh rolled from somewhere deep in his chest. "Who said anything about *involving* Harlow? Just steal some of her treasure."

Calem launched to his feet, kicking his chair out from under him. "Did you not hear that thinly veiled threat earlier?"

"That was thinly veiled?" I mused. Noc chuckled.

"I thought you were on my side!" Calem whined. I raised my hands in apology, but giggled just the same.

"Calem," Noc said, voice still light but tinged with the hint of a command. "You were a thief before I raised you. You know Harlow. There's no one better to steal her treasure than you. I bet you can even think of a suitable item."

Calem hissed. Dragged his nails down his cheeks. "You're all dead to me."

Oz couldn't keep the grin off his face. "Well, how about it? Got any ideas?"

With a begrudging nod, Calem let out a huff. "Yes."

"Right before we leave, then. We don't want her to notice its absence until we're already gone."

"You owe me. All of you." Calem made a show at pointing his finger at each of us, and then stormed away toward our quarters.

Oz stretched his hands to the sky as he stood, mirth still evident in his eyes. "We should probably all rest while we can. Stock up on sleep." He nodded a good night, and then strolled off in the same direction as Calem, leaving me alone with my *anam-cara* for the first time in days.

Noc grinned as he watched Oz leave, but as his attention shifted back to me, his smile warmed even more. Butterflies took flight in my stomach as I simply stared. He reclined against the wooden railing, muscles stretched tight across his chest, visible thanks to the tight fabric of his midnight-blue tunic. His tousled hair grazed the top of his angular cheekbones, and he ran an errant thumb along his chiseled jaw. He looked like a god, and I almost forgot where we were. I longed to be with him, but our predicament had kept us running. And sharing rooms. And just entirely too clothed.

I let out a steadying breath, and Noc raised a sinful brow. Heat bloomed across my cheeks. I was still flustered by the man I loved— and he wasn't even trying. For the first time in days, he smirked, and I nearly melted on the spot.

"Come here," he said, voice smooth and low. I obliged and he wrapped me in a soft embrace, fingers dancing about my waist. Sagging into his chest, I let his honeyed scent envelop me in a blanket of security.

"We need a vacation," he said.

"Do you think we'll ever get one?" It was meant to be a joke, but Noc's answering sigh was heavier than I'd anticipated.

"Yes and no. When we take the throne...life will be different. Are you sure you're ready for that?"

For a moment, I didn't speak. I simply listened. To the steady beat of his heart. To the cadence of ocean water crashing against the ship's bow. To the creak and groan of ropes and flapping canvas sails. The sounds of the night were soothing, a stark contrast to the storm of emotions raging inside me. I'd agreed to become the queen of Lendria, not because I was eager to take the throne, but because standing beside Noc was something I'd always do. Ruling was still so new to me, and I had little in the ways of guidance. Even so... I glanced upward and caught Noc watching me. He believed in me. He and all the Charmers and assassins. Maybe we could actually change things for the better. For all Lendrians. The churning uncertainty in my mind lessened, and I smiled.

"I know it won't be easy. But we'll do it together." I placed my hands against his chest. "You know, we never celebrated becoming *anam-cara*."

He tilted his head, a question in his probing, ice-blue stare. "What does that entail?"

"A celebration that spans several days. Lots of food and dancing with friends and family while the sun's out, and lots of personal time for us at night." I bit my lip and looked up at him. "It's nice. Kaori would perform a private ceremony for us, too, with tea from the sacred liefera plant found near the falls of Hireath. It's not as stuffy as it sounds, and the little sweets are delicious."

Noc grinned. "Is that why Calem suddenly drinks tea?"

"Probably."

Pinning my chin between his fingers, he brought his lips just inches away from mine. "Sounds similar to a royal wedding celebration in Wilheim. When all this is over, we'll blend our traditions and the whole country will come together. And we'll get some damn private time."

He kissed me then with enough passion that adrenaline flooded through my fingertips. Looping my arms around his neck, I slanted my lips over his and relished in the feel of his tongue intertwining with mine. A delicious tingling spread over my skin as his fingers dug deeper into my hips, and a wondrous moan slipped from the back of his throat.

He pulled away a fraction, breath heavy and tantalizing against my neck. "I love you."

"I love you, too." I traced the crescent-moon scar along his cheek. "You sure we need to wait until then for this 'private time'?"

"I'm sure we'll find a moment before then, but as for now..."

He glanced around, taking stock of our surroundings and the crew. Drawing attention to ourselves was the last thing we wanted. Both to preserve Noc's identity and to keep the spotlight off us so it was easier for Calem to steal when the timing was right. "Come on. Let's get some rest."

As much as my body rioted at the idea of merely sleeping beside him, I followed him without complaint. There would be time for us eventually. For now, I could take solace in the feel of his hand in mind. In the feel of his chest against my cheek while we slept. It would have to do. And when the time was right, I'd keep him to myself until I was satisfied several times over.

SIXTEEN

YAZMIN

Fury pumped through my veins as my booted feet slammed against the tile. We'd only just returned to Wilheim, and already I found myself pacing in the Queen's Respite. Varek and Darrien were somewhere in the castle—the king fuming and going on about our failings, Darrien apologizing profusely and acting like a subservient aristocrat rather than a deadly assassin. Somehow, Leena had outsmarted the Prentiss. She'd survived. And while Noc visiting another ruin site made Varek furious, it had little effect on my plans.

That's right. Breathe. This is all inconsequential. Exhaling deeply, I slowed my progression and stared at the hauntingly beautiful tree. When Varek learned I could've pursued them with the help of one of my flying beasts, he'd been outraged. But the risk was too great. There was no way for me to transport all of us, and I refused to put myself in jeopardy, attacking them alone or with minimal forces. I had important work to do here, like raising Ocnolog and finding the missing Charmers. Fortunately, pacifying Varek simply meant transferring another lowly beast—this time, without any conditions—as a show of my continued "devotion." His greed outweighed his anger, and he'd dismissed me without another harsh word.

A boon, considering he then turned his ire on the Sentinels. He was currently forcing them to run drills under his strict supervision to ensure they were still up to the task of serving him. Which meant, for the moment, I was able to visit the Queen's Respite without escorts.

Folding my arms across my chest, I frowned at the tree. What was it about this place that kept pulling me back? At first, I'd chalked it up to ancient magic similar to my own. But what if it was more than that? I'd scoured every nook and cranny of this gods-forsaken castle. Turned the place upside down in search of my brethren. And yet, nothing. Nothing, save this strange pull I couldn't ignore.

Splaying out my hand, I wrenched open the beast realm door and summoned my Canepine. The wolflike beast appeared, and she circled me once before ramming her head into my hip. Full grown with ivy-green fur and powder-blue eyes, she was a talented tracker. Aside from those I'd traded to Varek, I'd been careful not to summon my beasts in the castle. It wasn't illegal to do so, but I didn't want to take unnecessary risks. Any perceived threat could've landed me in a cell and squandered my plans. But desperation to find my brethren outweighed the danger of being seen, especially since an opportunity like this was unlikely to happen again.

Fingering the indigo flowers that grew along the underside of her neck, I angled her head upward. "Can you feel it? Is there something here? Something like me?"

I let her sniff my hand. She inhaled deeply and then pressed her snout to the floor, stalking an invisible scent. Minutes stretched by as her nails clicked against the tile. An occasional huff expelled from her nostrils. Once, her ears flicked up to the ceiling, and she went stock-still before riveting her head to the tree. Slowly, she stepped off the tile and into the soft dirt surrounding the trunk. Navigating around roots, she inched closer to the tree. Snarled.

My breath caught in my chest. "What is it?"

She growled in answer, flattening her ears against her skull and staring intently at a knot in the wood. Moving to her side, I crouched before the tree. My heart pounded in my ears as I reached out and placed my fingertips against the spot. The tree shuddered beneath my touch. A few of the roots around us receded, and dirt fell away to reveal a set of wooden, bark-covered stairs that disappeared into darkness.

Opening the beast realm door, I sent my Canepine home and stared into the newly visible hole. The scent of mulch and soil met my nose. An iridescent glow began to throb from the walls. Moss lit up like foxfire, illuminating the narrow staircase fully, and I descended into the earth. There was silence, save the soft thud of my feet against the wood. The stairs eventually gave way to a flat path of pressed dirt and stone, and I followed the cramped, twisting trail for what felt like ages. Every step sent my pulse racing. Anxiety ratcheted in me as the walls started to widen. What would I find? A horde of corpses? Gruesome displays of the royal family's abominable transgressions?

Finally, the path widened into a rounded cavern, and I came to a complete stop. Roots from the tree puckered through the ceiling. A strange glow, similar to the moss's dim light, pulsed from each tendril. They trailed down the walls and spread like veins, casting the whole space in a faint, pale-green light. On one side, two desks were pushed together, topped with endless scrolls of parchment. Some were tied off with twine, others opened to reveal scribbled notes. On the other side...cots. Filled with bodies.

I knew it. Heat flooded my limbs, and I stepped toward the closest one. On it lay a woman with faded-brown hair and soft wrinkles across her forehead. Her hands were clasped together atop her stomach. And there, resting along her collarbone, was her bestiary.

Still intact, thanks to Celeste's magic. Only a Charmer could remove a bestiary—no one else. Her skin was abnormally pale, but there was a slight flush to her cheeks. A subtle rise and fall to her chest. Thin tree roots had reached down and attached themselves loosely to the crown of her head. Light pulsed from the tendrils, and for a brief moment, lit up the veins along her face, neck, and shoulders. But nothing else happened.

I told them. I told them, and they didn't listen. My hands balled into fists, and my nails pricked against my palms. The room swam out of focus for a moment as my breaths hit hard and fast.

Uncurling my hands, I grazed the fabric of the Charmer's off-white blouse. The fashion was outdated but recognizable. It was heavily embroidered with flowers and beasts, a bit thicker than the flowy garb most Charmers wore now. Perhaps something my mother would've chosen. How long had this woman been here? Despite her lack of color, her body hadn't decomposed in the slightest. My gaze shifted to the tree roots around her head. To the steady pulse of life from those dripping tendrils.

They were *preserving* them. I grabbed the nearest roll of parchment and scanned the cramped writing. Blood magic. I recognized a handful of glyphs inked along the top of the page. Beneath the spellwork was a detailed section written in Lendria's common tongue. They were keeping the Charmers alive so they could experiment on them and learn about our powers. The parchment fell from my hands as a wordless shriek burst through my lips. All this time and I was *right*. Rage turned my vision scarlet as I thought of the king in his courtyard, overseeing forces he didn't deserve to command.

I would kill him. I would bring this whole gods-damned capital to the ground. And I would laugh as Ocnolog's fires completely erased these Wilheimians from history.

Consumed by bloodlust, I gripped the Charmer's arm without

thought. The action tugged at her collar, revealing three puncture marks at the base of her neck. The holes were impossibly deep, and the veins around the wound were black. Poisoned. For a moment, my fury subsided.

I recognize that bite mark. Touching my hip, I fingered the small bumps of raised scar tissue where a mirror wound had long since healed over—one I received while charming an Uloox. I'd been fortunate in my taming. The deadly snake's three fangs deposited enough venom to completely immobilize its prey, no matter the size. It had only bit me once, but if it'd struck again... Gently, I peeled back her shirt to find two more wounds.

My hands trembled. They'd used an Uloox against her, tortured her with a beast knowing she'd resist harming it. Where was it? My gaze traveled over the cavern, but there was nothing indicating they'd tamed such a creature. No discarded rodent bones or glass enclosure to keep the beast from escaping. Just a motley collection of old books, jars, and vials. As I shifted, my toe nudged the parchment I'd dropped.

Maybe the beasts were kept elsewhere. Retrieving the document, I scanned the inked writing in the hopes of unearthing more. Instead, I found her name, injuries, and... Ringing sounded in my ears. The already-dark cavern seemed to devolve into total blackness, and I forced myself to breathe. She'd come here *willingly*. As my vision returned, I dragged a finger over the parchment's contents. My eyes narrowed. Willingly, but...

I moved to the next body and searched for wounds. Slash marks that'd spanned his stomach had been neatly stitched and healed. By all accounts, he should've been released. Like the woman beside him, his records detailed an acceptance for "treatment" against life-threatening beast injuries. And yet, here he was. Fully healed, from the looks of it, and still lost in a deep slumber.

With cautious fingers, I pulled away one of the tendrils attached to his head. The beating light died, and the man began to sputter. His eyelids fluttered erratically, and he fell into convulsions that nearly sent him flying off the cot. Panicked, I placed the tree root back on his forehead, and prayed the rhythmic, glowing light would return. Slowly, it did, and the man fell back into a calm, peaceful slumber.

I gritted my teeth. Ruddy-red light ruptured from my Charmer's symbol as emotions raged beyond my control. I didn't know how to overcome this. I wasn't a healer, and while I recognized some of the blood magic glyphs, I had no idea how the spellwork interacted with these mysterious roots. This was beyond me, and worse, it meant I couldn't use the Charmers like I'd planned. Who better to join my cause than those wronged by our enemy? But now... They were just bodies. Incapacitated, unmoving bodies.

Charmer after Charmer turned up more and more bestial wounds, long since healed. Ears pounding, I studied each one. Varek would pay for this. I would make sure of it. When the time was right, I'd end his life in front of his precious kingdom. I'd drain every last drop of blood from his body until he was cold and lifeless. And then I'd put his corpse on display outside the castle walls so that no one would make a move against a Charmer—against me—ever again.

Finally, I came to the last two bodies. The first, a woman with dark-brown hair and full lips. Something about her features gave me pause, and I forced my power to recede. She'd suffered a serious stomach wound, as if something with razor-sharp teeth had taken a bite out of her side. Notes indicated the healer had grafted burdyuk leaf over the wound, but some of the muscle damage had been irreparable. The man on the cot beside her shared a similar scar, and his head was tipped in her direction.

Gently, I unclasped his bestiary. Magic hummed beneath my touch—without his permission, it would be near impossible to open it—but the golden, miniature scripture on the binding was still apparent. Grabbing a nearby magnifying class, I examined the lettering. A rush of adrenaline surged through me as I recognized his name. I did the same for the woman, and my excitement crested.

Leena's parents. I reached for the parchment on the bedside table and scanned the cramped handwriting. In addition to the wounds, they'd both almost drowned before washing up on shore outside Ortega Key.

An idea started to form in the back of my mind as I pocketed their bestiaries. *I can use this.*

Setting the notes down, I backed away from the cots and headed toward the stairs. I already had everything I needed to raise Ocnolog. And now I had a bargaining chip that could turn the tide of this impending war. And I'd be damned if I wasn't going to use it. A faint smile pulling at my lips, I ascended the stairs and headed toward my quarters. Leena and Noc had to return to Hireath eventually, and when they did, I'd destroy whatever resolve she had left. By killing Gaige, I'd seeded doubt in her mind. I saw it plain as day in the Kitska Forest. She had no idea if she was doing the right thing, and now with the irrefutable proof of her parents' trapped existence...

She'd never be strong enough to stand against me.

SEVENTEEN

NOC

In the dark hours just before dawn, Calem had exited our hidden cabin and snuck into Harlow's sleeping chamber in search of some treasure we could use. Ozias, Leena, and I had all remained behind so as to not draw further attention to Calem's plans. Only when the early morning rays slanted through the stained windows did we rise and dare to enter the main area of Harlow's quarters. Calem had exited her room just as we'd exited ours. With a wide grin, he lifted a small pouch to the ceiling in triumph before hiding it in one of the inner pockets of his coat. Relief sang through me. He'd gotten what we needed, but more importantly, he was safe.

"What now?" Ozias asked.

"We wait," I said, placing a finger against my lips. The last thing we wanted was to discuss our plans in the open or let Harlow know we'd stolen from her. From beyond her door, I could just detect the sounds of her waking. A long, exaggerated yawn. Feet padding against the floor. Any minute now, she'd emerge ready to escort us to our rowboat.

Leena shifted, facing the windows stretching across the back wall. Kings Isle loomed before us, a slate-black mountain jutting out of the ocean and reaching toward the sun. Right at the curve of the bay, where water sucked into a hidden crevice leading to Yuna's Ruins, stood three massive statues made of soapstone and lime. The child, the mother, and the elder. Not quite as tall as the island, they stood guard over the mage's burial site, and for a moment, I smiled. My mind rewound to the night I'd had dinner with Leena while journeying to Ortega Key, how I'd quizzed her about these very statues.

She'd stolen my attention from the moment I met her, with her determination, her passion, the way she never backed down from what she thought was right. As she studied the ocean, I looked at her. Deep-brown hair fell around her face in waves. Her hazel eyes were full of wonder and worry. She was easier to read now. Less of a puzzle than she used to be, but somehow more intriguing. Her gaze snagged on the statues, and she stilled. Then, she turned my way and tossed me a knowing grin.

Harlow's door opened, and the captain appeared fully dressed with a bright smile on her face. None the wiser, it seemed, about Calem's theft. "Ready to get the hell off my ship?"

A loud clank sounded as the anchor dislodged from the side of the boat and rushed toward the seafloor. Her crew was directing the passengers to the prow of the ship. A sightseeing distraction so we could slip away unseen.

Calem draped his arm over Ozias's shoulder and offered her a blazing grin. "Lead the way, Harlow."

She turned, hair bouncing against her shoulders, and strolled out onto the deck. As promised, there were no people to be found. We could hear their voices carrying over the ocean breeze—a mixture of breathless exclamations and adoration—as crew members shared the lore of the statues. Still, we were careful to move quietly and quickly, following Harlow in a single line until we reached our rowboat. It had already been lowered into the calm waters below, and a ladder hung off the side of the *Sea Mare*.

Harlow gave me a curt nod as she folded her arms across her chest. "Pleasure doing business with you."

The trade routes. I'd almost forgotten. I schooled my irritation into a look of indifference. Pirate or no, she'd gotten us out of Invere safely. "Thank you for your assistance."

Ozias shimmied down the ladder first, dropping into the rowboat and steadying himself before reaching up to help Leena.

Harlow watched them go. Just as Calem started his descent down the ladder, she caught my gaze. "I'll be waiting for those trade agreements."

"I'll send them as soon as I can." I nodded a goodbye and then followed after my family. The moment my feet met the wood, Calem and Ozias thrust the oars into the ocean and guided us away from the *Sea Mare* and Harlow's weighted stare. Once we'd put some distance between us, I finally allowed myself to breathe.

"You think Harlow will come after us?" Leena asked, eyes still locked on the ship.

"Most definitely." Calem's proud grin stretched his lips tight. "Not now, though. She's got a schedule to stick to with all those nobles aboard. Let's just hope she doesn't notice the conch is gone until after they've set sail."

"Conch?" I asked.

Calem paused in his rowing to extract the pouch and toss it to me. "Queen Jessamine's Conch."

I blinked, fingers tight against the cord. "She had that?"

"Yup."

Leena sidled up beside me and pressed her chin to my shoulder. "What is it?"

Gently, I undid the cord and removed the conch. Larger than my fist, it glittered in the morning sun. Rows of white diamonds alternated with chocolate ones, highlighting the dual tones of the shell beneath. A small sapphire indicated the clasp, and I opened it to reveal the iridescent, pale-pink interior.

"It was my great-grandmother's. My great-grandfather had it made for her as a wedding present. No one knows where it ended up."

"Well, until now." Calem smirked.

Leena's eyes went wide. "It's beautiful."

"It's yours." I handed it to her, and she let her fingers dance across the shell, hesitant. "It was meant to be passed on from queen to queen."

Her hand stilled. Her gaze, full of quiet warmth, met mine. She looked at me as if I'd just given her the world. Just knowing that she would rule over Lendria with me, the very same woman who'd eradicated my curse, who brought joy to my life and my family, who cared more about everyone else than herself... There'd never been a better queen in the making. If only I was a better king. Taking the pouch from me, she secured the conch shell to her waist and smiled. She, at least, was determined to take on the world.

"Where exactly are we heading?" Calem asked.

I shook free the lingering self-doubt and took in the mountain behind him. Slate layered upon slate created a sheer surface, but there was a small sliver of darkness. A crack where two faces of rock had crashed together and then fallen away.

"There," I said, pointing to the entrance.

As we approached the hidden crevice, we passed the first statue: the child. Waves crested against her calf as she stood on one foot, the other kicked out behind her. With one hand upstretched and face upturned, she reached for the heavens with a blissful smile. She was the symbol of innocence and wonder. More than that, of pure, unrestricted belief. A necessary conviction any ascending prince or princess needed to have in order to become a ruler of Lendria.

You are the child. Tyrus's words rumbled through my mind, low and demanding. *You possess pure belief.* I frowned. I'd never once *believed* I was the best ruler for this country. His conviction still baffled me, and yet... I cut a glance to my *anam-cara*. To her wide-eyed wonder and heartwarming smile.

I believed in *her* unconditionally. In the good she'd bring to our kingdom. And maybe I could even believe in the man she inspired me to try to be.

Something warm ignited in my chest.

Next came the mother. Still smiling, but a bit more subdued. Her expression was one of love as she looked upon the child. Hands clasped before her, she watched after her family with total devotion. That, too, was a necessary trait to becoming king or queen—compassion and dedication to one's people.

You are the mother. The warmth in my chest spread to my limbs. *You love fervently.* This, I believed. I would die for my brethren—had died for my country—and I would do it again if it meant the people I loved were safe. And Leena felt the same, that much I knew. My desire for her to be queen wasn't just because she was my *anam-cara*. It was because her benevolence, her kindness and compassion, knew no bounds.

And finally, the elder. She looked at no one. Instead, her gaze was cast far out to sea, scanning the horizon for what had yet come to pass. Her wisdom and the ability to consider not just her current predicament but the future as well was what, above all else, it meant to be a ruler. To think critically, to act appropriately, to make hard decisions to ensure prolonged happiness for her people instead of immediate gratification that would fade with time.

You are the elder. Your decisions are guided by wisdom.

A deep sense of acceptance flooded my body. I'd always valued the counsel of my friends and family. I'd listened to people like Gaige and Kost as they'd strategized for a better future, just like my father had done with his own advisers. There were always other perspectives, other ways of approaching things, and true wisdom meant considering all viewpoints—not just my own. Maybe Tyrus was right. Maybe I did possess the values needed to rule. A slow-moving, cautious smile tugged at my lips.

"Noc." Ozias cleared his throat, pulling my attention to him. "Where are we supposed to dock?"

We'd reached the side of the mountain a few feet away from the crevice. Waves crashed rhythmically around us, and our boat nudged the sheer, water-slicked surface. There wasn't a single hold we could use to secure the boat with rope, and the water was much too deep for an anchor. Not that we had one to begin with. I doubted any royal previously visited this ruin without the comfort of a fleet at their backs, or at least one solid ship to drop anchor and await their return—warm cabins, food, and blankets at the ready.

"Selenis can hold the boat from beneath the waves while we visit the ruins, just in case we're unsuccessful in taming the Revmandra," Leena said, flexing her fingers. Rosewood light bloomed around her hand, and she summoned the Vissirena that'd helped us tame Jax and Lola, the Laharocks, so long ago. Selenis manifested before us and batted her fishlike tails against the waves.

Ozias grinned and tossed the rope off the side of the boat. "There ya go, Selenis. Hold onto it for us, will you?"

She flipped her seaweed and tentacle hair with one of her webbed hands before snagging the rope.

"Stay out of sight," Leena added. Her beast nodded once before diving deep into the ocean, her iridescent scales glimmering in the sunlight until she disappeared in the mountain's shadow.

Calem dropped his oar in the boat, drove his hand into the sea, and cursed. "We'll freeze our asses off."

Following suit, I dragged my fingers through the ice-cold water. A shiver raced up my arms. Cold wouldn't kill an assassin of Cruor. Touched by death, we could withstand dangerously low temperatures. It wouldn't be comfortable, but manageable. For Leena, though... My eyes slanted to her. She worried her lip between her teeth and stared at the choppy, blue-green sea.

"You should stay with Selenis and the boat."

She jerked her head my way and frowned. "No. We're doing this together, Noc. All of it." She pierced me with a fierce stare that had me swallowing my retorts.

Ozias grimaced and laid his oar flat across his thighs. "Plus, if the Revmandra shows up, she's the only one who can charm it."

Tension coiled tight in my shoulders, and I rubbed the back of my neck. We couldn't afford to dally. If Harlow discovered we'd stolen the conch, she still had time to come after us. Not to mention, there was the very real threat of Varek. He'd coordinated an ambush at Tyrus's Ruins. But that force was just a small showing of the power he wielded. Varek had an entire armada he could've unleashed on us. And while they'd all likely returned to port for Winter Crest, that holiday had since passed. Which meant his ships could be lying in wait anywhere.

"All right. Let's move quickly. The sooner we're out of here, the better," I said.

"Agreed." Leena stood slowly, keeping her balance in the rocking boat. With nimble fingers, she took off her overcoat and let it fall to the floor. Her long-sleeved blouse and skintight breeches would do little to protect her from the icy sea, but wearing her leather coat would only weigh her down. Before I could warn her, she jumped into the water. Bubbles and foam rose to the surface as she sank down, and I gripped the edge of the boat. She popped her head up, wet hair floating around her in a halo, and yelped.

"Holy gods, it's cold!"

"I wasn't exaggerating." Calem glanced between her and me. "Here goes nothing." Jumping in after her, he sprayed us in a sheet of ice-cold water. He surfaced quickly with a litany of curses that sent Leena's brows skyward.

Ozias and I abandoned ship together. Needles pricked at my skin the moment I submerged, and a deep tingling started in my extremities. Kicking to the surface, I treaded water near Leena. "You okay?"

"For now." Her teeth began to chatter. "Let's just hurry."

"We'll stay above water as long as we can. But when I dive, you all need to dive, too. There's an underwater current in the crevice that will drag us straight to the ruin. It's the only way we'll make it there and not drown. Understood?"

They nodded their agreement, and I began to swim toward the ruin's entrance. Blue-green water shifted to ink-black the moment we passed into the mountain. The farther in we swam, the darker it became. Soon, the morning sun was just a blip at our backs, a glittering reminder of where to go once we returned. I tossed a quick glance behind me to check on Leena. Visible gooseflesh covered her flushed cheeks, but she didn't complain. Instead, she nodded my direction and kept swimming. The path narrowed until I reached a point where I could graze the mountain on either side of me with my hands.

"Here," I said, treading water. "Make a chain so we don't lose each other." Grabbing Leena's hand, I indicated for her to do the same. She snared Ozias's forearm, and he gripped Calem's wrist. "Take a deep breath and hold on."

We all gave an audible inhale, and then dove beneath the surface. The current snatched us, dragging us under and forcing air out of my lungs and through my lips. Bubbles danced around our heads as each one of us fought to hold our breath. Still, we were swept farther and farther beneath the surface. All light disappeared. My senses jumped into overdrive. The beat of my heart frantically crashing in my ears. The roar of raging water as we were thrust farther into the crevice. Leena's hand in mine. I held on to her with everything I had, too afraid to consider what would happen if I let go.

My lungs started to burn, and I fought against the desire to try to escape the current. Doing so would result in our deaths. We were far beneath the mountain now, and the only way to survive was to wait this out. Seconds felt like hours, until finally a faint, pale-blue glow bloomed to life before us. Lichen covered the walls of the massive, underwater cavern, and their luminescent bodies showered our surroundings in light. The sandy ocean floor became visible beneath our feet, covered in thousands upon thousands of shells, all varying colors and sizes. A shoal of silver fish swam by, causing a ripple in the water across the surface above our heads.

Surface. The current died, and I kicked upward with all my might. My muscles screamed from lack of oxygen, the burn of exertion chasing away the cold of the water. Finally, we emerged, each one of us gasping mouthfuls of air.

"Never. Again," Calem sputtered.

Ozias coughed and then rolled to his back, allowing himself to float atop the surface. "Well, at least one more time to get out of here."

Leena pushed hair out of her eyes and shivered. "Let's hope we can charm a Revmandra instead. Trust me, riding one is much more preferable than that."

"First," I said, nodding toward the small island within the cavern, "let's do the ritual so I can ask for a pearl."

They turned, following my gaze. An altar made entirely of dusty-purple, rose-shaped coral stood tall over the limestone statue of a kneeling woman. Her hair, dotted with shells and glittering opals, fell in a frozen wave down her side. And she was smiling. A bemused, soft grin, as if she were privy to a joke we'd never hear. But perhaps the most stunning part of the entire display was the endless amount of pearls. Pale-pink and lustrous, they clung to the altar and statue like bubbles.

Leena swam to the shore and hoisted herself out of the water. Dripping wet, she stood before the statue, backlit by the glowing lichen, and ran a delicate finger over one of the pearls in Yuna's hair. "These will work for the taming."

"Good. One less thing to worry about." I joined her side and wrung out the edge of my tunic, dousing our feet. Calem and Ozias followed after us. Once safely on the island, they sat on large pieces of driftwood and removed their shoes to dump water across the sand.

"I'll get our bag from Tok," Leena said, moving away from the altar as she splayed out her hand. Her soaked, white blouse was nearly see-through, and I tracked the progression of rosewood vines as they climbed up her arm. Flowers bloomed and framed her temple, and finally, the beast realm door opened. She stepped into the flood of light and disappeared temporarily from our world. A minute or two later she returned with a canvas duffel in her hands.

She set it on the ground before her and closed the beast realm door, allowing her emblem to recede. "You guys go on ahead and get out of those wet clothes. I'll wait until after we tame the Revmandra. I have to get back in the ocean to do it, and I only have the one spare set." Her teeth chattered, and she rubbed her hands along her arms.

"At least start a fire to keep warm in the meantime," I said. Ozias, Calem, and I stripped out of our clothes and slipped into new ones. Given we were still using borrowed attire left behind by travelers, the trousers and linen shirt were a bit snug. I tugged at the collar before shoving my feet back into my boots.

As soon as he'd dressed, Ozias broke apart some driftwood and stacked the pieces like a cabin. Satisfied, he snagged two stones and struck them together until a spark caught. Hungry flames devoured the wood and cast an immediate warmth around us. Sighing, Leena crumpled before the fire and held her palms out to the heat.

Calem plopped down beside her and ran a hand through his wet locks. Looking at the altar from across the flames, he gave me a nod. "You ready?"

"No turning back now." Moving away from the warmth and security of the fire, I walked toward the altar. Each step forward was one step closer to a future I'd never wanted, but one I'd started to accept. I let out a weighted breath. Listened to the snarl of the fire and the steady, if not heightened, heartbeats of my family at my back. The occasional drip of water sliding off stalactites and splashing into the ocean below. It was almost peaceful here. Safe.

And the safety and security I felt deep in my bones was something I wanted my family, everyone in my kingdom, to feel. Varek couldn't continue his reign. Not when he wielded borrowed power like a tyrant. Employing Harlow to steal for his own personal gain was an abuse of power, but that action only scratched the surface of his misdeeds. Not to mention allying with Darrien and Yazmin. He was a paranoid king obsessed with preserving his power, likely because he was never meant to occupy the throne. He locked away people without trials. Imposed high taxes so he could continue to fortify his castle on their bits. And if there *were* captured Charmers imprisoned in his city...

He wasn't a king of the people. He only fueled the divide the First King had created centuries ago when he'd sacrificed his children, splitting our world in three.

But I...I wanted what was best for everyone in Lendria—Charmers, undead assassins, and Wilheimians. And that, apparently, was Leena...and me.

"The fifth bows," I mused aloud, words barely a whisper. And yet that was enough. A sudden influx of magic swirled from the depths of the altar and shot outward in a visible, fine mist of bright-blue particles. The glow of the lichen throbbed like a heartbeat, and a faint aura formed around the statue. It grew outward with every pulse until Yuna appeared, an astral projection of the stone woman before me. Noble and all-knowing, she stared without moving, bemused smile still on her lips.

"*Aleksander Nocsis Feyreigner.*" She tilted her head slightly, temporarily casting her gaze to Leena, Ozias, and Calem. "*And family. Welcome.*" They remained quiet, but I caught glimpses of their nods in my periphery. Not silent, then. A message for all witnesses to hear.

Returning my focus to the mage, I dipped my chin to my chest. "Yuna. I'm here so that I may ascend to king."

"*You have a fight ahead of you. It will not be easy.*" Her smile faded, and sadness touched her eyes. She clasped her hands before her. "*But it will be worth it. This kingdom needs you...and your pair bond.*" Raising her hand, she beckoned to Leena.

Craning my neck, I watched as she strode forward, chin angled high. She was so confidant, so *regal*. When she reached my side, she offered a reverent bow before intertwining her fingers with mine. I hadn't even prepared her for this. Hadn't thought to. The mages never called upon those outside of the royal family. Yes, she was my pair bond, but by blood she had no claim to the throne. Yet this couldn't have felt more right. Peeking at me out of the corner of her eye, she smiled and gave my hand a tight squeeze.

"*Leena Edenfrell,*" Yuna said.

"You know my name?"

"Yes. I am a conduit for the gods. Celeste sends her blessing." Slowly, Yuna extended her hand and cupped Leena's face. Eyes wide, she stared back at the mage, and she sucked in a sharp breath. Yuna's expression softened. *"The world is ready for you."* She tipped her head my direction as she let her hand fall away. *"Both of you."*

"We will protect Lendria. Together." Placing a kiss on Leena's temple, I pulled her closer.

Yuna smiled. *"Stop the fires and unite your people. Come together to undo the past and restore balance to your land."*

Immediately, my mind went to Zane and his sister, Mavis. They had been sacrificed during the First War against Charmers. Zane and his troops rose from the dead to become the first assassins of Cruor. And Mavis... Her blood bestowed to the castle guards transformed them into Sentinels and granted the people of Wilheim prolonged life. But the First King's actions had cursed Lendrians. Instead of one unified country, factions rose out of bloodshed. And even though he'd caused the rift, even won his war, the First King was paranoid they'd one day return for his crown. And so he'd banished the assassins and Charmers, keeping only the Sentinels for protection, and solidified the divide.

But with Leena as queen and me as king...

Yuna gave me a knowing look. *"Together you will unite this land once again."*

Her hair fell over her face as she bowed, obscuring her lips, but her words were clear as a bell. *"I bow to you, Aleksander Nocsis Feyreigner, and also to your pair bond, Leena Edenfrell. The gods have acknowledged both of you as the rightful rulers of Lendria."* She straightened and placed one hand on either of us—just above Leena's heart and on the right side of my chest. *"The people will know."*

I didn't have time to warn Leena. I'd braced for this myself, but hadn't expected Yuna to call upon Leena to stand beside me. Searing heat splintered from the mage's fingertips, followed by a white-hot glow. Black spots danced across my vision. Leena cried out in pain but held her ground, fingernails digging into my hand so hard they drew blood. My pulse roared in my ears as adrenaline flooded my body. Then all at once the pain subsided, and I blinked several times to clear my vision.

Gingerly, Leena pulled back the deep cut of her collar to reveal a midnight-blue griffin emblazoned on her skin. The royal family's crest. I didn't have to pull back my shirt to know the very same mark now claimed a spot on my chest as proof of the gods' blessing. It was the very thing my people would need to see in order to abandon Varek. For a moment, I held my breath and waited for Leena to meet my gaze. I prayed she was still in this with me, that the permanence of what just happened didn't scare her from my side.

She looked up at me, eyes glassy and full of emotion, and offered me the most genuine, beautiful smile I'd ever seen. The urge to kiss her senseless rushed over me. I cupped her cheeks and slanted my mouth over hers. Tasted her breathy exhale, felt the sudden flux of heat from her body against my skin. She broke away first, resting her forehead against mine. Then, she turned her attention to Yuna.

"I know it's forbidden, but may we have a pearl? It's...it's for a beast."

"*A Revmandra,*" Yuna mused. "*They often frequent these waters in the hopes of stealing one of these.*" She removed a fist-sized pearl from the altar and handed it to my *anam-cara.* "*No doubt this will attract one. Good luck, Leena Edenfrell, Charmer Queen of Lendria.*" With that, she disappeared, and the magic that had flooded the cavern dissipated. The lichen returned to their normal, steady glow. Adrenaline abandoned me, and my shoulders sagged. I had finally completed my rites to become king. My parents would be proud. I only hoped that if they were watching over me, they understood why it'd taken me so long to accept my birthright. That in the end, this long, winding path to the throne—full of war and death, curses and oaths—was the very thing I needed to endure in order to heal our kingdom. To find *her*.

Leena bumped her hip against mine. "How does it feel to be king?"

I grinned. "How does it feel to be queen?"

"Am I?" She frowned and passed the pearl between her hands. "I mean, yes, to the gods. To you. But to the people? They don't know who I am. They already know you."

"They'll love you. This," I said, grazing my fingers along the edges of her griffin tattoo, "will help. And so will a ceremony to formally introduce you. All that can wait, though."

"Please," Calem said, standing and stretching his hands to the ceiling of the cavern. He and Ozias had been silent throughout the entire exchange with Yuna, merely watching as she bestowed our new titles. "You're already Crown of the Council. One extra title is nothing."

Ozias offered a sheepish but sincere smile. "You've been a queen in my eyes since the day I met you."

Leena blushed. "Oz. Stop."

"Seriously, you make the rest of us look bad." Calem side-eyed him, and then he gave Leena a suggestive wink. "You already know how I feel about you. There's no need for words."

"Gods, Calem." She rolled her eyes and then smacked him on his chest. "Do you ever stop?"

"No."

Leena shook her head and then kneeled in front of the fire. Setting the pearl before her, she undid the pouch at her waist and extracted the glittering conch shell. Two out of the four necessary taming ingredients ready and waiting.

"Fish and seashells, right?" I asked, sitting beside her.

She nodded. Some of the light in her eyes had faded. How she must have felt, knowing she was about to attempt to tame the very creature her parents had supposedly been after. There was no way of knowing if a Revmandra had caused their deaths. Or if they'd even died at all. Still… I brushed Leena's cheek with my knuckles, and she leaned into my touch.

"We'll be right here with you. I promise," I said.

She angled her head toward me and smiled. "I know." Touching her hand to her chest, she rested her fingers over Wilheim's emblem. "I'll always be with you, too."

A familiar tinge of pain sparked in my chest, but I buried it deep. We'd already witnessed what raising Gaige had done to his beasts. Leena's life would be fleeting in comparison to mine, but I wouldn't let that fear consume me. Not anymore. Not when we had each other. Wrapping her hand in mine, I held on tight. For now, the time we had together would have to do. And I'd protect it with every fiber of my being so that my queen could stay by my side for as long as the world would let me have her.

EIGHTEEN

LEENA

O z, Calem, and Noc made quick work out of capturing the fish needed for taming the Revmandra. Still as statues, they stood with their boots barely in the water and called forth slim shadow blades that they sent careening into the deep. Smoky tendrils remained wrapped around their fingers, and with subtle yanks, they retrieved the speared herrings from the water. As they hunted, I scoured the shallows for an array of shells and dumped them on the shore.

"That enough?" Oz asked as he added another fish to the pile.

"Yes." I rubbed my hands together as I eyed our haul. Reaching for a net I'd secured from Tok, I arranged the herrings, shells, Queen Jessamine's Conch, and the pearl safely in the middle. Then, I tied it off into a makeshift sack. It, along with my presence, would act as a lure. With some spare rope, I fashioned a belt and looped the bait around my waist.

Calem plopped onto the beach beside me, kicking his feet out before him. "Good. Fishing is boring."

Oz rolled his eyes before settling on a piece of driftwood. "I find it relaxing. Real fishing, though. This was kind of cheating."

I chuckled. "Well, sorry this couldn't be more leisurely. We're in a hurry."

Noc came to my side and peered at the bag. "How, exactly, is this going to work?"

"I'm going to jump into the water, wait for a Revmandra to appear, and then tame it. It's pretty simple." I tried my best to keep my voice level, to downplay the risk associated with this taming. I wasn't lying—in theory it *was* simple. But Noc saw right through my words. His jaw ticked as he folded his arms across his chest.

"Leena."

Sighing, I met his hardened gaze. "I'm not lying, it's just... It's going to look...violent. But I swear, I'll be fine." I threw up my hands as I talked, speeding through my words to try to make my point before any of them could interject. "Revmandra are attracted to treasure. More than one will appear, and they'll fight for the right to claim the treasure as theirs. Only one will win. I will be able to tame that one."

For a long moment, no one said anything. Finally, Oz cleared his throat, brows inching together. "Then why did you say charming one is dangerous? It's not like they're attacking you, just each other."

I chewed on the inside of my cheek. "Sometimes Charmers can get grabbed in the process. A Revmandra might try to steal me rather than fight the others, which will cause the others to attack it, and I might get a scratch or two."

Noc's words were ice. "*Might* get a scratch or two?"

"Sneaky bastards," Calem muttered.

Oz clasped his hands together and toed the sand with his boot. "What if we just jump in and pull you out?"

"That won't work." I shook my head, begging them to understand. "If you intervene, you'll be perceived as a competing Revmandra. One of two things will happen: you'll either die, or you'll successfully save me and the Revmandra will scatter. Since you'll have 'won' the treasure, I won't be a viable lure and I'll be unable to charm one."

"We'll just take the boat, then. No sense in you getting hurt over this," Oz said.

"He's right." Noc gave his brother an appreciative nod. "We can take the current back to the surface. It won't be pleasant, but at least we'll be safe."

"And then what?" I turned to him, placing my hands on my hips. "Row our way to Rhyne? That should be our last resort. What if Harlow is waiting for us? Or Varek and his fleet of ships?"

Noc didn't say anything. Only stared.

I took advantage of his silence and kept going. "We can't outrun a fleet, not without a Revmandra. And you said it yourself, Varek *knows* you'll be visiting this ruin site, one way or another." Slowly, I moved toward him and gripped his hands in mine. "We *must* make it to Rhyne. We need their help. You know I can do this. I can tame this beast."

He pressed his eyes closed for a moment, then opened them and let out a quiet sigh. "I know you can."

"It's the only way." With light fingers, I lifted his chin. "You can't intervene. Do you understand?"

A muscle feathered down his neck, but he nodded. "Just be careful."

"I will." Planting a quick kiss on his lips, I backstepped into the water. I swallowed a curse. The biting cold felt like needles threading through my skin, but I kept going until only my head remained above the surface. I moved away from the shore and Yuna's Ruins, treading slowly to keep myself from sinking. I'd have to submerge eventually, but not yet.

Minutes stretched by. My heart pounded in my ears as I waited.

Had my mother or father tried to tame a Revmandra? I glanced over my shoulder at Noc. His entire frame was rigid, and thin shadows dripped from his fingertips, barely restrained. Maybe it was impossible to tame this beast with one's *anam-cara* standing by. Had my mother been pulled under and my father reacted? Had he died trying to save her, only for her to be accidentally mauled in the process? A shiver raced through me, completely unrelated to the cold. I wouldn't blame Noc if he came storming into the ocean after me. I don't know if I would've been able to stop myself if our roles had been reversed.

Turning my back to them, I closed my eyes and focused on my Charmer's magic. A subtle warmth rolled through my limbs, chasing away the sting of the frigid water, and a pale glow bloomed around me. I was a living lure, using the possibility of my Charmer's Bond to attract interested beasts.

The steady cadence of water droplets dripping from stalactites filled the cavern as time crept by. And still I waited. My magic continued to pulse outward with every beat of my heart, until finally something grazed my calf.

My breath caught in my throat. No matter how prepared I'd been, there was no avoiding the unsettling feeling of something monstrous lurking below. Or the knowledge that I couldn't outswim it. Circling beneath my feet along the ocean floor, the Revmandra moved with a fluidity few creatures could match. The giant, salamander-like beast was the size of a small whale and just as ferocious. Three horns similar to moose antlers grew from the base of its neck. In the glow of the lichen-covered cavern, the creature glimmered. Which was no surprise, given its entire back was covered in treasure. Revmandra hoarded shiny objects and permanently affixed them to their hides via a sticky, unbreakable adhesive they could secrete on command. This one was covered from head to tail in gold aurics and rare stones—a testament to its prowess in battling other Revmandra for treasure.

A few seconds ticked by, and four more appeared. They encircled me slowly, snapping at one another as they made their rounds. Any minute now, the battle would begin. After one final look at Noc, I sucked in a sharp breath and allowed myself to sink beneath the surface. That was the only signal the beasts needed. They attacked in a flurry, bodies sliding over each other like eels and white water churning the surface. Vicious snarls were somehow audible even with water filling my ears. They struck without restraint, gleaming white teeth cracking against glittering hides. Those with fewer treasures glued to their backs were vulnerable, and soon, a muddy-red haze filled the ocean.

One Revmandra slithered closer. Unlike the rest, it wasn't engaged in battle. Which only meant one thing: I was about to be snatched. I braced myself for impact just as the beast lunged. With one of its webbed hands, it sank its claws into the soft flesh of my thigh. Stars exploded behind my eyes as pain ruptured deep in my muscles. Blood bloomed in a cloud around me, the scent alerting the other Revmandra to my predicament. My captor drew me close to its body and then bolted, knocking the air out of my lungs in a flurry of bubbles. The remaining beasts abandoned their battles and raced after us. It didn't take long for a larger Revmandra to crash into us. The force of the hit set me free, and I hurried to the surface to refill my lungs before submerging again.

Chaos reigned around me. Enraged, garbled roars and the nerve-racking scrape of nails on metal filled my ears. Pain throbbed in my leg in time with every beat of my heart. But I was alive, and the Revmandra had started to dwindle. The smaller, injured beasts swam off to lick their wounds and seek treasure elsewhere.

Finally, only two remained. They rammed each other with their horns with such force the water trembled. One managed to get its claws beneath a piece of treasure on the other's hide, peeling back the layer of aurics and stones to reveal tender, pink flesh. The beast howled, and, rather than sacrifice treasure it'd already accrued over the years, submitted, rolling over to expose its soft white belly—the one space Revmandra didn't adorn with jewels so they could fool their prey while swimming above their heads. The winning beast released its grip and slunk through the ocean to float before me.

Quickly, I undid the sack at my waist and first presented the fish to the Revmandra—food to replenish the energy it expended while fighting for the right to claim me. It ate quickly, expectant eyes tracking the remaining treasure. With one webbed claw, it poked at the seashells, knocking some to the side. Once it was pleased with the selection, it rubbed its bare snout against the shells until they affixed in the few open spaces along its hide. The beast did an excited barrel role when it spotted Yuna's pearl, and the force of the unexpected current nearly sent me crashing into the island wall. Like an otter, the Revmandra dragged its claws over its skin until it found a hole and then placed the pearl there.

Finally, I presented the beast Queen Jessamine's Conch. The Revmandra went incredibly still. A pirate's bounty. It was a treasure no Revmandra could deny. The beast snatched the conch and ran a claw along the diamond surface, nail clicking against the stone. Gently, it dipped its head down to reveal a clear spot at the base of its horns. It was as if the beast had been waiting for a prize worthy enough to occupy the most protected part of its body. Tiny, bubble-like droplets of tacky secretion formed along its skin, and it held out the treasure to me. I didn't hesitate, and I swam closer to place the conch against its hide. I channeled power into the Charmer's emblem on my hand. Rosewood light blossomed around us, and the Revmandra willingly accepted my charm. With our connection solidified, my beast gently nudged me to the surface, mindful of my injured leg, and I gulped down air.

Noc, Calem, and Oz stood at the edge of the island. Shadows festered and lashed out around Noc's hands. His entire body was rigid, muscles ticking in his jaw. Oz had a firm grip on his shoulder to keep him from moving, but there was no mistaking the concern racing through his stare, either. Calem, too, had sidled closer, as if waiting to latch on to Noc in case he'd decided to come into the waters after me. Mercury had flooded his normally muted-red irises, and there was an air of frantic energy about him. But somehow, he'd maintained his human form. Somehow, we'd all managed to do exactly what was needed to tame the Revmandra.

Relief washed over my assassins like a wave the moment they locked eyes with me. Oz's arms went slack as he released Noc from his grip, and he immediately went to our bags to start extracting healing ointments and bandages. Calem closed his eyes and forced out several slow breaths. When he opened them again, the mercury hue had receded. Noc rushed to the shore and helped me out of the ocean, offering me his arm so I could lean against him and keep weight off my leg.

"That was...brutal," he said, voice low and full of emotion.

I cracked a tired smile. "Worse than when I tamed Onyx?"

He paused as if in thought. Then shook his head. "No. That was worse because I wasn't expecting it."

An old pang of guilt threaded through my stomach. When I'd tamed my Myad on our first, fateful journey together, I hadn't told any of them what it would take to charm the legendary beast. I'd tricked them and immobilized them. Rendered them useless while a ferocious creature nearly killed me. Maybe it had been then when Noc realized how much I meant to him—when he thought he'd lose me forever.

We'd both denied our feelings longer than we cared to admit. But not now. Not anymore. Gripping his arm tight, I gave him a reassuring squeeze. "I'm fine. Let's get this wound dressed so we can get the hell out of here."

Noc eased me to the ground while Oz measured and ripped bandages to care for my injury. The beast waited in the shallow waters with a contented look in its amber eyes. It was the largest Revmandra to appear—and the most decorated, covered in precious stones, gold aurics, and pearls of every shade. The beast was worth more than its weight in bits. Not that anyone would ever be able to remove its possessions and live to sell them.

Calem peered at my Revmandra. "Do we just hop on its back?"

"Not quite." Wincing, I shimmied out of my trousers with Noc's help and extended my leg to Oz. He didn't miss a beat, quickly wiping off the gash and applying a healing balm before wrapping it tightly several times. The pressure alleviated some of the lancing pain, and I sighed. Taking the offered pair of fresh breeches from Noc, I slipped them on, then swapped my soaked blouse for a dry pale-pink one.

"Then where?"

I pointed to the scoop-shaped antlers protruding from the water like high-backed thrones. "There. The Revmandra can produce an air bubble that will attach to its rack so we can safely travel underwater and avoid detection." Rising to my feet, I hobbled toward my beast with Noc by my side. "I'll show you."

As I moved to the edge of the water, my beast slithered forward, his belly etching a groove into the sandy bottom. I crouched before him and placed my hand against his massive snout. Gold bits scratched against my palm. But between the glittering, protective barrier, glimpses of slippery skin were still visible. And so were the tiny bubbles full of oxygen just waiting to be expanded.

"Hey, there." My mind whirred as I tried to think of a name suitable for such a magnificent creature. He was majestic. Powerful.

Clearly, he'd ruled over these waters and amassed a great deal of treasure. "I'm going to call you Magnus. Can you produce a bubble for us? We'd like to leave this cavern."

One by one, tiny bubbles lifted off his body and rushed toward each other, forming one massive sphere that rose out of the water and hung just above his head. Satisfied with its size, Magnus then trapped it with his antlers. The bubble shifted, expanding to encompass the horns and lock in air. He rested his snout on the shore and let out a wet huff.

Stepping lightly, I walked across the flat of his skull and pressed my palm against the bubble. Instead of it popping, a peculiar slurping met my ears and my hand passed right through the barrier up to my elbow. Turning my head, I offered my assassins a grin.

"Let's go."

I passed through the dome, a tad sticky thanks to the residue of Magnus's adhesive keeping the bubble intact, but otherwise dry. Maneuvering to the first antler, I hoisted myself up and relaxed, then beckoned to Noc, Calem, and Oz with a playful wave.

Noc followed immediately, taking the same steps I did and clambering up into the antler beside me. Draping one arm around my shoulders, he pulled me against his chest and placed a kiss on the crown of my head. Oz quickly grabbed our things and then tiptoed across Magnus's head to the center antler.

I held back a laugh. "You're fine, Oz. Trust me, he can carry our weight and then some."

"Just being nice is all," he said with a smile. Shoving the bag up first, he climbed onto the horn and settled in. Calem was right on his heels, and he strolled over to the third and final antler. With all of us securely in place, Magnus let out another huff.

"Take us south," I said to my beast. "We're heading to Rhyne."

Magnus plunged beneath the surface and took off in the

direction of the underwater current we'd rode in on. It had mysteriously switched directions, as if the gods had altered the water's path for the ascending king and queen to exit the same way we'd arrived. We didn't need it, though. Magnus swam parallel to the swirling channel into the depths beneath the mountain. The lichen died off, and so did the pale-blue glow they provided. We were thrust into darkness with nothing more than a bubble to protect us. But Magnus was unfazed, and within a few minutes, we escaped the belly of the island to waters doused in sun. Light filtered through the blue-green ocean, a handful of boat-shaped shadows marring the sandy floor beneath us.

Noc's grip on me tightened. "We've got company."

My gaze snapped upward. "Harlow?"

"I don't think so." His eyes narrowed as he studied the small fleet of rowboats heading toward our vessel. I spied Selenis immediately, still safely hidden within the shadow of Kings Isle. Her head was angled toward the approaching ships, and aside from the constant flutter of her finned tail, she barely moved.

Extending my hand, I opened the beast realm door. "Good work, Selenis. Come home." Her gaze riveted to me and she smiled before releasing the rope and disappearing into the realm. I let my hand fall to my side, thankful she hadn't been spotted.

"Our rowboat will act as a good diversion," Noc said, jerking his chin toward the few ships anchored a short distance away. From the underside, it was impossible to tell who they belonged to. But the location of these hidden burial sites wasn't public knowledge, which meant we were more than likely lurking beneath Varek's forces.

I signaled to Oz and Calem, pointing to Magnus's rack. "Hang on tight." Gripping the edge of his antler, I urged my beast forward. "Get us out of here as fast as you can."

He swam in earnest then, pressing his arms and legs flush with his body and rocketing away from the island like an arrow sailing through the air. Fish scattered, and the world around us became an indecipherable swirl. Sand kicked up behind his tail, but as the minutes stretched by and we raced farther and farther away from the threatening forces, the tightness in my chest lessened. Finally, the boats' shadows disappeared altogether, and we were left with nothing but filtered sunlight streaming through clear water.

I gave his antler a gentle pat and reclined back. "We're okay now. You can take it easy."

He let out a whalelike guttural groan followed by a whistle as he slowed, allowing his webbed claws to leisurely drag beneath his body.

With a blazing grin stretching from ear to ear, Calem leaped to his feet. "That was incredible. Can we do that again?"

"Maybe later," I called.

"Whoa. Look at that." Oz's awe-filled words pulled my attention to the surrounding ocean, and my mouth went slack. We were swimming above a coral reef teeming with life. Colonies of brightly colored fish darted between flowerlike coral structures, and vibrant blue starfish and ruby-red crabs crawled over stones in search of food. Tangerine-colored anemone with white tentacles snared small fish in the passing current. Jellyfish floated through it all, not a care in the world as they tumbled over one another on some hidden path. Every inch of the seafloor was covered in flowering plants, and I itched to touch them all. Shoals of herring swam beside Magnus, and he lazily snapped at a few, enjoying a quick snack without breaking his stroke.

Noc looked over Magnus's antler with me and smiled. "I've never seen anything like this."

"It's incredible. No wonder Queen Jessamine loved the sea so much."

He trailed a light finger down my arm. "Is this the farthest you've ever ventured from Hireath?"

"Yes."

A shelf had formed below, the coral reef coming to an abrupt halt and an endless, deep-blue void stretching farther than my eye could see. A pod of beasts I didn't recognize hung around the ledge. At first glance, I'd mistaken them for manta rays, but they had extra flippers and long necks that extended outward as they snatched nearby fish.

My hand went to my bestiary, and I pictured all the beasts I'd encountered. The ones I'd tamed and the ones I hadn't. There were so many more out there. Beasts we'd never even imagined. Before becoming Crown of the Council, it'd been my dream to travel the world. To discover every creature. Now... My gaze slanted to Noc. My dream had evolved into something more. One that involved him, and Oz, Kost, and Calem. Everyone back at Hireath and Cruor. I still wanted to see the world, to travel and expand upon my beast knowledge, but I wanted a life with him—with my family—too.

Noc studied my face for a long time. "You know, being queen means establishing relationships with foreign countries." He placed his hand over mine, right on top of my pendant. "I'm sure we could extend those trips from time to time and go on some beast hunts."

Warmth radiated outward from his touch, and a lightness invaded my chest. I knew all along he never expected me to stop charming beasts, but hearing it made me smile just the same. Snuggling closer to him, I inhaled deeply and savored his signature honeyed scent. "I'd like that."

"Me too."

And even though we were hundreds of feet under water and swimming toward enemy shores, I'd never felt more secure about my future.

NINETEEN

NOC

Traveling beneath the ocean waves was surreal. Leena had given me so many firsts in my life, and this was no exception. We'd breached a few times during our journey to Rhyne, allowing Magnus to recharge and store oxygen in his hide. He'd then channel it into our protective dome so we could continue to move undetected underwater. He was fast, too. His nimble body cut through the water and shaved days off our travel time, though we still had to sleep beneath the stars in the middle of the ocean twice. At first, it had unnerved me. But Leena assured me no creature would dare disturb a predator like Magnus, and after the first night proved uneventful, I was able to relax. At one point, Leena summoned Blitz—her wolflike Canepine pup—to purify the ocean water for us to drink. We fished for food. Swam in the cool sea to bathe and relieve ourselves. Not entirely ideal, but a great deal safer than any ship I could've chartered.

Still, my body ached for a real bed and the comfort of a fire. So when we encountered the characteristic kelp forest marking the shores of Rhyne, I couldn't help but sigh. Even if Queen Elianna wanted me dead in the name of justice, we'd at least get a night of reprieve at a local inn before I had to face the crown. And I wasn't the only one who needed it.

Leena had done well to hide her fatigue from Calem and Ozias—which was fairly easy, given we were mostly separated by the tall height of Magnus's antlers—but she couldn't hide her exhaustion from me. Sweat had long since dampened the collar of her blouse. She was gaunt, cheeks hollow and eyes heavy. She was still nursing the injury on her thigh, and of course, there was the issue of Magnus. Never before had she kept a beast in our world for as long as she had with him. She assured me that it was easier with him than any of her other creatures because of his own well of massive power. But still, his connection to this world was tethered to her. And she'd used up every last ounce of energy keeping us all afloat for the past several days.

The moment we could stand in the waters, she sent him home. And then collapsed in my arms. Incoherent and slightly feverish, she curled up against my chest and immediately fell asleep. For a moment, I was thrust back to the first time I'd carried her after she'd depleted all her power taming a beast for Kost. She'd always push her limits when it came to us.

"Is she okay?" Ozias asked as he rushed over, water splashing against his thighs.

"She overexerted herself," I said, trudging toward the shore.

Calem blanched and picked up his stride to walk beside me. "She never sent Magnus back to the realm."

Worry ate away at my insides. "Not once."

"Shit." Ozias wrung his hands together and then picked up the pace. "Do we even know where the Polished Goblet is?"

"No." My fingers pressed tightly against Leena's slumbering frame. "We'll use the shadows and stay out of sight while we look."

My feet hit the black sandy beach as we exited the ocean. Night had fallen a few hours ago, and the shores were deserted. Warm, buttery lights blurred against the dark backdrop in the distance, marking the edge of Rhyne's capital—Veles. The hairs on the back of my neck raised. I was across the ocean, hundreds of miles away from my brethren, and practically knocking on our enemy's door. Too much could go wrong.

Together, we slipped into the world of shadows. Smoky dark tendrils enveloped us as we strode across the beach in the direction of Veles. Ozias and Calem stayed close to my side, and Leena never stirred. The dirt roads were quiet, but not empty. Locals sat outside their modest houses on wooden rocking chairs with blankets draped across their laps and mugs in their hands. Steam curled upward from their drinks and framed their smiling faces. Low, friendly words passed between them. They were the perfect picture of rest and relaxation, and longing stirred in my chest. Since I'd met Leena, we'd been constantly running. Fighting. Doing *something* to protect ourselves and our family. When this was all over, I'd find a way to get us the break we deserved.

Soon, the dirt pathways transitioned to cobblestone streets, and the flagstone manors grew more opulent in design. The prized jewel of the city, though, was the royal castle. It towered above all else, and hundreds of floating orbs fueled by rycrims cast a warm glow over the jade stone. Molten-gold veining crawled upward toward the spires and practically pulsed in the light. It looked almost... alive. And though it was mesmerizing, we avoided it at all costs. We needed to visit Queen Elianna, but not yet. Not before we had a chance to regroup with Kost.

Sticking to dark alleyways, we avoided people but kept our ears open. Listened for any detail about taverns or inns, desperately picking apart conversations in the hopes we could find our destination. We followed one group of intoxicated locals only to wind up at a tavern full of boisterous patrons. Their loud tune about warrior maidens followed us into the night as we retraced our steps.

After what felt like hours and absolutely zero luck, I came to a halt and bit back a sigh. "We'll never find it like this. Ozias, ask someone for directions."

"You sure about that?" Calem asked, peering around the corner at the constant flow of locals. We hadn't prepared for this kind of nightlife. Gone were the quiet residences on the outskirts of the city. Here, it appeared, no one ever slept. Endless shops and watering holes lined either side of the cobblestone path, all open for business. People dressed in shimmery slacks and tunics with foiled-gold patterns filled the streets. Their fashion wasn't too different than Wilheim's, but even in the dead of winter, Rhynelanders favored clothing that exposed skin. Everywhere we looked there were slits along thighs, bare midriffs, and plunging collars. In our days-old travel gear—ill-fitted and stiff with salt from the sea—we were bound to stick out.

"They won't know either of you. It's me who needs to stay out of sight."

"It's fine. I'll do it," Ozias said. His eyes roved to Leena, and he frowned. "We need to get her someplace safe." Then, without looking, he abandoned the shadows and stepped into the main street of Veles—right into a fast-walking blond. She stumbled backward but recovered quickly, shooting fire with her umber gaze.

"Watch where you're going."

"S-sorry," Ozias mumbled, immediately ducking his chin to his chest. Rubbing the back of his neck, he met her unrelenting stare. "Can you tell me where the Polished Goblet is?"

She was tiny in comparison to him, and yet when she straightened her back, she somehow managed to tower over him. "What business do you have there?"

He shrank away. "It's a tavern, right? I just need a place to stay for—"

"You're not from around here." Her eyes narrowed as she took a step in his direction. "You sound...odd."

A rock formed in my throat. We spoke the same language as Rhyne, but our accents were different. Their words carried a smoother, softer intonation than ours. Not by much—something I'd only grown accustomed to after my time with Amira—but apparently Ozias's speech was just different enough to catch this woman's attention.

"Odd?" His grin was sheepish. "Well, you're right, I'm a traveler."

She raised a single manicured brow. "Why are you here?"

"Uh... Isn't that my business?"

Placing her hands on her hips, she leaned forward. "As part of the Queen's Guard, it's my business to know about everything that happens in my city. So yes, your business *is* my business."

Tension corded tight in my shoulders. I remembered the Queen's Guard from my time as prince. Even though she was only a princess, Amira never went anywhere without them. They were an elite force of soldiers dedicated to protecting the crown, much like our Sentinels. My gaze caught on the gilded lion stitched into the fabric of the woman's olive-green coat. There was no mistaking the royal court's insignia.

"Shit," Calem hissed. I motioned for him to be silent and took a careful step back. The shadows masked our presence, but I wasn't in the mood to be surprised by something unexpected. Just knowing she was part of the Queen's Guard was enough for me. Even worse, I couldn't find a weapon strapped to her body. No sword sheathed against her hip. No dagger attached to her belt. Nothing. Which meant she was either skilled at concealing weapons, or deadly enough not to need one at all.

Ozias swallowed thickly and shot a fleeting, worried glance

our direction. The woman stiffened, and then leaped in front of him, staring directly into the mouth of the alley where we stood, protected by shadows. For a moment, none of us moved. We barely breathed. Her brows pulled together, and she slowly turned away before pressing an accusing finger against his chest.

"What were you looking at?"

"Nothing, I swear." Ozias held his hands up. "It's just… Veles is larger than I expected, and I got lost."

She studied him without moving, her gaze traveling from his salt-soaked tunic to his worn boots. Satisfied with her once-over, she relented with an exaggerated sigh and turned on her heels, beckoning over her shoulder. "C'mon. I don't have all night."

Ozias practically tripped over his feet to fall in line beside her, and we snuck behind them under the cover of our shadows. She power walked with force, driving her feet into the ground and making a path through the throng of people without ever breaking pace. And judging by the way they naturally moved away from her advance, the locals knew she wasn't someone they wanted to upset. One interaction with her was all it took for me to think the same.

Hooking a right off the main street, she led us toward a quieter strip of shops and taverns. "So, what's your name?"

"Ozias." He clasped and unclasped his hands, then let them fall by his sides, only to start all over again.

Beside me, Calem rolled his eyes. "You should've sent me out there."

"He's fine." Though the first beads of sweat forming along Ozias's hairline seemed to defy my words.

"Not going to ask my name?" the woman asked, cutting Ozias a hard glance.

"Oh. Um. Yeah."

She scoffed. "Wow. Not the most eloquent person, are you?"

Coming to an abrupt halt, she turned to face Ozias and jerked her thumb over her shoulder. "Here's the Polished Goblet. Don't do anything to catch my eye again."

Ozias blinked up at the swinging, golden sign hanging above the heavy oak door. The curtains along the windows were pulled back to reveal a well-lit interior with only a few patrons and a horde of open tables. One man sat alone at the bar, rotating an empty glass in place with two fingers. He had a strikingly familiar pompadour styled to perfection and neatly pressed clothes.

Kost. Relief surged through me at the sight of my brother. It was as if the very thought of his name summoned his stare, and he tilted his head upward only to freeze when he spied Ozias through the window, and then the Queen's Guard, and then us. I nodded once in reassurance, and he relaxed a fraction, waiting for us to make our move.

Ozias cleared his throat. "I won't. Thanks for bringing me here."

"At least you have some manners." She shook her head and then started off in the direction we'd just come from, boots thudding fiercely against the paved stones.

"Wait!" Ozias took a step her way and then stopped. Gripped the back of his neck tight. The woman paused, tilting her chin back toward him. "You never told me your name."

"Did you even really ask?" Her breathy laugh was a stark contrast to the way she assaulted the streets with her stride. Shaking her head, she continued forward and spoke just loud enough for us to hear. "It's Isla. Hopefully you'll have no need to remember it."

"I hope not," Ozias mumbled to himself.

As soon as she disappeared from view down a nearby street, Calem emerged from the shadows and socked Ozias in the arm, wide grin threatening to split his face in half. "Holy shit. You played that *terribly.*"

"Shut it." Ozias shoved him away, but Calem only tipped his head to the sky and laughed.

"He got us here, didn't he?" I shot Calem a stern look as an ache started to throb against my skull. We'd been in the shadow realm so often on our journey, and my power reserves were all but depleted. Adjusting Leena's sleeping form in my arms, I took quick stock of our surroundings and then sent the shadows away.

Before Calem could respond, Kost opened the tavern door. Holding it wide with one hand, he gestured for us to enter with the other. Uniform mahogany tables with matching cushioned chairs spread across the tavern floor. In the corner, a lone musician strummed a soft, pleasing melody on a harp that filtered through the hushed conversations of patrons. There weren't many, just a few groups littered throughout, and they sipped drinks out of jeweled goblets and sparkling glasses while poking at artfully arranged platters of food.

Calem frowned. "This is...different than our usual haunt."

Kost let the door shut behind him. "As I mentioned, I wasn't familiar with Veles. I picked the only tavern I'd heard of. Gods forbid we stay in a nice establishment for once."

"It's fine." I nodded toward Leena. "Let's get her to a room."

Worry framed Kost's eyes, and he pursed his lips together. "This way." He led us around tables to a grand set of polished stairs at the back. After one flight, we peeled off down a brightly lit corridor full of landscape paintings and potted plants. Their thick leaves stretched toward the rafters and bordered rows of closed doors. Kost stopped when he reached the last one on the right and fished a shiny key out of his breast pocket. The lock clinked open, and we stepped into a spacious room with elegant white oak furniture and a small sitting area.

Gently, I laid Leena on the bed and draped a blanket over her.

She let out a contented sigh and gripped the blanket tight, rolling over into a mound of pillows.

Kost hovered nearby and dragged his fingers along the bedside table. "What happened to her?"

"We crossed the ocean on one of her beasts." Satisfied she was comfortable and safe, I sank into the settee at the foot of the bed and let out a tired groan. My whole body ached, but it was likely nothing in comparison to what she felt. "She kept him out the entire time and used too much of her power."

"That explains why you're here so soon. I wasn't expecting you for a few more days at least." Kost shook his head at Leena and then sat in the high-back armchair across from me. Crossing one ankle over the other, he took a moment to study all of us. He sighed. "Not an easy journey, I take it?"

"Not in the slightest," Ozias said. He sauntered over to the fireplace, first warming his hands before the dying flame, then resting his arm along the baroque mantel. His shoulders sagged.

Calem sprawled out in the other chair, draping one leg over its arm. "Varek, Darrien, Yazmin, massively powerful beasts," he said, ticking off his fingers as he went. "Oh, and a crazed pirate who will no doubt try to murder me when this is all over. Noc had me steal from her."

Kost eyebrows shot into his hairline. "What?"

"I'll fill you in later. For now... It's just good to see you," I said.

"You too." Kost's smile was sad. "I only got here yesterday. I've had little opportunity to do any reconnaissance."

"That's okay." Ozias abandoned the fire to clap a hand on his brother's shoulder. "We're just glad to see you."

"I'm happy to see you, too." Kost let out a long exhale that did little to alleviate the tension in his shoulders, but he didn't pull away from Ozias's touch. "I do think our timing is fortunate, though."

"Why is that?" I asked.

"Queen Elianna's daughter just got engaged. There will be a public celebration tomorrow evening." Kost tilted his head to the ceiling, studying the ornate, oversize chandelier laden with candles. "The amicable mood just might help our cause. Not to mention, we'll draw little unwanted attention to ourselves with so many people rejoicing in the streets. We can approach the queen after the announcement without suspicion. Many will offer gifts, and we can fall in line with them."

"And say what? 'Congrats on your upcoming nuptials, let's go to war!' Hell of a wedding present, Kost," Calem said.

He barely deigned to give him a glance. "I would never phrase it that way."

"Of course you wouldn't." Calem rolled his eyes, but a warm, almost relieved smile touched his lips. No doubt Kost's response was exactly what he wanted to hear. Proof that the brother we all knew and loved hadn't changed.

"We'll figure it out. In the meantime, I think we could use a good night's rest," I said.

"And some food," Oz added, giving Kost's shoulder one last squeeze before stepping away.

Calem wrinkled his nose. "And a bath. My stench has stench."

Kost stood and brushed his hands along his vest. "I took the liberty of bringing you spare clothes, which, it seems, was the right thing to do. Your things are in your rooms. Save the formal attire for tomorrow evening's celebration."

"Yessir," Calem said, rocketing to his feet. "Now, about these rooms..."

"I'll show you to them. Reconvene downstairs for a meal in half an hour?" Kost asked.

Looking over my shoulder, I found Leena's sleeping form and

gave her ankle a gentle nudge. She didn't move. "I'll bring some food back for her. I don't think she'll be waking up any time soon."

Kost nodded and moved toward the door, Ozias and Calem on his heels. "See you shortly."

As soon as they left, I kicked off my boots and climbed into bed next to Leena. I pressed the back of my hand against her forehead, thankful to find that her temperature had dropped back to normal. The steady rise and fall of her chest chased away the last of my concern, and I scooched closer, tucking a few strands of hair behind her ear. She barely stirred, shifting slightly toward the middle of the bed and curling in tighter on herself. I could've forgone dinner altogether and simply lain by her side, but we had plans to formulate. And now that I knew Leena was safe, I wanted to spend some dedicated time with Kost. We all needed to be in the right mindset going into this war, and I wanted to ensure that he was truly okay.

TWENTY

LEENA

By the time I awoke, late-morning sun was slanting through the ivory curtains drawn loosely over the window. While the fire in the hearth was dead, there was a stuffy warmth in the air that suggested it'd only recently gone out. I peeled back the blankets and wrinkled my nose, mad that I'd fallen asleep before bathing and sullied the sheets with a layer of salt and grime. Stifling a yawn, I surveyed the quiet room. The thick rug stretching across the wooden floorboards muffled the tavern sounds just beyond the heavy door. A scrap of neatly folded parchment waited for me on the nightstand, and I quickly scanned Noc's looping, familiar handwriting.

> *Downstairs in the tavern. Join us when you're ready. There are spare clothes in the armoire and fresh linens in the bathroom.*
>
> *Love,*
> *Noc*

I set the sheet down and immediately spied the ornate oak door leading to what I assumed was our attached bathroom. A dull pain throbbed through my skull, and I rolled my neck from side to side to try to loosen the knotted muscles. Limbs full of lead, I stood up on my toes and stretched before I made my way to the bathroom and filled the gilded claw-foot tub with steaming water. As water poured from the faucet, I closed my eyes and focused on the connection I had to my Revmandra. The beast realm door creaked open a fraction in my mind, and I found Magnus fast asleep beneath one of the realm's many oceans. I smiled at the steady flux of energy that pulsed down our bond and then opened my eyes, eager to chase away the last of my lingering pains.

There was no denying the ache in my body, but it wasn't as deep as I'd expected. I'd overclocked myself a few times during my journeys with Noc, but I'd never kept a beast outside the realm for as long as I had with Magnus. I'd chalked it up to adrenaline and drive, knowing that we'd likely die if I couldn't safely get us to Rhyne's shores. Magnus's own expansive well of magic had made it easier to keep him in our world. And yet... This pain hardly compared to the time I'd taken Noc to the beast realm, or even my run-in with Felicks before I'd tamed him for Kost.

Sinking into the tub, I frowned as the soothing water lapped against my shoulders. Why? I recounted the last few tamings I'd performed, starting with how easily Tok had joined my side back at Oslo's Ruins. Even Reine, my legendary feline and apex hunter. They'd both chosen me, and while I'd followed the necessary prerequisites for charming Magnus, I'd expected it to be harder. Especially knowing a Revmandra had supposedly killed my parents. Dragging my fingertips across the surface of the water, I stared at the ripples as I tried to piece together the ease of the tamings and the lack of pain in my bones. My hand moved to my chest, and I paused over the freshly inked griffin.

"Celeste sends her blessing." The memory of Yuna's words

rattled through my mind. Had she been helping me all along? Warmth purled outward from my touch, separate from the heat of the bath. The gods rarely interfered with our lives, but perhaps once Yazmin had started down this path, she'd forced Celeste's hand. For the sake of our people, our beasts, our world. If Celeste were on my side, and the gods on Noc's, then maybe we had a chance to stop Yazmin.

After dressing quickly in a simple getup of breeches, boots, and a long-sleeved blouse, I made my way downstairs to the first-floor tavern. For the most part, it was empty, with only a single bartender floating between patrons. Dimly lit chandeliers hung low over circular tables surrounded by ornate high-back chairs. Noc, Oz, Calem, and Kost sat near a window in the front, their heads bent low in quiet conversation. I crossed the room and slipped into the empty chair between Noc and Calem.

Noc straightened his back and offered me a warm smile. "How are you feeling?"

"Surprisingly okay. Hungry, though." I eyed the near-empty plates before them. Oz scooted a platter with two hefty potato wedges slathered in cream and chives my direction. I snatched one and finished it in a matter of seconds, fingers already reaching for the remaining morsel.

Kost signaled the bartender with a pointed nod. "We'll get you a proper meal. We're not in a rush."

Something loosened in my chest. Seeing Kost again, having him sit across from me with a look of concern and quiet protectiveness for his family, for me, felt right. I could still detect the ghost of pain in his eyes, a line of worry that seemed permanently etched between his brows. But he was coping. He was here. And I knew we couldn't do this without him.

"Thanks, Kost."

He glanced my way and allowed for a tired smile, just as the bartender approached our table. I gave the menu a quick once-over and ordered while Noc poured me a glass of water from the pitcher on the table. As soon as the bartender left, Kost cleared his throat.

"We'll be approaching the queen tonight."

"Really? Already?" My brows shot upward, and I glanced around the table. Oz only shrugged and Calem toyed with the tumbler between his fingers, eyeing the amber liquid sloshing up the walls. "Did I miss something?"

"No, took us by surprise, too," Noc said. "But the timing is right. Queen Elianna's daughter announced her recent engagement this morning. Here, it's tradition to celebrate with a reception line for gifts and a night of festivities."

"The positive atmosphere, the lack of attention we'll draw... It makes sense. We won't have to formally approach the castle in order to gain an audience with the royal family." Kost took a sip of his water. "We'll just ensure we're the last ones in line in case our appearance requires a more private discussion after."

"You mean 'when,'" Calem said. He leaned back into his chair and gazed at the ceiling. "I'm still not sure about this."

"The guard will be light." Oz braced his forearms on the table and rubbed his hands together. "That much we've gathered from our reconnaissance this morning. Of course, the queen and her family will be attended by the Queen's Guard, but overall they're well loved. They're not concerned about threats, and many of the soldiers will be participating in the festivities."

I popped the last of the potato wedge in my mouth and chewed slowly, mulling over their words. "Seems like a good plan. What's the etiquette on gift giving? Do we have something appropriate?"

Kost stiffened ever so slightly. "There's no etiquette per se."

Noc grimaced. "People give what they can and, if they can't, offer warm wishes. All are received with grace and thanks." He paused for a moment when the bartender returned to drop off my creamed soup served in a bread bowl. The aroma of thyme and parsley flirted with the scent of portobello shrooms, and my mouth watered. I dove in the moment he set my meal down, but kept my eyes glued on Noc.

"Then what's the problem?"

"We were thinking that the gift should be reflective of what we're asking for in return." Kost nudged his empty plate forward, not meeting my gaze. "Something of great value to help sway the queen in case she still harbors ill will toward Noc for Amira's fate."

"For gods' sake," Calem said, rolling his eyes and draining his glass of its contents. "They want a beast."

I paused midspoonful. "A beast?"

"That was just an idea." Noc shot him a hard look. "We're not committing to anything."

"Plus, gifting a beast could set the wrong precedence," Kost said. "Assuming we make it through our current...predicament, we don't want other allies of Lendria to expect beasts in the future."

Slowly, I brought the spoon back to my lips. Swallowed the savory soup and dropped my gaze to the table. "What other options do we have? I agree with Kost, we have to consider what gifting a beast would mean in the long run."

Oz frowned and propped his elbows on the table. "Bits aren't really feasible. Rhyne is pretty well off. They've had a good harvest this year, from what we've heard."

Noc nodded. "If the queen didn't hold a grudge against me, we'd be in less of a bind."

"So here we are," Kost said, finally meeting our stares. "What gift is worthy enough to inspire trust *and* forgiveness?"

A beast would work, but was it the right thing to do? I'd sworn to never sell one again, but gifting was different. The problem was, I didn't *know* Queen Elianna or her daughter. Promising to gift them a beast without understanding who they were or what their intentions were… Not to mention, there wasn't a single creature I'd tamed who wasn't already bonded to me.

I ate another bite. "What's the princess like? If I were to agree to gift a beast—and if we think that's the smartest move—I'm assuming she'd be the recipient."

Kost nodded. "Correct. I imagine Princess Jayla's exactly the type of person you'd be comfortable gifting a beast to, and I'm not saying that to try and sway you."

"Some call her the Dove," Oz said. "All the decorations going up today have that symbol on them."

"She's a peace bringer." Noc watched me closely. "She cares deeply for her people, working hand in hand with a number of groups to reduce poverty and provide housing for the homeless. She has virtually no enemies, but perhaps she's too trusting."

"We think that's why Elianna hasn't handed off the crown yet," Kost added. "She worries other countries will perceive her daughter as weak and move against Rhyne." He removed his spectacles and began polishing them. "A strong beast to protect her might make the territory-hungry countries bordering Rhyne think twice about attacking."

"In addition to an alliance with Lendria," Noc said. He dipped his chin my direction, not an ounce of pressure in his ice-blue eyes. "There have been skirmishes in the south. Countries testing the new leadership to see what they can get away with. Offering our soldiers in support might be enough to entice Elianna." He ran a soft thumb along my cheek before letting his hand fall away. "You don't have to trade a beast if you're not comfortable with it. I promise you we will find another way."

Setting my spoon to the side, I tore off a bit of the bread bowl and rolled it between my fingers as I considered our options. There weren't many, really. These were the best circumstances we could've asked for, and yet there was still the glaring truth that it could all go horribly wrong. Elianna had lost her older sister, Amira, to Noc, intentionally or not. That kind of pain didn't just disappear. But she also had a family, a daughter to consider. If we could show her how much we were dedicated to the future of Rhyne, to Princess Jayla, then maybe she could set aside the decades-old heartache she likely felt for her deceased sister.

"First, I want to be very clear about something: this will not be a standard negotiating tactic moving forward."

Noc nodded. "Of course."

"Second, if such a situation arises again, I get full discretion on whether or not a beast trade is acceptable." My first decree as queen, and it wasn't something I would ever bend on. No one knew beasts like me. No one could make this decision but me. I rounded my gaze on Noc, on my king, and was met with nothing but understanding and love.

He placed his hand on my knee and gave it a squeeze. "Agreed."

"Good. That said, I don't have a beast to gift Jayla," I said, dropping the remnants of bread and folding my hands together. Kost nearly deflated, but recovered quickly, adjusting his spectacles and giving a firm nod. Noc must have sensed there was more, though, because he waited without moving. "But, I can promise to tame one for her. If, and only if, I feel she's fit to own a beast. That's the best I can offer."

Noc smiled. "That's more than enough."

"When do we approach her?"

"The celebration will start at sundown," Kost said. "In the meantime, we'll continue to survey the city from the shadows and plan for quick exits in case we need to escape."

A chill swept down my spine. "Is that likely?"

Noc shrugged. "There's no way to know until we try. Rhyne has had no contact whatsoever with Lendria since my death. At least not from the royal family. The number of tourists between our countries has slowly climbed over the years, apparently." He tilted his chin Kost's direction, who nodded his agreement. "Our accents might give us away, but it shouldn't be a problem."

"Like with Isla," Oz muttered.

Calem raised a playful brow. "Plans on reconnecting with your lovely escort?"

"No." His chin dipped toward his chest and he averted his eyes.

Before Calem could goad him further, Noc shot him a stern look and cleared his throat. "Reconnaissance. Four hours, starting now."

Calem groaned, but stood up from the table without hesitation. Cracking his neck, he gave us a parting devilish grin before slipping out the front door and then presumably disappearing into the shadows. Noc only rolled his eyes, then turned his attention to Oz. "Go with him. Don't let him get into trouble until after we've had our audience with the queen."

Oz let out a belabored sigh, but there was a hint of warmth to it that suggested he didn't really find it troubling to look after his rambunctious brother. "Can do."

"And," Kost interjected, "be sure to drag him back with plenty of time to change and prepare for the evening. Formal attire is required. We must abide by every custom to gain as much favor as possible."

"Whatever works." Oz smiled and gave a lazy wave before weaving around the tables and heading out the door.

Kost tracked him until he'd disappeared, and then he deflated.

Sinking into his chair, he rested his lifeless hands on the table before him. His carefully constructed expression of control slipped away, and his faraway gaze targeted an indistinct spot on the floor. I glanced at Noc, asking a silent question, and he pressed his lips together.

"Kost." His voice was soft. Gentle.

"I'm fine."

"No, you're not. You haven't said a word about Gaige since we arrived."

Kost winced. "There's nothing to report. I've shadow walked to Hireath at least twice a day since the...incident. There have been no signs of him."

If it were possible, he somehow shrank further away from us. My heart ached at the sight, and I reached across the table to wrap his hands in mine. He remained still, but finally raised his chin to meet my eyes.

"This isn't your fault."

"But it is." His voice wavered, and his fingers started to tremble. He swallowed several times, as if even coming up with the words to articulate what happened was agony. Finally, he shook his head once. Let loose a shaky breath. "Calem was right about me. I'm too cold. When Gaige tried to confide in me... I just threw my life experiences at him. I didn't *listen*. And then he just walked away and never came back. I did this. I'm the reason he's gone." He withdrew one of his hands to slip his fingers beneath his glasses and obscure his face, but nothing could hide the muffled, broken exhale that escaped his mouth.

He was carrying so much guilt. Giving his hand a tight squeeze, I implored him to feel every ounce of love I had for him. Our hard-won relationship had gone through so much before we trusted each other. Cared for each other. My life would never be complete without Kost—without any of my assassins, really. And I needed him to know that I would always be there for him. We all would.

"Gaige is a grown man. He's going through a lot, but don't for one second blame yourself for this." I ducked my head lower, trying to keep Kost's eyes in my line of sight. "Even if he walked away from you because of that conversation, that doesn't mean his disappearance is your fault. We don't know what happened beyond that."

Noc placed a hand on his brother's back. Then, he pulled Kost into a one-armed hug. Kost slumped into him as a wordless sob shook his entire body. Noc shouldered it all. Even tilted his head against Kost's, ensuring Kost had warmth, love, from every angle possible. For a long while, we simply sat and waited, allowing Kost to let loose his feelings without ever saying a word. And when he finally pulled away, eyes red-rimmed and puffy, his jaw was set. Gaze hard. Determination flitted through his expression, and he straightened himself while running his hands down his vest to smooth any wrinkles.

"I will find him."

With a soft smile, I nodded. "I know you will."

"Right." He cleared his throat and stood up, hips already pivoted toward the spiral staircase leading to the second story. "I'm going to collect myself and then begin reconnaissance. What will you two do?"

Noc glanced at me, concern evident in the weighted look we shared, and I knew he wanted to stay with Kost. But he didn't want to abandon me, either, given I hadn't set foot outside the tavern. Yet, right now, I didn't need him like Kost did. Even if nothing else was said, I knew just how important being surrounded by family was, how healing it could be.

"Actually, I need to spend some time in the beast realm. After that, I should probably rest up. I'm still feeling a bit tired, and I'd rather be prepared in case we run into any problems later on."

Kost gave a curt nod.

Noc leaned in and claimed my lips with a soft kiss. "Until this evening, then."

"See you then."

After leaving a handful of bits on the table to cover our meal, Noc stood and the two of them headed for the stairs, presumably toward Kost's room. As I watched them go, I wrapped my fingers in the chain of my bestiary. The hum of power reverberated through my fingertips, and warmth sparked through my Charmer's symbol. The soothing relief I felt just from that simple action was something Gaige would never experience again. I could understand his agony, his despair. I hadn't even thought what it would've been like for him to return to Hireath. And then to argue with Kost... I let my hand fall away. I wouldn't let Kost search alone. We'd find Gaige, no matter what.

TWENTY-ONE

NOC

Despite Kost's best efforts, we had no chance of blending in with Rhynelanders. Not because our attire was lacking in any way—he'd done his due diligence and selected ivy-colored outfits trimmed in gold, the collars of our fitted tunics plunging down our exposed sternums—but because Leena was so regal in her presence, it was impossible not to look. Her emerald sleeveless gown was more polished than a gemstone and moved with the fluidity of water, clinging to her every curve. With each step she took, an exposed slit of skin flashed along her thighs. Tantalizing. Mesmerizing. Even with my arm around her, I couldn't get enough. I was painfully aware of how little time we'd spent together. How much I wanted to let my fingers explore every inch of her. To taste the curve of her neck and feel her breath against me.

We'd only just left the tavern, and already I was dying to carry her back to our room.

Reaching up, she dragged her fingers along the wide brim of my formal hat before giving it a tug, casting a shadow over my eyes. "I could get used to this. It's mysterious."

"I wouldn't count on it," I said. The hat had been Kost's idea, and while I wasn't accustomed to wearing one, it expertly hid my white locks and shrouded my features.

"Leena, my sweet, you're a sight to behold." Calem sidled up beside us and gave her a suggestive wink. He tilted his head in my direction, catching death in my glare, and laughed before throwing his hands up in mock apology.

She only rolled her eyes as she draped a light shawl over her shoulders. "Your antics are getting old, Calem. I'm not even sure you have game anymore."

He pretended to be affronted but couldn't hide his grin. "I've never given it my all with you. You have no idea how charming I can be."

Without warning, Leena's emblem ignited in a soothing, rose-wood glow, and she raised a coy brow. "Don't bait a Charmer. You'll never win."

"Enough, you two." Kost inched closer, nodding to Leena's symbol. "Let's not give the locals something to gossip about." Sheepishly, Leena clasped her hands together and capped her power. The light faded instantly, and she offered Kost an apologetic smile.

Ozias surveyed the swelling crowd. "Seems like the whole city is out tonight."

He wasn't wrong. Before us, the streets were packed with bodies, all of them dipped in gold in some fashion or another. Flecks were dusted across their skin and paint dripped along their cheeks. It was magnificent. Where vendor stalls had been earlier, makeshift daises now held their place. Musicians and dancers took center stage, ensuring that there was always something to catch the eye. The beats were rhythmic, the foreign tunes full of rejoicing. And even though a chill had descended as the sun fell below the horizon, there was no escaping the heat of so many bodies pressed tightly against one another, or the plethora of fires contained within barrels that lined the streets.

Slowly, we moved with the crowd in the direction of the castle. And Leena drank everything in. Her hazel eyes devoured sight after sight, her smile impossibly wide. She'd even sway to the music if we stopped long enough to hear a full song, and she gasped each time the dancers performed an impossible twirl or dip.

Craning my neck toward her, I whispered against her ear. "Enjoying yourself?"

"Definitely." She was breathless. Radiant.

I ran my knuckles along her jaw, then angled her chin toward me. "Good. Maybe tonight..." Dragging my thumb across her lip, I felt her startled inhale. A sudden, sharp hunger flooded her stare.

"Yes." She kissed me fiercely, leaning into me with the full weight of her body. My heart rammed into my chest, but I slipped my hands around her waist. Gripping her tight, I fought back the groan threatening to escape my throat.

Ozias coughed and averted his gaze while simultaneously nudging my side. "We're approaching the procession."

Reluctantly, I broke away from Leena and stared at the castle gate before us. A winding trail of patient locals zigzagged through the boisterous crowd. At the very end stood Queen Elianna, Princess Jayla, and her betrothed. The princess and her pair bond sat in regal high-back thrones dotted with emeralds. Their pleasant smiles were genuine, and as each local stopped to pay their blessing, the queen-to-be took their hands in hers and offered words we couldn't possibly hear, but were somehow still obviously full of warmth and gratitude. With a calm, reassuring smile, Queen Elianna stood by her daughter's side. She nodded at each guest, but allowed Jayla to handle the greetings.

"That line is massive," Calem said with a whistle.

"Indeed." Kost's eyes flitted across the crowd. "We should wait until the end. For now, it's best we simply blend in."

Leena couldn't hide her excitement and immediately dragged me toward one of the many tables laden with food and drink. We followed her lead, securing candied apples and spiced ales before moving toward one of the stages full of dancers. Time slipped by quickly as I watched her simply *be*. We hadn't really celebrated anything. Not our declaration as *anam-cara*. Not our ascension to king and queen in the eyes of the gods. Nothing. So to see her grin so broadly, to dance and move among the crowd without a care in the world... I wanted to give her everything. I wanted to see her free to smile like this, dance like this, laugh like this. Her happiness was infectious. The locals were drawn to her, and they all moved and celebrated together.

Standing on the fringe of it all with Kost, Ozias, and Calem, I was content to simply take in the sight of her. Not to mention, it was necessary to keep my presence quiet. It'd been ages since I set foot in Rhyne, and while the general public likely didn't recognize me, I'd caught a few lingering stares and furrowed brows. It was only a matter of time, though, before we approached Queen Elianna, and my return would no longer be a secret.

"Do you think it's her Charmer's lure?" Ozias asked, pulling me from my thoughts. His gaze was locked on Leena as more and more people gathered around her to join in her impromptu dance.

I lifted a shoulder. "Maybe."

"I'll admit to feeling compelled to join her myself." Kost folded his arms across his chest. "Of course, I would never, so it must be her lure."

Calem snorted. "Lighten up, Kost. You might find a little dancing could lift your spirits."

"I'm fine right here." Even though he was already still beside me, he somehow stiffened further and rooted himself to the ground.

As if she'd heard our conversation, Leena twirled toward us, snaring the first pair of hands she could grab—Ozias's. She grinned up at him. "Dance with me."

He blinked in shock, but didn't put up a fight as she yanked him into the crowd. It only took a moment for the tension in his muscles to loosen, and soon he was spinning her about and laughing in earnest.

"Good to see he has *some* moves," Calem chuckled.

"The only hopeless one here is you, Calem." Kost shot him a teasing look, and Calem let out an indignant huff.

Leena and Ozias danced for the length of two songs before he offered a playful bow and rejoined us, grin slowly slipping off his face. "The line is dwindling. We should go now."

My gaze darted to the gilded gates. The hour was late, and only a handful of people remained in line. Most of the locals were either dancing in the streets or had moved off to the sides, too drunk on spiced ale to move but unwilling to call it a night. Gone too were the countless youngsters who'd pushed between us throughout the evening. Calem had grinned at their games all night long, never once complaining if they knocked into him too hard.

Moving toward Leena, I slipped my arm around her waist and gave her a twirl before bringing her in close. "Time to go."

Sweat clung to her forehead and dampened her neck, but it did nothing to lessen her beauty. Haphazardly, she wiped it away and then adjusted her shawl, ensuring the griffin tattoo beneath her sternum remained hidden. With Calem, Ozias, and Kost, we moved toward the procession and took our place at the end of the line. It was quieter near the castle gates, the lilting music a gentle backdrop to the soft tidings offered from reverent Rhynelanders to their princess. But as kind as Jayla appeared, I couldn't help the tightness in my chest. My gaze flitted to her mother, a stoic statue who was both foreign and familiar to me. I saw Amira in her, in the golden locks of her hair now streaked with silver and in the round shape of her eyes. But she lacked Amira's dimples and button nose, and she was taller than her sister had been. Still, her likeness was enough to make my stomach plummet to my feet.

My grip on Leena's waist tightened. This was a horrid plan. While I knew little of the political landscape of Rhyne, I knew Elianna's life hadn't been easy. Kost had gathered enough details about her past before we arrived to illuminate as much. It's why we'd asked Leena for help with a beast. Yes, I'd taken Amira from Elianna at a very young age, but it was more than that. She'd had the throne thrust upon her not long after her parents fell ill. They passed quickly, but she was only thirteen at the time. And the countries along Rhyne's borders saw her misfortune as an opportunity to attack.

Elianna had always been cunning, though, and somehow survived. She'd held Rhyne's borders and proved herself to her people. Even married someone of noble birth from one of the countries some years later to maintain peace. His death had been equally unexpected, leaving Elianna alone with a newborn child and no one for her daughter to call father.

Gentle fingers grazed mine, startling me from my thoughts, and I glanced down at Leena. She tilted her head to the side in question, and I offered a strained smile as we took another step forward. Another step closer to my past. Bad plan or not, it was the only one we had.

"Hey, Ozias. Isn't that Isla?" Calem asked beneath his breath.

Ozias stilled, then swallowed thickly. "Yes." The same woman from earlier had made her way through the remaining crowd to approach the royal family. Unlike the rest of the locals, she was wearing the same outfit she'd donned when we'd first encountered her. Ever the Queen's Guard, apparently, and still very much on duty. Standing on her toes, she whispered something into Queen Elianna's ear. She nodded once, unperturbed by whatever insight Isla had shared. Isla seemed content with her response and was about to take her leave when she did a quick sweep of the line, her gaze snagging on Ozias. Her eyes narrowed. Instead of leaving, she folded her arms across her chest and stood by the queen.

"Thank you so much for your kind words. Maddox and I would be honored to stop by your bakery for breakfast," Princess Jayla said, gesturing to her husband-to-be. She then bowed her chin slightly in gratitude and bade the portly man before us a good night, leaving us to stand before Rhyne's royal family.

As I'd never seen a portrait of Jayla's late father, I could only assume she took after him. The bronze glow of her skin was beautiful against her mostly sheer, golden gown. She shared her mother's smile and the round shape of her eyes—Amira's eyes—but her braided hair was dark and tumbled to her waist. She clasped her hands together and placed them in her lap as she leaned forward slightly, inviting us to step closer.

For a moment, I couldn't move. All I could do was stare. At Jayla. At her mother. At Amira's family. Elianna's brow furrowed at my hesitation, and her gaze raked over me. Cautiously, I removed my hat. The queen glanced at my hair. At my eyes. At the subtle scar on my cheek. And then she paled, sputtering wordlessly as she gripped the back of her daughter's throne.

"Mother?" Princess Jayla asked. Beside her, Maddox stood and immediately moved to the queen's side. He offered his arm, the perfect gentleman, but she refused to take it. She only stared at me.

"Murderer."

In less than a breath, Isla closed the gap between us and the royal family, positioning herself in front of the princess. Something sparked in her umber stare—a flicker of magic that mimicked a flame—and I immediately tensed. *Mage*. No wonder I hadn't spotted a weapon on her; she didn't need one. Kost, Ozias, and Calem must have picked up the same thing, because they froze, each of them staring at the woman's hands. What kind of mage were we dealing with? Did she have compulsory powers like Eryx? Or perhaps something more destructive? My mind rewound to the time I'd faced off against a mage during our war with Rhyne. I'd nearly died, thanks to that woman's sparking, electrical wave of magic.

Isla spat at our feet. "I knew something was off about you."

"We mean no harm," Kost said, voice level. "We've come to offer our blessing to the princess and her betrothed."

Maddox inched closer to his lover, dark eyes alight with caution. "Who are you?"

Jayla poked her head around Isla to get a better view of us. Her brows pulled together, and she tilted her head toward me. "Are you a murderer?"

Instead of returning her gaze, I looked straight at Elianna. "Yes."

"That *man* is responsible for the death of your aunt. And countless others who fell before him on the battlefield so many years ago." Elianna's voice shook, but she braved a step forward. "You are supposed to be dead."

"I did die." Slowly, I raised one hand, palm upward. I called forth a single shadow and allowed it to slip between my fingers. "Your soldiers succeeded. But unbeknownst to my family, to all of Lendria, I was brought back. I made no moves to reclaim the throne and instead lived in the shadows. I stayed hidden because I didn't want to reignite a war."

With curious eyes, Jayla tracked the movement of my shadow. "You're Aleksander. The reason we don't trade with Lendria."

I winced at the name and allowed my shadow to disperse. "I go by Noc now, but yes."

"Your presence here is an insult," Elianna seethed. No longer afraid, she stormed forward to stand beside Isla. "Arrest him."

"Mother, wait—" Jayla started, but the heavy groan of an invisible door swinging open rushed over us. I pressed my eyes shut. Leena was half-hidden between Kost and me, obscured from the royal family's view, but wouldn't go unnoticed for long if she'd just summoned a terrifying beast. But Onyx didn't come barreling before us, and the stunned glances of the royal family didn't sway Elianna's conviction.

"I said arrest him!" she barked.

Isla didn't hesitate, but as she made a move to grab my wrist, her hand smacked into an invisible barrier. A ripple cascaded outward from the impact and traveled across the dome, and at once I knew what creature Leena had summoned.

With quiet authority, she cleared her throat and nudged me to the side. "I wouldn't do that." There at Leena's feet sat Quilla, her Asura. The beast had planted two hands firmly on the ground with the rest extended around it, firmly securing the near-unbreakable dome that covered us. Ten milky-white eyes stared endlessly into the ink-black night, and Quilla let out a quiet huff.

Before us, Isla's hands dropped to her side and her jaw fell open. Even Elianna was unable to hide her shock. Her wide eyes stared at the beast, then traveled upward to Leena. Jayla abandoned her throne all together and joined her mother to get a closer look at our group. Maddox remained an inch behind Jayla with a tense hand poised to pull her back in case of danger.

"Quilla won't hurt you," Leena said, gently patting her beast's head. "She's only here to protect us."

"You..." Elianna's eyes first roved to the bestiary dangling against Leena's collarbone, then to the exposed wing of the midnight-blue griffin tattoo on her chest. Her shawl had slipped from her shoulders as she'd reached down to praise her beast. Elianna's gaze snapped to me, and I tugged on my collar to reveal the same mark emblazoned on my skin. She'd know exactly what our matching symbols meant. "So much for not retaking the throne."

"He hasn't. Yet." Kost's voice was level as he addressed the queen. "However, that is part of the reason why we've come."

"Part?" Jayla asked. Unlike the rest of her family, her initial shock had faded, and she'd crouched to the ground to be at eye level with Quilla. A slow smile pulled at her lips.

"Jayla." Elianna's warning was unmistakable, but her daughter ignored it.

"Shall we take this conversation indoors?" Kost asked, jutting his chin in the direction of the street. While the procession had died, there were still citizens about. Prying eyes had fallen on our group, and the steady thrum of music had come to a halt. Guards who'd been lingering on the fringe of the festivities inched closer, steely stares targeting us.

I cleared my throat. "We would, of course, be willing to be escorted by your guards. Our intentions are honest. We're not here to hurt anyone."

"And the beast?" Elianna asked.

"Quilla's abilities are purely defensive. She can't—" Leena tried, but the queen cut her off without even deigning to give her a glance.

"The very fact that you expect me to trust you proves how naive you are. I will not allow a threat into my home. Not now, not ever."

Jayla stood slowly and turned to her mother, placing a soft hand on her shoulder. "They would've already attacked us if that'd been their plan. I believe them."

The queen bristled. "You believe everyone, Jayla. This…this

monster"—she spat in my direction before glancing at her daughter— "nearly destroyed our kingdom. And now you want to entertain the notion that he's here for what? To offer his blessing?"

"A trade agreement," I said softly.

"And maybe another gift," Leena said as she touched her bestiary. There wasn't an ounce of hesitation in her voice, but I caught it in the way her fingers tensed over her pendant. In the subtle way she tangled the chain before letting her hand fall away. While she'd agreed in theory to trade a beast, determining whether or not Jayla was an appropriate recipient was something she had to do in person—and on her own.

With cautious eyes, she studied Jayla. And then, without warning, opened the beast realm door and sent Quilla home. As soon as the groan died—along with the protective dome Quilla had magicked into place—Leena took a step forward, putting her within easy grasp of the mage. A dull ringing started in my ears as I watched her. Slipping my hands into the pockets of my trousers, I willed my nails to elongate and poised them over my palm. I wouldn't allow Isla to harm her. Even if it meant sacrificing a potential alliance with Rhyne.

For a moment, no one moved. We became statues in a standoff, each one of us daring the other to break first. And with every second that ticked away, my heart raced faster. A nail pricked my skin, and blood lined the creases of my palm. Waiting. Ready to do my bidding. Finally, Jayla extended her hand toward Leena.

"Welcome to Veles, Charmer. I would be most honored to have you in my home."

Leena nodded and shook her hand, allowing the slightest of smiles to claim her lips. "Thank you."

There was no masking the anger on Elianna's face—and I highly doubted she even tried—but she turned on her heels and stormed toward the castle gates, guards immediately flanking her sides. Isla positioned herself behind us to bring up the rear, and Jayla and Maddox led us after the queen.

Slowly, I let my nails recede and the blood dry. I glanced at my brothers and gave them a tight nod, ordering them to follow the royal family. Together, we walked toward the jade castle. It had been tense, but we'd overcome the first obstacle—gaining an audience with the queen. Now all that was left was the much more difficult task of convincing her to join a war she had no idea was brewing in the first place.

TWENTY-TWO

LEENA

Aside from the keep in Hireath, I'd never been inside a castle—and the one in Veles did not disappoint. The subtle beauty of it all was breathtaking. My heels clicked against the marble tiles with rich, dark veining, and we passed countless stone columns wrapped in jade vines. A glass dome ceiling provided an unobstructed view of the indigo night. Thousands of stars winked from above, adding their light to the dangling, golden chandeliers. Queen Elianna and her daughter sat at the two high-back thrones beneath an ornate arch. Guards lined the perimeter, and Isla positioned herself faithfully at her queen's side, her hard gaze flitting between Noc and Oz. Maddox stood at his lover's side. One day, he'd sit where Elianna did, but not until she relinquished the crown.

We'd come straight here from the gates, and none of the tension had dissipated from Elianna's expression. With a pinched mouth and her arms firmly crossed over her chest, she glared at us with an intensity that made me sweat. Noc, for all his worth, seemed unmoved. Or maybe he was. Stock-still beside me, his expression was perfectly masked and his hands tucked in his trouser pockets. The only inkling that he was experiencing any sort of discomfort was the errant muscle feathering his jaw. Beside him, Kost mirrored his stance, and Calem and Oz stood by me.

"Speak," Elianna said. "And make it quick."

"We'd like to propose an alliance between Lendria and Rhyne. Before everything happened…" He let out a long breath, gaze softening. "Our countries were prosperous, thanks to unfettered trade. I'd like to reopen those routes, as well as set up a treaty ensuring we come to each other's aid in the event of a war."

Elianna's voice was flat. "We don't need your alliance or your trade."

"Mother," Jayla cut in as she leaned toward the queen, "don't be so hasty. What about our southern borders? There's—"

"Enough." The queen's voice rose, silencing her daughter. "We will not forge an alliance with the man who murdered my sister."

"I didn't kill Amira," Noc said.

Elianna's knuckles turned white as she gripped the armrests of her throne. "Lies."

"I'm not lying. I *am* a murderer. I *am* responsible for the death of many, including your sister. But I did not kill her." He looked directly at the queen, never faltering. "Amira died because of a curse that'd been placed on me. I didn't know the extent of it; otherwise I never would've put her in harm's way."

"Twist your words however you want," Elianna fumed, "but you won't manipulate me into accepting a treaty we don't need."

Noc cleared his throat. "Are you certain? We're aware of the mounting problems you face in the south, and we're committed to helping. Now and in the future."

In exchange for your immediate help against a threat we can't possibly face alone. The thought rattled around in my head, and a weighted silence followed Noc's promise, as if the queen knew there was something more to this bargain. Her mouth twisted as she studied him, her expression hardening by the second. Finally, she scoffed.

"You're not even the king of Lendria, last I checked. How can you offer such assistance?"

Noc didn't blink. "My pair bond and I are retaking the throne. You have my word that we will honor whatever agreement we come to here."

"Do you take me for a fool?" Her words cut like the edge of a blade.

"No."

"Mother," Jayla tried again, her voice firmer this time. "Please, we should at least listen to—"

"What my daughter fails to see," Elianna cut in, snapping her gaze to Jayla before returning her ire to us, "is the nuances that you're conveniently leaving out. The nuances that would drastically affect us and could leave us completely open to an attack from our southern neighbors you seemingly know everything about."

She stood then, hands shaking by her sides. "You plan to reclaim your rightful place on the throne. As you've been blessed by the gods"— she indicated with a sharp nod the tattoo on Noc's chest—"you hope your people will fall in line. But there's no telling if Lendria's army, the Sentinels who've pledged their loyalty to King Varek, will come to heel. And you need backing to convince them. Backing from an army you don't have and one you think we'd willingly provide.

"And so you stand before me, before my daughter, and attempt to take advantage of our current state of affairs. Wrap a treaty and trade agreement in a bow and call it a wedding present." Seething, she took a step forward. Isla moved with her, a shadow behind the crown ready and willing to strike if her queen were in danger. "Tell me why I shouldn't execute you here and now, not only for this ridiculous notion, but for *killing* my sister so many years ago."

"Because if you don't help us, you'll face an enemy even greater than the countries to the south." The words fell from my lips with a quiet authority that silenced the room. Countless eyes turned to me, and I raised my chin so I could meet Elianna's damning stare. "I promise you, we're not trying to mislead you. I wouldn't be standing here asking for your help, asking Noc to face his past, if it weren't absolutely necessary."

Before her mother could speak, Jayla stood and addressed me directly. "What danger do you speak of?"

"You met one of my beasts tonight, so you must know what I am." Gingerly, I touched my bestiary and felt the weight of her gaze as she followed the movement of my fingers. "My name is Leena Edenfrell, and I am Crown of the Charmers Council. The former Crown, Yazmin, has aligned herself with King Varek and intends to awaken a beast that will turn our world to ash. If we do not stop her, everything and everyone will fall.

"There won't be skirmishes along your border anymore," I continued when neither Jayla nor Elianna moved to interrupt me. "No trade. No prosperity for your country. There will be nothing but fire. This I can promise you."

Silence stretched around us, filling the throne room. My proclamation sat heavy in the air, and I waited as emotions coursed through Jayla's gaze. Uncertainty. Fear. A glimmer of determination. Her mother, on the other hand, had gone cold. There was no telling what thoughts lingered behind her icy stare.

"I love my pair bond," I said, turning to offer Noc a warm smile. "But I would never lie about something like this simply to aid his efforts to retake the throne. He didn't want it to begin with. I know you likely won't believe that, but it's true."

Finally, Jayla spoke. "There's no stopping this Yazmin?"

"We've tried." I dropped my gaze to the floor. "I'm afraid the only option left at this point is to retake the throne from Varek before she raises Ocnolog, the dragon beast, and unleashes his fury."

"And if it's too late?" Elianna asked, her voice surprisingly low. "If you can't stop Ocnolog from rising?"

I looked at her and prayed she heard truth in my words. "Then we truly will need every ounce of help we can get to stop Yazmin and Varek before they inflict their will upon the realm."

Shaking her head, Elianna stared at some indistinct spot over our heads. "This isn't our war."

"But it will be," Jayla cut in.

"Jayla..." Her mother let out a long sigh full of burden. "Blind faith is dangerous. We can't just trust their word. *I* can't trust them. Not after what he did to my sister."

Noc's arms hung loosely by his sides. "I wish there was more I could say or do to prove my innocence." Remorse racked his expression, and an ache formed in the back of my throat. I hated to see him like this. For a brief moment, I entertained the idea of summoning Onyx. If he judged Noc's claims and found him to be worthy, then maybe Elianna would, too. Except... My gaze roved to the queen. She wouldn't value a beast's approval like Charmers would. With Onyx's invisible flames and the private commune he'd hold with Noc, Elianna wouldn't even *see* anything. There'd be no physical confirmation of Noc's truth, other than a purring legendary beast, which could just as easily be a sign that Onyx liked Noc. I even doubted a Nezbit—a rare, bunny beast that could discern truth from lie with its radar-like ears—would convince her.

Jayla tipped her head toward Noc. "Tell me exactly what happened to my aunt."

With quiet sadness, Noc recounted the story of the time he'd crossed a high priestess. She'd used dark magic, sacrificing her own life to curse his existence, making it impossible for him to truly love another being without condemning them to death.

"When I finally realized the extent of my curse, I was already dead. There was no point in trying to come forward with this information. The war was over." He looked up at Elianna, taking in her stoic expression. "I'm not sure anyone would've believed me, anyway."

The queen remained still. Her shrewd gaze never left Noc as he spoke. A minute stretched by before she shook her head. "You've had decades to come up with a story for your crimes. I simply can't accept it."

"I...understand," Noc said.

With a tight expression, Isla took a tentative step forward. "You mentioned dark magic."

"Yes."

"That kind of spellwork leaves a trace that can never be removed." Slipping one hand into her coat pocket, she extracted a quartz crystal orb no larger than a river rock. "One of my kind crafted this. It can detect the presence of dark magic. If your story is true, then the stone should react." She tipped her head in a bow to Elianna. "With your permission, of course."

"Do it," Jayla said. She gave her mother an apologetic look. "Please."

Neck stiff, Elianna relented. "Fine."

Isla's gaze bounced between the two royals before she finally extended her hand. The spherical gem lifted into the air, hovering first above Isla's palm before floating to a halt before Noc's chest. I held my breath as we waited for the stone to react. Aside from the one interaction I'd had with Eryx, I'd never known another mage, let alone experienced their magic.

Within seconds, a dark swirling ink filled the stone. The darkness was absolute, so much so that the sphere looked more like a void waiting to consume our world. Isla grimaced as she snatched the gem and tucked it in her pocket. "He's telling the truth. Dark magic was used against him."

Elianna's mouth went slack, and then she slammed it shut. With a hard shake of her head, she looked away. "This...this proves nothing. We have no way of knowing if his curse—"

"Mother, stop." Jayla's voice grew in strength, and she angled her chin high as she stared down the queen. "There is no one I respect more than you. No one wiser. I have spent my entire life learning from you. If this were anyone else, anyone but Noc, you'd believe them. He's spoken the truth, and so has his queen." She looked to me, her eyes softening, before once again regarding her mother. "We must acknowledge that Ocnolog is real and that our country is in danger. We need to protect our people, even if that means forming an alliance with Lendria."

Elianna's jaw hardened, but she said nothing.

"Give the queen and me some time to discuss this," she said, turning back to us. "You may stay in the castle tonight and rest. Isla, escort them to our guest quarters and see they are cared for. We'll have our answer for you first thing in the morning."

"Thank you," I said with a bow. Noc, Kost, Oz, and Calem followed suit, tipping their chins down before straightening. Pressing her lips together, the queen left without another word. Several guards took off after her, and Jayla closed the short distance between herself and our group, Isla and Maddox on her heels.

"I appreciate your honesty." A warm smile graced the princess's lips, and she bowed before me. "Please forgive my mother. She's been through nothing but dark times her whole life."

"I understand," I said. "And I'm grateful both of you were willing to hear us out, no matter the outcome."

Jayla nodded. "Isla, their rooms."

"This way," the mage said tersely. With a jerky wave, she indicated the closest corridor lined with brass light fixtures and smooth walls. Jayla bade us good night and then looped her arm through

Maddox's, following the same path her mother had taken minutes ago. No doubt they were in for a longer night than either of them had expected.

The winding hall deposited us in a wing of rooms manned by guards. Isla said nothing more to us. Instead, she simply nodded at each door and waited as we entered our respective rooms one by one. When Noc and I stepped into our quarters, we caught some muffled orders from her to the other guards, but nothing unexpected. None of us were permitted to leave, they were to notify her if anything out of the ordinary happened, and something about shift rotations. We were still a threat to the queen and to be treated as such, even though we'd been granted reprieve for the night.

Sighing, I turned my back on the door. Our modest room housed a bed, a pair of nightstands, an armoire, and a rycrim heater. The slate, conical structure dotted in red gems gave off a faint glow, and heat simmered around it. Somewhere in this city, a larger core must have existed. And for a brief moment, I wondered if Isla or her family had a hand in the magical developments of Rhyne. Mages used to call Lendria their home—as well as those like Eryx who visited our island country in secret—so their leftover artifacts and magical objects weren't completely foreign. But here? I had no idea. Clearly, at least one mage had aligned herself with a country other than Allamere.

Another question for another time. Isla's alliance with the royal family was her business, and as far as we were concerned, she was a Rhynelander. We'd need her support, along with the rest of the Queen's Guard, in the days to come.

Letting out a long exhale, I made a beeline for the canopy bed. Sheer fabric was draped from the simple wooden beams and tied back to the posts with a maroon cord. I sank into the mattress and let out a sigh. After discarding his overcoat and hat on a rack near the door, Noc joined me, and I leaned my head on his shoulder.

"Are you okay?"

"Yes," he said. "I expected Elianna to react that way. If I were in her position, we'd probably already be locked up or dead."

"I don't know if I believe that."

He frowned. "Why not?"

I peered up at him, taking in his inquisitive stare. Noc had changed so much since I'd first met him. He'd once been cold and unapproachable, thanks to the priestess's curse. And even after he'd eradicated that, he'd been forced to deal with the darkness of Cruor's Oath. It'd twisted his mind and shattered the control he'd worked so hard to maintain. But now he was entirely free. And all those admirable traits he'd kept hidden away—his unflinching devotion to his family, his compassion, his drive to create a better world—flourished.

He was my partner. My *anam-cara*. And he would always strive to do the right thing.

"Because I don't think you'd let your pain, no matter how great, place your people in harm's way."

With light fingers, he tucked a loose strand of hair behind my ear. "You always see the good in me. Every day, I'm grateful you walked through my door. Even if you held Kost hostage at the time."

It felt like ages ago that I'd strolled into Cruor with Kost as my bargaining chip and demanded Noc lift the bounty off my head. Gingerly, I dragged my fingers along his wrist where that damning black mark used to be. The one that leaked poison into his mind and convinced him to kill me.

Now, we'd moved on to our next impossible feat.

Pulling his hand to my lips, I kissed his knuckles one by one. He sighed before cupping my chin and angling my face toward his, then, he captured my lips and stole the breath right out of my lungs. A shiver of pleasure raced through me, and suddenly I was acutely aware that we were alone. In a room all our own, with no family to keep us apart and nothing but time to kill until we heard Jayla and Elianna's decision. We'd been told to rest, but...

My hands acted of their own accord, gripping either side of the deep cut of his tunic as I climbed into his lap. His hands went to my waist, anchoring me in place, as he let out a quiet, dark laugh. The warmth of his breath skirted along my neck, and I sucked in sharply.

"Trying to seduce me the moment we're alone?" His playful accusation was full of heat, and he slipped a hand beneath the slit of my dress, caressing my thigh with barely restrained fingers. I ground into him, pleased to feel the evidence of his growing arousal. He groaned and pressed his forehead against mine.

"We haven't been alone in...too long." I bent my lips to his neck, tasted his skin, and reveled in the scent of him. A delicious hiss escaped his mouth, and satisfaction bloomed inside of me. Kissing his sternum, I moved my hands to the waistline of his shirt. With a forceful tug, I removed the garment, and was left with nothing but smooth skin to admire. The grooves and contours of his chest, his abdomen, called to me, and I traced each line with light fingers. A trail of gooseflesh rippled across his skin in the wake of my touch. Before I could travel further south, he captured my wayward hands and held them in place.

"You're stopping me?" I asked, barely recognizing the whine of my own voice.

His answering smirk did wondrous things to my heart. "No, but I think we should get you out of that gown before I destroy it and we're left to explain to the royal family why we can't appear before them tomorrow." His arm circled my waist, pressing me flush against him. "Unless you'd rather attend naked, but I doubt that'd help our case. Or maybe it would. Couldn't say."

I couldn't help but laugh at his reasoning. Reluctantly, I stood and turned my back to him. "You're in charge of the lacing." Earlier, I'd goaded Kost into helping me tie up the back of my gown, insisting he was the only one meticulous enough to ensure it'd be done correctly. He'd conceded and, of course, done an excellent job. Which meant it was impossible for me to get out of the damn thing without another set of hands.

Noc stood with me, first sweeping my hair off my neck before dragging his fingers down my spine. I couldn't help but shudder. The scrape of his nails. The tug of the string as he slowly undid the artful ties. Anticipation ratcheted in me, and I swore he slowed down, intentionally taking his time with each eyelet and teasing my skin. He bent his nose toward the crook of my neck, and his breath tickled the curve of my ear.

Groaning, I nudged against him with my backside.

"In a hurry?" he asked, words gravelly and full of dark humor.

"No, but you're so colossally slow."

"It's fun." He kissed my shoulder and then nipped at my skin, sending a wave of longing through me. Finally, he reached the final tie just above my tailbone. His fingers dawdled there for a moment before he grabbed the fabric of my dress and slid it down my skin, taking my undergarments with it. Heat flooded me as his hand found my behind and he gave it a firm squeeze.

Thoroughly undressed, I spun around and pushed him onto the bed, then wasted absolutely no time in removing his breeches and drawers, much more eager to devour the sight of him completely bare. Gods, he was beautiful. Hard muscles cut from granite, shock-white hair just begging to be tugged. Endless ice-blue eyes full of love. Of desire. I never felt like anything less than wanted in his presence, and it was intoxicating. I kissed my way up his chest and felt him tense beneath me. By the time I got to his lips, he was just as impatient. He moaned before capturing me in a deep kiss, our tongues brushing against each other. Straddling his hips, I hovered over him. His gaze was full of hunger, and I offered him a coy smile before slowly positioning myself against him.

Grasping my hips, he slid into me and all rational thought fled. Every sensation narrowed to the feel of him, to where we were joined together as one. He angled my hips against him, deepening his thrusts, and stars bloomed behind my eyes. I couldn't get close enough. Couldn't possibly touch him enough. My fingers raked along his chest, leaving scratch marks in their wake. His answering growl was anything but a complaint. Need coiled tight in my belly, and I moved in time with him to try to relieve the building ache in my core. My name was a breathless exhale on his lips, full of heat and want. Sweat glistened along our skin as we moved faster, harder.

I called out his name as release shot through me, sending unending waves of heat through my limbs and turning me to liquid. He let out a curse as his own release joined mine. Our bodies trembled as I remained on top of him for a moment, only sliding off after placing a gentle kiss on his lips. Rolling to the side, he snared my waist and cradled me against his chest. His fingers drew lazy circles up and down my spine, and I sighed.

For the first time in days—weeks, even—I was content. And as he continued his progression along my back, I felt my eyelids grow heavy. The steady beat of his heart was a lullaby I didn't have the power to deny. Slowly, sleep chased away the worries of our world. There was no telling whether or not we'd be successful in our tactic to secure Rhyne's aid, but at least for now, we were safe. We had a roof over our heads. And Noc and I were together.

TWENTY-THREE

NOC

Waking beside my still-slumbering *anam-cara* the next morning was a sight that warmed my soul. It's not that we hadn't shared a bed during our travels, but to see her tucked against me in total relaxation was something else. Ruling would demand many more hard nights from us, so being able to find even an ounce of reprieve was a gift. Gently, I brushed a strand of hair off her cheek. Her bare skin was silk against mine, and I resisted the urge to rouse her just so we could enjoy each other all over again. I was content to simply lie there until she awoke when a loud knock on our door shattered the illusion of a slow, lazy rise from sleep.

"Yes?" I didn't bother to hide the annoyance from my tone. Judging by the faint light slanting through the cream-colored curtains, it was still early. There was no doubt in my mind that Elianna and Jayla had spent several more hours discussing our proposition, which had left me to assume we'd have a later start to our day. Apparently, I'd been wrong.

"Pardon the interruption, but Princess Jayla has requested an audience with Leena," an unknown feminine voice called through the door. Leena groaned, scooching closer to me and burying her nose in my chest.

"She's still sleeping," I said, tucking the sheets tighter around her. "Come back later."

A minute passed, but the just-visible shadow beneath the door didn't disappear. Finally, the attendant braved another attempt. "I'm sorry, sir, but Princess Jayla insists."

A wordless growl rumbled in my chest, but Leena pressed a finger to my lips. "Please tell her highness that I will join her shortly."

"Yes, my lady." And with that, our lazy morning went down the drain.

Bleary-eyed and clearly still longing for sleep, Leena yawned. "Duty calls."

"I suppose so."

"Don't look so sour. You don't have to go anywhere." Sighing, she peeled back the sheets and stretched her hands to the ceiling. Her muscles tensed and loosened, and then she stood, picked up her discarded clothes from the night before, and shimmied into her undergarments. After pulling her gown up to her waist, she touched her chin to her shoulder and glanced at me. "Do me up?"

"And if I say no?"

She rolled her eyes. "What happened to my calculating, tactical pair bond? He'd never go along with me slighting the princess of Rhyne."

"He's still sleeping," I mumbled. "This pair bond wants his love to join him in bed."

"Another time." Her smile was soft, if not a little forced. Clearly, she didn't want to be awake any more than I did. But she was right, and if speaking with Jayla before our larger meeting today resulted in a greater possibility for success, then getting out of bed was the best thing to do. Relenting, I came to the edge of the bed and laced her up as quickly as I could. I hadn't been able to replicate the exact way the strings had been threaded before, but I gave them a tug for good measure and the dress seemed to hold.

Running her fingers through her tresses, Leena untangled a few knots before skillfully tying it all back with a thick lock of her hair. "How do I look? Presentable?"

She was ravishing, as always. Leaning forward, I gave her a quick kiss. "Beautiful."

A blush crawled over her cheeks, and she waved me off. "See you soon." And with that, she made her way to the door and left. I'd hoped I'd be able to fall back asleep, but the rapidly cooling space where Leena used to be was jarring. I tossed and turned, contemplating all the reasons the princess would ask for Leena to speak with her privately. Perhaps she didn't trust me. I couldn't blame her— there was no telling what her mother had told her over the years. And while entering into an alliance with Lendria inherently meant trusting me to some degree, maybe Jayla felt she'd be more willing to do so if she understood the woman who stood by my side. In any event, at least it gave Leena a chance to determine whether or not Jayla was worthy of owning a beast, if it came down to that.

But when the minutes dragged by and the sun rose fully, darker thoughts slipped into the recesses of my mind. There was no reason for Rhyne to take Leena prisoner. Or worse, harm her. Elianna might have fashioned Leena's capture as some sort of revenge plot for what I'd done to Amira, but not Jayla.

I'd long since abandoned the bed, dressed, and started to pace. Senses straining, I listened to the sounds of the castle waking—the scuttle of feet on stone, muted conversations between attendants, idle chitchat from the guards. Nothing out of the ordinary. I was just about to give way to the shadows, to attempt to sneak through the foreign castle, when another knock sounded from my door.

"Prince Noc? The royal family is ready to meet now."

The attendant had barely finished speaking before I'd wrenched open the door. "Take me to them."

Kost, Ozias, and Calem joined one by one as we passed their rooms, their silent, wary gazes speaking volumes about their concern for Leena's absence. I offered one slight shake of the head. One tense action in the hopes they'd remain calm—or at least as calm as I was pretending to be—until we found out more.

Instead of the throne room, the attendant ushered us into a small library with a polished oak table centered beneath an unlit chandelier. A semicircle of bookshelves enclosed the space, broken up only by large picture windows open to the morning light. A warm glow filled the space, and Elianna, Jayla, and Maddox watched us quietly from their seats at the table. I scanned the room, surprised to find only two unknown guards manning the door. Before I could consider what that meant, my gaze snagged on Leena. She was lingering, unharmed, by the nearest bookshelf and fingering a stray tome. She turned as we entered and offered a reassuring smile. My hand found hers in an instant, and the worry that'd clawed up my throat died.

Taking the seat directly across from Elianna, I slid into my chair just as Leena slipped into the one on my right with Ozias beside her. Kost and Calem sat to my left. Elianna glanced at us all before allowing her hard stare to settle on me.

"We're concerned about what aiding Lendria would incite with our southern enemies," she said, voice terse but not overly argumentative. A flicker of hope ignited in my chest. Not an outright no, then.

"Understandable," I said. "I wish circumstances were different. I wish I could offer forces to eliminate those threats first before requiring your assistance. Unfortunately, I don't have the power to do so until I reclaim the throne—an action that requires your backing."

She pressed her lips into a fine line. "I know. But I cannot budge on this matter. If we send forces to Lendria to aid you in your cause, we leave ourselves vulnerable for an attack. What's to stop them from invading?"

I turned to Kost, and he lifted a stiff shoulder. "We could offer them some of our numbers, but that defeats the purpose of why we came. We need all our strength focused on Varek and Yazmin."

With a tight nod, I looked back at Elianna. "What is the scale of the threats you face? How brazen are they?"

"A few ransacked villages, their stores depleted." Elianna tapped her fingers on the smooth table. "We've been fortunate in our haul of grain and were able to replenish those towns from the capital's reserves, but there's only so much more we can take. The local guard can't seem to keep the raiders from returning, so we're looking into stationing some of our forces for their protection."

As I grappled with a solution, I snuck a glance at Leena. She hadn't seemed surprised by the news, and instead reached beneath the table to give my knee a gentle squeeze. My brows drew together. What was she trying to tell me? What did she know? My gaze turned to Jayla, who was studying me with a calm look. There was no telling what information had passed between them, but if there was no chance of this working, Leena would've been more distraught. Instead, she held her chin high and regarded Elianna with conviction.

"You're looking for a show of strength."

"To a degree," Elianna answered, her words edged. "War with the southern countries would be costly. They're testing the transition of the crown to see what they can get away with. If we show them—"

"If you show them an unyielding throne, it all goes away." Leena removed her hand from my knee and braced her forearms on the table. "That's what you really need. A way for Jayla to be viewed as a powerful queen beyond contest. Soldiers will quell the threats for now, but what if I can provide something much more…lasting?"

Elianna raised a purposeful brow. "Such as?"

"Such as a beast worthy of a queen."

She dropped the words with such certainty that the room was stunned to silence. And she didn't dare break it. Instead, she waited, letting the gravity of her offer sink in. Finally, she touched a finger to her bestiary. "With your permission?"

Eyes tight, the queen gave a single, definitive nod.

Rosewood light blossomed from the back of Leena's hand, surrounding us in a soft, warm glow. But out of that wondrous, peaceful beauty came a deep, bloodcurdling growl that would've sent the hairs on my arms skyward if I'd not grown accustomed to Onyx's call. He emerged from the beast realm just as the light receded. My mind raced as I tried to keep my expression indifferent. Summoning Onyx made little sense. Leena would *never* offer him to Jayla. And when she stood to greet her beast, she only further solidified that belief by pressing her forehead to his and running a gentle hand down his neck. He pulled away then and shook out his feathers so they stood on end. And…realization struck my gut with unexpected force.

Onyx was *regal*. He stood beside his queen, black coat glossy and feathers shimmering in the morning light. Fierce eyes full of power and wonder. He even outstretched his wings, nearly knocking over the closest bookshelves in the process. He was a force and Leena knew it. She knew what it would look like to see something like him standing on the battlefield. The wonder and fear. Jayla's enemies wouldn't know how to act. And that was the very feeling, the very truth, Leena demonstrated with Onyx by her side.

Elianna's mouth had fallen open, and she white-knuckled the edge of the table. After a minute passed, she collected herself. Swallowing hard, she asked, "You're offering this beast to my daughter?"

"No." Leena clasped her hands together. "Onyx is already bonded to me. But Princess Jayla already has a beast in mind. And I have the ability to charm it."

The queen's brows shot to the ceiling. She targeted her daughter. "Since when do you know anything about beasts?"

"I don't." Jayla's voice was cool, but her eyes were alight with mischief. "You always chastise me for spending so much time away from the castle. But did you know there's a strange, unexplained phenomenon that's been happening in Goldwind?"

"My attention has been focused on replenishing grain stores, as should yours," she responded.

"I *was* checking on the grain silos of our nearby towns to see how much we could reallocate if need be." She let out a belabored sigh. "Anyway, the people there told me of a strange sight they'd noticed over the past few weeks—what they thought was a shooting star. But it was far too regular for that. I'd been looking into it when the presence of Leena's beast last night got me thinking... What if it's a beast?"

"I'll need to see for myself, but if Jayla's descriptions are correct, we're likely dealing with a Vyprale." Extending her hand, Leena once again channeled power to her symbol and opened the beast realm door. Onyx disappeared from view, along with the rosewood glow, and Leena retook her seat by my side. "It's a winged, snakelike beast with extraordinary powers. All Jayla would have to do is show up to one of these border skirmishes atop its back, and your enemies would flee."

"Rumors of her power would travel fast," Kost mused. "Since the First War on Lendria, no one has dared to cross a Charmer because of their beasts. I imagine the same would hold true here."

I nodded my agreement. "If Leena is willing to tame the Vyprale and gift it to Jayla, do we have your support in our war against King Varek and Yazmin?"

A heavy silence fell over the table as all eyes turned to the queen. She reclined into her chair and formed a steeple with her fingers, bringing them to her lips. For a long time, she didn't move. Hardly seemed to breathe. Her stoic expression was unreadable. I was used to these games, to hiding my intentions while letting my enemies sweat. It was always a fantastic way to gauge their weaknesses and learn how quickly they'd crack under pressure. I wouldn't give Elianna that satisfaction, and the rest of my family held fast. Not even Calem twitched. Together, we presented a united, unrelenting front. Both a strong ally and potentially a strong adversary if things went south.

Fortunately, they didn't. Dropping her hands to her lap, Elianna let out a tight breath. "We will form an alliance with Lendria under the rule of King Noc and Queen Leena, assuming my daughter is presented with a suitable beast and the aforementioned trade routes are established once this mess with Varek and Yazmin is cleaned up.

"But," she continued, cutting me a hard glance, "I will not send my entire army to your aid. Not now. I still need to station forces across the towns spanning our borders. Jayla can't be everywhere at once, even with this beast. I can spare three of our ships, the crew needed to sail them, and as many soldiers as can fit. In addition, I'll send Isla with them. As a show of good faith."

Not as many bodies as we'd wanted, but it was a great deal more than we'd had before venturing to Rhyne's shore. Isla was an interesting development. A mage wasn't someone I'd ever turn down, especially not in battle, but no doubt Elianna was sending her closest guard to keep an eye on us and Rhyne's interests. Still, we had no room to argue. "That's reasonable. We accept these terms."

Queen Elianna stood, and the rest of us followed suit. She strode around the table until she came to an abrupt stop right between the exit and me. "I don't trust you. I don't know if I ever will. But..." Her shoulders slackened, and she looked at Jayla. The ice in her voice ebbed. "Holding onto grudges won't help my daughter rule over Rhyne. You might. Your pair bond certainly will." She extended her hand to Leena. "Do right by my daughter, and you will always have my favor."

Leena grasped her hand in return. "I will."

Elianna tipped her chin in a subtle bow and then left, taking the two manned guards with her. Jayla practically skipped to Leena's side and gripped both of her forearms in excitement. "So, when do we go searching for this beast?"

Leena grinned. "We can leave today if you'd like."

"I'd like nothing more." Jayla spun on her heels and threw her arms around Maddox, who'd been largely silent for the duration of our negotiation. He seemed as unsurprised by the turn of events as his bride-to-be, but there was an unmistakable air of caution to his movements. Not as trusting as Jayla, but not as standoffish as Elianna.

"Goldwind is about a half day's ride from here." He looped an arm around her waist and glanced at Leena. "What supplies will you need?"

"Not much. Some gold paint and bright feathers will do. The art of taming a Vyprale has more to do with the bait than the dressing, so to speak." Leena gave a nonchalant shrug—one that fooled the royal family, but not me. I'd never heard her speak of such a beast before, which meant she was relying on knowledge passed to her from one of her fellow Charmers. Unease simmered in my gut. She'd had no experience with the Revmandra until she'd tamed it. It was safe to assume she was being light on the details to minimize any fear on Maddox or Jayla's part.

Plus, I didn't like the way she said *bait*.

Slipping my hands into the pockets of my trousers, I pressed my lips into a fine line, then tipped my chin ever so slightly her direction.

She gave her head a subtle shake. Suspicions confirmed. Biting back my words, I turned my focus back to Jayla and Maddox.

"We'll get them together while you gather your things," Jayla said. Threading her fingers through Maddox's, she dragged him out the exit.

Once the door closed behind them, I let out a forceful sigh. "Bait?"

"Oh, not me." Leena smirked. "For once."

"Then, who?" Kost asked, not bothering to hide his confusion.

"You four can draw straws." She waved her hand as she made her way for the door. "That's the safest option, anyway. I highly doubt Maddox would agree to participate, and it must be a man. Based off Jayla's description, we're dealing with a female. And let's just say she'll only descend from the heavens if a suitable mate presents itself." Hand wrapped around the handle, she paused at the threshold. "Hence the feathers and paint. I'm going to bathe. See you soon."

And then she left, a light laugh trailing behind her.

Calem found his words first. "She's officially gone crazy."

"We asked her to consider a beast for Jayla. She's done us that courtesy. We can't be picky about the semantics." Kost slipped his fingers beneath his glasses and pinched his nose. "Though admittedly, I'm not keen on this."

"Me either," Ozias mumbled.

Chuckling, I extracted one hand and summoned a wispy shadow. I willed it to separate into four separate threads and then fisted them as they solidified, hiding their lengths. "Fair is fair."

"So long as you're not cheating and know which one is the shortest," Calem hissed.

"On Zane's blood, I wouldn't dream of it." I grinned. "But just to satisfy you, I'll take whatever's left."

Calem lunged for the first shadow straw before anyone else could move. Ozias fidgeted for a full thirty seconds before finally caving and choosing next. Kost extracted his with much more dignity, and I opened my palm to let the final straw roll to the tips of my fingers. One by one, my brothers did the same.

With a loud gulp, Ozias palmed his face as the shortest straw rolled from his hand and clattered to the floor.

TWENTY-FOUR

LEENA

Taming the Vyprale was a relatively quick process, thanks largely to Oz's role as bait. At first, he was as uncertain of how to behave as he was with women. Restless and fidgety, he couldn't help but swipe at the gold paint covering his body, smearing it so badly we had to apply a second coat and reattach the vibrant, teal feathers dangling from his clothes. After that, it took nearly an hour of coaxing to get him to shimmy appropriately—a necessary tactic to draw the Vyprale's eyes to the flashy feathers— and nearly twice as long for him to perform an acceptable birdcall. At one point, he attempted a "sexy" caw that had us all rolling on the ground in tears. But eventually, his antics worked, and the radiant beast had appeared. Oz had only suffered a few wounds, too, which I counted as a total success. The stories I'd heard of Charmers taming Vyprales almost always ended with missing limbs. But his ability to slink into the shadow realm at a moment's notice made it possible for us to avoid that unfortunate outcome, and I was able to drop out of the sky atop Onyx and tame the confused Vyprale the second Oz disappeared.

And despite it all, he never complained.

"I think I need a drink," he muttered for the tenth time since we'd returned to Veles. I only shook my head and smiled. He certainly deserved one, but we had more important things to worry about, like our impending return to Lendria. Maddox and Jayla had flown home ahead of us atop her beast to set everything in motion. Apparently, the moment Elianna caught sight of her daughter, she'd honored her deal and set Rhyne's forces in motion. Ships were already readying in the harbor off the city by the time Noc, Calem, Oz, and I arrived, and troops had seemingly amassed out of nowhere. Their jade armor was intimidating. Instead of smooth lines hugging the shape of their bodies, the cuts of metal were sharp. Severe. As if their armor was a weapon in and of itself. They marched with deadly precision toward the waiting ships, and I was immediately thankful we'd gained such a promising ally.

We waited in the courtyard just inside the castle gates, while Jayla and Maddox circled above us. Her Vyprale was stunning and powerful. Its slender, snakelike body was covered in shimmery, reflective feathers that made it hard to look at directly. With a falcon's head and lustrous mane that trailed the length of its form—not to mention a pair of wings that spanned the width of a decent-sized house—it was a beast of legend. And that was before it even unleashed its devastating attack. Channeling power from the sun, it stored energy in its wings and rained magic arrows down like hellfire on its prey.

I was only somewhat disappointed I hadn't been able to keep the beast for myself. Large enough to fly several people at once, incredible strength... But it had to be done, and I had every faith Jayla would show it nothing but love and devotion. The Vyprale wouldn't have agreed to join her side otherwise. They were picky like that, and I was silently relieved to tame a creature that would ease my decision in gifting a beast to a near-stranger.

Sharp steps sounded at our backs, and we turned to find Queen

Elianna moving down the walkway toward us. She approached alone, save Isla at her side, and motioned to the sky for her daughter to join her. The Vyprale descended, somehow floating just an inch off the ground, and extended its wing in a makeshift slide for Jayla and Maddox to dismount. As soon as their feet hit the earth, Jayla sent her beast home and they joined Elianna.

"You've managed to keep your first promise," she said, voice level.

It was hard not to be intimidated by the queen of Rhyne. She was as resolute as the army she wielded, and she stood before us without so much as blinking. But even with her stoic mask firmly in place, there was a glimmer of recognition in her faded-amber stare. I wouldn't go as far as to call it trust, but it was something.

Noc gave a tight nod. "We'll continue to honor our agreement. We can't stress enough how much your support is appreciated."

"My forces are not to be taken lightly." She clasped her hands together. "Isla will lead them under your direction, but if at any point she feels your plan is inadequate, she will recall them to prevent inconsequential loss of life. Understood?"

"Understood," Noc said.

"Don't mistake this alliance for friendship...or forgiveness." She pursed her lips. "I will always be watching you, Aleksander. And I hope my daughter will carry that same vigilance when she takes the throne."

Noc didn't bristle. Didn't stiffen. Didn't react at all, really. But when he finally spoke, his words were somber. "I'm sorry, Elianna. I know those words will never be enough, but you deserve to hear it anyway."

She considered him for a long moment, and then turned to me. Her gaze softened. "Thank you for gifting my daughter a formidable beast. I look forward to our continued relationship. Now, if you'll excuse me." She gave the slightest bow before turning her back on us and signaling to her daughter and Maddox. "Jayla and I have a strategy to formulate regarding her presence along our southern border. I expect weekly reports on any developments in Lendria, as they relate to our alliance and my troops."

"Of course, my queen." Isla bowed low, only straightening once the royal family departed. Her hands formed neat fists by her side, and she power walked right through our group, leaving us scrambling to keep up with her. "We head for the docks. Now. As it appears you came to Rhyne with few belongings, we've taken the liberty of stocking some things for you."

We moved quickly down the city streets, passing opulent houses and shops that shifted in style the closer we got to the water. The quaint manors were more open, a bit larger with bay windows and wide doors to allow greater access to the sea breeze. A few locals meandered from vendor stalls to handle their morning shopping, and the scent of fresh fish collided with the salt in the air. A heavy chill rolled in off the ocean, and I rubbed my arms to try to spark warmth. Hopefully, these supplies Isla spoke of included clothing better suited to winter. The thin blouse and breeches I'd secured before taming the Vyprale were doing little to combat the weather.

When the docks came into view, Kost upped his gait to match Isla's. "We should discuss our plans for landing once we arrive at Lendria."

Isla glanced over her shoulder at us, then frowned. "I'm assuming we'll need to dock in secret to avoid Varek's detection."

"Yes," Kost replied. "Though our options are limited."

"Penumbra Glades?" Calem offered. "The small trading town there doesn't get nearly as much traffic as Ortega Key."

"That won't work," Noc sighed, gripping the back of his neck. He glanced out at the horizon, his gaze snagging on the ships.

"There are still a good number of people who live there, and word travels fast. Varek will hear of our landing before we have a chance to regroup with our brethren and formulate an attack."

"And anything along the eastern coastline is too close to Wilheim. There's no way we'd go unnoticed," Oz said.

Isla halted and whirled in place, planting her hands on her hips. "I can end this mission before it even starts. If you have no plan to get my troops safely into Lendria, I'll call them back right now."

Kost ran his hands along his vest before giving the hem a forceful tug. "I said our options were limited, not impossible. Jumping to conclusions helps no one."

A spark ignited in Isla's gaze. An unspoken threat. "Is this how you speak to everyone?"

"Is the leader of Rhyne's army prone to rushed judgments?" Kost frowned.

"Okay, okay, enough of that." Calem shouldered his way in front of Kost, giving him a forceful nudge toward Oz. Oz only slapped a thick hand over his face, effectively muffling a sigh. We were used to Kost's nature, but there was no doubt in my mind that this fiery mage would consider everything out of his mouth an insult. I had at first.

"The issue is," Noc said, cutting a hard glare to Kost and silencing his second-in-command, "that no matter where we land, it's only a matter of time before we're found out. Currently, our troops are in Hireath—a place Yazmin knows well. It's no secret we've made the beast city our stronghold. For now, it's protected enough. It's just a matter of getting us there."

"Have the ships make anchor on Hireath's western coast," I said as I tried to sift through my memory of the land. "There isn't a place to dock, but we can take rowboats to the shoreline. There's a hidden path there to the city."

Noc nodded. "Varek won't think to patrol there, at least not at first. There's no clear place for an armada to land, and no coastal towns. If you can guide us, then it'll work."

"I can do it."

Isla rounded her stern stare in my direction. Despite her diminutive stature, there was no way in hell I'd ever underestimate this woman. Her umber gaze was not to be taken lightly, and that had nothing to do with the errant spark of magic that would sometimes flare to life across her irises. Finally, she relented with a quiet huff. "All right. We'll chart an exact course once onboard. Shall we?"

"Lead the way," Noc said. Isla strode forward once again, her quick pace effectively ending the conversation, and we followed after her in silence.

The moment we hit the docks, Isla directed us toward the nearest ship and then left to attend to her forces, stating she'd rejoin us within the hour in time for launch. Waves crashed against the creaking wooden boards, and the soft breeze I'd felt in the city transitioned to a full-blown wind that smacked into my face with icy force. Shivering, I sidled closer to Noc. He looped an arm around my shoulder and guided us onboard. Sailors moved about the deck shouting orders and readying the sails. Barrels of drink, crates of food, and other cargo were loaded in an orderly fashion. For the most part, no one even bothered to acknowledge our presence. Just the occasional gruff "hello" or "move," and the one chipper soul who directed us to the captain's quarters.

Once we were safely inside the warm cabin, I sank into one of the armchairs across from the captain's desk. My muscles practically melted into the worn upholstered fabric, and I kicked my feet out in front of me. Calem did the same, sprawling out in an identical manner, as Kost came around to the table to examine the maps already laid out against the mahogany wood. Noc leaned against the back of my chair, his fingertips dancing idly along my shoulders.

Rubbing his head, Oz scooted toward the desk. "So, what kind of mage do you think Isla is?"

I tilted my head. "Kind?"

Noc's fingers tensed, then resumed their dawdling. "There are different types of mages. Depending on their class, they can only wield a certain type of magic."

"I only know of two, no, three types, thanks to our encounter with Eryx," Kost mused, his gaze glued to the maps. "Those who can make things out of magic's essence, like Noc's old ring. Those who can project magic like a weapon. And, apparently, those who have compulsory talents."

"The exact mechanics of their magic system are a bit of a mystery to me." Noc shifted to drop his hands lower and began to massage the base of my neck. My head rolled forward, and he chuckled. "Regardless, their magic is not to be underestimated. As for Isla... I can't say for sure. But, I did encounter a mage who could fire off offensive magic during a battle with Rhyne. That's actually how I met Kost."

Kost allowed himself a small smile. "She would've killed you if I hadn't gotten to her first."

"Maybe she was a relative of Isla's?" Oz's thick brows drew together, and he folded his arms across his chest.

"Maybe. Maybe not. A lot of time has passed since then, though it is odd a mage would call Rhyne her home. There's likely a reason why she's not in Allamere." Noc gave my shoulders one last squeeze, then let his hands fall away.

"And that's our cue to zip it," Calem said as he tapped his ear with one finger. A minute later, heavy footsteps crested on the other side of the door before Isla strolled in, a bit of redness to her cheeks. A freezing wind whipped in behind her, and I slouched down in my chair to avoid the brunt of the gust. She slammed the door shut and stalked toward the table, finally taking a seat across from us.

"You're welcome to use this cabin as your room for the duration of our travel. I'll be staying with my soldiers. The sleeping chamber has several cots," she said, yanking her thumb in the direction of a door tucked between some shelves. "Your things will be here momentarily."

"Thank you," Noc said.

She braced her forearms against the table, and her blond hair fell in a wave over her shoulder. "Once we get closer to Lendria's shore, I'll be counting on you to guide us to a safe place to anchor."

"Of course," I said, straightening in my chair.

She glanced between us, then abruptly stood up. "Well, if there's nothing else, then I need to make sure everything is in order."

"Wait…" Oz tensed, and then he slammed his mouth shut as if he hadn't meant to speak. Shuffling his feet, he studied an indistinct spot on the floor. The rest of us stared at him. Calem had to bite his lip to keep his smile from claiming his entire face, and Kost's eyebrows nearly disappeared into his hairline. Never before had I wanted to leap from my chair and give Oz a hug as badly as I did in that moment. When we'd been out together in Ortega Key and he'd been shy around the ferryman's daughter, at least there'd been something—food—for them to bond over. Something to smooth the embarrassment and awkward, stilted conversation. But now…

"Yes?" Isla prompted when Oz didn't add anything further.

He refused to meet her gaze. "What about…rations?"

I winced just as Calem let out a bark of a laugh that he tried to disguise with a cough. Noc threatened to murder him with his stare. Isla blinked. Slowly.

"We have plenty of food for the journey, if that's what you're asking."

"Good. I mean, no. I mean, yes, that's good. But I was offering my help. In the kitchens. You know, if you need it." Sweat developed along his hairline, and he wiped it away. "Not that I'm suggesting you need my help. You've clearly got it figured out."

Isla snorted. "Clearly. Anything else?"

Oz shook his head violently. "No."

"Are you positive? Because you have a habit of stopping me every time I'm going to walk away."

"There's nothing," he muttered, ducking his head. "Really."

"Sure," she drawled, a wicked smile tugging on her lips. "I'll be back in a bit to discuss our route more in depth."

Calem exploded into howling laughter the moment the door closed, and Oz's shoulders slumped forward. Kost only rolled his eyes before once again turning his attention to the maps.

"Oh, Oz," I said, voice soft.

"I'm fine." His brittle, forced laugh was far from assuring.

"Keep up with the antics, and we'll have a 'training' session that will not end well for you." Noc leveled Calem with a glare, and he threw up his hands in mock apology. Still, there was no hiding the mirth in his eyes.

"It's fine, I promise." Oz rolled his head from side to side and let out a sigh.

"Honestly, I don't know why you're laughing so hard. These days, Leena is the only one who puts up with your antics, and we all know she'd never act on your half-hearted advances. Perhaps you're losing your touch." Kost tipped his head upward, just enough so I could catch the glint of mischief in his green eyes.

"It's true," I said with a mock sigh. "What's the problem, Calem? Can't find it in you anymore? Maybe someone has already stolen your attention?"

Noc's brows rose as Oz chuckled.

Calem waved me off and reclined in his chair. "Hardly."

"Sure," Kost responded, clearly unconvinced. He abandoned the maps and glanced toward the door Isla had indicated was full of cots. "That aside, I think I'll take my leave for a bit."

"Since we've got time, I'll shadow walk back to Hireath and check on the recruits," Oz said. "Need to make sure Emelia, Iov, and Raven are getting on fine."

"I'll come with." Calem pushed out of his chair. "I'm not tired, and there's nothing to do around here."

"Good idea," Noc said. "Check in on the assassins. See if…" He glanced toward Kost, then let his eyes fall. "See if there are any new developments."

New developments clearly meaning any word of Gaige. A rock formed in my throat, and I forced it down with a hard swallow. Kost managed a tight nod and then hid himself away in the sleeping chambers.

Oz looked after him as if he wanted to follow, but instead shook his head. "I'll also let them know we're on our way and where we plan to anchor."

Just then, a knock sounded at the door, followed by a gruff voice announcing the arrival of our trunks. Noc strolled over and let a stout sailor in. He yanked a heavy trunk into the center of the room and then took off without a word, leaving us to sort through its contents. Mainly, enough clothing to get us to Lendria. I pulled out a thick indigo coat and wrapped myself in it. As I sank back into the chair, the weight of the days' activities—meeting with the royal family, my night with Noc, taming the Vyprale—caught up with me, and my eyes slipped closed. Better to sleep while I could, because the moment we returned to Hireath, we'd have to focus our attention on Yazmin, Varek, and Darrien.

TWENTY-FIVE

OZIAS

Calem and I manifested on the open lawns outside of Hireath just as Iov and Emelia were about to start evening drills. Newly raised assassins waited before them, some with shadows already slipping between their eager fingers. I missed being the one to help them form blades out of smoke, to reassure them as they moved through the process, but Emelia and Iov were good replacements. I'd trained them myself years ago and had been immediately impressed by their prowess. One woman with short, spiked hair bounded to the front of the lines. Astrid. She was just as capable as the twins had been from the get-go. The three of them rounded their gazes on us, cautious smiles on display as they took in our sudden appearance, and I grinned back. The worry lines etching the sides of their eyes faded. Just here for a check-in, nothing to be alarmed about.

Before they could pull away from the troops, I waved them off. "We'll come back after drills. Keep at it."

"Fine," Iov said in a mock whine, dragging his words. He pivoted toward the assassins and called forth a single, dark tendril and fashioned it into a hovering blade that glittered black against the purple sky.

"Too bad we can't spar in this form," Calem mused. He rolled up his sleeves and flexed his hands, as if somehow that would make it possible for him to join in on the action. The shadows around him flared in response. "You got all the fun with the Vyprale taming."

I cocked a brow. "You call that fun?"

"I didn't hear you complaining."

Footsteps crunched against grass at our backs, and we turned to find Kaori and Raven approaching us. Dark circles shadowed their eyes, and they moved briskly across the lawn. Beside me, Calem stiffened. His eyes tracked Kaori's frame, lingering on the fidgeting hands that toyed with the hem of her cloak. Raven's expression was tight, and she came to an abrupt halt before us.

"Your timing is impeccable."

"What's wrong?" I asked.

"We're not entirely sure," Kaori answered. She frowned and cast a glance behind her toward the keep. "We have something to show you."

"Wonderful," Calem said, voice dark. They led the way, maneuvering through the courtyard and around the trickling fountain. When we reached the open archway to the first floor of the keep, they strode into a small foyer just off the entrance where a white oak desk was centered over a circular moss-green rug. Bookshelves lined the walls, along with a handful of high-back upholstered chairs. Kaori and Raven made straight for the desk. Right in the middle was a small parcel wrapped in brown parchment and tied with twine. Neither of them made a move to touch it.

"A package?" I folded my arms across my chest. It didn't seem dangerous, and yet Kaori and Raven were giving it a wide berth, as if a violent beast were about to pop out.

"It's addressed to the Crown." Kaori clasped her hands and swallowed thickly.

Sauntering forward, Calem crouched before the desk. Shadows spired around him, but nothing happened. "Seems like a regular old package. Who's it from?"

"Doesn't say," Raven bit out. "But considering there are only a handful of people who know of Hireath's exact location..."

"Exact enough to bypass the Kestral and deliver a package to our doorstep without alerting the Dreagles or being seen," Kaori added, her gaze temporarily leaving the box to look first at me, then Calem. "We're guessing Yazmin."

Calem stilled. "Did you open it?"

"Does it look like we opened it?" Raven raised an incredulous brow. "No. We were debating what to do when you two arrived."

The small, seemingly harmless parcel dominated my vision, and my stomach churned. Yazmin was cunning, that much we'd learned. Maybe there *was* a small beast lingering inside, just waiting to leap out and kill us. Or maybe it was a different trick. Some way for her to gain leverage if we simply opened the box.

"What does it mean? Could it be a peace offering?"

Raven snorted. "I highly doubt that. But, I suppose anything is possible."

Kaori shifted from one foot to the next, her gaze darkening. "What if... What if it has to do with those Charmers she mentioned? The missing ones?"

"I'm not so sure about that." Calem's voice was soft, gentle. Concern and something else I couldn't quite place filled his gaze.

"I agree with Calem," Raven said. She dropped her hands to the table and rapped her painted nails along the wood. "Yazmin has proven to be nothing but manipulative. I doubt those Charmers even exist."

Kaori shut down completely, all emotions wiped clean from her face. She gave one definitive nod and said nothing more. Inching closer, Calem dared to ghost his fingers along her arm. Smoky tendrils grazed her skin where his touch would've been, but she didn't react.

Clearing my throat, I nodded toward the package. "Let's wait for Leena to open it. She'll want to know about it."

"Sounds like a plan," Calem said, attention still focused on Kaori. Dropping his voice an octave, he spoke only to her. "Let's take this to her room, yeah?"

"Okay. I'll station a beast there, too, to keep an eye on it until she arrives." She scooped up the package and held it close to her chest before exiting the room. Calem gave us a quick nod, then strolled out after her.

Raven deflated, shoulders softening and eyes falling to the desk. "She's not taking this well."

"The box?"

"No, the thought of Charmers still being out there." Raven straightened and then brushed her hands along her faded-brown coat. "Kaori's always been tight-lipped about her past. I'm not entirely sure why this is triggering her."

My eyes narrowed a hair. Raven was skilled at masking her emotions, but not perfect. I could see the concern lingering in her gaze, too. The way she kept flexing her hands and twisting her neck as if it were aching. No one liked the idea of their family being held captive. If anyone from Cruor, even one of the newer recruits I'd barely gotten to know, had been captured, I doubted there was any force in this world that could stop me from going after them. Rounding the table, I placed a hand on her arm. She eyed the shadows that lingered on her skin.

"Come on. Let's see how the assassins are doing with their drills. Probably better than you, considering you're not out there."

She huffed and batted away my hand, tendrils dispersing and re-forming. Her cold stare warmed. "Whatever."

I chuckled as we left the keep, making our way toward the still-training troops. It was easy with Raven, just as it had been with Leena. I wasn't entirely sure why. Was it their Charmer's lure? Or was it because they'd never expressed a desire for something more with me? My thoughts rewound to Zara, a budding recruit I'd trained not long ago. She wasn't much of a fighter, instead choosing to spend her days painting and helping out around Cruor, but I hadn't forgotten how she'd attempted to flirt with me. How one moment I'd been in complete control of my thoughts and words and the next...nothing.

"What's going on in that brain of yours?" Raven asked, poking my side and sending my shadows outward in a flurry. The sudden disturbance was enough to bring me out of my reverie.

"Oh, nothing."

She cocked her head. "Sure. You know, it's okay for you to have problems, too. You don't always have to take care of us." She gestured widely to include all the assassins training on the lawns. Even some of the Charmers who'd elected to participate along with them.

I could've deflected. Could've shifted the conversation to Eilan and her grief—the one thing she never discussed—but I knew she'd come to me in time. And I didn't want to close that door before it opened, because what good would that do? How could I comfort someone who didn't want it? So instead, I sighed. Looking out over the assassins and Charmers, I paused when I found Zara lingering at the mouth of the communal tent. She was locked in an animated conversation with another assassin, hands waving about her body.

I looked away. "It's not a problem. Not really."

"Spill." Raven positioned herself in front of me and leaned forward with her hands on her hips. "You're not leaving until I hear what's bothering you."

A memory of Isla surfaced in my mind. To the swish of her blond hair as she turned her back on me after yet another dumb comment. Heat flushed to my cheeks. *Bother* was hardly the word I'd use. "It's this...woman."

Raven raised a brow. "And?"

"And I don't know how to talk to her," I said in a rush. "Anyone, really. Aside from you and Leena. I get all tongue-tied."

She pursed her lips together in thought, but there was a glint of mirth to her stare. "You like her?"

"Yes. No. I don't know, I hardly know her. But I want to know her. I want to be better with people."

Raven frowned. "Ozias, you're great with people." She gestured loosely to the assassins. "They've done nothing but sing your praises since you left."

"New people, then. I just... I just don't want to flounder when I talk." My ears still burned from my earlier moment with Isla. *Rations.* Even now, it sounded dumb. And Isla was so...confident. She commanded attention the moment she entered a room. And when she spoke, people listened. She was magnetic.

And I was the complete opposite.

"Just don't analyze it so much." Raven lifted a shoulder. "Better to speak your mind and fumble over words than say nothing at all. You never know when it might be your last chance." Her eyes clouded over with sadness, and she jerked her chin away. My own insecurities died, and I inched closer to her.

"Raven."

"I'm fine." Her curt words did nothing to hide her pain. She took several breaths and then straightened. Emotions hidden behind a stoic mask, she nodded toward the assassins. "Look, they've finished with their drills."

I glanced over her head just as Iov and Emelia strolled toward us. Astrid followed with them, sweat clinging to her hairline but a happy grin stretched wide across her face. As much as I wanted to press Raven further, to show her that she could be vulnerable with me, I let that desire fall away. When she was ready, I'd be there for her.

"You ready to come back yet?" Astrid asked. "These two are good, but not Ozias good."

Emelia jabbed her with a playful elbow and then flicked her braided ponytail over her shoulder. "As much as it pains me to admit, Astrid is right. The newbies could use your guidance."

I smiled at them, happy to shift the conversation for Raven's sake. "Yes. We'll be back in a few days. Drills going smoothly?"

"They're swell." Iov side-eyed Raven, then grinned. "You missed out today. What, was this morning's sparring match enough for you?"

Raven hissed. "Sweep my legs again and I'll end you. I promise."

I didn't bother to muffle my laughter. "Good. And the sentries? Any news to report?"

Emelia stiffened slightly and shook her head. "No. No news, no sightings."

The warmth in my chest died along with my smile. No sightings. Not even Yazmin, assuming she'd been the one to deliver the package in the first place. Of course, there was always the possibility she'd sent a beast into the city, and with so many Charmers calling on their creatures at any given time…there was no way we would've detected hers among the crowd.

It also meant they hadn't found Gaige. Bile soured my tongue, and I rubbed my jaw for a moment before letting my hand fall away.

"All right. Add a few more sentries to the watch. We had an unexpected development today. We'll be back soon."

They nodded in unison, and Emelia and Astrid immediately left in the direction of the communal tent, presumably to seek out more sentries to join those already stationed in the Kitska Forest.

"I'm off to find Calem and report back to Leena and Noc. Maybe you two should practice recovering from the ground."

Raven glared at me so fiercely I swear she somehow pierced the shadows. But Iov leapt at the opportunity, cracking his knuckles and regarding Raven with excitement. She shrugged out of her coat and waved a goodbye over her shoulder, focus already locked on Iov.

As much as I wanted to share in their temporary reprieve, to feel the burn of muscles and beads of sweat along my skin, I couldn't. My relief would have to wait. For now, I needed to find Calem and report back to our family. Knots formed in my stomach at the thought of that conversation, but they needed to know about this mysterious parcel and Gaige's continued absence. Between the anxiety and pain this news would bring, I wasn't sure I even wanted to return. But I had to. And I would be there for my family like always to shoulder whatever I could.

TWENTY-SIX

CALEM

Kaori had dismissed the attendants stationed nearby the moment we'd hit the floor dedicated to the Crown's quarters. Save for the ever-present crashing of water from the nearby falls that filtered through the closed window, Leena's room was quiet. And so was Kaori. She'd placed the package on the low coffee table before the fire and sunk into the settee to stare at it. With light fingers, she absently tracked the mercury veining on her inner wrist.

"Kaori?" I tried, moving to her side. It killed me that I couldn't touch her while shadow walking. Not really. I desperately wanted to grip her hands in mine. To give them a squeeze and offer her some of my strength. "What's wrong?"

After a long moment, she finally looked up at me, but her gaze was somewhere far away. "Nothing. I'm fine."

"You're not fine." She'd always been a bit reserved. Quiet. But nothing like…*this*. "Tell me what's going on."

"There's nothing to tell."

I bit back a sigh. Her stubbornness was beyond irritating. "I don't believe you. Something is up."

She lifted one shoulder, but the action was stiff. "Yazmin is attempting to manipulate us yet again. Something is certainly 'up.'"

Tossing my hands in the air, I rounded the couch to position myself in front of her. "Right. This is about the box."

She blinked. "What else would it be about?"

"You're as dense as Kost," I mumbled, pinching the bridge of my nose before sighing. "Sorry, I didn't mean that. He's far and away worse."

I'd hoped my jest would get her to smile. Just a small curl of her lips would've been enough. But she continued to look at me as if I weren't really there, face devoid of emotion. Her fingers endlessly trailed along her wrist. My hand itched to clamp down on hers and stop their progression.

Shifting my weight from one foot to the other, I scoffed. How could I get her to open up? To share with me when she'd done so little of that before? I owed Kaori my life. I valued her more than I could put into words, and yet most of our conversations had centered around our inner beasts. We'd discussed my triggers at length and how to rein in my temper and practice control. But the more I thought about it, the more I realized she'd never shared anything of herself with me. Nothing about her past. Nothing about her triggers. I'd been so focused on my own recovery, on learning to strong-arm the beast in me, that I'd failed entirely at asking more about her.

And the fact that I wanted to know more, beyond an amicable friendship or flirting, was startling enough to bring my fidgeting to a standstill. *Get a grip. She's family, that's why you're worried.* Worried. That was it. I drew in a slow breath and pushed away my scrambled thoughts. Thoughts that had absolutely no place in my mind. Not now, not ever. Kaori needed support. And I could give that to her.

Crouching before her, I rested my hands on my knees. "Kaori, I need to know that you're okay."

"I'm okay," she responded all too quickly.

"No, you're not."

"Are you insinuating you know what I'm feeling?" A glimmer of annoyance colored her voice, and I almost jumped for joy. Anything was better than the statue I'd been dealing with moments before.

"No; of course not. But I'd like to know."

She considered me for a long moment. Her dark eyes were full of emotions I didn't have the ability to place, but one thing was certain: there was a storm brewing in her stare. One that wasn't necessarily directed at me. There was an age-old hurt masked behind her wall of indifference. And gods if I didn't want to know what'd caused it. Slowly, she dropped her gaze. Dug her fingers into her skin. When she sighed, her shoulders rolled forward.

"This is...difficult for me to talk about."

I was almost too scared to respond in case it silenced her all together. "I'll hear whatever you're willing to share."

She nodded. "You remember Wynn?"

A familiar heat raced through my veins, and my inner beast stirred. The rage I'd felt at seeing what he'd done to Leena, a member of my chosen family, had sent me into a murderous frenzy. But now was not the time to give way to my beast. I wasn't even entirely sure what would happen if I shifted while shadow walking, and it wasn't something I was eager to test.

With a deep, steadying breath, I nodded. "Yes."

"He wasn't the first one who went rogue playing with dark magic." Her words were barely a whisper, as if she'd had to coax them out against their will. She pressed her eyes shut. Went entirely still. "My parents were."

For a moment, I did nothing. Simply waited. I had my own complicated memories of my parents, particularly my mother. She'd destroyed me in ways I didn't ever care to examine. If any inkling of my mother's presence was somehow thrust before me again, no matter how tangential, I'd already be a beast rampaging through the Kitska Forest. Pushing that thought aside, I placed my hand over Kaori's fingers. Shadows caressed the mercury veins, and she looked between them and me.

"What does this have to do with them?" I asked.

"I don't know. Probably nothing. It's just…" She curled her fingers upward, as if trying to intertwine them with mine. "Wynn primarily experimented on humans. My parents…experimented on *everything*. What if…what if the missing Charmers are because of them and not Wilheim?"

My throat went dry. "We don't even know—"

"They were exiled when I was young, supposedly sent to some prison off the coast of Allamere." She interrupted me in a rush, her words gushing like water that had just been freed from a dam. "But they were powerful. So powerful. And dangerous. They could've escaped, could've made an alliance with the king of Wilheim somehow. Maybe they've been helping him capture Charmers all along. What if they're…what if they're experimenting again? What if…"

"Kaori, breathe."

Glassy eyes met mine, and she inhaled sharply. "I'm sorry."

I let go of her hand and stood up. "Get up."

"What?" She blinked.

"Stand. Up."

Slowly, she pushed herself off the couch. "I don't understand."

Before she could say anything else, I wrapped my arms around her and tucked my head against her neck. I knew she wouldn't be able to feel the warmth of my touch, but I willed the shadows to encircle her and provide as much comfort as I possibly could in this moment. At first, she didn't move. Then, she started to tremble. Her tremors sent ripples through the inky tendrils, but I commanded them to stay in place. Finally, she cradled her head in her hands and let out a quiet sob.

As gently as I could, I spoke directly into her ear. "It's going to be okay. I promise."

"But what if I'm right?" she whispered between her fingers. "I don't want to be right."

My chest tightened. "Then we'll take it one step at a time. But we don't know anything yet, and if we focus on what we can't control…" I sent a soft tendril snaking through her fingers. She pulled her hand away to watch its progression as it danced along the silver veins of her wrist. "Then the beast wins."

Tears lined her face, and she looked up at me through thick lashes. Something shifted in me in that moment. Not my beast. Not anything I could really name. But it was warm and full and entirely too much. For the first time since we'd arrived in Hireath, I was glad I wasn't physically there. Otherwise, I didn't know if I would've been able to restrain myself in that moment. My fingers burned to brush away her tears. To cup her face and hold her close. To…

A tremble raced through me, one I was thankful she couldn't feel.

Just then, a small, insistent shadow slipped beneath the door and raced across the floor toward me. Ozias. So absorbed in my conversation with Kaori, I hadn't realized that he was waiting outside. A strange mixture of relief and irritation brewed in me. Relief because I didn't have to stay and examine whatever the hell was going on in my brain, and annoyance because…

I let my arms fall away and took a small step back. "Ozias is waiting outside."

Kaori nodded and rubbed her hands along her arms. Right where my shadows had been. "Thanks, Calem."

"Any time." I flashed her a grin because that's what I did best—hide behind a smile. And with that, I headed for the door, eager to put some distance between me and the woman who'd turned my thoughts upside down.

TWENTY-SEVEN

LEENA

I knew the moment Oz and Calem returned that something was wrong. They'd pulled Kost, Noc, and me into our sleeping chambers—a few dark tendrils still clinging to their frames from their shadow walk to Hireath—and closed the door. With quick, stilted words, they revealed that a mysterious package, one likely left by Yazmin, had made its way undetected into the keep. Kaori and Raven had discovered it first, then showed it to Calem and Oz so they could inform me. For the time being, the parcel was safely under guard in my quarters, unopened and awaiting my return.

But that was days ago, and while Isla insisted we were making great time on our journey back to Lendria, it felt more like an eternity. Anxiety gnawed at my insides, and I often found myself pacing, unable to focus. All I could think about was that parcel, and my mind continuously served up horrendous worst-case scenarios. What if the box contained some disastrous beast just biding its time, waiting to unleash fury the moment I pulled open the twine? Or maybe it contained proof that Gaige wasn't missing, but rather captured by her hand—or worse, killed. Noc had tried to soothe me, but there was little that could assuage my fears short of unboxing the damn parcel myself.

So when Hireath's western cliffs finally came into view, I was hit both with relief and a renewed sense of restlessness. Noc, Calem, Ozias, Kost, and I took the first rowboat toward the sheer, gray cliffs with Isla and her troops following suit behind us. The aroma of salt and seaweed filled my nose as tumultuous waves crashed into the slate rock face, obscuring the hidden staircase from view. Only a Charmer would know how to safely pinpoint the entrance. After rounding the bend, the rocky slabs making up the winding stairs came into view, and we were able to safely deboard on the water-slicked stones. It would take time to ferry all the troops and supplies, but a safe return to Lendria was more than worth it.

The moment we reached the open lawns of Hireath, Isla began barking orders at the troops behind her. They worked quickly and efficiently to erect tents and set up camp, and a handful of them returned to the boats to usher in more soldiers and supplies. The Cruor assassins looked on from their own encampment, uncertain whether or not to help. Oz signaled for Emelia and Iov, and they appeared in a plume of shadows beside us. He gave them orders to assist in any way possible, pointing out Isla as their leader, and they disappeared as quickly as they'd came.

"Welcome back," Raven called as she approached us from the direction of the keep, Kaori beside her. "Glad to see Rhyne has joined us."

I allowed for a tight smile. "Thanks, I'm glad everyone is holding up here. Where's the package?"

Kaori grimaced. "In your room."

"Thank you for handling that." I glanced around at the flurry of activity. There was so much to do, so much to organize. Noc watched me closely and let his fingers graze the back of my arm. Just the smallest of reassuring touches. "I'll open it shortly."

Kost cleared his throat. "No word of Gaige?"

Another punch to the gut, and I sucked in a breath.

Raven shook her head once. "No."

Noc eyed his brother, a glimmer of sadness in his gaze. "Go on. Speak to the sentries. See if they have anything more."

"I'll come with you." Calem clamped a hand on Kost's shoulder. "We can do a quick perimeter check. Maybe they missed something."

Kost nodded without speaking and backstepped into shadows, Calem a breath behind him. Both Oz and Noc tracked their invisible progression before sharing a somber look. Noc rolled his head from side to side, easing tension from his shoulders.

"We'll find him," he said.

Raven clenched her jaw tight. "I hope so. Though, he's going to get an earful from me when he does return."

"The transition is hard. Even more so for Gaige," Oz said. He eyes lingered on the plethora of beasts intermingling with the Charmers. Their presence was a constant reminder of what Gaige had lost. It would be enough to send me running from Hireath, too.

"Yeah," I said. For a moment, we simply stood in silence and let the sounds of the clearing wash over us. The crashing falls were a constant backdrop to the bustle of activity on the lawns. Canvas flapped against the breeze as Rhyne's troops erected tents near the assassins. Isla moved away from the closest one, her confident steps thudding against the ground, and approached us. Beside me, Oz stiffened. Raven quirked a brow as she took in his sudden stillness, and then she rounded her gaze on Isla.

"We'll be done setting up in no time. Are there any strategy meetings planned for this evening?" Isla asked.

"No. We have a separate matter to attend to first." Noc peered at me for a moment, and I nodded. I didn't know what was in that package, and the last thing I wanted was to put our new ally in danger. Noc and I could examine the contents ourselves and report back to the group after. "We'll convene in the morning," he added. "Once everyone has had some rest."

"Good. If I could get a tour of the place, that would be appreciated." Isla nodded to the castle and the surrounding woods. "I'd rather be prepared in case we get any surprise visitors."

"I can do it," Oz blurted out, then blanched.

Raven stared at him for a long minute before pivoting toward Isla. "How about we show her together? I'm more versed in the castle layout than you. I'm Raven, by the way."

Isla gripped her extended hand tightly and smiled. "Isla. That would be wonderful, thank you."

"Come on, Ozias." Raven beckoned over her shoulder as she and Isla strode away, first in the direction of Cruor's forces. "Why don't you introduce her to some of your brethren?"

Oz practically tripped over his feet as he went after them, leaving Noc and me alone with Kaori. Noc's gaze followed his brother, a slight smile tugging at his lips, before returning his focus to us. His expression sobered.

"Let's deal with the parcel."

Kaori glanced between us. "If…if you could just fill me in as soon as possible…"

There was a slight quiver to her tone that stole my attention, and a tightness formed in my chest. Her face was carefully blank. Forced, even. Only her voice betrayed the worry she felt. Worry I also shared, but I wasn't entirely certain it was for the same reason.

"Of course. Why don't we plan to have the Council meet in the library within the hour to discuss its contents?"

Placing a hand over her bestiary, she nodded. "Thank you." And with that, she strode off in the direction of the library, her glossy black hair swaying behind her.

"You ready?" Noc asked, jutting his chin in the direction of the keep.

Chewing the inside of my cheek, I stared at the towering castle nestled against the falls. From the outside, it appeared peaceful. The network of homes tucked away in the trees were full of life, and a warm, buttery glow flickered from the windows. Charmers and beasts alike milled about the wooden bridges. Despite the horrors we'd faced, we were surviving. Finding joy where we could. I couldn't let Yazmin jeopardize that. And if she truly did send the parcel...I needed to know what she was planning.

"Let's go." Hand in hand, we walked toward the keep and made our way to my quarters. Attendants tipped their chins in polite bows before dispersing, giving us privacy as we closed the double doors to my room. Unmoving, a Havra stood near the exit, her four, deerlike eyes riveted to the low table in front of the hearth. This must've been the beast Kaori had stationed to monitor the package. With the ability to materialize through walls, the Havra would've been able to safely flee if something dangerous had emerged. Fortunately, that hadn't happened, and the small, slender beast took one look at me before fading into the wall, presumably returning to Kaori.

With the beast gone, the fist-sized parcel stole my focus. Resting on the coffee table, it appeared unassuming enough. Just a box wrapped in faded-brown paper and tied off with twine. A tiny bit of parchment was attached to the string—addressed to Hireath's new Crown—and I kneeled before it to get a closer look.

Noc inched toward it. "How do we know it's safe to open?"

I assumed Kaori and Raven had done their due diligence, perhaps summoning a Dosha to test the paper for poison before bringing it here. But I doubted they examined the contents further out of respect for my privacy. Channeling power to my Charmer's emblem, I focused on the beast realm door and wrenched it open.

After searching for a few moments, I found my Bockular munching on grub beneath a shade tree and called him to my side.

He manifested on the table and looked up at me with giant, glass-blue eyes that dominated most of his tiny face. No larger than a teacup, my hedgehog-like beast rolled onto his hind legs and shook out his rainbow quills.

"Hey, Cushy." I gently poked his soft underbelly, and he let out a playful squeak. "Can you examine that box for me?"

Snout rounding on the parcel, he gave it a quick sniff before placing his abnormally large hands on its sides. His eyes homed in on the package, and his body went still.

"What's he doing?" Noc asked.

"Checking its contents. Cushy can see through barriers, so long as he's touching them. Though anything beyond a few inches and it's much harder for him to get a clear picture. Either way, he'll share what he finds with me like Felicks does with Kost." I tapped my temple, waiting for an image to form in my mind.

When it finally appeared, my breath caught.

Cushy released his hold on the parcel and crawled toward my frozen hands. With a quiet chuff, he nudged my fingers.

"Leena?" Noc asked.

I couldn't think. Couldn't breathe. All I could see was the outline of two book-shaped pendants wrapped in cloth. Panic clawed up my throat. They were bestiaries. *Bestiaries.* Our pendants could only be removed by a Charmer's hand, which meant this gift had to come from Yazmin. Even worse, it meant there were Charmers in the capital.

Living Charmers.

Slowly, I extended my shaking fingers and opened the beast realm door. I sent Cushy home without a word before dropping my hand to the table.

Noc settled to his knees beside me and grazed my arm. "Leena, what's wrong?"

I couldn't bring myself to answer him yet. Not until I knew for absolute certain, with my own eyes, what was inside. Gently, I tugged at the twine and peeled back the paper. The lid was all too easy to remove, and I peered down at the very thing I'd hoped I'd never see: two bestiaries laid upon ivory cloth, just as Cushy had shown me.

Noc stilled, his hand on my arm going rigid. He'd know exactly what it meant to receive a "gift" like this.

Ears ringing, I brought shaky fingers to the first of two bestiaries, their chains still intact. I could feel the grooves of a name etched into the leather, taunting me with a truth I wasn't sure I wanted to unearth. Tilting it toward the crackling fire, I examined the gold lettering of our ancient language.

Verlin. I inhaled sharply, dropping the pendant back into the box. Slowly, I willed myself to examine the second one.

Sabine.

My world slipped out from under me. I barely remembered my parents, but I'd never forget their names. My aunt had made certain of that, always reminding me that they'd been named after members of the first Charmers Council. She wanted me to know where I came from. And now, with my mother's bestiary clasped tight in my hand, I could feel her. It was as if she were there, running gentle fingers through my hair as I bounced impatiently in her lap. I heard the soft hum of a long-forgotten lullaby. Felt the warmth and security of her hug, as if she'd be able to protect me from anything.

Noc curled his fingers over mine and held my hand tight. "Who do they belong to?"

Rounding my gaze on him, I didn't even try to stop the flood of tears. "My parents." A sob racked my chest, and he pulled me to him. Burying my head in his tunic, I tried to lose myself in his embrace. To find security and stability when the very foundation of my world had just been annihilated. They were still alive. My parents were *alive*. Snaking my free hand back to the box, I secured my father's bestiary and held it close. I could *feel* their power humming from the pendants. Their ties to the beast world. If they'd died, the books would've gone with them. But here they were, warm against my palms.

Yazmin had been right. She'd found them.

Suddenly, my ratcheted breathing halted. A wet cry died in my throat.

How many others had she found?

Over the years, a number of Charmers had "died" on beast hunts. Wilheim couldn't have possibly captured them all. But...I didn't know. And if there was a small force of Charmers being held captive in the capital, how could Noc not have known? His parents?

I jerked my head upward and took in my *anam-cara*'s expression. Pain. Sadness. Concern. And yet... "You didn't know. Promise me you really didn't know."

He didn't flinch. Didn't balk at my need for reassurance. Instead, he pressed a feathery kiss to my forehead. "I swear on my life, Leena, I didn't know."

My eyes slipped closed. There was no way he would've lied to me about something like this. But someone was responsible. Someone knew.

Varek. Even if he wasn't the first one to capture Charmers, he was still aware. He was the one holding them prisoner after they'd been missing for decades.

The grip on my parents' bestiaries grew tighter. As much as I wanted to rush off and confront him immediately, to find my parents and release them from whatever hell they were living in, something felt...off. How did Yazmin get their bestiaries in the first place? Did they willingly give them to her? Or did she remove them by force?

There were too many variables at play, and I wouldn't be a pawn in her games. Not anymore. With the backs of my hands, I rubbed the tears from my cheeks. She wouldn't win. Not now, not ever. One way or another, I'd stop her and save the Charmers locked away in Wilheim. And I wouldn't do it alone. Gazing at Noc, I let out a steadying breath before pressing my lips to his.

Together. We'd handle Yazmin's latest ploy together.

TWENTY-EIGHT

LEENA

The library was quiet, thanks to the late hour. The clusters of bookshelves softened the creak and moan of the winter wind seeping through the walls. But at least it was warm. A rycrim heater hummed nearby, dumping heat into the space and eliminating the need for a fire. Something we never would've dared to light for fear of accidentally igniting the massive tree trunk that housed our library.

Kaori had a book open in her hands, but she flipped the pages absently, her eyes focused elsewhere. She tipped her head in greeting to Noc and me as we entered before returning it to a shelf. Reclining in the nearest chair, Calem quietly watched Kaori's stiff movements. Oz and Kost sat next to him, and a low, inaudible conversation flowed between them. Raven bustled around lighting a handful of floating rycrim orbs, their somber glow basking the space in a soft light.

Sliding into one of the wooden chairs, I placed my parents' bestiaries on the table.

Kaori's eyes went impossibly wide. Raven froze as Kost and Oz's conversation came to a screeching halt. Calem's mouth fell open. Noc was quiet behind me, his hand heavy on my shoulder and fingers tense. Pulling strength from his touch, I swallowed once before meeting each of the Council members' gazes.

"These belong to my parents."

For an eternity, no one spoke. Only stared. Then, Kost cleared his throat. "You're absolutely positive?"

"Yes." The word soured my tongue, and I swallowed thickly. "Even if they weren't, would it matter? Yazmin has clearly found the Charmers she said Wilheim has been hunting. My parents can't be the only ones."

Kaori blanched and gripped the chair before her for support. Calem subtly in shifted her direction, the beginnings of a crease forming along his forehead.

Raven bit out a curse. "Leena's right. It's not like Yazmin just found a pair of bestiaries to send us. They burn away soon after the Charmer dies."

A memory of Gaige's bestiary turning to ash sparked in my mind. It'd been such a horrifying moment, but only because he'd been there to witness it. Rebirth, apparently, wasn't something we were ever supposed to experience.

"Which means they have to be alive," Oz mumbled. He looked at me then with such sorrowful eyes that it was hard to maintain composure.

Calem dragged his gaze away from Kaori to glare at the pendants. "So, what do we do?"

"I'm not sure we can do anything." Noc was barely audible. "Not yet."

Something snapped in Kaori, and she pushed away from the chair to brace her hands on the table. "Are you out of your mind?" Her fingers turned bone white as she leaned forward more. Her outburst was everything I wanted to feel. Everything I wanted to express. But I was strangely numb. My limbs were lead, and every-one was speaking through cotton. I knew what they were saying. Knew how it was supposed to make me feel, but it just didn't regis-ter. It was all dull compared to the all-consuming anguish inside me. I'd had parents all these years, and I never knew.

Noc's words were measured. "We would love to free them immediately. But I think this is Yazmin's way of trying to bait us into a compromising situation."

Mercury veins—so like the hue of Calem's eyes—crept down Kaori's right hand and wrapped her fingers like rings. The wood beneath her grip gave a definitive groan. Calem immediately stood and moved closer to her. He placed his hand over hers and gave it a squeeze. She blinked, then shook her head, and the veins receded.

"I'm with Kaori on this one," Raven said, jaw ticking. Ire flashed through her eyes. Her desire for vengeance hadn't subsided, and her words were edged. "I said I'd fight anywhere, under any circumstances. Now seems like a good time to me."

Oz grimaced. "We can't do that, Raven."

"And why not?" she ground out.

"I want Yazmin to get what's coming to her just like you do," Oz said, giving her a long look, "but we need to think about this. She's playing at something, we just don't know what."

Kost pushed his spectacles up the bridge of his nose. "Did the note say anything else?"

"No," I said. "Nothing." No one spoke. This was a riddle we couldn't possibly solve, and suddenly all I wanted to do was scream. Gone was my inability to process, to feel, and now I was hot all over and angry. Angry at the world for taking my parents. Angry for the Council exiling me when they did. For Yazmin turning against us. Years of injustice piled up and I just wanted to knock it all down. My hand formed a tight fist by my side, and power flooded to my emblem. Rosewood light exploded around me, and for a moment I just reveled in it.

"Leena." Noc's words were soft against my ear. "It's okay."

"It's not okay." My glow harshened. I stood up and paced, unable to sit still any longer. "None of this is *okay*. I don't know what to do. How am I supposed to fix *this*? How do I know she won't kill them like she did Eilan and Tristan?" Raven winced at the mention of her deceased lover, but didn't interrupt my tirade. I turned to Noc then, tears lining my eyes. "Tell me what to do. Tell me."

Noc's expression broke, and he placed both hands on my cheeks. "I wish I knew."

A hot tear slipped down my face, and my power receded. I wanted to get lost in his eyes, but I couldn't. I couldn't escape this awful truth. Before I could think of anything to say, Noc went rigid. He jerked his head toward the open entrance of the library. A moment later, a smooth, deep voice that was achingly familiar floated through the air.

"I might have an idea. If I'm still allowed to speak."

Everyone turned then. There, standing a few feet away, was Gaige. With wild, unkempt hair and bags beneath his eyes, he was a little worse for wear, but otherwise sound. His tunic was torn, as if something had slashed through the sleeves. Shadows dripped from his frame, still far from being completely controlled. But he'd somehow masked his presence, at least from me. Noc had detected him, but only a moment before he appeared. Kost inhaled sharply as he took a hesitant step forward.

I don't know where the urge came from, but one moment I was standing frozen in utter shock and the next I was bolting toward him. My arms clutched him so tightly he coughed in my ear. I burrowed my face into his cloak. At first, he didn't respond. His hands wavered above my back before finally connecting, and he dipped his head to my shoulder.

Voice gruff, he spoke only to me. "I'm sorry I took so long."

"I don't care. I'm just glad you're here." Stepping back, I wiped away tears with the back of my hand and gestured to the group. "We all are."

"You foul, horrible, terrible"—Raven's feeble attempt at anger broke as she strode toward us—"insane idiot. I'm so fucking glad you're back." She forced a hug out of him, too, and then released her grip. "You don't know... You don't know what it was like without you. What it did to me...to the Charmers." She recovered quickly, but there was no mistaking what she'd clearly meant to say. For someone who'd lost so much already, having Gaige essentially walk out on her was a blow she hadn't prepared for.

"Gaige." Kaori's exclamation was near breathless. "Thank the gods." She was much slower to come around the table, but eventually met us halfway and wrapped him in a quick hug.

"You're certainly a sight for sore eyes," Calem said with a slight smile.

"I didn't mean to cause so much alarm. I just... Well, I found something, but it's not as important as this. We can discuss it later." His fingers absently grazed his jaw before he turned his steel-blue gaze on Kost. Aside from his initial shock, Kost hadn't moved a muscle. Tension racked his frame, and unspoken emotions raged in his eyes.

Noc glanced between the two of them before joining us and offering Gaige a firm handshake. "The transition is tough. On *all* of us."

He didn't need to target Kost with his words for me to understand that last part was meant for his second-in-command.

Gaige seemed to catch on, too, and relief soothed some of

the lines forming canyons across his forehead. "Thank you for understanding."

"I think I pummeled a few innocent assassins for looking at me wrong when I was first raised," Oz said with a shrug. "Calem was worse."

"Hey now," Calem exclaimed. "Let's not go there."

"The point is," Noc said, regaining control of the conversation, "you're back. And you're certainly still a member of this Council in my book."

"Absolutely." I nodded and gripped Gaige's forearm, dragging him toward the table. "And we need your insight now more than ever."

Gaige's eyes found the bestiaries. "I heard most of what you were discussing before I emerged from the shadows. I do think Noc is right. We can't rush at this problem headfirst. Yazmin is trying to provoke us. She wants you to race to the castle in search of them so she can dispose of you before you interfere again."

"You think we should leave them there, too?" Kaori asked, voice stiff.

A glimmer of understanding passed between them. I wasn't sure exactly what it was. My friendship with Kaori was fairly new, but Gaige had known her for years. He understood things about her past, about who she was beneath her calm exterior, that I couldn't possibly guess at.

He let out a long sigh. "I wish it were different, but the truth of the matter is we don't know what we'd be walking into. We don't even know what state they're in."

"State?" Kost wielded the single word like a blade.

Gaige met his icy stare. "Yes. State. It's very rare for a Charmer to willingly give up their bestiary. For example, I've only done it twice." He gave me a knowing look, and I recalled the time he'd handed me his bestiary as we searched for ways to eradicate Cruor's Oath from Noc's wrist. "Did she harm them to get the bestiaries? Were they already harmed? Or did they give them up willingly? We simply can't say. Attacking without that knowledge is dangerous."

Kaori's chin slumped to her chest. "I hate it when you're right."

"But there might be another way to use this to our advantage." Gingerly, he picked up the closest bestiary. My father's. "I'm not sure Yazmin realizes the gift she's unintentionally given us."

"What are you talking about?" I asked.

"The beast realm." He glanced at all of us, waiting for us to catch on. When we didn't, he set the bestiary down and began to pace. "There are a few things we know to be true about the realm. One, when a Charmer visits the beast realm, they will exit at the exact same point where they entered. In other words, we can't magically travel across this world by doing so in the realm. Two, the realm is massive. It's rare to spot another Charmer—unless that Charmer is one's *anam-cara* or related by blood."

He came to a full stop before me and waited. Thoughts clicked into place in my mind like cogs in a wheel, one by one. Adrenaline crawled slowly up my limbs, and my lips parted in disbelief. "I can reach my parents through the beast realm. But how, if they're not there?"

"It's a theory that's never been tested, but you have their bestiaries. You can travel to the realm and try to connect with their beasts. And one of them—"

"Can force their way out," I said, words tumbling out in excitement. I thought of all the times Dominus had opened the door on his own, how young Charmers just learning to hone their skills often lost control of their beasts entering and exiting the realm. How it happened with Calem and Effie, Oz and Jax.

"More than that, there's a chance you can follow them through the door when it opens," Gaige said.

"This"—Kaori struggled to find words—"is unheard of."

"Is it really possible?" Raven echoed, her words no more than a whisper.

"We won't know until we try," Gaige said. "I've never been able to verify the theory because Charmers so rarely remove their bestiaries, and only family members even have a chance of encountering each other or their beasts in the realm."

"How is this the first time we're hearing of this? As Council members?" Kaori asked.

Gaige lifted a shoulder and offered a weak smile. "Because I never told the Council? It's a family secret. Supposedly one of my ancestors performed the act to get back to their loved ones. It's an old story we were all told when we came of age and were sworn to protect it. Again, I haven't proven it, as the only 'family' I have left is you all here."

Power once again surged through me, and I channeled everything I had into my symbol. Rosewood light fractured around me as the sound of the beast realm door opening washed over us. "I'll test it right now. We can save my parents. We can save all the Charmers in Wilheim. They can even join us in our fight, assuming—"

"Wait." Noc gripped my arm and begged me to meet his pleading gaze. "We need to think this through."

Slowly, Gaige nodded. "He's right. I'm not saying we don't give this a shot. Otherwise I wouldn't have mentioned it. But we don't even know exactly where your parents are. What if you suddenly appear in the very throne room of Wilheim?"

My gaze flicked between them.

"I'm not saying don't go, don't try..." Noc let his hand fall away. "I would never rob you of that. But I'm asking you to take some time before you rush into this. Please."

Taking a deep breath, I considered his words. I wasn't just a

Charmer anymore—I was the Crown of the Council and soon-to-be queen of Lendria. My responsibility was first and foremost to my people. All of my people. If I raced off to rescue my parents, I would be putting myself in danger. All Noc was doing was looking out for my safety so I could continue to guide and protect others. We needed a plan, and then we could act. Calling back my power, I wrapped an arm around his waist and nodded.

"Okay, Noc."

He held me tight and placed a featherlight kiss on the crown of my head. "Thank you."

"Yazmin won't do anything rash right away—that would be counterproductive. She's baiting you, Leena." With that, Gaige let out a sigh that suggested he hadn't slept in days. "For now, I'd like to clean up and get some much-needed sleep. I suggest you do the same in case we do move forward with this tomorrow. Let's regroup in the morning."

"Works for me," Calem said through a stifling yawn.

"We'll need to meet with Isla, too, at some point about our joint strategy with Rhyne's forces." Noc rubbed the back of his neck, attempting to chase away the tightness that had gathered there. "There are a lot of moving parts."

"Sounds like we all need to be well rested, then." Kost abruptly made his way toward the exit. "See you in the morning." He walked out without another word.

If Gaige was flustered by Kost's sudden departure, he didn't show it. In fact, he already appeared half-asleep as he too mumbled a good night and left the library, Kaori, Raven, Calem, and Oz close behind him.

Pulling me tight against his chest, Noc wrapped me in another hug. There was nothing but love in his embrace, and I never wanted to jeopardize that. Nuzzling against him, I breathed in his honeyed scent and the last of my rattled nerves settled. I wasn't sure how much sleep I'd actually get, knowing my parents were out there, but at least he was by my side. We'd come up with a plan. We'd use my parents' bestiaries to sneak into Wilheim and rescue not only them, but all the captive Charmers.

TWENTY-NINE

LEENA

There were a few things to consider when it came to opening the beast realm door through my parents' bestiaries. First, we didn't even know if it was possible. Second, if it was, I'd still have to find their beasts, and that could take time. Time that would eat away at my power, making it more and more difficult for me to remain in the realm. Third, we didn't even know where the Charmers were. Yazmin had always insisted that Wilheim was behind the disappearance of our kind, but she wasn't exactly trustworthy. We'd seen her with the Sentinels and Darrien, but that didn't mean she hadn't discovered the Charmers on her own elsewhere. While it seemed unlikely, there was no telling until we actually traveled through the realm and exited the other side.

Which brought up a fourth sticking point that Noc couldn't get over: sound. The obvious, glaring truth that, whenever one of our beasts exited the realm, the sound of the door opening couldn't be muffled.

"If your parents are being held captive in Wilheim, presumably with guards, it will alert them to your presence immediately," he said for the fifth time, his hair practically standing on end from how often he'd shoved his fingers through it. "I don't want you walking into a trap."

After hours of back-and-forth, only Gaige, Kost, Noc, and I remained in my quarters within the keep. Originally, everyone from last night had gathered here for a light breakfast to discuss a strategy, but with no end in sight, the others had left to meet with Isla and check on our forces. Noc had made it a point to rise early and greet her, just in case our own private predicament took longer than anticipated. He couldn't be an absent king when our alliance with Rhyne was so new. Isla needed to believe he was as invested as his comrades, but I knew that one quick morning recap would only tide her over for so long.

"There's no way around it." Gaige sighed and reclined into his plush armchair. We were seated around a low coffee table littered with empty mugs and plates, the fire across from us on the verge of dying out. No one had moved to replenish the wood.

"I hate this." Noc let his head fall into his hands.

My heart was heavy as I glanced at my love. I hated to make him worry. But at the same time, this wasn't something I could walk away from. I had to get to my parents, one way or another.

"So come with me, then," I urged. I knew he had responsibilities here. He needed to be a more prominent leader with his men, to show Isla that Rhyne's alliance wasn't misplaced. Yet, in my very core I knew he wouldn't be himself if he thought I were in danger. He'd be distracted. Possibly reckless. And that wasn't the image we wanted to portray, either.

Gaige scraped his fingers along his trimmed beard as he tipped his chin upward. "It could work. Accessing their bestiaries and opening the door can only be done by you, but I don't recall any restrictions about who can actually pass through said door. Of course, no one has been daft enough to try."

"Why would that make me daft?" My brows knit together. "Noc has gone to the beast realm with me before."

"And exited with you the same way you entered." He leaned forward, bracing his forearms along his knees. "That's not unheard of. The problem is, this whole theory is simply that—a theory. We don't know what we're dealing with. What if you're able to slip through the door because you're their daughter, and Noc is left in the realm? No one has ever been trapped there before. We have no idea what could happen to him."

At that, Kost stilled. "You can't afford that risk."

The muscles racing along Noc's neck tensed. Slowly, he lifted his head. "But I should let her go alone?"

"You are the guild master of Cruor. The rightful king of Lendria. The person waging this gods-forsaken war. If you die or get stuck, what do you think would be the result?" Something sharp and fierce flashed through his eyes. "Forget about Rhyne's allegiance. Forget about Cruor. Forget about everything all together, because Varek will have gotten what he wanted, and Yazmin, too. She'll rain fire down on a land that has no means to protect itself. That's what will happen."

"But sacrificing the queen of Lendria is more justifiable?" Ice dripped from his words, and he clasped his hands together.

Kost didn't flinch. "No. I don't want Leena doing this either, but as she's the only one who can, I don't have a choice."

Tension snapped tight between them, and I slid closer to Noc on the couch we shared. Placing my hands over his, I rubbed a thumb along his bone-white knuckles. "Noc, he's right."

He didn't respond. Only glowered.

Kost sighed and removed his spectacles, pinning them between his forefinger and thumb. "Leena must go. But if she finds her parents there, and they do happen to be imprisoned in Wilheim's castle or nearby, she should leave them there for the time being."

"What?" My voice rose an octave. Now it was my turn to share the anger Noc felt. Kost had been right about him staying behind, but this was a step too far. "I'm not leaving them in some cell."

Kost replaced his lenses. "Only for a short while. I've been thinking on what...Gaige said last night." He didn't look at the Charmer seated across from him, but tripped over his name just the same. "If this theory proves true and they are being held in the capital, Yazmin has handed us an incredible advantage. A back door into enemy territory.

"And you should take someone with you now, so we can find out if it's possible for more to accompany you in the future." His green eyes hammered deep into my skull, and a tingling sensation rushed over my limbs. He was asking me to leave my parents in Wilheim's clutches because it would be advantageous for us in the coming war. We'd theoretically have a way to funnel at least a small, elite troop of fighters right into the castle. There was merit in his approach, and judging by the way he implored me to consider the idea with his weighted gaze, he knew it. He always knew it. But to leave my parents behind when they'd be within my reach? Could I even do that?

I glanced at Noc, but his anger had softened into something much worse—remorse. Agony. Distress. All of it plain as day on his face. He couldn't come with me. And he couldn't deny Kost's logic.

The world swam out of focus as my chest tightened. "And if Yazmin kills them before we can attack?"

At that, Kost averted his eyes. "It's a risk. War is full of them."

"Leena." Gaige's tone was soft. "We're running out of time." It was all he could muster, but it was enough to prove that he agreed with Kost. Toying with Okean's key around his neck, he looked away.

"This is a sacrifice I'm afraid you'll have to make. I don't envy you." Kost kept his voice low. Apologetic. I hated it. "Your parents, or the possibility to turn the tide of war? To save everyone else?"

"But saving them would add numbers to our forces. Yazmin wouldn't be able convince them to join her side," I tried, gaze frantically bouncing between Gaige, Kost, and Noc. None of them met my stare.

"We don't know how many there are," Kost finally said, "let alone what kind of state they're in."

"But what about Yazmin?" I grasped at any argument I could, hoping one would be sound enough for us to rescue my parents instead of leaving them behind. "If we rescue the Charmers, then she'll have no reason to raise Ocnolog. That's why she's doing this, right? We can show her that everyone is safe. We can avoid war altogether."

Gaige let out a shaky breath before raising his chin to look at me. "Leena. You don't believe that. You *can't*. Do you really think she'd stop now? After everything she's done?"

No. But I didn't want to say it out loud and give merit to his reasoning. Apparently, my silence was enough, though, and he shook his head.

"Yazmin has everything she needs to raise Ocnolog. The captive Charmers might be the reason she went down this path in the beginning, but they're not why she's still on it. Otherwise, she would've returned with them already."

"She wants to see the kingdom burn, Leena." Noc threaded his fingers with mine. "We need a way to stop her before that happens. If we can sneak into the castle without her or Varek knowing, then we have a chance to end this."

I wanted to take his logic and toss it out the window. Let it crash with the falls and be buried under the weight of the water. Wrapping my arms around my stomach, I stared at the floor and fought back tears. Why? Why did it have to come to this? One life shouldn't be more important than another. But if I picked saving my parents and the captive Charmers over my people—everyone who inhabited Lendria—that's exactly what I'd be doing. Placing value on their existence over an entire country full of innocent people. Only a ruler would ever face such a predicament.

"This is too hard," I said, my voice breaking.

Noc moved then, wrapping me in a hug and tucking my head against his chest. The collar of his tunic caught my tears as he ran a loving hand down my back. "I'm sorry."

I allowed myself one minute. One minute to hold Noc and pretend that I could just be Leena. That I was just a girl who only had a few people in her world to worry about—not the queen of Lendria or the Crown of the Council. Not someone forced to make impossible decisions that chafed no matter what direction I chose.

But once that minute was up, I pushed away from my love and straightened my back. Wiped away tears and set my chin high. I wouldn't let Yazmin win. I wouldn't let her break me. The only way to save my parents, and my people, was to push forward—regardless of how difficult the path before me was.

"Okay. I'll find one of my parents' beasts, have them open the door, and then we'll finally know where they are and what we're dealing with."

"And I'll go with you." Kost stood and brushed his hands along his vest. "Noc isn't expendable, but I am. And I can protect you with my life, if need be. Lendria won't go without her queen."

"Expendable," Gaige whispered in an indignant huff. "You're a prick, you know that?"

"It's my decision," Kost responded a little too forcefully. He shot Noc a quick look. "Assuming it's all right with you."

"None of this is all right with me." He clenched his jaw tight. "We can send someone else."

"There's a logical thought," Gaige muttered.

Kost barely deigned him a look before returning his attention to Noc. "And who would that be?"

Noc's answer was resolute. "We'll find a volunteer."

"*I'm* volunteering," Kost said. "I have knowledge of Wilheim. I have a connection with the beast realm, thanks to Felicks. Maybe that will help, maybe it won't, but I'm not sure it's a risk we should take."

Gaige tossed his hands to the ceiling as he stood. "This is ridiculous. Cruor can't afford to lose you. I..." He let his voice trail off, biting his lip and forming fists by his sides. "You're second-in-command. Your presence is needed here."

Kost didn't miss a beat. "As a Council member who just abandoned their duties for several days, I'm not sure you have grounds to argue that. We won't be gone for nearly as long."

"But you could die!" Gaige barked.

"And you couldn't have?" Kost rounded on him, anger finally cracking his collected facade. Tendons along his neck jumped as he spoke. "We had no way of knowing that you were okay. This isn't any different."

Tension crackled around them, neither of them willing to say anything more. Pushing off the couch, I stood between them and placed a gentle hand on their arms. "Take a breath. Both of you."

Staring at Gaige, Noc stood and let out a forceful sigh. "I don't like this any more than you do." His jaw tightened as he swallowed thickly. "I don't know what I would do if I lost either one of you. Let alone both of you."

The stiffness in Kost's frame finally deflated, and he gave Noc a long look. "I wouldn't suggest this if I didn't think it was absolutely necessary. We'll be careful. We *will* return."

Noc dropped his head into his hands. Several minutes passed, and then he dragged his fingers down his face. "If I'm going to ask you to make impossible decisions, I'll have to do the same."

"Well, now that *that's* sorted, I'll be off." Gaige practically kicked his chair into the wall as he moved toward the door. "Kaori asked to see me when we were done."

"Promise you won't disappear again?" I couldn't keep up with his erratic emotions, but his sudden show of displeasure worried me. Was this all it had taken for him to walk away before? I couldn't stand to leave with Kost—risk losing him—if it meant losing Gaige, too, in the process. We needed him. Not just Kost, but all of us. He'd become part of our family, and I'd already lost him once, thanks to Yazmin's attack. Twice, if we counted his disappearance. I wouldn't do it again. *Couldn't* do it again.

"Everyone seems to be forgetting that I found my way *back*." His steel-blue glare targeted Kost, who held Gaige's gaze for a moment before he lowered his head, hiding a grimace. Gaige studied him for what felt like ages before finally glancing my way. "But I'm not going anywhere. I look forward to your return."

With that, he stormed out the double doors of my room and into the halls of the keep. Stiff as a board, Kost ignored his exit, only allowing the smallest sounds of displeasure to slip between his pursed lips. Noc stood slowly, the entire weight of the world—and then some—on his shoulders.

Moving to my side, he pulled me into a tight hug, then angled my chin upward so he could slant his lips over mine. I never wanted to break that kiss. I had no idea what I'd be walking into. If I'd see him again. And no doubt he felt that way, too, because there was a hint of desperation in his embrace. Slowly, as if he couldn't bear to say goodbye, he pulled away. "Please, be safe."

"We will. I promise."

Reaching around me, Noc tugged Kost toward him and wrapped him in a hug. "Nothing happens to either of you. Understood?"

Emotion filled Kost's eyes, and he nodded into Noc's shoulder. "Understood."

After Noc released him, I extended my hand toward Kost as excitement and despair warred with each other in my mind. We were going to see my parents. My *parents*. But I'd have to leave them there. We didn't know if Kost would make it. We didn't know if I'd be walking right into a guard-filled prison. We knew so little, and yet I couldn't deny the tingling in my fingers.

"Shall we?"

"It's now or never." He took my hand, and I activated my power. The tree on the back of my hand bloomed to life, branches and vines racing up my forearm to wrap around my neck and frame my temple. As I wrenched open the beast realm door, the last thing I saw before the world was wiped away in a rosewood glow was the ice blue of Noc's desperate gaze.

THIRTY

NOC

T ime passed slowly as I made my rounds, visiting my brethren
and mingling with Rhyne's forces. Isla and her people were
formidable soldiers. They'd joined Oz's troops in training and
had little difficulty keeping up with his rigorous drills. Raven had
taken to instructing the Charmers with more basic directions, as
many of them had never held a blade before. When it came time to
fight, they'd still rely on their beasts, but it was better to be prepared
for anything—especially if they had to recall one of their creatures to
the realm to heal, leaving them open for an attack. But as pleased as
I was with everyone's progress, it wasn't enough to distract me from
Leena and Kost's absence.

Abandoning the lawns in favor of the courtyard outside the
keep, I made my way to one of the stone benches surrounding an
ornate fountain. An alabaster maiden poured sparkling water from
her vase into a shallow, circular pool at her feet. The shrubs and
flowers surrounding the structure were dormant, save one twig that
was already sprouting a leaf. Spring was almost upon us—and so
was the anniversary of Celeste's death. We needed to march the
moment Leena and Kost returned.

Footsteps sounded on the marble path leading to my seat, and

I glanced up to find Gaige approaching me. Okean, his legendary water feline, strolled beside him. His twitching, finned tail swished back and forth like a broom. It was nice to see that Gaige's transformation had only startled his beast initially. Now, Okean was as playful as ever. He rammed his head into Gaige's hip and let out a yowl, and Gaige responded by reaching down to scratch behind his ears.

"He seems happy," I said with a nod.

"Indeed." Gaige gave him a loving pat before the beast leapt into the fountain and began rolling around in the water. "He's keeping me distracted."

"I see." My fingers tapped restlessly against my thigh.

Gaige rubbed his jaw before sinking onto the bench beside me. "I'm sorry for my outburst. This is all very new."

"It's understandable. You've only been raised for a short while."

"Even so, the thought of them sneaking into Wilheim or being trapped in the realm..." His voice was thick with unspoken emotion. "I don't like it."

"Me neither, but it was the right thing to do." Or maybe it wasn't. Their reasoning for going was sound, and had it been anyone else, I would've agreed without hesitation. But this was too much. Regret wormed through my gut as I stared at the trickling fountain. Losing one of them was unimaginable. If I lost both... An errant shadow flared to life in my palm, and I let it flow between my fingers.

It simply wasn't an option.

Gaige watched me closely. "They won't be gone long."

I wasn't sure if he was saying it to convince himself or me, but his words didn't hold the conviction I needed to believe him. Standing, I silently commanded the shadow to disperse before pivoting toward Cruor's camp. "We should alert everyone to begin packing."

We'd never leave without Leena and Kost, but I needed

something to do. Something to keep my mind off all the horrible things that could be happening to my family. And a small, irrational part of me insisted that readying ourselves now would somehow make them appear that much faster.

"Yes, well..." Gaige's eyes slanted to the Kitska Forest, as if he were searching for something. "Before we set off, I should inform you I found—"

A plume of shadows exploded to life before us, and Emelia stepped out of the snarling mess of black tendrils. Wide-eyed, with a smile pulling tight at her lips, she practically bounced on her toes. "Kost's plan worked."

"What?" My heart stutter-stepped in my chest. They'd only just left. How? He couldn't have possibly succeeded that quickly. I'd hoped they'd be swift in their journey, but there was no way he'd seek out Emelia before me.

"Oh, right. He may not have told you, given all the craziness that's been going around." She couldn't help but glance at Gaige. "Before Kost met you in Rhyne, he stopped by Midnight Jester. Paid a bunch of travelers to visit Wilheim and spread rumor of your return.

"Apparently, it worked. Not as quickly as he'd have liked, but a troop of soldiers under the lead of one Sentinel arrived at Midnight Jester just this morning. They're here to see if Prince Aleksander lives. And if so, rally to his side."

I blinked. Of course Kost would put a plan like this into motion. A way to seed dissent without risking my life. I'd suggested somehow presenting myself to the people of Wilheim, but there was no possible way I would've survived. Simply spreading a rumor wasn't as powerful as showing my face, but clearly it resulted in at least one brigade joining our side. Assuming I could prove to them I was alive. A quick shadow walk to Midnight Jester would solve that problem.

"How do you know they're there?"

"Part of my and Iov's duty. We were told to shadow walk there every couple of hours until we marched, just in case forces showed up." She clasped her hands before her and rocked back on her heels. "I can go back now if you want me to. Let them know you're here."

"No. I'll go. I need you to find Oz and Calem. Tell them to break down camp and ready our forces." I did a quick sweep of the area, calculating how long it would take us to move out.

"Understood." Emelia tipped her chin to her chest and then took off in the direction of Cruor's camp.

Touching the key around his neck, Gaige sent Okean back to the beast realm. "If it's all right with you, I'd like to tag along. I have business near there I need to check in on."

I couldn't help but frown. "Business?" I'd always known that Gaige juggled a variety of contacts. The mage, whoever he connected with during trips to Wilheim... But I wasn't keen on any of his "business" interfering with our plans for war.

"I can explain after the meeting," he said as he stood. "Besides, what's the harm in having another ally by your side to present a strong front?"

I didn't have time to argue, and part of me wondered if he was looking for a way to keep his mind occupied. I was glad for the opportunity to act, to busy myself with our war efforts while Kost and Leena did the same. Relenting with a tight nod, I turned on my heels and strolled briskly through the courtyard in the direction of the keep. Gaige kept up easily, his long strides laced with shadows. He still wasn't in control. Not fully.

"Shadow walking is usually something more practiced assassins attempt. It isn't an easy feat."

His brows drew together. "I may have done it accidentally already. Imagine my fear, floating above my body and not knowing how to get back. I'd prefer to have someone with me for this next go-around so I can learn."

Accidentally? I cut him a glance. It'd certainly happened to others before, but his talents were developing at an astonishing rate. If he didn't learn to control them soon... I tracked an errant tendril that looped around his forearm and crawled down his fingers. He could end up swallowed whole. Permanently locked in the shadow world, unable to walk among his family and friends. In my life, I'd only seen one assassin fall prey to such a fate. He'd been on the verge of disappearing completely when Talmage slit the man's throat. It had been a kinder fate than an endless life all alone.

I hadn't forced anything on Gaige as the guild master of Cruor. Not yet. I wanted to give him time to adapt, and I wasn't sure how keen he'd be on suddenly deferring to me as his leader. But when this war was over, I'd force him to train. I would not let him be consumed by darkness.

For now, what little instruction I could give him about shadow walking might aid in his control. "Fine. But we don't have time to dally. If you don't get it after a try or two, I'll need to go on ahead to greet the Lendrian soldiers myself."

"I'm a fast learner," he said, and we quickly made our way into the quarters Leena and I shared. The room had been cleaned by attendants since our earlier meeting, and the polished coffee table was bare of empty mugs and plates. Gesturing to the upholstered couch, I waited for Gaige to lie down.

"I'll walk you through projecting your spirit. If we succeed, you'll just have to wait a moment while I do the same. Then, we'll travel to Midnight Jester together."

"Right." He adjusted a throw pillow beneath his head before settling his hands on his stomach. "Ready when you are."

"Close your eyes." I watched as he obliged, letting out a quiet sigh. "First, I want you to flex your muscles, then let them relax completely. Allow them to melt into the cushions and focus on taking slow, deep breaths."

His body went rigid, then sagged into the couch. Measured, weighted breaths slipped from his parted lips, and the rise and fall of his chest slowed to a point where it was almost imperceptible. Minutes passed and I simply let him be. Let him soak in the rest he so desperately needed. But if I didn't interrupt him soon, he was more likely to fall into slumber than project his consciousness.

Pitching my tone low, so as not to disturb his peaceful state, I continued. "I want you to think about your right hand. Picture how it looks, how it feels to control. Think about curling and uncurling your fingers, but don't physically move them. Let your mind take over."

He didn't move, but shadows began to pool beneath him on the floor. They licked at his hand and beckoned his consciousness to grab hold.

"Feel for the shadows. Embrace them, and then allow yourself to detach completely. Don't be afraid."

I'd been afraid the first time I'd separated from my body. The shadows had raced over me in a way I'd never experienced before. It was like losing control completely, feeling their icy kiss against my very soul instead of my skin.

A whoosh of shadows rushed over Gaige, and then suddenly he was there, a wispy projection of himself. I hid my amazement—and my worry—behind a stoic face. He'd grasped the notion so *quickly*. Yes, he'd mentioned doing it accidentally before, but to successfully project himself without a single hiccup... Gaige blinked, then turned his gaze to his unconscious body. A smile tugged at his lips.

"This is amazing." His frame wavered with his words, and I nodded.

"Don't move. I'll only be a moment."

Crossing the room to the bed, I lay down and closed my eyes. Repeating the same instructions I'd given Gaige in my mind, I welcomed the rake of cold shadows along my consciousness. A moment later, I'd pushed myself out of my physical body and was standing before him.

"Now, traveling." I rolled my neck from side to side more out of habit than need. There wasn't much tautness to be felt in my shadow form, just the ever-present sensation of cold. "Picture Midnight Jester in your mind's eye. Focus on the concrete details of the exterior and will your mind to go there. There's no way for me to hold on to you and drag you with me. You have to do this on your own."

A flicker of uncertainty passed through his gaze. "If I get lost?"

"Don't." I pressed my lips into a fine line. "You'll return to your body eventually, but I won't know where you went and won't be able to help you."

"Well, here goes nothing, then." He closed his eyes again, and an invisible wind gusted through the space between us. One moment his projection was standing beside me, and then next it was gone. Completely wiped from existence.

Clenching my jaw, I took off after him. I pictured myself flying through the keep, across the open lawns and deep into the Kitska Forest before finally reaching the quiet establishment known as Midnight Jester. The black market tavern was the same as always. Shuttered windows closed tight against the winter air. A sturdy door with an iron knob just waiting to be opened. A few dormant shrubs near the cobblestone path. Muffled conversations slipped through the cracks, and I caught wind of a more reserved, authoritative voice than those who typically trafficked at the tavern. Likely the Sentinel Emelia had alluded to.

I took a few steps to the side of the building and froze in my tracks. A small group of soldiers—maybe fifty or so strong—loitered around a handful of campfires, their belongings still unpacked. They hadn't set up camp just yet, likely waiting to confirm my existence before fully committing to our cause. I scoured every face from a safe distance out of sight, hoping to find some familiarity among those loyal to me. But it'd been so long since I'd been the leader of a Lendrian army, and while some likely were the sons or daughters of people I had fought with, I couldn't tell at first glance.

Just then, a whirl of shadows announced Gaige's arrival, and the sliver of worry that had been eating away at my insides disappeared. He'd made it.

"That's a reassuring sight," he mused.

"Indeed. There's a Sentinel inside. Let's start there." Turning away from the group, I made my way toward Midnight Jester and floated through the door. There was no sense in pretending to open it when I couldn't grip the knob, anyway. Gaige did the same, and we came to a halt once inside. A few patrons startled at our appearance, but most who frequented the tavern knew of Cruor and our tendency to walk with the shadows. The circular, rickety tables were near full, thanks in large part to the handful of lucky soldiers who'd managed to bargain their way inside with their captain instead of lingering by a campfire.

"I suppose I have you to thank for this uptick in business." A gruff voice rose above the din of conversation, and I turned my head toward the bar. Dez, the bartender, leaned against the countertop on his forearms, a damp rag in one hand. There was no malice in his greeting, but I couldn't overlook the stiffness of his shoulders. The muscles coiled tight in his neck.

"Possibly," I said, my cool response garnering a rush of whispers from the closest tables. "Though it wasn't entirely expected on my part."

Dez tilted his head toward Gaige. Frowned. "Last I remembered, you were alive."

Gaige lifted a shoulder in feigned nonchalance. "Things change."

"Things change for Leena, too?" His question was too harsh. Too demanding. I fought back the urge to snap at him. Leena wouldn't want that.

"She's still very much alive, but that's not why we're here." I jerked my chin toward the tables. "I'm looking for the Sentinel in charge of these soldiers."

"What, don't recognize me without my armor?" a woman drawled, swinging around on her barstool so she could face me instead of Dez. Her brown eyes sparked with a familiar mixture of frustration and fondness—like a parent who couldn't help but love their rambunctious child, even after a severe scolding. She ran a broad hand through her cropped blond hair. My breath came up short. *Madeline.* Whispers of wrinkles framed her eyes, but I'd recognize that gaze anywhere.

She'd been one of the three Sentinels assigned to me when I'd turned myself over to Rhyne all those years ago. More than that, she'd been a constant in my life. A nagging presence I'd resented. A stand-in mother on the battlefield and a constant source of reprimand. She'd aged gracefully, thanks to the magic Mavis's blood had bestowed on all the people of Wilheim. And I couldn't have been happier that she'd turned up here.

"Madeline." I closed the distance between us, Gaige on my heels. "You're alive."

She raised a brow. "Any reason I shouldn't be?"

"No, it's just been years and—"

"I'll let Death know when I'm ready for him." She took a long swig from her ale, then pushed her empty mug to Dez. He sauntered away to fill it. "Though I half expected your father to end my life when I came back with the news of your untimely end."

I flinched. "Sorry about that."

Her eyes narrowed. "Do you have any idea how long I searched for you? I spent years cursing myself for not following you that night." She never broke her gaze as she accepted her refilled ale from Dez and took a hefty swig. "I swore that if there was ever even a rumor of your existence, I'd root out the truth. It was my job to protect you, and I failed."

"You didn't fail." The shadows around my form wavered with a gust of wind as someone exited the tavern. "What happened was my fault—no one else's. Besides, I did die."

"I see that." She studied my appearance, and the sternness in her expression faded. "Never thought I'd see you again. But then one night I'm having drinks with my men, and this traveler comes into the tavern whispering about you. About how you're a powerful, undead assassin who's been blessed by the gods to retake the throne. Not only that, but you've somehow done what no leader has before—allied yourself with Charmers.

"At first, I paid him no mind. It was a ludicrous tale." She took another long drink before setting her mug down and leaning toward me. "But then I remembered that time the city went on full alert when a dark-haired, black-eyed assassin slipped through our gates. I thought it was strange how Varek reacted."

I recalled that fateful day when I'd brought Leena, Ozias, and Kost to Wilheim. We'd hoped a beast just beyond the city's limits could lift Cruor's Oath, but we'd been led on a fool's errand by Yazmin herself. "That was me. My appearance had been masked because, at that time, I had no intentions of reclaiming the throne."

She nodded once. "The king has been on high alert ever since then. Ratifying forces, bolstering our defenses... He's expecting a war. I figured I owed it to your parents to find out exactly who I was supposed to be fighting."

"And now?" I asked, my voice no more than a whisper. In my peripheral vision, I saw Gaige stiffen. I hadn't thought about the possibility of a Sentinel coming here under Varek's orders to gain insight on my whereabouts. Madeline couldn't hurt us in this form—and we couldn't harm her—but she'd be able to take her forces and retreat before I could dream of moving my men here to stop her.

"Now..." She gave me a long look. "I intend to uphold my promise and protect the prince—or in this case, the king—of Wilheim."

A sudden lightness raced through my fingers, and a slow smile spread across my lips. "That's good to hear."

"King, huh?" Dez asked, palms flat against the bar. He'd barely moved since I'd entered his tavern, save to refill Madeline's drink. Despite this newfound knowledge, he scowled with the same apprehensive look, and I couldn't help but respect him for that.

Gaige let out a light chuckle. "Surprising turn of events, isn't it?"

"Doesn't change how I feel about him in my tavern, that's for sure." He shook his head, then sighed. "Speaking of, should I be expecting more soldiers on my lawns? They ain't exactly great for business."

Standing, Madeline fished a handful of bits out her coat pocket and thrust them on the counter. "I doubt it. The others don't believe the rumors and aren't willing to face treason if they're caught investigating."

"Unfortunate, but expected." I gripped the back of my neck, then nodded toward the door. "I caught a glimpse of your brigade before I entered. My forces are about a two days' march away. We'll join you as soon as we can."

"So there is to be a war?" Her brows crawled to her hairline.

"Yes. I'll fill you in on the details, but we have several hundred men from Rhyne, the Charmers, and Cruor assassins on our side." We reached the door and she pushed it open, the aging hinges creaking loudly. Gaige and Madeline exited first, and I paused to glance back at Dez.

Everything good in my life started right here, even if I hadn't known it at the time. If not for Midnight Jester and Dez, there was a chance Leena and I would never have crossed paths. At one point, this place had been home to her, too. She'd want to protect it at all costs.

"Dez."

"Yeah?"

"I'll make sure these soldiers don't bother you or your patrons." I gestured to the tavern before slipping my hands into the pockets of my trousers. "And when this is all over, Midnight Jester will continue to run as usual."

He barked out a laugh. "Are you saying that as the king of Lendria, or as the guild master of Cruor who used to rely on my services?"

I couldn't help but smile at that. Two parts of my life so very much at odds with one another, and yet I knew in my core I'd always turn a blind eye to this place, so long as nothing too egregious occurred. If not for me, then for Leena.

"Both, I guess. Thanks, Dez. For everything."

He snorted and averted his gaze, glancing instead at the rafters. "You've got nothing to thank me for. I run a tavern. That's all."

"Yes, well..." I tipped my chin in a bow just the same. "We'll be back."

"Yeah, yeah." He gave a flippant wave and then turned his back on me. I slipped through the door and joined Gaige and Madeline on the other side. She was curiously eyeing one of Gaige's errant shadows as he detailed the nature of our existence to her.

"So our corporeal bodies are back in Hireath. When we return with our forces, we'll be very much in the flesh."

"I see." She poked a shadow. "Can you feel that?"

"No, but it is distracting." He took a step back and then caught my eye. "Ah, Noc. Shall we?"

"Let's."

Madeline straightened and wiped all traces of interest from her expression. Stoic and reserved, she transformed into the Sentinel I'd always known and walked with purposeful, lengthy strides toward her troops. The authority she commanded was palpable, and there wasn't a single person who didn't stand at attention when she passed. When we reached the nearest campfire, she barked orders to set up camp, and everyone flew into motion.

"I only have fifty or so soldiers, but one of mine counts for five of any other brigade. That I can guarantee." She folded her arms across her chest and watched as tents went up without hesitation.

"We appreciate the support, no matter—"

A lonely, grating howl erupted from the depths of the Kitska Forest, and several of Madeline's soldiers flinched. Even I cut a glance to the jagged treetops. Being that Cruor was nestled within this cursed wood, I'd grown used to the errant calls of monsters throughout the years. But this one was hauntingly close. It reminded me of the time Yazmin had used a monster to distract us from an ambush and Gaige had paid the ultimate price. I couldn't let that happen again. We couldn't afford to lose any more people before the war even started.

"Are those calls fairly common around here? They've got us all on edge." Madeline flattened her lips as she too scoured the dense wood.

"You have nothing to fear," Gaige said, voice surprisingly calm. I expected him, out of everyone, to be more concerned about the danger such beasts posed. "They won't harm you."

I narrowed my eyes. "How can you be so sure?"

He pulled at the collar of his tunic, despite the fact I knew he couldn't feel it chafing against his neck. Not in this state. "Because I'll tell them not to."

Madeline blinked slowly. "Is that another power of the undead? Controlling monsters?"

"No. Care to explain?" I asked.

"I'll show you on our way back to Hireath," he said.

Madeline rubbed her chin as she glanced between us. "Well, I won't keep you two from that. I have enough proof of your existence, Noc, to take up arms against Varek. We'll await your return."

Setting aside my frustration with Gaige, I turned to Madeline. "Thank you. Your support means more than you could ever know. We'll return quickly, I promise."

"See you then." She hoisted the nearest crate full of supplies and joined her soldiers to set up camp. Slowly, I dragged my gaze back to Gaige. He twisted the key about his neck, flashed me a quick look, and then started toward the darkened wood.

"Follow me."

With that, I took off after him, and we sped through the trees in search of the haunting, bloodcurdling calls we usually avoided at all costs.

THIRTY-ONE

LEENA

I didn't know how long I'd been in the beast realm, just that my power was waning, and a cool sweat had started to dampen my hairline. Kost had been dutifully silent while I'd sat cross-legged on the ground, eyes half-closed as I held my parents' bestiaries in my open palms. Seeing other beasts in the realm was rare, but as I focused on my well of power, allowing light to bloom around me, I hoped the bestiaries and my magic would lure my parents' creatures to me. My beasts had arrived almost immediately—they'd abandoned their homes and rushed to the open plains where I rested. The forest was alive with their calls, birds dancing along the branches and creatures of all kinds weaving around trunks. Even those who preferred the mountains or remote dunes had come, and they'd stayed with me for support.

But as the minutes ticked by, my doubt grew. If I couldn't lure them out, what was I supposed to do? Wandering the great realm wouldn't do me any favors. I'd figured simply staying put—making my location steady and known—would make it easier for my parents' beasts to track me down. I'd even asked my creatures to spread the word, a lesson Wynn had taught once. Beasts talk, he'd said. And no one knew the realm better than them. A few had disappeared after I'd whispered my task into their ears, but none had returned. Nothing had happened, really.

Tipping my head upward, I stared at the puffy clouds dotting the clear blue sky. Onyx, Dominus, and Reine lingered a few feet away, each of them stretched out with their bellies turned toward the sun. A cool breeze ruffled the tall grass, and Reine sneezed. They were utterly at peace. And as much as their presence soothed me, they couldn't slow the drain of my power.

"Your mark is receding," Kost said quietly, the first words he'd uttered since I'd shared my plan with him and sunk to the ground. He lingered beneath the shade of a willow tree with Felicks at his feet. His own beast seemed largely unconcerned with our presence and, like my legendary felines, had opted for a nap.

I let out a huff. "I know." Poof, my Groober, inched closer to my thigh. His soft, pink fur was soothing to the touch and had helped to keep me grounded, but I'd been careful to avoid his ears. The last thing I wanted was to accidentally scratch them and perfume the air with valerian and lavender. I'd only end up drifting off to sleep in the realm and possibly miss my parents' beasts entirely.

Kost picked a stray piece of lint off his ebony vest and flicked it away. "Can I help somehow?"

"No. Not unless Felicks has shared something insightful with you that I'm unaware of."

"No." He gazed at the amethyst orb atop his beast's head. Now, it was clear and free of smoke. When a new future was brewing, it would cloud and Kost could tap into what his beast saw every two minutes. But, since Felicks had fallen asleep, the orb nestled between his ears had stayed woefully clear. No telling the future when he wasn't awake to view the events unfold.

"At this rate, I'm worried that even if we do find my parents' beasts, I won't have the energy to get us home." I held my arm out before me and studied the network of rosewood vines and leaves visible through my white, long-sleeved blouse. Between that and my skintight breeches, I'd opted for comfort in case we ran into trouble and needed to move quickly once in Wilheim. But now, I wasn't even sure we'd make it there.

"How much longer can you hold out?" Kost asked.

"I can't say for sure... Maybe an hour?" I curled my fingers around my parents' bestiaries. I didn't think it would take much energy to follow one of their creatures through an open door into our world, but I'd still have to summon my Telesávra once there so we could quickly and safely return to Hireath.

"I see." Kost frowned. Bending down, he smoothed Felicks's fur. His grim expression worried me more than I cared to admit. We'd moved so quickly in order to take advantage of the gift Yazmin had unknowingly given us. But what if we hadn't worked out all the details quite right? What if Kost ended up stuck here? From the moment I'd awoken, I'd pushed Noc to make this happen. Maybe I pushed too soon, too hard.

I chewed on the inside of my cheek. We could call it. Go back to Hireath and try again once we knew more. Dousing my lure, I made a move to stand when the blades of grass before my feet shifted. Fable, my Gyss, appeared. Her mossy hair fell over her shoulder, draping across her leaf dress, and she pushed it aside to offer me a wide, mischievous smile full of sharpened teeth.

"Fable. Did you find anything?" I spoke aloud for Kost's benefit rather than pushing my thoughts to her. He straightened and left his spot in the shade, coming to my side and crouching before Fable.

She placed her hands on her hips, and the wisp of smoke where her legs would've been shifted with the motion. *See for yourself.* She jerked her head over her shoulder, and my gaze roved to the thicket of trees bordering the plains.

At first, I didn't see anything—just the swaying leaves dancing in the faint breeze. But then something shimmery appeared, like a haze over a desert horizon, followed by a lengthy arm that solidified in shape and color. A slender, near-invisible beast that didn't belong to me emerged from the shade of the forest, and a grin split my face.

"An Iksass." One of my parents had tamed the same creature as me. Unfurling my fingers, I thumbed the bestiaries' spines and jolted at the sudden spark of warmth that flared to life when I grazed my father's name.

I told him what you were trying to do, and he followed me here. The rest is up to you. Fable dusted her hands before her, clearly proud of herself for finding my father's beast.

Excitement swelled in my chest, and I brought my attention to her. With a gentle finger, I poked her belly. "Thank you, Fable."

She giggled in response, lovingly pushing my touch aside before waving me off. *Don't get caught.* Parting through blades of grass, she headed for the forest.

Kost stood and I followed suit, taking a careful step toward the Iksass. "Hey, there. I'm Leena, Verlin's daughter."

The beast inched closer. With a tender limb, he pushed aside a lock of hair covering the mark that had crawled up my neck. Soon, it would disappear down my shoulder and retreat back to my hand. We didn't have much time and connecting with this beast was likely my only chance at seeing my parents. The Iksass's watery scent teased my nose as I held still. I wasn't exactly afraid, but I didn't want to spook him, either. The memory of my father was so faint, so distant, that I had no other way to reassure this creature that I was, in fact, Verlin's daughter. I also had no idea when my father had tamed an Iksass. Had this beast been around when I was a child? Did he recognize me? I couldn't say for sure, but when he let his arm fall away, a strange, almost reassuring sigh scraped through the air.

"It's been a while since you've seen him, hasn't it?" I asked.

The beast nodded.

"Can you take us to him? Force your way out of the beast realm?" Calling on my power once again, I allowed my lure to bloom around me. I wanted my father's Iksass to trust me, to feel the light and love I was offering and know that I'd never harm him.

He hesitated and then reached forward to nudge my father's bestiary.

"He's in trouble." My voice broke, and I squirmed my eyes shut for a breath. "I know it's not normal to do something like this. But I promise I'm not trying to deceive you. I *am* Verlin's daughter, and I have to get to him." His beasts never would've thought to try this without my aid. Only newly tamed beasts or those with new masters occasionally forced their way out of the realm, and so his Iksass—along with all his other beasts—would've continued to live peacefully here.

Tilting his head to the side, he studied me silently. Each second that passed felt like a decade.

Please. Please believe me.

Finally, he pressed my fingers firmly against my parent's bestiaries and let out a soft, reassuring moan. Tears welled at the back of my eyes as relief surged through me.

"Thank you," I said, calling back my power and tucking the pendants into my pocket.

Raising a single arm, he wrapped his tentacle-like appendage around what appeared to be an invisible doorknob. His muscles locked tight, and he gave it a forceful yank. A loud, grating whine rolled over us, and I cringed. It was so drastically different than what I typically heard when summoning my beasts, as if the hinges were in need of a good oiling.

So many years of disuse. My stomach dropped as I watched my father's Iksass struggle to wrench open the door. It fought him every inch of the way, but there was a sliver of blinding light that had appeared. A slice of the other world peeking through to the realm. A few more tugs, and it'd be large enough for us to pass through with this beast's help.

The Iksass gave one last heave, and the door sighed as it finally gave way. He let go of the doorknob and extended his limb toward me. An invitation to join him as he forced his way through.

"Are you ready?" I reached for Kost. He stared at my open hand, expression tight. We had no idea what would happen. If he'd be able to follow me through or if he'd be stuck here. And if he got stuck, what that would mean. Would we be able to find him? Or would he simply disappear? Kost never shied away from difficult decisions, even ones that put him in harm's way, but as his hands fidgeted over his tunic—pausing for a brief moment to rub the space above his heart—I couldn't help but wonder if he'd maybe acted too rashly when it came to this one.

"Leena... Tell him I'm sorry."

Gaige. Kost refused to look at me, but I could hear the remorse in his weighted words. The guilt.

"Tell him yourself."

Finally, he took my hand and gripped it tight. Nodded. "Let's go."

Forming a chain, we followed my father's beast toward the column of light...and stepped right into it. Entering the beast realm through normal methods was actually quite peaceful. It was almost like a warm embrace, and then my feet would gently touch down in the realm as the light faded away.

This was nothing like that.

This was as if the bones in my diaphragm were fracturing, splintering into my lungs and making it impossible to breathe. Fire raked over my skin as we hurled through space, and I grasped Kost's hand for dear life. I could still feel his fingers, see his white-knuckle grip. But his tortured expression shook me to my core.

I'd never seen Kost in agony before. Not like this.

His eyes had rolled to the back of his head, and his entire body was impossibly taut. If he jerked too quickly, if we came to an abrupt halt, I feared his muscles would snap and his bones would shatter.

Mustering every ounce of strength I could, I squeezed his hand.

His fingers barely pressed into my wrist in response.

Shit. Panic spiraled in me, warring with the nausea brewing in my stomach. The world around us spun uncontrollably, and my neck cried out in pain as I craned my head toward my father's beast. Fortunately, his experience seemed far less excruciating. He was *meant* to go through this tunnel, whereas Kost and I were not. Every second we spent moving toward Lendria felt like an eternity, and the pain in my chest only increased in severity until I was certain my lungs would collapse.

Kost's fingers went slack in my grip, and I dug my nails into his skin. His head had lolled to the side, unconscious, and the harrowing vortex seemed to tug him in the opposite direction.

No. I gritted my teeth and then let out a wordless scream.

I would not let him go. I'd *never* let him go.

Power surged from deep within me as my Charmer's emblem ignited in a rosewood light. With a sudden sense of renewed strength, I yanked Kost closer to me. My magic battled against the surrounding tunnel, somehow alleviating a sliver of my pain and chasing away the breathlessness in my chest. Beside me, Kost twitched.

Almost. I pushed more power outward, blanketing us in a protective shield of light and warmth. *Almost.*

I was being wrung out like a rag, and my power was being drained away faster than I could hold on to it. Just when I thought the vines on my forearm would recede completely, the tunnel opened up and we slammed into packed earth and stone. Stumbling against what felt like a cavern wall, my knees shook as the world swam out of focus. A pale-green light ate away at the dark splotches, and after a moment, my vision returned.

"Kost," I croaked. He'd fallen in a heap on the ground, and I rushed toward him. With shaky hands, I hoisted his back against the wall and then gripped his tunic, giving it a forceful shake. "Kost."

His eyes fluttered open. "Leena."

"Oh, thank the gods." I slumped before him, hands still entrenched in his shirt.

Wincing, he let out a pained exhale. "That was...unpleasant."

"That's an understatement. I was afraid I'd lose you." I finally released my grip on him. The scent of mulch and soil hit the back of my tongue as I steadied myself with a deep breath.

"And your father's beast?"

The Iksass had crouched beside us, completely unharmed. I gave his arm a gentle pat. "He's fine."

"Good." Kost adjusted his glasses and looked over my shoulder. His body went rigid.

"What's wrong? Are you hurt?"

"No. Look." His nod was sharp. Definitive.

I turned, unease stirring in my gut, and froze. There, lined along the cavern wall, was a row of bodies draped in stark-white linens. Bile crept up my throat as a heady ringing crashed through my ears. Not one of them moved. Tree roots dripped from the ceiling and attached to their heads. A strange, pulsating light traveled through each tendril, illuminating the veins along the Charmers' faces and necks. My father's beast crossed the room to stand before a cot at the end and let out a heartbreaking groan.

"Dad." I rushed to his side. At first, I couldn't bring myself to look at his face. What if I didn't recognize him? What if I *did*? The guilt of realizing he'd been alive all this time and I'd done nothing to seek him out... Something cleaved my heart in two. Tears burned the back of my eyes, and my breathing ratcheted several notches. If I'd known... Swallowing the rock in my throat, I held back a sob. It didn't matter. The only thing that was important now was finding a way to save him and my mother. Wrapping my fingers around his lifeless hand, I forced my gaze upward.

Charcoal-black hair curled around his oval face, and thick lashes lined his closed eyes. A light smattering of freckles dusted across the bridge of his long nose, and slow, even breaths slipped through his parted lips. With shaky fingers, I grazed his cheek. Memories I hadn't even known existed rushed over me. Him chasing me across the bridges of Hireath, shouting playfully while also urging me to be careful. Late-night treats he'd sneak with me on the back porch while we looked at the stars. A soothing song he'd sing to distract me as he'd cleaned up minor scrapes and bumps on my knees.

My chest heaved, and a hot tear escaped down my cheek. I'd buried so *much*. Everything, really. The pain of losing him and my mother at the same time had been too great, and I'd ignored those emotions, kept them locked away in a chest, because that was the only way I knew how to cope. I was too young to do anything else. And as the years had passed and life grew more complicated, the memory of my father had faded. I swallowed thickly as I studied his face. At least he seemed peaceful, though his head was angled toward the cot behind me.

Without letting go, I looked over my shoulder and gasped.

Mother. She was stunning, even in her slumbering state. Walnut-colored hair, smooth skin. We shared the same, angular cheekbones and full lips. There wasn't a doubt in my mind that I was her daughter, and my heart thundered in my ears. It was almost too painful to look at her. Seeing her had the same effect as my father, and the memories came swift and hard. My whole body was trembling by the time my hand found hers, and I let out a wordless sob.

"Leena." Kost's voice was soft. He'd moved to the other side of my mother's cot and was holding several sheets of parchment. His eyes flew over the page as he read. "She was attacked by a Revmandra and brought here for treatment. But..." He frowned. Paled. And then tossed the parchment to the floor, as if he couldn't get the damned paper out of his hands fast enough. "They were tricked. They were supposed to be released once they were healed, but have been placed in some sort of coma-like state for testing. The king himself signed off on it."

Slowly, I bent down and picked up the parchment. With every word I devoured, heat crested inside me. Varek's notes about my parents, about these wonderful, caring people, were so...inhuman. Dry. Despicable.

"*Vessels for magic, nothing more. Continue testing and...*" My throat burned as I forced myself to read aloud. To acknowledge the true breadth of his wickedness. Swallowing, I tried again. "*And terminate once powers are successfully extracted.*"

My vision blurred, and I let the parchment fall to the floor again. Kost let out a rare curse. "I would've never expected this."

"We have to get them out." I spun toward the cavern wall, eyeing the tendrils that had rooted into their scalps.

Kost flinched. "Yes, but—"

"I know I said we'd wait, Kost." I moved toward the crown of pulsing vines lining my mother's forehead. "But I can't leave them. Not like this. Not when he plans to kill them."

"Leena—"

I didn't give him a chance to sway me. With one quick tug, I yanked the roots away from my mom. The foreign, pale-green light receded, and my mother started to shake. Not a light tremble. Not a quiver of her hand. But uncontrollable, full-body shudders. Her eyes raced beneath her closed lids, and her breathing turned erratic. Frantic.

"Leena! Put the roots back." Kost rushed to the cavern wall and reached for the tree, yanking the tendrils toward my mother's head. I'd frozen entirely, my hands like statues above her face. He pushed me aside, breaking my trance, and reattached the roots. The rhythmic, glowing light returned, and my mother's convulsions stopped. Slowly, she fell back into a calm, sedated state.

"What the hell?" I whispered.

"I don't know." He clenched his jaw tight. "But until we figure out how to safely wake them, we must leave them here."

Tears lined my eyes. I couldn't leave them here. I *couldn't*. And yet, I had to. What's worse, Yazmin had been right. Wilheim had been capturing us. Testing our abilities for their own gain. Did that mean she was right about everything? About raising Ocnolog and setting the world on fire? The room turned. I was supposed to be the queen of Lendria. The queen of...*this*. My throat closed, and I took several steps back. I had to get out. I had to run and fight and... Anger replaced panic, and everything steadied. A strange calm soothed my frayed nerves, and a drive like I'd never experienced before settled deep in my bones.

I had to kill Varek.

I glanced around the room until I spotted a staircase and stormed off, Kost and my father's beast a breath behind me.

"Where are you going?" Kost whisper-yelled as he tried to grip my arm.

I shook him off and ascended quickly. "To find Varek."

"And do what?" The narrowness of the dark stairwell forced him behind me, and I didn't slow. I would've vaulted up the stairs if the light hadn't diminished to something dim and near impossible to see through. Nothing else mattered except getting out of this hell-hole. I didn't give a damn what I was about to walk out into. Varek would answer for this. They all would.

"Make him pay."

"Leena, listen to yourself. You sound like Yazmin," he tried. "Think about what you're doing. I know you're upset, but doing something like this won't help anyone. Not even your parents."

I whirled in place, towering over him from the step above. "I'm supposed to just let that injustice go? Forget what I saw? Yazmin was right." I exhaled sharply and formed fists by my side. "Maybe she was right about everything."

"No. Never." Kost gripped my arms tight. "We all want revenge for something. We've all lost *something* to this war already. If we rush out there now with no plan, we'll be ripping away everyone else's chance at justice. Noc's. Raven's... Gaige's."

The riddling anger I felt stalled. *Gaige.* Eilan. Countless others. So many had already died for this. The heat in my palms trickled away, and my shoulders drooped. As much as I wanted to find Varek and make him pay, immediately, Kost was right. I didn't want him to be. Gods knew I wanted to storm up those stairs and end this war right here and now. Especially if we were lucky enough to find ourselves in Wilheim's castle. But if that were the case, then we'd no doubt find ourselves face to face with Sentinels, Darrien's assassins, and Yazmin. As alluring as the idea was, it was just as futile.

Grinding my teeth together, I slumped against the cavern wall. "So, what now?"

"Now we go back to Hireath. Regroup." Gently, he released his hold on me. "We need a plan."

Rather than speak, I answered with a small nod.

"We'll come back, Leena. I promise." Kost opened his mouth

as if to add something further, but heavy footsteps slammed into the earth above us, cutting him short. A faint layer of dirt dusted the top of our heads. We both fell silent and craned our necks upward. Apparently, we'd climbed up quickly enough to near the exit, though the bend before us obscured any potential door. Muffled sounds like conversation drifted our way, but it was impossible to make out what was being said. At least for me.

Kost's eyes widened, and he mouthed one word. *Yazmin.* He wrapped us in a cocoon of shadows as an added layer of protection. The muddy-brown walls and earth tones shifted to dark charcoals and ebony tendrils. My father's Iksass remained outside the shadow realm, but disappeared entirely to protect himself from the threat above. Only when Kost was satisfied with our now-masked presence did he dare to whisper.

"She's speaking with a guard." All the muscles in his neck strained, and he tilted his ear toward the ceiling. "He's calling her away."

Between the shadows and our underground position, I heard nothing, save the heady beat of my heart in my ears. Minutes ticked by as we waited in silence. Tightness swelled in my chest, and I wrapped my fingers in the chain of my bestiary. Try as I might, I couldn't siphon any warmth from the beast realm. Couldn't soothe my amped-up nerves with a tingle of power. While I was hidden away in the shadow realm, my beasts were definitively out of reach.

Finally, Kost let his shadows recede. "She's gone."

Peering around the bend in the staircase, I eyed what appeared to be a dead-end covered in gnarled tree roots. "Let's see where this leads, and then we'll leave. Before anyone notices we're here."

Kost's brows furrowed as he contemplated my plan. When he didn't outright decline, I kept going. "We need some sort of idea of where we are so we can be better prepared when we return. For all we know, we might not even be in the castle. This could be a crypt outside the gates. Or even somewhere further away, and that would do us no good if we want to use it as a back door later."

He relented with a sigh. "Fine, but summon your Telesávra first. We need to be ready to escape at a moment's notice."

Splaying out my hand, I opened the beast realm door and called forth my Telesávra. The dense earth muffled the signature groaning of hinges, but I still held my breath, ears straining for potential footsteps thudding against the earth over our heads. A minute dragged by. Nothing. Letting out a tight exhale, I reached down and patted my Telesávra's head before signaling him to stay close to my side. Then, I inched forward, Kost a shadow behind me. And while I could no longer see my father's Iksass, the beast let out a quiet grunt, signifying he was still bringing up the rear.

Gently, I stroked the nearest tree root. A quiet creaking filled the space around us as it retracted into the dirt. And then another one followed, until all the roots were moving to reveal an open hole above us where daylight streamed through.

Gripping the densely packed earth, I poked my head up just enough to catch a glimpse of the massive room. It was strangely beautiful and serene, with nothing more than the tree above us stretching toward an opening in the castle ceiling. But the quiet splendor of the room was lost on me the moment I spied four Sentinels stationed on the far side of the room near the exit. With their backs turned our direction, they hadn't noticed the subtle shift in dirt near the tree's trunk.

"We're definitely in Wilheim," I said.

Kost tensed as he peered over the edge of the hole. "There are griffin emblems etched into the columns. It's safe to assume we're somewhere in the castle."

"What do we do?" I itched to investigate more, to get a better sense of the layout so that when we did return, we'd be prepared. I felt rather than saw my father's Iksass slink up beside me, his watery scent heavy in the air. My Telesávra remained close behind in the tunnel. Slightly parted, his jaw was poised to crack fully open and summon the portal back to Hireath at any moment.

"We should leave." Kost barely breathed. "I can't safely hide us from Sentinels. Their magic…"

Loud footsteps crashed against the polished tile, and Kost went silent. We both jerked our heads toward the entrance in time to see Yazmin storm into the room. Her gaze cut from Sentinel to Sentinel, and she let out an agitated huff. Smoothing the length of her gown, she hid her frustration with a placid smile. The four guards approached her, temporarily barring her entrance and pulling her focus. After a moment, she ushered them toward the exit, turning her back to the tree.

"Let's go. Now," Kost hissed, snaring my wrist. "We can't let her know we've discovered this place."

With fast, quiet steps, we retreated the way we came. Roots wormed through the dirt above our heads, obscuring the exit and once again sealing us away beneath the earth. My father's Iksass shifted so I could see him, and I gave him a tight nod. "Go back to the realm and wait for me. We'll return in a few days to save the Charmers. Okay?"

The beast realm door groaned open, and I froze as the Iksass disappeared. "Do you think—"

Kost immediately pressed a finger to my lips. Shadows danced around us, waiting to cocoon us in safety, but his gaze flicked to my Telesávra. It wouldn't protect him. Seconds ticked by. My heartbeat thundered in my ears, and I prayed Yazmin hadn't heard the telltale sound of the beast realm opening.

Yazmin's muffled footsteps filtered through the earth. She was so *close.*

I took one look at my Telesávra and commanded him to send us home. "Let's go!" His jaws flew open, and a flickering portal sparked to life. I grasped Kost's hand and pulled us through, just as the roots above our heads once again began to move. But as the blinding light washed away our surroundings, I knew we'd made it out safely.

And there'd be no stopping us when we came back.

THIRTY-TWO

NOC

After shadow traveling through the Kitska Forest, Gaige and I came to a halt in a small, secluded clearing. What had felt like merely a few minutes to us would've taken hours on foot, and I glanced around to get a grip on my bearings. Though try as I might, it was damn near impossible. There was nothing but dying grass beneath our feet and the same scene of gloomy, gnarled trees no matter where I looked.

"What are we doing here?" Slipping my hands into the pockets of my trousers, I glanced at Gaige. "We need to be getting back. Kost and Leena might already be waiting for us."

"This will only take a moment." He took a few steps into the clearing until he was at its epicenter. "After my...*tiff* with Kost, I went for a walk in the woods. I was so wrapped up in my thoughts I hadn't realized how much time had passed—or how far I'd traveled." He gestured wide to the forest and sent a river of shadows outward. They slunk across the floor and disappeared into the haunted wood.

A hair-raising howl sounded from the surrounding forest, and the trees began to tremble. The pinesco pods dangling from their limbs jittered in a frenzy, their strange pattern like wild eyes darting left and right. More terrifying calls joined the first until there was a cacophony of screeching, unsettling cries all vying for attention.

"What did you do?" My gaze roved along the edge of the clearing. I doubted monsters could hurt us in this form, but I wasn't keen to test the theory. No one had been brazen enough to willingly put themselves in striking distance of a Kitska creature before.

"I'd like you to meet Boo." Cupping his hands before him, he summoned a swirling shadow in his palms. With a quiet whisper directed solely at the thin tendril, he said, "Bring him to me."

The shadow soared through the air like a bolt of lightning, cutting through the woods until it disappeared from view. Not a moment later, a loud roar shook the trees.

A dominating creature rushed into the clearing, knocking aside errant branches and vines to come to a lumbering halt before Gaige. Glowing red eyes glowered at us through his bone helm, and a fine mist curled outward from his open maw.

My throat dried. "The Gigloam." Spittle dripped from the beast's fangs as he let out a threatening growl, and I took an involuntary step back. "Is this the same one as before?"

"Yes. The one Yazmin provoked the day I died." Curling his fingers, Gaige beckoned to the beast. "Come on. It's all right." Inching his muzzle toward Gaige, the beast inhaled deeply. He let out a disappointed chuff before suddenly poking him with one of his massive, stag-like antlers. My breath froze. But Gaige's form merely wavered and re-formed once the antler was removed.

"None of that." Gaige gave Boo a stern look. "It's me, I promise."

At that, the beast fell onto his haunches and let out a groan.

It took me a moment to find my words. "You charmed him? But how? I thought Charmers couldn't tame Kitska monsters."

Gaige shook his head. "I wouldn't say 'charmed.' These beasts are different. I have earned his trust, though." He gave Boo a pat on the nose, though his hand fell clean through the creature's snout. Gaige frowned, but shook it off. "He didn't take to me at first. Gave me his fair share of wounds. Fortunately, I heal pretty quickly, thanks to you."

With an incredulous look, I stepped closer. "Are there others?"

"Oh, yes." Gaige turned and gave a flippant wave to the trees. Outlined figures of foreign beasts appeared, but none were brave enough to enter the clearing with Boo. "Some are more trusting than others. You see, my whole predicament—me being undead—got me thinking. It's basically the same for these beasts, right?

"They died during the First War, and they were cursed for some reason to live again in this wood rather than return to the earth. My theory is that Zane didn't know the extent of his power when he founded Cruor, and his presence here caused the beasts to rise again." He strolled toward the forest line, and a few beasts dared to extend their snouts and sniff at his shadows. He paused before each one and offered them a soft word before moving to the next. "That same power resides in me now, too. It corrupted my Charmer's lure. Because when I tried calling to them, all that happened was this."

Shadows swirled around him in a turbulent vortex and then shot outward like they had when we'd first come to the clearing. As they snaked through the surrounding woods, a cacophony of bestial calls rose above the treetops.

"They're drawn to me because we're the same. My shadows are my lure now."

"That's incredible." I held the back of my hand outward to Boo, and he gave it a good sniff. He let out a disinterested huff before sinking to the ground and closing his eyes.

Gaige came back around to us. "It took time, and I couldn't

just leave them without seeing it through. They've been on edge for centuries, Noc. Can you imagine?" His pleading eyes found mine. My face fell. For these beasts, living in the Kitska Forest without any purpose or direction or love had to feel like being consumed by the shadow realm—lost without any way to get back to the life they once knew.

"So they'll find peace now?" I crouched before the bear beast, all at once wishing I could solidify my hand and run my fingers through his fur. When was the last time he'd been stroked? Loved? My heart twisted. I'd once locked myself away in a prison of my own making, away from human contact and emotions, just to protect those around me. These creatures had been suffering a fate far worse than that—and for longer.

"I don't know." He clasped his hands together. "At least I can give them something to hold onto. And the Kitska Forest is vast—there are many more out there still roaming." Sighing, he tipped his head to the sky. "The good news is, I think they'd be willing to help us fight in this war. They gave their lives for their masters, only to be cursed to this wood. I'd say they'd love to see balance restored to our world."

Standing, I tilted my chin in his direction. Gaige had never given up on our mission, not even in death. Even when he was struggling to come to grips with his new reality, he found a way to hold on. To find purpose in these beasts and keep moving forward. And now, we had an army of Rhynelanders with a mage as their captain, a band of assassins, a troop of Lendrian soldiers headed by a powerful Sentinel, the Charmers of Hireath, and the beasts of Kitska Forest on our side. We were an army of scattered peoples and creatures, but together we would present a force strong enough to take down a kingdom.

The hope I'd been feeling earlier at the sight of Madeline and her men grew, and I let a slow smile claim my lips. "Gaige, we just might have a chance at this."

He grinned. "I know. Now all we need is for Leena and Kost to return." His smile faltered as his words registered. Kost. Leena. Their names tempered our excitement, and my shoulders tensed. We still didn't know if they were okay.

"Let's go." Turning on my heels, I waved at him over my shoulder. He was right—we needed Leena and Kost. And as much hope as had built in the past few hours, I knew that if anything had happened to them, everything I felt right now in this moment would die. I needed them in my life like these Kitska beasts needed Gaige. They were everything to me, the reason I pushed forward, the reason I tried to be something better than I was.

Allowing the shadows to devour me whole, I sped through our world and rushed back to Hireath where my body was waiting. Gaige appeared in Leena's quarters only a minute after me, and together we reentered our bodies. The feeling of silk sheets beneath my fingertips hit first, followed by the soft down of the pillow against my head. Once all my senses returned, I swung my feet over the side of the bed and stood up.

Gaige sat up on the couch and tenderly rubbed one of his temples. "Why does my body feel so...strange? Heavy?"

"You'll get used to it. After a few more successful projections, you won't even notice the difference when your consciousness returns to your physical being." Extending my hand, I helped him up off the couch. He wobbled for a moment, then straightened.

"Now what?"

"Let's see if Leena and Kost have returned. Then, we'll check on our forces and make sure they've begun preparations to march." I let go of his hand and crossed the room, pushing open the double doors into the keep's hallway. We descended to the ground floor side by side, our booted feet thudding against the stone floor in unison. Charmers rushed all around us, barely offering nods or hurried apologies if they bumped into one another—a good sign things were moving along as I'd instructed. When we exited the keep into the surrounding gardens, we stepped into a world of flurry.

Not only Charmers, but Rhynelanders and assassins rushed from one end of the clearing to the other, breaking down camp and barking orders at one another. A litany of beast realm doors groaning open and closed was the backdrop to it all. Beasts helped carry trunks and crates as Charmers joined in, organizing belongings under the watchful gazes of Kaori and Raven. They stood on the outskirts of it all and helped direct where they could, though Ozias and Calem had a good handle on our brethren and Isla's forces were as orderly as Lendria's Sentinels.

"There you are," Raven said the moment we approached, a slight scowl on her face. "Skipping out on hard labor?"

"You caught me," Gaige said. "Any news of Leena or Kost?"

Kaori trailed the mercury veins on her wrist. "No. Nothing yet."

My stomach knotted several times over. They should've been back by now. While we hadn't set an exact time frame, hours had passed since their departure. Every minute that dragged by was an opportunity for Varek or Yazmin to find them.

Assuming they'd even made it to Wilheim to begin with.

I winced, unwilling to consider that outcome. "They'll be back."

"Yes." Gaige's face was ashen. "They can handle themselves."

Raven swallowed audibly. "Well, we'll be ready to move when they return."

"Good. Lendrian troops are waiting for us at Midnight Jester to join our cause, thanks to Kost." Even saying his name brought about a wave of panic. Shifting from one foot to the other, I scoured the assassins in search of Calem and Ozias. Maybe they'd heard something.

"Oh?" Raven's brows arched. "That's wonderful."

"Enough men to turn things in our favor?" Kaori asked. She glanced at the Charmers rushing around us. We'd been surprised by how many had come to our side and pledged to fight in the war. But there were still those who couldn't take up arms or who simply didn't have the beasts to do so.

"Certainly more than I expected, but only a small fraction of Varek's army." I rolled my neck from side to side, stretching the tight muscles coiled there. "Have either of you seen Calem or Ozias?"

"They're with Isla, helping her soldiers pack," Raven said.

"Got it. Thanks." I was making a move toward my brethren when a sparking, white portal crackled to life before us. The air surged with energy, and the hairs along my arms stood on end. Two figures stepped out of the glowing abyss, followed by a Telesávra, and the portal immediately disappeared. Kost. Leena. My heart soared at the sight of them. Beside me, Gaige visibly sagged as anxiety fled his frame. He let out a huge breath, uttering a soft "thank the goddess," and tipped his head skyward.

I rushed toward them, my hurried gait eating away at the distance between us in no time. "You're okay. You're both okay."

A bit harried but otherwise unharmed, Leena took one look at me and flew into my open arms. "We're fine."

I held her tight for a moment and dipped my head to the crook of her shoulder. The faint aroma of lilac and vanilla teased my nose, soothing my frayed nerves. After a long, steadying breath, I craned my neck upward and spied Kost. Only when I yanked him into our hug did the last of my fear ebb away.

He broke away, a faint blush touching the tops of his ears. "Honestly, did you think we couldn't handle this?"

"It was never a question of your skill." Gaige approached slowly, as if fighting the urge to rush over like I had. "It was danger-ous. We're glad you're alive." Raven and Kaori nodded their agree-ment as they joined our side.

Kost shifted uncomfortably, but his gaze held none of the anger or frustration it had this morning. Instead, there was a rare soft-ness to his expression as he regarded Gaige. "Yes. Well, we were successful."

Leena nodded as she gripped my hands. "We found them."

"What happened?" I asked.

"Can we have everyone gather in the throne room? All the Charmers deserve to know what we found." Something dark clouded her eyes, and she flexed her hands.

"I'll gather everyone immediately." Kaori left without another word, snagging attendants as she went and urging everyone to head for the keep.

Leena watched her leave. "It worked, though. We can get to my parents, and Kost made it there with me."

Kost righted his glasses before giving an affirmative nod. "It was a touch uncomfortable on my part, traveling through the beast realm door, but manageable."

"A touch?" Gaige's brow quirked upward.

"More than a touch," Leena corrected. "But once I used my magic while we were traveling, it shielded us from some of the... discomfort. If I do that from the beginning next time, I think we'll fare better."

"I still can't believe any of this was even possible." Raven let out a low whistle. "What about Yazmin? Varek?"

Leena stiffened against me. "She was there, but we escaped before she could find us." Slipping out of my embrace, she crouched before her Telesávra. He let out a happy croon and then rammed his head into her extended hand. "This little guy did wonderfully. I can't thank you enough, Raven, for gifting him to me."

"You're welcome," she said.

Leena lifted her chin and tracked the flurry of activity around us. "Did something happen?"

"In a sense. We've gained more troops. We need to leave right after you address everyone in order to meet up with them," I said.

"More troops?" Kost asked.

I nodded, tilting my head his direction. "Thanks to you. A Sentinel has abandoned her post with Varek and brought her soldiers in search of the true heir to Wilheim. They're waiting for us at Midnight Jester."

"I'll make it quick then." Leena stood, sending her Telesávra home and pivoting toward the throne room. "Have the Rhynelanders and Cruor join, too."

Gaige and Raven didn't hesitate to follow the Crown's orders, and they each took off—Gaige in the direction of the assassins, and Raven toward the captain of Rhyne's tent.

"Are you okay?" I asked.

Hazel eyes resolute, Leena gripped her bestiary. "I will be once we win this war."

And with that, we set off toward the throne room so Leena could share the horrors of what she'd found in our country's capital—and how we planned to stop them.

THIRTY-THREE

LEENA

Whispers filtered through the throne room as Charmers, Rhynelanders, and Cruor stood in packed rows before the dais. With our combined forces, there wasn't enough space to accommodate everyone, and people clambered around the entrance and surrounding lawns. Countless wary gazes studied me as I waited for everyone to settle in. Once the rest of the Council had made their way to the dais, Gaige gave me a tight nod, signifying all our people were in attendance. I stepped forward, and a hushed silence fell over the room.

"I've discovered something I wish weren't true," I said, projecting my voice. "But I wanted you to hear it from me. Yazmin was right. Many of the Charmers we thought missing or dead are being held prisoner in the capital."

A collective sharp gasp sounded from the crowd, and the sea of faces before me turned parchment-pale. Even the Rhynelanders and assassins flinched. Then, the questions came flying at me in a flurry.

"How many were there?"

"Are they okay?"

"What's happened to them?"

I waited until their voices faded before clasping my hands in front of me. "Twenty or thirty of our people have been placed in a deep sleep somewhere in Wilheim's castle." My gaze bounced from face to face, and I inhaled deeply. "King Varek is experimenting on them in the hopes he can learn more about our magic so that he can take it."

The outraged cries that splintered the air sent shivers racing down my spine. Beside me, Kaori had turned to stone, her face stricken. Shadows spiked around Gaige in deadly spires, and Raven... Raven was ready to murder. Her entire body trembled, and Oz sidled closer to her. Though he was concerned for his friend, I could see his own anger in the bulging veins along his neck and arms, as if he were trying to hold back his rage. Calem's eyes had turned into dangerous pools of mercury, and Kost placed a tight hand on his shoulder.

On my other side, Noc peeled back his lips in a grimace. "*Varek.*"

As much as I wanted to give in and join the Council in their anger, I couldn't. Not yet. Succumbing to that rage is what Yazmin had done—and it's what we needed to avoid at all costs.

"We *will* save them," I said, voice rising as I stepped off the dais to walk among my people. "I will not rest until we do. But we will not make the same mistake that Yazmin has." The enraged outcries faltered, and I kept going. "Because while Yazmin was right about Varek's egregious activities, she is also wrong.

"We are angry, but we cannot raze the world in fury. We cannot hope to create a better future for us, for *all* of us, if we burn everything to the ground." I paused when I came to a section of the congregation where Charmers, Rhynelanders, and Cruor alike had all meshed together. I stared at each one of them as I spoke. "She would put a wall between us—or worse, kill us. All because she doesn't believe we can live together peacefully." Dipping my hand into the pocket of my breeches, I extracted my parents' bestiaries and gripped them tight.

"We can't let that be our future. We belong to this world. Unifying with Cruor, with Lendria, even with Rhyne"—I found Isla standing beneath the open archway leading out to the lawns and tipped my head in a bow—"is how we can save the captive Charmers and set right the wrongs of the past."

A strange energy seemed to pulse from the crowd. It built with every second that passed, climbing higher and higher, until the whole room surged with electricity. Determined eyes, shining and raging, stared at me as I came to a halt.

"We are *done* hiding in Hireath. Our goddess is with us." I thrust my hand toward the statue of Celeste behind the thrones. Her face had always been upturned, but now I swore her lips had curved up in an approving smile. Her half-open eyes stared into the future—our future—and the rightness of what we were doing settled deep in my bones. This was our war. And we would not shy away from it.

The congregation let out a resounding roar in approval, and every Charmer raised one hand to the ceiling. Hundreds of groans crashed around us as beast realm door after beast realm door opened in a flood of blinding, rainbow light. Beasts answered the call, their war cries carrying from the realm to our ears, and hot tears pricked the back of my eyes.

Every Charmer, save the sick and the young, pledged to join me in that moment, even those who'd initially held out. We were in this *together*. And we would end this together. Raising my own hand, I summoned my rosewood glow and wrenched open the beast realm door.

"For Celeste. For our beasts. For *us*."

When I turned back to my Council and found them all kneeling, hands fisted over their chests, the tears that'd been brewing streamed down my cheeks. And I knew with every fiber of my being that if they believed in me, if my people believed in me, then we could do this.

It was time to march on Wilheim.

◆

Arriving at Midnight Jester several days later was like coming home all over again. It was strange to think that three separate places— Cruor, Hireath, and here—could all have that effect on me, but they did. Each place owned a piece of my heart, and my favorite black market tavern was no exception.

Madeline, the Sentinel who'd defected with her brigade to join our forces, had greeted us immediately and commanded her soldiers to help us set up camp. Given the size of our troops, it'd taken us longer to reach the tavern than expected. Trekking through dense wood and thickets of thorn-covered vines—all with little to no visibility, thanks to the network of tree branches overhead—made for slow travel. And, there was the matter of our quick detour to Cruor.

After everyone had dispersed from the throne room, I'd found myself lingering by the statue of Celeste and Ocnolog. I'd trailed my fingers over the prophecy, hesitating for a moment as I read again about the fires Ocnolog would bring. And as I traced those ancient symbols, a deep, unsettling weight dragged my stomach to the floor. A cold sweat immediately gathered along my hairline, and uncontrollable shivers raced over my skin.

Noc had taken one look at me and rushed to my side, shadows already swirling around us in case he'd needed to protect us from danger. But there wasn't any immediate threat—just the unbearable sense of dread that seemed to stem from the prophecy itself.

Or rather, Ocnolog. One look at his gleaming, ruby eyes and the symptoms amplified a hundred times over.

"We need to get everyone out," I'd said. "Even those who aren't fighting. No exceptions."

I don't know if it was the fear in my voice or the obvious, visceral reaction I had to the statue, but no one questioned me. The Council backed my order, and they dispatched all available hands to quickly pack up any lingering Charmers. We still had no intentions of forcing them to fight, though, so we'd stopped by Cruor where Noc could safely lock down the residence and keep them out of harm's way.

Now, we just had to orchestrate our attack with the forces we did have.

Madeline had gone into Midnight Jester ahead of us, clearing the place out so we could strategize without interruptions. Other than her, Isla and the Council, the only person who remained inside the tavern was Dez. He reclined on a barstool and eyed us as we entered one by one. His eyes lit up the moment he saw me, his crooked grin pulling at the jagged scar along his face. I crossed the creaking floorboards and threw my arms around his shoulders. He smelled like stale ale and peppermint oil, and I couldn't remember the last time I'd simply hugged him. When we'd said our goodbyes before, there'd been so much happening. An enraged Noc threatening to hurt him. Dead bodies on the lawn. My whole life packed up in a duffel bag—the very belongings he'd painstakingly kept safe for me in case I ever returned. We'd parted ways with some semblance of reconciliation, but I hadn't realized how much I'd missed him until I felt the coarse fabric of his tunic against my arms.

"Hey," he said, returning my embrace. "This won't get me killed, right?"

I chuckled, then broke off our hug. "No. I promise." Noc and the rest of the Council took seats at a large table centered in the room, along with Isla and Madeline. Mugs were already positioned before the rickety chairs, and Calem snatched his and took a long swig.

"It's good to see you," Dez said, resting his hands on his thighs. "Been awhile."

"A lot has happened."

"No kidding. Well, I won't keep the queen from her subjects," he finished with a smirk. Heat flushed my cheeks, and I batted his arm before moving to the table and taking my place by Noc's side. I should've assumed Dez would put two and two together, but it felt weird to have him acknowledge me as anything other than "Leena" when I used to rent the room above his tavern.

The first hour of conversation consisted of Noc recapping events, the threats we faced, and our newfound allies in Rhyne. When he'd finished, Madeline shared what had been happening behind the capital walls: the extra fortifications Varek had constructed and the ever-vigilant watches he'd established. She had little information about Darrien and his men or Yazmin, as apparently the king kept them close and they didn't mingle with the rest of the soldiers. Isla weighed in on the strengths and weakness of her forces, but revealed absolutely nothing about her own magical abilities. In general, mages were fiercely protective of their powers and shared little about the intricacies of how it all worked. Isla was no different.

When all our mugs had been drained, Dez sauntered over and refilled each one from a ceramic pitcher, then laid out a few platters of his more edible dishes. An assortment of cheeses and fruit, hunks of bread with oil for dipping, and potato slices fried in lard.

"So," Calem said, popping a grape into his mouth, "if Varek has gone to all this extra effort to fortify Wilheim, how are we going to get to Yazmin before she raises Ocnolog?"

"I'll set my Telesávra's hearth point to wherever we make

camp. From there, I'll transport a small group of elite fighters directly into the castle through the beast realm." An image of my slumbering parents surfaced in my mind, and the potato wedge I'd been nibbling on turned to glue. "When we've stopped her, we'll return through the portal."

"We have to act quickly." Gaige's fingers traced the whorls and grains in the wood as he spoke. "The anniversary of Celeste's death is only a few days away."

A few days. It would take us that long just to move our army from Midnight Jester to Wilheim's doorstep. And the moment we left the protective shroud of the Kitska Forest, we'd be exposed. "We'll leave tomorrow, then. If we can get to Yazmin before she raises Ocnolog, then we'll only have to worry about defeating Varek."

"I don't think that's a good idea." Kost rubbed his temple as he stared at the tarnished silver candle manning the center of our table. "The castle will be teeming with soldiers. How many people do you think you can safely escort through the realm?"

I chewed on the inside of my lip. "Ten, maybe fifteen if we interlock arms and I project my magic long enough. More than that, though, and I'd worry about us losing our grip or the realm door closing since the beast will have already made its way through."

"Right." Kost sighed, then met my gaze. "Fifteen elite fighters would still be no match for all of Wilheim."

"He's right. When I left, there were at least ten soldiers stationed per hall." Madeline smooshed a wedge of cheese between two chunks of bread and tossed it into her open mouth.

"Is it possible she'd simply be on the battlefield?" Calem asked.

"No." Gaige folded his arms across his chest. "My guess is she'll have convinced Varek of her need to remain behind while summoning Ocnolog. She won't risk injury or interruption for a spell as great as this."

"We need a distraction," Noc said. "Something to pull Varek's attention away from his city and force his troops to look outward."

"An enemy army ought to do that," Isla mused. All our gazes rounded on her, and she shrugged. "I know you want to get there sooner rather than later, but what if you wait until we make our stand? If he thinks we're going to attack through the front door, he'll be less likely to guard the back."

Running a thick hand over his shorn hair, Oz glanced at her. Then Gaige. "Can we make it there in time? Before Yazmin can raise Ocnolog?"

"It'll be tight, but it's doable." A muscle twitched in Gaige's brow. "Celeste died during midday, according to legend, so I imagine Yazmin will try the spell around the same time. If we can get there the night before or even the morning of, we'll have a small window of opportunity."

Tension knotted in Noc's shoulders, and he grimaced. "I don't like it. Too many things could go wrong. But, we can't push our forces any faster. They need to be alert and rested when the time comes."

"Agreed," Madeline said. "So, who goes with Leena, then?"

"I will." Raven's answer was swift, harsh. Anger flashed through her yellow eyes. "Yazmin needs to pay."

Gaige shook his head. "I understand your desire to go, but I think you should stay."

"And why is that?" She nearly chomped his head off with her curt reply, but Gaige didn't shrink away.

"For the same reason I won't be going," Noc said, voice soft.

My breath hitched, and I clenched my jaw tight. We hadn't discussed it, but somehow I'd known we'd be separated during this war. The very thought put me on edge. How could I not fight beside my *anam-cara*? What if something happened to him? What if I didn't get to say goodbye?

No. My fingers curled toward my palms, and I rested my hands on my knees. I wouldn't think of goodbyes. We'd survive this. We had to.

He pinned Raven with a gaze full of emotion and understanding. "There's nothing I want more than to be by Leena's side. But I can't, because I'm expected to lead these forces. They need to see me. They need to know that I'm willing to risk everything, because that's what they're doing—risking everything.

"And while Leena would normally be expected to do the same, she's the only one who can take people into Wilheim. Someone has to inspire the Charmers in the same way she would. Someone who's been training with them. Supporting them. They need to see you on the battlefield, Raven. Perhaps more so than my men need to see me, as it's been centuries since Charmers took up arms."

Silence filled the space around us. Raven held his gaze the whole time, never blinking, until she deflated with a sigh. Oz, who'd taken a seat beside her, placed a gentle hand on her shoulder. She leaned into his touch for a moment before pulling away.

"Fine. Then the question still stands—who goes?" she asked.

"I'll send my finest swordsman with you. He'll have knowledge of the castle's layout, which will be helpful," said Madeline.

"The bulk will likely come from Cruor," Noc said, tilting his chin toward Oz. "Emelia, Iov, a few others."

"They'll go without question." Oz braced his forearms on the table and clasped his hands together. "What about us?"

"You should stay for the same reason Raven is. The new recruits trust you." Kost brushed his hands along his vest and then righted his glasses. "I'll go. I'm already familiar with the process."

"I'll join," Kaori said. Gaige opened his mouth to argue, but she cut him off with a frosty glare. "I have no reason to stay behind, and we should send at least a few of our own. We might have the skill set to aid the Charmers imprisoned there."

"I agree," I said, and Raven nodded along with me. Gaige let out an agitated huff, but didn't fight us further on the matter.

"Well, fuck it. I'm in then." Cradling the back of his head with his hands, Calem smirked. "Sounds like fun."

"I'd offer my men, but I'm not sure that would be wise," Isla said. She pushed her blond hair over her shoulder and leaned back into her chair. "They don't know you well enough to implicitly follow your orders."

"That won't be necessary. We can fill the remaining spots from our respective troops." Noc reached for my hand and gripped it tight. "We'll leave at first light. Make sure everyone is rested and ready to go."

Chairs scraped along the uneven floorboards as we all stood. Gaige straightened the collar of his tunic, then tilted his head in our direction. "I need to gather the Kitska beasts. I'll be back in a few hours."

During our journey to Midnight Jester, Gaige had revealed where he'd disappeared to—and the beasts he'd encountered. He'd summoned a few of them while we'd traveled, and the Gigloam he'd named Boo never left his side. The beast's presence had startled everyone at first, but he'd quickly won over almost every assassin with his insatiable curiosity and love of chasing shadow blades. Once we'd arrived, he hung back, hiding in the safety of the trees bordering the black market tavern.

"Be safe," I said. Gaige waved me off with a smile as he maneuvered effortlessly around tables before strolling out the door. Kost's eyes trailed his movements, lingering a fraction too long on the exit. When he caught me looking, the tips of his ears turned red, and he left with a mumbled excuse of checking on the assassins. Calem and Oz followed quickly after him to do the same.

"We should notify the Charmers of our plans," Kaori said, gesturing to Raven.

"Same here. I'll need to ensure my forces are ready to march." Isla stood, and the three of them exited without another word.

"Well, we have a plan." Madeline lifted her mug to the rafters above our heads before draining her ale. She set the mug down with a loud thump when she was finished and grinned. "Nothing like the thrill of battle to make me feel young again."

At that, Dez moved toward our table and began gathering empty plates and glassware. "Think you might have room for one more in your ranks?"

A sinking feeling brewed in my stomach. "Dez, no. Who will look after this place?"

"I have a new tenant. A barmaiden in need of work. She can manage it while I'm gone." He moved to the bar and unloaded the dirty metal plates and mugs on the countertop. Dusting his hands over it all, he turned back to face us. "What do you say?"

"Can you wield a sword?" Madeline asked, giving him a once-over. She placed her hands on her hips and studied him with interest.

"I'm better with a battle hammer," he said. When my mouth fell open at his response, he merely shrugged. "I wasn't always a tavern owner. And this seems like a war worthy of my time."

"Dez, please." I stepped toward him and gripped his hands in mine. "I don't want you to get hurt."

He raised a thick brow. "How weak do you think I am?"

"No, it's not that, it's—"

"Leena." The way Noc said my name made me want to scream. It was quiet. Soothing. I didn't want to be soothed; I wanted my friend safe in the confines of his tavern. "It's his choice."

I whirled in place and gave him my best glare. "Don't take his side."

"There's no side to take." He slipped his hands into the pockets of his trousers. "If you say no as his queen, I will stand by you without question. I will never contradict your rule. I'll place men at his door to keep him from joining if I have to. But I just want you to consider if that's the right thing to do."

Letting out a wordless groan, I fisted my hands by my sides. I didn't want my first ruling as the queen of Lendria to involve putting someone under lock and key. Even if it was for their safety.

Moving to stand in front of me, Dez placed both of his hands on my shoulders and ducked his head to meet my gaze. "Don't make me beg."

"You'd beg for this?" As I stared into his round eyes, I realized that maybe I didn't know Dez as well as I thought. The time I'd spent with him before I'd run into Noc had been filled with flirtatious banter. I'd appreciated his boyish charm, his rugged looks. But every time he'd tried to form something deeper, I'd shied away. Bolted, really. I had been so scared of trusting anyone that I'd never taken the time to really get to know him.

And that realization wrecked me in a way I didn't expect. Especially if he planned to join our war where his life would be at stake. Where the very possibility of getting to know the real him would be stripped from my fingers.

A rock had formed in my throat, and I forced it down with a hard swallow. "Just don't die, okay?"

His wide, toothy grin dominated my vision. "Not on your life." He wrapped me in a hug that lifted my toes off the floor, and then set me down. Looking over my head, he nodded his thanks to Noc.

Madeline strode up beside Dez and clapped her hand on his

back so hard he stumbled in place. "I've got a spot for you in my ranks, assuming that's fine with Noc."

"Fine by me," Noc said with a wave. "I'll leave you to it." He shifted toward the door and extended his hand my way. As much as I didn't want to leave Dez to settle into his new role as soldier, I couldn't deny him his choice. With Noc's hand in mine, we left the tavern and made our way toward the makeshift camp. The troops had erected tents quickly, and with setup done, they were mingling around campfires and preparing to retire for the night. Evening was already upon us, and the first twinkling stars had appeared against the indigo sky.

Noc wrapped his arm around my waist as we walked. "Are you ready?"

"Is anyone ever truly ready for war?" The concept of preparing for it felt so foreign to me. Likely from my years of upbringing as a Charmer, where the very thought of fighting made us cringe. There would be no shortage of blood. Of death. And while I'd seen more of that during my time with Noc than my whole life, I still wasn't sure if *ready* was the right word.

"I suppose some people live for it." Noc tipped his head to the sky. "I'm not one of them. I'm not particularly 'ready' for this, either. I just hope we can stop Yazmin before everything comes crashing down."

"Me too."

For a while, we simply walked in silence. The air around us was thick with the scent of pine and moss, and it quieted the uncertainty within me. There was beauty here, even on the eve of battle. Peace. Crickets chirped a gentle lullaby, and the swaying pinesco pods clattering in the breeze carried over the muted conversations of soldiers. The last of the frost had melted during our journey here, and the grass beneath our feet was slowly inching its way from brown to green. We were fighting to protect this—the very world we lived in—because if Ocnolog rose, he'd burn it all to the ground.

Toward the back of camp and nestled against the tree line of the Kitska Forest stood a tent considerably larger than the rest. Noc stopped before it and peeled open the deep-blue fabric, ushering me inside. Rugs had been draped across the earth, and several round cushions were arranged around a low oak table filled with maps and parchment. Further back stood a makeshift bed of soft hides and plump, feathery pillows.

Raising an incredulous brow, I bit back a laugh. "What is this?"

"Madeline insisted." Noc let the fabric close behind him. "It's similar to the tent I used to sleep in as the prince of Wilheim before I died."

"Nothing but the best for the king," I said.

"And the queen." Slipping his hands around my waist, he rested his chin on my shoulder. His warm breath teased my ear, and gooseflesh raced over my skin.

Craning my neck to give him better access, I leaned back against his chest. "I suppose it has some benefits."

"That it does." His hands wandered upward, slipping beneath my blouse to trail along my stomach. Biting my lip, I closed my eyes and focused only on his touch. Tomorrow, we would march. Tomorrow, we'd begin our attack. Tomorrow, we had to focus on the war. On everything else other than us.

But not tonight.

Turning in his arms, I stood on my toes and pulled his face down to mine. His lips slanted over my mouth, and I felt his soft exhalation as his whole body melted into me. It was as if touching me filled him with life. With hope. And touching him filled me with such a deep, fulfilling sense of love that it was hard to breathe. No matter how many times we'd felt each other's embrace before, coming home to his arms always had this effect on me. And the need to explore every inch of his body, to reaffirm what I knew lay beneath his clothes, was so carnal and real I could never dream of denying it.

Lifting me up, he carried me across the room until we reached the bed. We eased down onto the blankets together, each of us stripping the other's clothes, until nothing but our bare skin remained. Lying down beneath him, I let my fingers trail along the contours of his chest. Felt the hard granite of his muscles as they flexed beneath my touch. Noc was so beautiful. Ardent. The way he looked at me, as if I were the only thing in this world, was something that would fill my dreams for years to come.

As he braced himself on his forearms on either side of my head, he brought his lips to my collarbone. "I love you, Leena."

"I love you, Noc."

He moved to my breast at the same time we connected, and I thought I would explode from the pleasure. Heady moans slipped from my throat, and I draped my hands around his neck, digging my fingers into his hair. I never wanted this moment to end. Because right then we were safe. We were happy. We were suspended in a moment created entirely by our love, and there wasn't anything that could jeopardize it. And as much as I knew it couldn't last forever, I still prayed to the gods that they'd find a way to stretch time for me, just this once.

We came undone together in a breathless exhale, our limbs tangled and bodies sweat-slicked. There wasn't a need for words. We said enough with our lingering touches, the soft trails our fingers working along the expanse of our arms. Chest. Stomach. And when Noc peppered light kisses along my neck, his tongue slipping between his lips to tease the soft spot behind my ear, we gave in to each other again. Now was the time to indulge, to feel. To relish in these last few moments of peace before the morning sun inevitably claimed the sky and pulled us from our bed.

I didn't know how much time had passed before we finally allowed ourselves to rest, but as I nuzzled against his chest and let the drum of his heartbeat pull me toward sleep, I forced myself to hold on to the happiness Noc stirred inside me. I wasn't sure what the coming days would bring, but at the very least, I had this.

THIRTY-FOUR

NOC

By the time we arrived that third morning, Wilheim was already waiting for us. We didn't even make it to the train tracks marking the outskirts of the city before we caught sight of Varek's army. Sentinels upon Sentinels in their full mercury-tinted armor stood before countless soldiers with midnight-blue banners proudly displaying the silver griffin emblem. We'd stopped a safe distance away, but that didn't put a damper on the threat. With no more than the flick of his wrist, Varek could command them to attack, and they'd be on us within minutes.

Settling into my Zeelah's saddle, I stared out at the motionless army. When we'd stopped by Cruor to leave behind some of the Charmers, we'd emptied our stables and provided those we could with mounts. Even with Madeline's existing horsemen, we couldn't compete with Wilheim's riders. They sat atop massive, glossy steeds covered in plated armor and gripped broadswords at their waists.

The air was unnaturally still. No breeze dared to disturb the open plains stretching between our two great forces. No birds greeted the midmorning sun with high-pitched trills. It was as if the very earth was holding its breath. It was so starkly different from my last battle outside Penumbra Glades. From the whipping wind and steady cadence of drums echoing through my bones. That show of strength should've rattled me, but it'd only emboldened me. The silence we faced now—the unknown—was far worse than any war cry.

Tugging on my Zeelah's leather reins, I turned my mount around and rode through our quiet troops. We didn't have unifying colors or armor. We didn't wield the same weapons or rely on the same skills. The only thing we shared was our mission. Our purpose.

I came to a halt before a brigade decked out in black leathers. Cruor. My family. Slipping out of my saddle, my feet touched the ground and I handed my reins to a nearby assassin. Kost, Calem, and Ozias gave a tight nod as I approached, each one of them wearing the same ebony attire as their brethren.

"It's time," I said. Instinctively, I went to toy with the pommel of my sword and my hand faltered. It'd been decades since I carried a physical weapon, but apparently the impending war had a way of stirring up old habits. "Where's Leena?"

"With the Charmers," Kost said, nodding toward the troop of soldiers beside us. My gaze cut to them. They'd opted to remain in their regular attire—flowy pants, loose blouses, leather boots—for the sake of comfort. Raven had argued against forcing them to wear armor when the weight of a sword was already foreign to them and would be challenging enough. And when presented with the opportunity to wear mail, they'd politely declined. Hopefully, their beasts would be protection enough.

As far as beasts went... My gaze roved to the Kitska monsters bringing up the rear of our procession. Their appearance alone was enough to strike fear into even the bravest of men. Ruddy red eyes. Drab matted fur. But even more than their terrifying talons and fangs was the aura that simply hung over them. It stank of rage and despair, and while I'd grown used to their presence over the course of our journey, there were many who still couldn't bring themselves to look at the beasts.

Gaige had managed to subdue a number of them, and his presence soothed their normally aggressive nature. He'd straddled Boo's massive back and gripped tufts of fur on either side of his neck for purchase. Leaning over, he gave the beast a heavy pat on his neck before whispering something into his ear.

"I'll be back. Keep everyone calm," I said, returning my focus to Ozias. He gave a stiff nod as Calem, Kost, and I walked toward the Charmers. Without having to be summoned, Emelia, Iov, and the few others we'd selected for Leena's mission appeared in a plume of smoke. They'd been watching from a distance, waiting for the signal to join us.

As we continued forward, Charmers parted quietly to let us pass, each one nodding a silent greeting before returning their attention to their bestiaries. Many had them open and were reading through the floating, magical script projected before their eyes, as if making final decisions on what beasts to summon. Leena stood among them and whispered words of encouragement or advice, pausing when she caught sight of us.

She was ready for war and looked the part. Her black, skin-tight breeches were tucked into silver, thigh-high armored boots, and a single dagger was strapped to her leg. A matching polished breastplate was affixed over her chest, and when she went to wrap her fingers in the chain of her bestiary, she stalled to trace the etching of the griffin over her heart. The queen of Lendria, preparing for battle.

"You're a sight," I said, allowing a wry smile to claim my lips.

She answered with a grin of her own as she adjusted her vambraces. "You can thank Madeline. She wanted me to be properly outfitted like you." Placing her hand on my chest, she tapped the same griffin mark across my armor that identified us as Lendrians. The only difference between our emblem and the one the enemy's flag showcased was the small crown atop the creature's head. Only the royal family wore that crest.

Leena glanced at the men behind me and her smile vanished. "It's time, then?"

"Yes." I pressed my lips together. "Kaori?"

"Present and accounted for," she said as she bid a few Charmers goodbye before joining us. Kaori took her place by Calem's side and glanced up at him, intently studying the color of his eyes. He gave her a tight smirk, but I saw the sudden flare of mercury lining his irises. He'd never been in a situation quite like this, and controlling his beast would undoubtedly be a challenge. If control was even the best move. Maybe allowing his beast to take over and wreak havoc on the castle would prove beneficial.

Before we could think to cross through the sea of Rhynelander soldiers in their severe, jade armor, Madeline had pushed her way through with a single man by her side.

"This is Joel. He'll act as your guide once inside Wilheim," Madeline said, clapping one of her gauntlet-covered hands on the broad man's shoulders.

With his helmet tucked under his arm, he fisted his free hand over his heart and bowed. "I serve the true king and queen of Lendria." After a moment, he straightened and pushed his sandy-brown hair out of his face to reveal bark-colored eyes.

"Thank you, Joel." Leena dipped her chin to her chest. "We couldn't do this without you."

A blush dusted his cheeks. "Whatever you need, my queen."

Leena touched a solitary finger to her bestiary. "I've already set the Telesávra's hearth point to this location. All that's left to do is take everyone to the realm and onward to the castle. My father's

Iksass knows we're coming, so it won't take nearly as long this time to get through."

My shoulders tensed. "I guess this is it, then."

"Yeah." She looked up at me, her hazel eyes full and bright. An errant tremor feathered through her jaw. Gods, I hated this. I hated the way she looked as if she wanted to say goodbye. How much I desperately did not want to hear those words in case it was the last thing I heard.

No. I couldn't think like that. We'd be fine. We'd make it through this. We'd finally be able to *live.* Wrapping one arm around her waist, I pulled her close and cupped her chin with my free hand. Angling her face up, I kissed her with everything I had. Her lips quivered, and gods if that didn't kill me. I didn't want to let her go. Didn't want to send her away. I wanted any option other than this, but no matter how many times I'd discussed the matter with Kost privately, or tried in vain to plan out attacks that didn't involve her sneaking into enemy territory, I came up empty-handed. We were the king and queen of Lendria, and we had our parts to play.

So now here I was, holding the woman I loved and feeling her tremble in my embrace.

Pulling away, I brushed my thumbs along her cheekbones. "I love you."

She nodded. "I love you, too."

Neither one of us said goodbye. We just held each other for a moment longer before breaking away. Forming a chain with her group of fighters, she called on her power to open the beast realm door. Breathtaking vines and flowers framed her temple as she focused, and rosewood light flooded outward first from her hand, then the rest of her body. She gave me one last look full of so much weight and emotion that my chest caved.

And then she was gone, the outcome of her fate beyond my reach.

"Bring me the white flag," I said, voice soft but firm. One of the nearest Charmers rushed off and returned within moments, flag in hand. The crisp, stark linen hung limp against the wooden stake, and I gave it a shake. We weren't surrendering—far from it—but I had to distract Varek any way that I could. And if I forced him into a parlay, then perhaps I could get close enough for his men to see me and realize that the true heir was still alive.

I strode back toward my Zeelah and stepped into the saddle, swinging one leg over his back. Ozias rode up beside me on his own stallion, and we urged our mounts down the line. Only when Gaige, Raven, Isla, and Madeline joined us did we turn to face Varek's army.

Raising the flag high to the ever-rising sun, I gave a quick click of the tongue and guided my Zeelah forward slowly, so as not to be misconstrued as an outright attack. Holding the parlay flag up high should've been indication enough of our wishes, but there was no telling with Varek. I hadn't seen him since my days as prince. We'd both been so young then, but he'd aged and taken the crown—and become a horrendous ruler right along with it.

Across the clearing, one small group of soldiers broke rank and stepped out in front of the rest. A single rider coated in silver from the neck down led the pack. With his helm tucked beneath one arm, he used his free hand to lift a white flag of his own. Varek. And all around him stood men drenched in shadows.

Ozias white-knuckled the grip on his reins. "Darrien."

"Easy," I said, though I couldn't ignore the way my fingers twitched. "Don't let him rattle you."

We made it to the midway point first and were forced to wait on Varek. He held his horse at a slow trot, and Darrien and his men were on foot. Intentionally, of course. Easier to slip into the shadow realm and move with lethal accuracy. Varek was smart to bring them. Darrien already knew who I was—they all did—and they didn't give a damn if I was king. They wanted my head on a platter just the same. And, by leaving his Sentinels and soldiers safely at his back, Varek ensured not a single one of them glimpsed me in person, in case that caused dissension in the ranks.

When he finally stopped a handful of feet away, Varek regarded me with nothing more than disgust. "Aleksander. You have no right to be here."

"I have every right to be here," I answered coolly. "My father was the king, and his father before that. Wilheim is my birthright."

"Which you forfeited when you died. And since your parents passed before producing another heir, the responsibility of safe-guarding the capital fell to my father. And now, to me." He handed the flag off to one of the assassins, then placed his palm flat on his thigh. "Leave now, and I'll spare those who elected to follow you." His sunken eyes flickered to Raven and Isla. His face turned to ash at the sight of Gaige atop an undead bear beast, but he swallowed quickly and averted his eyes. When his gaze snagged on Madeline, he went rigid. "Except for you."

Madeline didn't deign to respond.

"I have a counter proposition," I said. "Relinquish the crown, and I'll spare your life."

He barked out a laugh, the action causing the end of his oiled brown locks to tremble. "Is that what you wanted to say to me? What a waste of our time." Beside him, Darrien smirked. His amber eyes were full of malice, and he summoned a shadow blade so he could roll it between his fingers.

"We can avoid death on both sides if we just end this now. If you won't agree to my terms, then battle me directly. One-on-one."

Looking down his hawkish nose, he sneered. "You have powers that put you at a distinct advantage. Why would I risk that when I'm sure to win if we go to war?" He made a show of looking behind me at the forces we'd assembled. "You're severely outnumbered, and all my pieces aren't even in play yet."

"Ah yes, Yazmin." I shifted in my saddle and glanced at his forces. "I don't see her among your troops. Are you even certain she's on your side?"

"Playing mind games, are we? *Tsk.*" He clucked his tongue. "I expected more out of you. Yazmin is exactly where she's supposed to be, rest assured. Now, are we quite done with this?" He reached for the flag and snapped it in half over his knee, letting the pieces fall to the ground. A sign no peace had been made and that a battle was inevitable.

I did the same, but when I broke my flag in half, I was sure to toss my pieces intentionally—one into Varek's unsuspecting hands, and the other at Darrien's feet. He hissed in response, and shadows flared to life in earnest around him.

Varek, much to my surprise, remained calm. Even allowed the shattered pole to clatter to the ground without a second glance. "Careful, Aleksander. Yazmin is intent on destroying your pair bond. I might have persuaded her to stop had this gone differently, but not now."

My laugh was brittle. "You don't know who you're dealing with."

"And you're out of your mind if you think you can win." Yanking on his horse's reins, he turned about face and galloped toward his army. Darrien and his men slunk away with the shadows, but not before he sent the single blade he'd summoned flying toward my face. I craned my neck to the side just in time so that it only sliced my cheek. Blood welled against my skin, and I willed it to form tiny needles that hovered by my jaw.

"You know how this ends, Darrien."

He snarled at the blood blades before taking off, leaving us alone in the middle of what was soon to be the battlefield. Darrien. Varek. Both men threatening my life and Leena's. The earlier uncertainty and anxiety I'd felt about the impending war was gone in a flash, replaced by an ire so reminiscent of my days under Yazmin's thumb that I half expected to see red tendrils flirting with the onyx shadows in my periphery. But this wasn't her anger—it was mine. Every breath I took stoked the flame inside me, and I thought of nothing more than seeing this through to the end.

"Let's go," I said, words harsh. We pushed our horses into a gallop and stormed back to our lines. Gone was the silence of the morning. Gone was the fear. Everyone snapped to attention then, and suddenly the nickering of horses and stomping of hooves filled the air. Gaige returned to his beasts and touched a finger to the key dangling around his neck. Okean came yowling out of the beast realm, not at all disturbed by the Kitska monsters, and clung to his master's side.

Madeline and Raven peeled off before their respective brigades as we made our way toward the end of the line—and the Rhynelanders. Isla yanked on her mare's reins, jerking herself into position ahead of her soldiers, and gave us a tight nod.

"We'll follow your lead."

"We're indebted to Rhyne," I said, tipping my chin in a bow. "You will always have my gratitude."

"Look out for the Sentinels," Ozias added abruptly. "They're dangerous."

Isla smirked, and magic flared to life in her pupils. "So am I."

With that, we raced back up the lines. People fisted their hands over their chests as we passed, and Ozias stuck close to my side, shouting at the assassins to prepare themselves for battle.

Finally coming to a halt before our brethren, I reached over the side of my saddle and snagged the bugle that had been strapped there. With one swift movement, I pressed the coiled horn to my lips. I think I emptied my lungs on that one call, and the low tone reverberated through my chest as it rolled outward over the plains.

"It's time to end this. All of this." I let the bugle fall to the ground and summoned shadows of my own. Too long had we been betrayed by those we once trusted. Too long had I spent my days away from Wilheim, from my home. Too long had I fought against the wishes of the gods. They'd known all along the good Leena and I could do for the kingdom, and now was the time to fight for our people. To give them a future and a home to be proud of.

I was Aleksander Nocsis Feyreigner, king of Wilheim.

And I would take back what was mine.

The last thing I heard as I charged into battle was Varek's answering bugle call, drowned out by the ominous groaning of hundreds of beast realm doors opening at my back.

War had begun.

Thirty-Five

LEENA

The process of getting fifteen people through the beast realm door was more painful than I could've ever expected, even with my magic shielding us, and we landed in the hidden prison in a heap on the floor. My whole body ached as if I'd been punched repeatedly on end for hours, and my skin felt like it'd been raked over with coals. Even the dull, pale light of the cavern was too much. My head pounded as my vision blurred, and I rubbed my eyes with the back of my hands. But at least we'd all made it in one piece. No one had been lost to the realm—that much I could tell, even through the haze. And fortunately, the aftereffects of such travel faded with each steadying breath.

"If I never have to do that again, it will be too soon," Emelia said through a wheeze as her fingers dug into the dirt.

"Agreed." Iov managed to push himself into a sitting position. He gripped either side of his head as if the world were about to give way beneath him.

Forcing myself to stand, I swayed on my feet before gripping the end of a cot. "I have no intention of ever repeating that, trust me." My vision started to clear, and I turned my head toward the makeshift bed. Mother was exactly how I'd left her. Relief was a cool splash of water on my burning skin, and I brought myself to her side. Gripped her hand in mine.

"Soon," I whispered. I would've tried to wake her right then and there, but the clock was ticking. We had to find Yazmin. At least here, the Charmers were safe.

The rest of the group stood, letting out stifled moans as they stretched and loosened their muscles. Kaori crept toward me, her gaze first locked on my mother. Then, my father. Her eyes grew wider by the second as she took in body after body. Whatever aches and pains she harbored from being tunneled through the realm seemed to disappear completely, and she rushed from cot to cot, hands frantically traveling over each Charmer and the roots crowning their heads.

"Kaori?"

She didn't respond.

"They're okay," I tried again. "They're not in any pain. They're just...sleeping."

She came to an abrupt halt when she reached the end of the room, her back to the stairs leading up and out of the hidden cavern. A tremor raced over her body. Releasing my mother's hand, I took a few careful steps toward Kaori. The rest of the group waited, uncertain how to proceed. Only Calem joined me. Worry lanced his gaze, and he quickened his pace to reach her.

"Hey," he said, stopping inches away from her.

She flinched before jerking her gaze toward him. Fury contorted her face into something disastrous. "This... This is their work. It has to be."

I glanced at Calem, but he didn't acknowledge me. He only focused on Kaori.

"We don't know that." Gently, he closed his hands around hers. But not before I could glimpse the growing network of mercury veins crawling up her arm. "Try to breathe. Think about—"

"I don't want to breathe!" she shrieked, yanking her hand away. Every vein in her body lit up like they'd been struck by lightning, and the dark hue of her irises bled outward, obscuring the whites of her eyes.

Her transition was just as sudden as Calem's, but instead of racing scales and bloodcurdling howls, the air around her shimmered with a crystalline glow. In an instant she was there, and the next there stood a creature both beautiful and terrifying. Her long, winding body took up the majority of the cavern. It curled and moved with the fluidity of water as she steadied herself on six legs. Glossy, mercury-tinted fur covered her entirely, and a mane of lavender hair traveled from the base of her skull all the way down to the tip of her tail. As she shook her wolflike head, her twin horns threatened to skewer the ceiling above us.

"Kaori..." Calem's hands went slack. He stared at her with unrestricted awe, as if this was the first time he'd ever glimpsed her beast.

She snapped her head toward him, let out one rumbling groan, and then took off. Her clawed feet gouged the earth, and she barreled through the tunnel toward the exit. All I could do was stare. I'd certainly reacted with similar anger when I'd first traveled here with Kost, but I'd never expected such a reaction from Kaori.

Kost rushed to Calem's side. "Go after her. Now!"

Calem didn't need any additional prompting. Summoning shadows to quicken his steps, he took off. Seeing him bolt spurred me into action, and I rushed toward the stairwell, Kost and the rest of the group on my heels. We ascended as fast as we could, but we hadn't even reached the exit before we heard the first startled scream, followed by a gurgled moan. When we emerged at the base of that lone tree, the surrounding tile was smeared in blood. A handful of soldiers had already fallen to Kaori's beast, and

Calem was close by, volleying blade after blade into the Lendrian attackers.

"Gods," Emelia said on an exhale as she took in the scene.

I didn't have a chance to answer her. A Sentinel had appeared, and he'd evaporated Calem's shadow blades with the force of his blinding, white magic. Arcing his sword high, the Sentinel brought it down heavy against Kaori's shoulder.

Her bone-rattling howl shook the leaves above us, and she jerked her head around to try to tear him off. He darted away before she could reach him, but hadn't thought to look behind him.

I think it was the sound of Kaori's cry that triggered Calem, because suddenly his gaze was pure mercury, and scales rippled over the length of his arms. With one clawed hand, he sliced clean through the Sentinel's armor and pierced his heart.

"You shouldn't have done that."

I didn't recognize his gravelly, foreboding voice. And then he shifted, his beast taking over right before our eyes until he was standing tall beside Kaori. He rammed his skull gently into her neck—the most tender thing I'd ever seen him do in that form—and she answered with a soft call of her own. Then, they pushed forward together.

"For fuck's sake," Kost said, allowing a rare curse to color his words. He slipped one hand beneath his glasses and pinched his nose. "So much for stealth."

"Come on." I raced after them, ignoring the bloody puddles, and forged a straight path across the tile. I paused only for a moment when I reached the large archway leading out to a brightly lit corridor. Smeared tracks indicated they'd hooked a left, and once the rest of the group caught up with me, we took the same path. Our thudding, hurried steps ricocheted off the polished stone walls, and the ornate chandeliers shook overhead with every bestial call from Kaori and Calem.

The corridor spilled into a large, open room and I came to a screeching halt. We were in the throne room. An ocean-blue runner trimmed in gold ran right up to the stairs of a raised dais, complete with a golden throne adorned with glinting leaves. Mosaic windows lined the far back wall, and massive, circular skylights took up most of the ceiling. Heavy sunlight poured through the glass, illuminating the subtle veining in the polished marble floor.

Calem and Kaori had paused near the throne, the hackles on the backs of their necks raised high. From across the room, the double doors had been thrown open and a stream of Sentinels and soldiers were swarming into the room.

Joel blanched. "That has to be the majority of the force that was left behind."

"Great," Kost muttered, shadows already gathering near his fingertips. "Our whole objective was to bypass them, not summon them." Emelia and Iov conjured weapons of their own, along with the other assassins who'd joined us, and Joel reached for the broadsword strapped to his hip.

The clattering of armored feet echoed off the walls, and Calem pinned his ears flat to his head. A low, warning howl slipped from his maw. His gaze snapped from soldier to soldier, as if he were calculating his attack instead of lunging headfirst without thought. But the enemy's numbers were too great for him and Kaori to tackle alone.

Thrusting my hand outward, I channeled everything I had into my emblem and wrenched open the beast realm door. Most of my creatures were waiting with bated breath at the threshold. They knew what I was facing, what we all were facing, and they were eager to help. But for now, I only needed one of them.

Lola, my Laharock, burst through the realm and landed on the floor before Calem and Kaori. Her bloodred scales glimmered in the sun, and she stretched her long neck tall to look down upon the impeding forces. Her pupil-less white eyes held nothing but fury as she glared at the entrance.

"Now, Lola!" I shouted. She responded with a war cry that shook the very room, and heat blasted from her in a deadly radius. Calem and Kaori retreated several paces, safely out of her range, but the Lendrian soldiers weren't as lucky. Earsplitting screams carried throughout the room as they tried to scramble backward, but they were blocked by their own men. They'd crammed too many bodies through the entrance, making their withdrawal clumsy and slow. The scent of burnt metal and flesh cooked the air, and I cringed.

A handful of Sentinels and soldiers opted to cling to the walls of the room, just barely out of Lola's range, and they rushed toward us with abandon. Emelia's halberd parried the first sword that came swinging through the air, but it only held for a fraction of a second. Soon, blinding light from the Sentinels erupted around us, and the very shadows my assassins wielded disappeared from existence. Emelia rolled to the side, dodging the attack, and yanked two silver blades from sheaths on her boots.

Kost let out a series of sharp curses, then extracted a slender sword from a scabbard at his hip. Knowing they'd likely be forced to face off against Sentinels, all the assassins had corporeal, secondary weapons stashed on their bodies. Joel joined in, slamming his broadsword against the back of one of his former brothers.

"Stop this madness! The real king lives. I've seen him," Joel tried, screaming above the clash of metal. Not a single one of his brethren acknowledged his claim. Instead, the soldier he'd attacked responded by raising his sword above his head, preparing to strike. Joel kicked him in the chest, and the man stumbled toward Lola. Blistering heat cooked him alive, and violent screams pierced the air as he crumpled to the floor.

Calem and Kaori joined in then, lunging from soldier to soldier and sinking monstrous fangs into flesh and armor alike. There was no stopping their attacks, and even if a blade managed to cut open their flesh, they kept moving. Kept fighting.

As I reopened the beast realm door, eager to summon another beast to aid my family, the high arc of a blade catching in the sunlight stole my attention. Kost parried it easily and continued to fight without stopping, but my gaze was locked on those damn windows in the ceiling. The ones depicting the sun crawling toward its highest point.

I jerked my attention back to the exit, still filled to the brim with soldiers. I had to get to Yazmin. But the path we'd taken to get here had no other offshoots or possible paths for avoiding the throne room. I scanned the space, even contemplated launching myself out one of the mosaic windows at the back, when I spotted another corridor across the room.

"Joel!" I shouted, pointing to the exit. "Where does that lead?"

He stuck his blade into the belly of a soldier, then glanced toward the hall. "East tower!"

My mind whirred. If I could make it to the top of the tower, I could summon Onyx and fly over Wilheim in search of Yazmin. I didn't have time to wait for this battle to end, and as much as it filled me with dread to leave my family alone with this threat, I had to trust that they'd be okay.

Kost ran his blade along the neck of a Sentinel, finding one of the few weak spots in his armor, and brought the man to his knees. The warrior let out a soft gurgle, followed by a blood-filled cough, then slumped to the floor. Kost whipped around before turning his gaze to me.

"Go."

It was the only prompting I needed. Screaming over my shoulder at Lola, I instructed her to hold her ground until Kost told her otherwise, and she answered with a trembling roar. My feet pounded against the tile as I ran, dodging soldiers' wayward attacks until I hit the wondrously empty hallway. A spiral staircase waited for me, and I kept running. Glittering platinum wall sconces held unlit torches, the oblong windows lining the walls providing all the light I needed.

My muscles throbbed as I continued to climb higher and higher. But adrenaline pushed me forward. Forced me to ignore the burn in my lungs and shortness of breath. Too long. I was taking *too* long. Panic ate away at my insides until I finally broke out onto the top of the tower. Without a roof to obstruct my view, the entirety of Wilheim was laid before me. The only thing that kept me from tumbling over the side was a series of stone columns and thick railing. I rushed to the edge and prepared to summon Onyx when I saw her.

Yazmin.

She was in the center of the courtyard Noc and I had traveled through on our mission to tame an Azad. Manicured lawns with fresh, budding grass sprawled out in a circular pattern around a tiered fountain. The statue on the highest layer was a kneeling, reverent king. The First King. Noc's ancestor. And Yazmin stood before him, a chilling smile on her upturned face. A basin full of shiny, red liquid and bones waited by her feet. Noc's blood and Wynn's remains. Two of the ingredients needed to summon and tame Ocnolog. Beside her, an Asura sat on the ground, one set of hands firmly on the earth, another pair stretched out to its sides, and the final two arms raised to the heavens. Which meant its invisible, protective barrier was fully intact.

Across the courtyard, a secondary tower loomed against the clear blue sky. And in its rafters hung a stunning, crystalline bell. One whose melodious gong had just started to ring out over the quiet city. Midday.

"NO!" I shrieked, forcing everything I had into my hand and heaving open the beast realm door.

Below in the courtyard, something flashed. A long, silver blade reflecting in the sun. Yazmin held it high in one hand, and then with a definitive swoop, plunged it deep into her own heart. Blood exploded outward and coated the base of the fountain before flowing into the basin. She immediately sank to her knees, smile still pulling at her lips. A glowing orb like a tiny, twinkling gem floated outward from her chest. It hung in the air, waiting for someone—*something*—to claim it. Onyx came barreling out the beast realm then, manifesting before me and letting out a series of angry caterwauls that competed with the gong of the bell.

But one sound drowned out all others.

One disastrous, horrifying, deafening sound. A bellowing, distant roar that forced my attention away from the traitorous Crown and toward the horizon. To Hireath.

An ominous cloud of black smoke bloomed against the sky, followed by a rumbling that sent tremors through our entire world. As if a mountain itself had crashed in a horrendous landslide.

As if Hireath had fallen.

I don't know how I knew that. But something deep inside me—a terrible, sickening sense of unbearable truth—fisted my heart and wrenched it tight. Yazmin had successfully awoken the very beast Celeste had given her life to subdue. And maybe that statue in the throne room of Hireath wasn't just an homage to the great creature of years past. Maybe it was the headstone to an actual tomb.

As the black cloud of smoke deepened and blanketed the horizon, a column of fire erupted straight up to the heavens. And against that fiery orange and burning red stream of color, the figure of a dragon rose into the air.

Ocnolog was here.

THIRTY-SIX

NOC

The harsh clang of metal screamed through the air as blades smashed against armor. There was no slowing the onslaught of Varek's army. They had numbers we simply did not. Arrows whizzed overhead, their deadly song ending with a definitive thud as their pointed tips met flesh or muck. Shields cracked. Beasts roared. Charmers, assassins, Rhynelanders, Lendrians—we all fought side by side against the power of the throne. Our battlefield was a sea of blood and carnage, the stink of copper heavy around us. But as valiantly as we fought, it was evident that we were losing.

Felled mounts and bodies marred the terrain, and Varek's tremendous forces had outmaneuvered us. They encircled us entirely, giving us no option for retreat. And still we fought. Still we raged against the Sentinels, the riders, the infantry. A few times I tried to call out to them, to prove that I was the rightful king, but Varek had ordered them to keep their distance until the battle had begun. And now, as we thrust our blades against one another, the only thing that mattered was survival. Blinding columns of white light detonated around me, decimating my assassins' ability to summon shadows. But not my blood blades. Deep gashes ran the length of my forearms, and I carried twin swords, unbreakable and devastating.

Still, it wasn't enough.

"On your left!" someone shouted, and suddenly a near-black war hammer came swinging through the air. The end of it smashed through the skull of a Sentinel I hadn't noticed in my peripheral, and Dez rushed forward. He gave his weapon a good yank, freeing it from the mangled helm of the downed soldier.

I nodded once in thanks before thrusting one of my blades into an enemy fighter. It cut clean through him, and he helplessly grabbed at my weapon until the life fled his eyes. Nearby, Ozias and his beast, Jax, battled against several soldiers. Bruises and swollen cuts obstructed Ozias's face, but he still cleaved into a man with the heavy swing of his sword. Jax protected his back, erecting a wall of volcanic rock that scraped and burned flesh.

Everywhere I turned there was chaos. Raven had summoned her legendary feline, Mika, and slender, slate-gray copies with the same power and ferocity as the original tore through the troops. Their numbers were dwindling, though, and many Charmers were sending their own beasts back to the realm to heal. The rainbow prism of colors as they opened the beast realm door showered over us, and even though they summoned new beasts to aid in the effort, their powers were waning. They couldn't keep up the endless stream of beasts forever.

Another Sentinel charged toward me, and I dropped to my knees, sliding across the muck and slicing one of my blades along the backs of his heels. He screamed and toppled forward, leaving him open to Boo's monstrous paws. One heavy swipe, and the man was dead. Gaige had managed to remain atop his Kitska beast, and Boo roared loud enough to send a few enemy soldiers scurrying backward. Not that it mattered—one nod from Gaige and the beast summoned a beam of moonlight that scorched a path right through them.

Gaige jerked his attention back to me. "What now?"

What now? My gaze raced over our surroundings. I didn't know. I couldn't see a way out of this. I couldn't—

An unexpected blade careened through the air and lodged itself in my shoulder. Hot blood spurted over my chest, and I screamed. Wildly, I flung my sword in the direction of the enemy soldier, scraping his armor. He took a step back, extracting the blade as he moved, and white-hot agony seared through my very bones. But before I could turn the dripping blood into a weapon that would certainly end his life, a vibrant orb of sparking magic flew right by my face. It cooked my cheek beneath my helm before exploding against the man before me.

Craning my neck, I tracked the trail of burnt grass to the feet of Isla. With her legs spread and hands thrust out before her, she flexed tense fingers that were still coated in what looked like hundreds of electrical currents. She'd projected the same type of magic as the mage I'd faced the day I died. I'd never been more thankful to see that devastating move again.

Without uttering a word, she summoned another orb of lightning and directed her attack at the approaching army. This time, though, instead of a single orb, she let loose an endless stream of crackling, electric-blue magic, and she mowed down the approaching line with ease—until her power ran out, and she fell to the ground on one knee, heavy breaths racking her frame.

One minute she was alone and the next, one of Darrien's assassins had appeared in flurry of shadows, blade held high. Isla only had the strength to lift her head in defiance. Before the blade could land, a vein of burning red streaked across the earth. And then a wall of rock and heat erupted before her. The assassin's blade struck stone. Then Ozias manifested behind him and thrust his blade deep into the man's neck.

We couldn't keep this up. Everywhere we turned, there was a new enemy with fresher legs and clean weapons and enough skill to beat us down. But I wouldn't give in. *Couldn't* give in. Somewhere in the castle, Leena, Kost, Calem, and our brethren were risking their lives to take down Yazmin. There was no other option but to press forward. If we wanted peace, then we had to keep fighting.

Preparing to lunge at a Sentinel, I pulled my blood sword back and held it parallel to my chest.

I never got the chance to strike. Instead, a chilling, otherworldly roar crested over the battle, silencing all our cries and bringing everyone to a standstill. An agonizing sense of dread flooded my limbs. Slowly, I turned toward the sound.

A massive black cloud covered the horizon, and at its swirling center was a column of fire that seemed to sear a hole right into the sky itself. Again, that horrifying roar bellowed from the depths of the maelstrom, and suddenly the outline of a massive dragon bled against the smoke.

I took one look at Gaige's stricken face and I knew: Yazmin had raised Ocnolog.

The beast's powerful wings thrust the cloud outward, and it crawled across the earth toward us like snakes in the grass. Soon, the sun was obscured behind a thick layer of charcoal smoke, a rusted-orange light barely illuminating the earth.

"Gods help us all," Gaige said, his hands going limp in his lap.

Ocnolog rose higher in the sky. As large as the mountain that Hireath was built into—and the same, alabaster shade—he soared toward the capital. In no time at all, he'd be upon us. What had taken us hours—days—to travel he conquered in minutes. Horns framed his skull and cut through the billowing smoke, leaving a thin trail of almost-clear sky in his wake. His jeweled, ruby eyes burned fear into my bones. And as he drew closer, he opened his maw. Roiling orange and red lit up the underside of his belly, speeding along his throat and forming a blast of horrendous fire that streamed from his mouth. He aimed his attack directly at us. That torrent of insatiable flame destroyed a third of our men in the blink of an eye, along with a large chunk of Varek's army. Ocnolog didn't care. He let out a roar that sounded more like a malicious laugh, and he flew over the scorched earth in the direction of Wilheim.

He circled the castle once before landing, crushing the marble and diamond walls with his monstrous, clawed feet. Extending his head to the ground, his snout temporarily disappeared from view, only to return a moment later with a tiny, humanlike figure standing between his horns.

Yazmin.

An excited shout erupted from the enemy forces, and for the first time since Ocnolog rose, I dragged my gaze back to the war at our feet. Varek had pushed to the front of the line and raised his sword high, a deranged grin visible thanks to the cut of his helm.

"The great dragon beast has chosen to aid Wilheim!" He turned his wild gaze on me. "You will not win this."

Maybe not, but I wouldn't let him win, either. Taking advantage of the stunned soldiers, I summoned more blood blades to my side and sent them flying through the air, directly at the king. He lifted his shield just in time, but the force of the hits knocked him off his steed. He rolled in the dirt, armor squelching against the blood and soil, and howled with rage.

Standing, he extracted his sword and directed his fury at me. He took several, threatening steps forward when a peculiar umber and gold mist gathered about his feet. So focused on me, he didn't notice the deadly warning. And then, the cloud billowed around him in earnest, and a rogue feline beast emerged. It sank its fangs deep into Varek's thigh, and he let out a pained cry. Releasing its hold, the beast stepped back and exhaled a deadly, gold-flaked mist. Varek stared in horror as his hands fumbled over the mangled flesh. But that damning mist easily seeped between his fingers, settling deep into the wound. His breaths turned ragged as the color drained from his face. Wild eyes raced across the battlefield, and he let out a scream as if to call for help, but his words ended in a wet gurgle. Stumbling forward, he reached toward his forces only to crumble in a heap. He let out one last shuddering breath, and then went still. Dead. My gaze riveted to the lingering beast.

Yazmin's Cumulo Leo. After witnessing what it'd done to Gaige, I'd recognize that creature anywhere. It disappeared as quickly as it'd come, slipping into the beast realm and escaping to safety.

And then Yazmin screamed at the top of her lungs. "They've killed your king! Fight! Show them the power of Wilheim!"

The enraged roar that bellowed from the enemy forces rivaled Ocnolog's call, and the soldiers surged forward with renewed energy and pure hatred in their gazes. I couldn't see Yazmin, but I swore I heard her malicious chuckle threading through the shouts. She'd killed their king and effectively taken command in the span of a breath. And no one questioned her. Ocnolog stretched his head to the heavens and then took to the skies. A disastrous, orange glow colored the underside of his belly. Soon, his fires would rain down upon us. Charmers and their beasts scattered, barely avoiding the destructive stream of flames as they ate away at the earth.

Unable to tear my eyes away from the sight, I shouted to Gaige, "How do we stop him?"

"You don't." His defeated tone destroyed what little hope I'd still harbored. We were surrounded by death and hellfire, bodies burning, beasts shrieking, people crying. I had no ability to restore my troops' morale. We'd given this war everything we had, and we were still shorthanded. And now, with Ocnolog flying lower over us all, there wasn't a damn thing that could save us.

Just then, a streak of black raced across the sky. A small, lithe form in the shadow of Ocnolog, but one I recognized all too well—Onyx. He let out a roar of his own, and I caught a glimpse of Leena pressed low to his back. Rosewood light exploded around her, somehow chasing away the smog that clouded the air. Sunlight streamed through the hole she'd created. The beast realm door was thrust open wide, the heady groaning angry and undeniable, and suddenly beasts manifested on the ground all around us. Aeon. Reine. Dominus. Iky. Kinana and Kapro, the ice and water serpent beasts she'd first summoned to battle Calem so long ago. And even more I didn't recognize.

She did one last circle, bringing herself just close enough that I was able to catch sight of her face. Rosewood vines, petals, and flowers had completely covered her skin, and she glared at the horde of enemy forces threatening to end our lives.

"For Celeste!" she shouted, her voice ringing out and reinvigorating us in a way I never could have. Her creatures roared, and Aeon grew to his full size. Mist poured out of his sieved body, and electricity brewed in his chest. He sent a streak of lightning directly toward the dragon beast, but Ocnolog hissed and jerked to the side before the hit could land.

And Leena rocketed after him in a streak of rosewood light like the damn beacon of hope that she was.

Pride and love filled my chest, and I shouted at the top of my lungs while raising my blood sword high. "For Celeste! For Lendria! For us!"

The answering shouts from my troops blended with bestial cries, and we once again stormed toward our enemy. Determination bright in their eyes, Charmers thrust their hands outward and pulled from whatever reserves of magic they had left. Beasts crawled out of the realm, their angry, violent snarls striking fear into the enemies before us. They stalled, and Cruor dashed ahead—shadows carrying their feet—and sailed through the air to take down the nearest brigade of Lendrian soldiers. Cruor's blades came away slick with blood, and they once again propelled themselves forward with shadows, targeting another set of soldiers. Rhyne's army thundered a breath behind them. Their heavy footsteps shook the earth beneath our feet, creating a cadence of hope that pulsed through our limbs. We were strong. We were united. We would prevail.

I charged forward, joining my brethren, when a gleaming, onyx blade found its home in my side. Crying out, I tumbled to the ground. I yanked the damn thing out and then watched it dissipate in my fingers as a haughty, laughing Darrien stood tall over me.

"Too long have I waited for this." He sneered and summoned a shadow, forming it with ease into a scythe. Gripping it with both hands, he chuckled. "I decided to take your advice and get my hands dirty this time. Save the arrows for someone else. I want a front row seat when you die, Noc."

I backed up quickly and stood, all the rage I'd felt now targeted directly at my former brother. The man who'd abandoned me when I'd needed him to help save the woman I loved. The man who'd attempted to kidnap Leena and steal Cruor right out from under me. The blood oozing from my waist responded to my anger, and I fashioned a two-handed sword as long and broad as my body. Even in the sickly light of the sun, my weapon shined like liquid.

"This ends here and now," I seethed.

"Agreed."

And with that we lunged at each other, knowing full well we wouldn't stop until one of us was dead.

Thirty-Seven

LEENA

Ocnolog flew into the dense, black cloud. With every beat of his impressive wings, smog furled outward around us until it was impossible to determine any sense of direction. All I could do was follow his gleaming, scaled tail and hope that he wasn't leading me into some unexpected trap. Below I could still make out the sounds of battle. The cries of beasts as they fought and the shouts of soldiers. It had been brutal, flying out over the open expanse to see Noc and my family encircled by an army more than three times their size. It'd set fire to my veins so that when I wrenched open the beast realm door, I'd summoned every creature I could. Every beast willing to stand and fight and defend our world.

I didn't know how much longer I could keep them with us. My body was already shaking, a cool sweat clinging to my forehead and neck. But I couldn't think about that. Couldn't focus on anything other than Yazmin and Ocnolog. When he'd arrived at Wilheim and he'd perched over Yazmin's crumpled form, he took one look at the floating orb of light and then swallowed it whole. I'd watched it move down his throat in horror until it stopped in his chest, right where his heart was.

And then Yazmin had let out a sharp gasp as her eyes flew open.

Kost had been right. She'd sacrificed her heart and became one with Ocnolog. And I hadn't been able to stop it.

Onyx let a worried yowl slip from his maw, dragging me back to the present. I'd lost sight of Ocnolog, which I'd thought was impossible, given his size. But there was nothing around us except for smoke and darkness.

"C'mon," I said, urging Onyx in the only direction I could think of—toward the muted sun. His wings beat fervently, tight muscles coiling and unfurling against my thighs, and suddenly we exploded through the smoke. Pure, brilliant sunlight poured over us. A sea of black fog stretched beneath Onyx's paws, and as we coasted over the expanse, his claws cut canyons into it. Guiding Onyx in a circle, I scoured the horizon for Ocnolog.

"Where are you?" I murmured to myself. I kept Onyx low against the smog, hoping the cloud would help camouflage him. A strange disturbance in the dark expanse caught my eye. Three puckered trails of smoke streamed toward us, as if a great creature lurked beneath the surface but hadn't yet emerged. Ocnolog's skull crested through the fog, fire already brewing in his maw, and he unleashed a geyser of flames directly at us. Onyx cut hard to the right. Heat seared the air, and my eyes watered as I clung to my beast. Instead of following us, Ocnolog submerged into the smoke. A haughty, gritty laugh—one that was vaguely reticent of Yazmin but somehow deeper—floated around us.

"*There's no escaping me this time, Leena.*" Her voice seemed to echo from every direction. It was bigger, too. More robust, more beast-like, and I shivered.

"I'm not going anywhere," I shouted back at nothing. The sunlight beat against my armor, cooking me alive, but it was nothing compared to the heat of Ocnolog's fire.

"*Why do you fight this?*" Her voice was a seductive purr,

and I slammed my hands over Onyx's ears. Dragon tongue. One of Ocnolog's many magical abilities. Rumor was that with just one thought he could control the will of all beasts and even some humans. Only Celeste's voice could counteract this ability. And since she was nowhere to be found, protecting the mind of my Myad fell entirely to me.

Beneath me, Onyx quivered. A strangled, warbled cry escaped his throat.

My pulse raced. How was I supposed to stop this? What was my plan? Again, Ocnolog erupted from the sea of smog, and again he sent a torrent of white-hot flames our direction. This time, Onyx barely avoided the attack. The scent of singed fur filled my nostrils, and Onyx let out a painful hiss.

"You had your chance to join my side." The voice rumbled from beneath the fog. Onyx shook his head back and forth. Bringing one paw to his face, he violently swept down, as if trying to get something out of his head. *"But instead, you allied with the Lendrians."*

I strained to hear every sound and watched for the churn of clouds that would mark his approach. Nothing.

"You've betrayed your kind."

"No!" I screamed back, frantically scouring the expanse.

Then, a dark chuckle. *"I wasn't talking to you."*

Beneath me, Onyx came to an abrupt halt. His wings continued to beat, keeping us afloat, but he simply hung there, his feet skating above the smog. When Ocnolog had attacked last, I'd been forced to grip the scruff of his neck to keep from falling, leaving his ears completely exposed. Slowly, he craned his head over his shoulder and skewered me with eyes that weren't wholly his. His pupils had bled wide. Worried chattering gurgled at the back of his throat. He was trying to fight Ocnolog's power. Trying to warn me.

But I didn't have a chance to find a way out.

Ocnolog rose from the smoke, Yazmin grinning wildly from her place between his horns. The smog swirled around us as his wings beat a ferocious gust in our direction, and Onyx did everything in his power to simply hold his ground. But I could feel his muscles giving. The slight loosening of knots as his wings started to shift.

"Let her go."

Onyx rolled and gave a definitive hard shake. And the next thing I knew I was falling. Plummeting through the fog and screaming at the top of my lungs as the sky rushed past me. My breaths came hard and fast. This couldn't be the end. I hadn't saved Lendria. I hadn't righted the wrongs the Wilheimians had committed against my people. I hadn't *lived* with Noc like we'd promised. Tears bisected my cheeks as the wind screeched by my ears. I'd finally careened out of the black cloud and was now heading straight for the hard, unforgiving earth.

There wasn't a beast I could summon to get me out of this. Most of them were already fighting in the battle below, and even then, Onyx was the only one that could support my weight.

Onyx. My tears thickened. I'd gone through so much to tame him. My journey started with him. Everything good in my life had happened because I'd sought him out. Because he was the beast that I needed. Because his faith in me had proven my innocence to the Charmers and my devotion to my creatures.

I would never see him again.

Gathering the last of my breath, I screamed as loud as I could. "Onyx!"

The ground rushed toward me. The soldiers below were becoming terrifyingly clear, their features more defined. The beasts, and Raven and Gaige and Noc and—

A thunderous roar broke through the howl of the wind. And then I saw him. My beloved beast. Wings pinned to his back in a dive, he sped toward me. But he wasn't alone. Behind him, an enraged Ocnolog also dove at breakneck speed, gathering fire in his belly and preparing to bury us in flames.

The clang of swords crashing against one another was close now. The cries louder, the ground closer. I didn't dare close my eyes. Didn't look to my demise, either, but instead stared at my beast. If I was going to die, then the last thing I wanted to see was him. The very creature who'd put me on this path and changed my life forever.

Onyx roared again and then suddenly he was there, snaking between me and the earth. I slammed into his back and he faltered for a moment before steadying himself and pulling sharply up, just in time. Relief crashed into me, and I let out a broken sob as I buried my face in his neck.

"You came." How he'd overcome Ocnolog's dragon speak I didn't know. But he'd saved me once again.

Fury colored Ocnolog's bellowing cry, and then fire rained around us. Onyx cut left and right, avoiding most of the flames, but his final maneuver wasn't quite fast enough. Scalding fire burned along our left side, eating away at his wing and causing my flesh to sizzle beneath my armor. Agony arced through me, and I screamed at the same time Onyx yowled. We crashed into the earth and rolled across the grass, squelching the fire but not the pain.

The world slipped out from under me. "Onyx," I managed, inching closer to him along the scorched ground. His answering cry was soft. Too soft. I ripped off my armor, eager to get the searing metal off my skin even if it left me exposed. We'd landed behind the battling armies, but close enough that I could still hear them. And yet they were still so far out of reach. The ground shook as Ocnolog landed a few feet away. His claws left canyons in the field, and his monstrous wings flared wide, casting my world in shadow. He beat them once, and the following gust knocked the wind out of my lungs before racing out over the plains. Rearing back, he snarled to reveal endless rows of sharpened teeth and a jaw capable of swallowing a Laharock whole.

Yazmin gripped his horns tight and leaned forward. *"I'm tired of your games."* Again, the voice somehow came from both of them. Her words were a strange amalgamation of her and the beast. Just how much control did she really have? There was a twitch to Ocnolog's muscles, an obvious shudder as he forced himself to look where she gazed.

Scrambling to my knees, I crawled along the earth to put myself between Ocnolog and Onyx. "Yazmin, stop this. If you keep this up, there won't be anything left but ash."

I gestured wide, wincing against the pain coursing through my side. The open plains outside Wilheim were burnt to a crisp. The very ground smoldered with heat, and there was no mistaking the heavy aroma of blood in the air. Atop the back of Ocnolog, she'd turned the thriving grasslands into a wasteland of death and decay.

It was horrifying. And yet...the burden of the crown, of wanting to protect your people at all costs, was something I understood in my core. But she'd turned to dark magic to do so, and it'd cost her more than she probably knew. Wynn had changed the moment he'd started dabbling in those spells. No matter how good his intentions had once been, there was no mistaking the corruption that followed.

As I looked upon Yazmin now, I knew the same could be said for her. But maybe she didn't have to suffer the same fate. Maybe there was still time.

"Please, think of your people," I tried, forcing myself to stand.

"My people?" Her sharp voice grated along my skin. *"My people turned on me. They didn't believe in me. Even though I'd been right all along."*

"I know."

She kept right on going as if I'd never spoken. *"And when I asked them to go to war, they rebuked me. But you?"* Even from atop Ocnolog's head, I could see the rage in her glare. *"They listened to you."*

"I'm sorry, Yazmin. I'm sorry they didn't listen, that *I* didn't listen. But I'm listening now." I took a few careful steps forward. "Celeste wouldn't want this. You have to know that."

"Do not speak that name!" Her voice trembled with fury, this time filled with so much raw heat and anger that I couldn't detect Yazmin's influence at all. Ocnolog stretched his neck high. *"She should never have shared her power with you. That was a sacred bond between her and us beasts. You are not worthy to wield her magic."*

Yazmin's face faltered, and she tightened her grip on Ocnolog. He didn't seem to notice.

"Why? We love our beasts with everything we have." While before I'd tried to appeal to Yazmin, this time I spoke only to Ocnolog. No matter that he was somehow connected to her, no matter that he'd destroyed so many already with his rage and fire. "Just as Celeste loved you."

"Silence!" he roared. He swiveled his head toward the battle. *"Come to me. Leave your Charmers behind. They do not deserve your devotion."*

The dragon speak was so thick I could practically taste it. I jerked my head toward the battle between us and Varek's army, and my stomach plummeted to my feet. The beasts had halted in their attacks and were now looking our way. One by one, they stalked toward us, completely unaware of the battle they were leaving behind. Charmers shouted at their beloved creatures, tear-filled cries screeching through the air. Not one of the beasts responded. They just continued to saunter forward until they formed a wall at my back. Dangerous, threatening growls filled the air as they targeted their wary gazes on me. Only Onyx remained in control, and he forced himself to stand between them and me. Ears pinned against his skull, he roared a challenge.

Yazmin had lost control entirely, and she was searching wildly for something in the folds of her cloak.

"You see," Ocnolog said, *"they're not as loyal to their Charmers as you'd think. The love you speak of must not be real."*

"That's not true!" My gaze bounced from creature to creature, until I found my beasts grouped together at the front of the line. They trembled under the weight of Ocnolog's compulsion, shaking their heads and snarling at nothing in particular. Aeon. Reine. Dominus. Iky. Kinana. Kapro. So many more. I wouldn't let Ocnolog convince them they weren't loved.

Turning back to Ocnolog, I called on every ounce of power I had left. Rosewood light fractured around me until I was drenched in an otherworldly glow, and I thrust both hands outward. The leaves, flowers, and vines along my arm bloomed to life, luminous against my skin. Celeste's magic lived within me, warm and soothing and *real*. Holding my chin high, I dared Ocnolog to tell me again how I wasn't worthy. Then, I wrenched open the beast realm door. The signature groan was a beautiful melody, proving Celeste had granted me access to the realm. To my beasts. To everything that made me, me.

"You might think I'm not worthy, but you're wrong." I took a definitive step forward, and Ocnolog hissed. "My beasts *choose* to be with me. I don't need dragon speak to compel them to stay by my side."

Thunderous roars sounded at my back, and I knew I'd broken through Ocnolog's magic. Without hesitating, my beasts rushed over and stood tall against the monstrous dragon beast of legend. They ignored the open door calling them to safety, and instead remained with me. Their love and devotion—the same emotions I felt for each one of them—washed over me, soothed the pain in my side and calmed the burn along my skin. Tears flowed freely down my face.

"You," Ocnolog said, his voice a dangerous whisper. He lowered his head so that his snout was only inches away.

"Enough of this!" Yazmin shouted, finally securing what she'd been searching for—the blade she'd used to pierce her heart. It was still coated in blood, and she pointed the tip of her dagger over the stained patch of red across her blouse. Right through the same slit in the fabric.

Beneath her, Ocnolog froze.

A wild laugh bubbled from her lips. "Remember who's in charge. You are bound to me, and I to you."

Ocnolog shuddered and cast one look beyond me to the battle-field. Charmers were still screaming, begging for their beasts to come back. They didn't care about power. They weren't looking to control their creatures. All they wanted was to know if they were okay. And with every bellow or heart-filled cry, another beast began to quiver in place. Confused groans simmered from the backs of their throats, and they swiped at their faces, trying to rid the dragon speak from their ears. One by one, they succeeded.

And then they abandoned their stations to rush toward their Charmers. Only when they were reunited did they dare to glance back, to stand defiantly in front of the person who loved them most, and snarl at Ocnolog.

Slowly, he swiveled his head in my direction and pried into my mind.

This woman was reason enough for me to believe that I'd been right all along. Celeste was the only one who could be trusted with such power. And yet... Ocnolog's voice was free of Yazmin's feminine tone, and his body gave a visible shudder, as if he were fighting to hold on to what little control he'd wrangled from her.

Yazmin pressed the dagger flush to her chest, and a rivulet of blood welled against the tip. Ocnolog's gaze went cold, all semblance of consciousness wiped away in a breath. Yanking his head back, he let out an earth-shattering roar. Spittle rained down on us from his open maw, and Yazmin laughed.

"Ocnolog…" I whispered. The agony he felt was palpable. Not just because Yazmin controlled him, but because he'd loved Celeste with everything he had. When the goddess had shared her gift with the Charmers, he'd felt betrayed and unleashed fury on the world.

What he didn't understand, though, was how deeply Celeste had loved him. How she couldn't bear the thought of ending his life, no matter how dangerous he had become. So she did the only thing she could—she sacrificed herself to grant him peace in eternal slumber. But when Yazmin awakened him, breaking the spell and proving to be everything he feared Charmers would become…

Fire and brimstone, just like the prophecy predicted.

The prophecy. The rosewood light around me sharpened as the words flashed through my mind. *A loving hand with the gift to break… Offers their heart…* It was as if Celeste herself whispered the words into my ears, and time seemed to slow. The goddess had given her life as a show of love for her beast. She'd broken their bond so that he could find peace.

Just like you. Realization slammed into me at the same time a wondrous warmth bloomed in my chest. I had broken bonds before. I had given beasts peace when they'd been lost or subjected to a Charmer's whims. Wynn and his Scorpex. Yazmin and the Vrees.

My hand had the power to break.

And as I stared into the endless ruby eyes of Ocnolog, I knew what I had to do.

THIRTY-EIGHT

NOC

The grating clang of metal on metal filled the air, punctuated by the chest-rattling roars of beasts and monsters. All of it was a din as I fought against Darrien, parrying swipe after swipe of his devastating scythe. I'd always pegged him for a warrior, but his skill was startling. So used to seeing him hide behind his bow, I hadn't been prepared for the swift arcs of his attacks, the whirl of his feet as they cleverly darted across the body-strewn earth. We moved with the shadows, bleeding in and out of existence as we tried in vain to outmaneuver one another. We'd each landed a few blows—a cut across his cheek, the gash in my arm, a smattering of bruises and welts—but nothing fatal. And every time I tried to send a droplet of blood racing toward one of his open wounds so I could control him, he'd deftly escape it. And then his skin would heal, just like mine, and we'd be back to hacking at each other all over again.

Rearing back, he brought his scythe swinging through the air. I thrust my blade forward, turning the broadside toward him, and effectively halted his attack. Our weapons scraped together, and I snarled.

He answered with a growl of his own. "I *will* kill you, Noc."

Pushing all my weight into my arms, I shoved him off and

sent him tumbling back. "All this because Talmage made me guild master? You went as far as to align yourself with Varek? Yazmin?" Fury burned through my veins. His arrogance had split my home in two. I'd murdered my own brethren because of him. Because of his actions. All for a title he thought he deserved.

"You'll never understand." He regained his footing and charged.

Shadows ensconced my feet, and I leapt away. "No, I won't."

Ocnolog's wild attacks had gone in our favor. While we'd certainly lost soldiers to his flames, Varek—or rather Yazmin, now that she'd murdered him—had lost more. And with Leena's beasts reinvigorating our forces, we'd begun to push the soldiers back toward the castle. Not to mention, the sudden appearance of Lola, Calem, and a lithe, mercury-colored beast I didn't recognize at the back of Varek's army had sent his men into a state of chaos. I could even feel Kost's presence through the shadows, and just knowing that my brothers were still alive and fighting gave me strength.

Racing toward Darrien, I aimed my sword right at his heart. He blocked the move, but the force of my attack sent him flying to his back. His scythe skittered to the side, and he squirmed in the mud to try to reach it.

I pressed my boot to his chest, holding him in place. "It's over, Darrien."

Fear flashed through his amber eyes.

As I raised my sword high, preparing to drive it clean through his sternum, a heartbreaking roar shattered the heavens and silenced our world. My gaze snapped to the sky, where I spotted a body free falling to the earth. A woman doused in a rosewood glow. Above her, a streaking bullet of black that could only be Onyx. And right on his tail, Ocnolog.

Darrien didn't hesitate to take advantage of my shock. With

a swift kick, he swept my legs out from under me and I crashed to the ground. I didn't care. Couldn't focus. All I could see was Leena, barreling toward the earth like a falling star. My heart thundered in my ears.

Darrien stabbed me through the shoulder with a blade and pinned me to the ground, bringing my attention back to him. Writhing beneath his weight on my back, I screamed. Not because of the lancing pain surging through my arm, but because I couldn't see her. Couldn't get to her. I had no idea if she was still alive. And even if she was, Ocnolog was right there. He'd end her before I could ever escape Darrien's clutches.

"She was always your weakness." He smirked and twisted the blade. Red-hot fire licked through my muscles. I'd lost so much blood throughout the battle that it was getting harder and harder to focus. Dark splotches filled my vision, and even though blood pooled beneath my arm, I couldn't force it to take shape. I hadn't given my body a moment to breathe, to heal. I didn't have time.

I felt a shift in the shadows before I saw him. Kost. He appeared behind Darrien, wild fury in his burning green eyes. Forming a slender rapier out of the shadows, he struck hard and fast, driving the tip right through the base of Darrien's neck. Hot blood spurted over me, and Darrien's eyes bulged. Wild and frantic, his hands flailed about the protruding blade. Then, they went limp as his face slackened. His legs gave out and he slumped to the ground.

"That's for Gaige." Ice edged Kost's parting words, and he shoved Darrien's lifeless body to the side. With the flick of his wrist, Kost commanded his weapon to dissipate, and then hauled me to my feet.

"Thanks," I said.

He opened his mouth to answer, but a low, demanding command tainted with dark power rumbled through the air.

"Come to me. Leave your Charmers behind. They do not deserve your devotion."

Ocnolog. All around us, the beasts stopped their attack. Slowly, as if being pulled by strings, they turned in the direction of the dragon and stalked toward him. Charmers called out to their creatures, their woeful cries pulling at my heart. Not a single beast reacted. They simply continued their march toward the grounded beast.

Toward Onyx and...

"Leena." I spied her standing before Ocnolog, armor cast to the side and body shaking. She was alive. Alive and alone.

Adrenaline surged through me, and the bone-deep fatigue I felt disappeared. I needed to get to her—now. Calling on my shadows, I bolted across the battlefield, focusing only on her. Her lips were moving but I couldn't quite make out what she was saying. Her beasts had come to her side, thankfully, but even with them beside her, they didn't stand a chance against Ocnolog.

Get out of there! Why aren't you running? I couldn't seem to move fast enough. I'd broken free of the forces and was sprinting at full speed in her direction, but there was still so much space between us. Too much. She'd stopped speaking, and Ocnolog had brought his snout inches from her face. Atop his head, Yazmin was laughing.

Any minute now, he'd burn her alive.

Any minute now, the love of my life would be gone forever. Even if I went against her wishes and raised her, I wouldn't be able to do so if there wasn't a body to begin with. If she was nothing but ash.

For a moment, she seemed startled. Then puzzled. And then a calm, serene look of utter certainty dominated her features. She stared at Ocnolog with so much understanding, as if she'd been let in on some private secret, and she reached for the blade strapped to her thigh.

What are you doing? My lungs burned. Every muscle screamed at me both to stop and to keep racing toward her. To save her. Something was wrong. Something was going to happen. I knew it like I knew the shadows. They whispered of death and streaked toward the source. Toward *her*.

She raised the blade high, and my world narrowed to that damn knife gleaming in the dusty, orange sun.

"Leena!" I bellowed her name with everything I had.

Pausing, she craned her neck toward me. A brilliant smile claimed her lips at the same time tears rushed down her cheeks. She mouthed one phrase. One disastrous phrase.

I love you.

And then she drove the blade deep into her heart.

The sickening sound of metal piercing flesh would play on repeat in my mind for the rest of my life. In that moment, I wished we'd said goodbye. I wanted that to be the last thing I heard from her lips. Because goodbye implied there might be a chance for a hello once again. But now... She crumbled to the ground as blood bubbled out over her hands. I got to her within seconds, but it didn't matter. The deed was already done. Sliding on my knees, I caught her before her head hit the ground and cradled her in my lap. Tears stung my eyes as I discarded my helm. Why? Why had she done this? I pulled her against me, soft sobs racking my chest.

Her smile was weak. "I had to do it."

"Leena." It was all I could say. All I could do. Her hazel eyes were full and glassy, but her stare was faraway. This was it. No amount of chest compressions or breathing air into her lungs could save her from this fate. Not like before. Her chest gave a heavy shudder, and her breath rattled. Blood trickled from her lips. And I knew in my core that I wouldn't raise her. Not after what happened with Gaige. I'd promised to honor her wishes, and as much as it pained me to let her go...I did. I simply watched as the light left her eyes and her body stilled. Gripping her hands, I pressed featherlight kisses to her fingers.

All around me, her beasts howled. Their heartbreaking cries dragged on forever as they tilted their heads to the heavens and let their emotions free. Wet fur lined the undersides of their eyes, and they gathered around us. Lying down, they curled their bodies up against her lifeless form.

In front of us, Ocnolog jolted in place as his nostrils flared wide.

Even if he'd threatened to unleash fire our direction, I wouldn't have moved. My throat ached and my whole body shook. I couldn't stop the tears from flowing. Nothing mattered anymore. I didn't care about the battle, about the war. I didn't care who ruled over Lendria. The only thing I ever cared about was gone.

A dark chuckle pulled me from my reverie. "I told her she couldn't win."

I jerked my head up, meeting Yazmin's tight stare. My bones quaked. I didn't care about the country anymore, but I did care about vengeance. About retribution. Yazmin would pay for the pain she'd caused.

Summoning blood from the still-closing wound in my shoulder, I formed a pointed spear and let it hover by my side. Aimed it directly at her center. "You will pay for what you've done."

She only smirked. "I don't think so."

Ocnolog reared back and opened his maw. Fire and brimstone and death brewed beyond his fangs, and I glared at it head on. I would burn away with my love. But not before I rid the world of Yazmin.

Just as I was about send the spear careening toward her, something strange happened. A beautiful sparkling light the size of a gem lifted out of Leena's body, right from the fatal wound in her chest. It hung low over her, then drifted toward Ocnolog's open maw. He considered it for a long moment before allowing it to travel through his mouth. All at once, the fire in his throat died. And that glittering, stunning light pulsed through his body, halting just over his own heart. And then it ruptured into a thousand tiny particles that rushed out over the clearing.

Abruptly, the smoke disappeared.

The fires that were eating through the grass were extinguished.

And Yazmin screamed.

An uncontrollable tremor overtook her body, and she lost her grip on his horns. She fell to the ground in a writhing heap, her hands wildly grabbing at her chest. Fresh blood bloomed between her fingers, and her face went parchment-pale.

"No!" she screamed, panicked eyes raking over the lawns until her gaze landed on Leena. "You. You did this." Trembling, she attempted to clamber to her knees, but her body gave out and she screeched wordlessly in anger. Clawing at the earth, she dragged herself forward, leaving behind a trail of smeared blood.

"You..." Her garbled accusation ended in a wet cough. Blood flecks shot from her lips, and she collapsed. She craned her neck upward, glaring at my *anam-cara* with nothing but sheer hatred, and reached a shaking hand toward her. It hovered weakly above the ground until her chest gave one last pitiful heave, and she went completely still.

A relieved sigh scraped through the air, and Ocnolog settled onto his haunches. Tipping his head to the blazing sun, he closed his eyes.

In my lap, Leena stirred. For a moment, I didn't breathe. Didn't look. I couldn't bring myself to hope that somehow she'd survived this. Not when I'd watched the very life leave her eyes. When I heard a startled gasp, I tilted my chin down. With a slight smile pulling at her lips, Leena looked up at me.

"Hey."

A choked sob escaped my chest. "Hey? That's all you have to say to me right now?"

Nuzzling her head against my collarbone, she chuckled. "It's done." She pulled me down to her and kissed me. Slowly at first, as if to reassure me that she was there, and then deeply and with so much passion that I forgot to breathe. She was *alive*. Somehow, despite everything that had happened, she'd made it. She'd won.

She'd saved us all.

Breaking our kiss, Leena pressed her forehead to mine before reaching out to her beasts. They'd leapt to their feet in excitement and were clambering around us, heads knocking into our sides and happy yowls slipping from their throats. She stroked their hides and laughed—the sound so pure and light and full of love that my tears threatened to start up again.

Once she'd calmed them, she turned back to me. "There's something I have to take care of." Standing tall, she regarded Ocnolog with a warm, motherly smile.

"You ready to go home?"

He peeled open his eyes, looking from her to the beasts at her back. *"Yes."*

Leena thrust both hands outward, and a flood of power unlike any she'd ever demonstrated before rushed from her center. Rosewood light raced across the open plains, and the vines and flowers lining her skin glowed like the stars. And for the first time in history, the beast realm door appeared right before our very eyes.

Suspended in the sky, the double doors were larger than any mountain and carved out of white oak. Platinum vines, flowers, and leaves adorned the wood in a magnificent pattern similar to the markings on Leena's skin. The gleaming handles shook as she worked to pull them open. A wondrous, rich groan coursed throughout the land, and then the beast realm was there. The rolling, endless hills of lush grass. The tall, snowcapped mountains and effortlessly blue sky. The doors stood open wide, and Leena beamed up at the sight.

Ocnolog spread his wings to take flight, then paused. There, standing at the threshold of the beast realm, was a being unlike any I'd ever seen. It took me a moment to realize I was looking upon a goddess. *Celeste.* She was magnificent. Ethereal. Her billowing hair flowed around her like a halo, and the vines and flowers racing across her skin changed color with every shift of her body. She cast her arms wide and, with a tender smile, beckoned to her beast.

A low, emotional groan rumbled from Ocnolog's throat, and he launched into the air. He passed through the realm and landed before Celeste, who threw her arms around him and cried. For a long moment, neither of them moved. Only after an eternity passed did Celeste turn her attention to Leena.

"Thank you." Her melodious voice rang out loud and clear for all to hear.

Leena wiped tears from her cheeks and nodded. "He's all yours."

And with that, the goddess and the dragon turned their backs on our world. Groaning to a close, the doors sealed tight and then disappeared from the sky, but not before Celeste's laugh and Ocnolog's happy sigh coursed over the land.

Leena smiled up at the space where they used to be, her grin only faltering when her gaze landed upon Yazmin's body. Her shoulders drooped, and she carefully moved to the former Crown's side.

"She was right in a way, you know." Leena's words were somber. "But she let her pain and her rage consume her. She went down a dark path in the name of protecting her people. I won't let that happen to me."

"I know you won't." I moved to her side and laced my fingers with hers. "What happened with her and Ocnolog?"

"I'll explain later. For now," she tipped her head toward Wilheim's castle, "let's put an end to this war."

And together with everyone's beasts at our backs, we walked back to the battlefield to sort out the mess Varek and Yazmin had started.

THIRTY-NINE

LEENA

When Yazmin died and Ocnolog returned to the beast realm, the war had come to a standstill. Without a leader to guide them, the Sentinels had ordered their respective brigades to stand down. We walked among them, hushed whispers floating around us, as they took in Noc's shock-white hair and ice-blue eyes. Casting aside his armor, Noc peeled back the collar of his tunic to display the griffin emblem on his chest. The Sentinels close enough to get a glimpse of the mark fell to one knee and stared at the ground.

"My king," they'd said, and one by one the rest of the opposing army followed suit.

Noc grabbed my hand and let his voice carry to those closest, knowing they'd pass the word along to their brethren. "Your queen, Leena Edenfrell." Murmurs of assent passed through the troops, and Noc gave my fingers a squeeze.

"It's really over, isn't it?" I looked out over the bloodstained field. Many had died on both sides, and it would take time for our world to heal. But their sacrifices would not be forgotten.

"Yes," Noc said. "It's over."

Everything after that was a blur. I'd gained immeasurable power by taming Ocnolog, but I'd spent it all just keeping my beasts in our

world. After sending them back to the beast realm, I did what I could
to help, arranging for healers to tend to the wounded and a small
party to seek out the captured Charmers. But my body was useless
and my brain mush. One moment I was sitting on the ground beside
an injured soldier and the next I was lying in a bed I didn't recognize.

Slowly, I pushed myself into a sitting position and reclined
against the upholstered headboard. Bandages had been applied to
my side where Ocnolog's fire had scalded my skin, but there wasn't
any pain—just a bone-deep exhaustion I couldn't seem to shake.
My eyes felt like sandpaper, but I forced myself to blink. To get a
sense of my surroundings. The room was entirely foreign to me. I
must've been in Wilheim, though, because I recognized the same
marble flooring from when I'd raced through the halls in search of
Yazmin.

I glanced about the space, taking in the quiet hearth with an
ornate stone mantel. A sky-blue settee was pushed up against the
foot of the bed, and a row of floor-to-ceiling windows dominated
the wall to my right. Sheer curtains were pulled tight over the panes,
but a soft, pink light still filtered through them. Gently, I brought my
hands to my bestiary. Then, I let my fingers wander to the scar just
above my breast. It was smooth and pale, as if the injury had happened years ago, and a sense of panic raced through me. Just how
long had I been asleep?

"The healers tried their best, as did Kost and Felicks, but they
couldn't completely get rid of the scar."

My gaze snapped to the doorway where Noc leaned against
the wall, one ankle crossed over the other. A light smile toyed with
his lips.

"How long have I been out?" I yanked back the silk sheets and
went to stand, but the world tilted hard and I fell back into bed.

Noc was beside me in a flash, strong hand steady against my

back. "A couple days. So like you to stick around for the thrill of battle, only to bail when the really fun process of rebuilding a city takes place."

"Oh gods," I mumbled, pressing a hand to my forehead. "I'm sorry."

He only chuckled. "I'm teasing you. Besides, there isn't really an expected recovery time for someone losing their heart."

That made my back straighten. Slowly, I raised my gaze to his, only to find that all semblance of humor had fled. Concern and worry filled his eyes, and I reached up to smooth the wrinkles lining his forehead.

"Ocnolog has it."

He raised a brow, waiting for me to explain further. I let out a sigh.

"It was necessary to tame him. I had to sacrifice my heart and tie my life force to him. Yazmin did the same thing, but..." I shook my head and dropped my gaze to the floor. "She only wanted to control him. Not set him free."

"So, what does that mean for you?" Timid fingers grazed the space where my heart used to be.

Placing my hand over his, I forced him to feel the warmth of my skin. The flush of heat his touch brought on. "It means that so long as Ocnolog lives, so will I. And since he's an immortal beast destined to remain by Celeste's side, that means I've got quite a few years ahead of me."

It'd been a risk, driving that blade through my heart on the battlefield. And falling into a pit of darkness, saying goodbye to Noc and my beasts, had been terrifying. But once I'd taken my last breath, an incredible sense of peace had settled deep within me. It was as if my tie to Ocnolog had chased away all my doubts. I would still get to live, and so would he. There'd just be a ball of light in my chest where my heart used to be. The connection point between me and Ocnolog.

At that thought, my skin glowed faintly beneath Noc's touch. Just enough to illuminate his fingers briefly before fading away. He stared at the space where his hand rested, and then he met my gaze with pure, unbridled joy in his eyes.

"Forever?"

I grinned. "Forever."

He crushed me with a hug and pressed kisses to my cheeks. "Good. Because I couldn't have turned you, anyway."

"I know, I made you promise."

"It's more than that." Pulling away a fraction, he took a blade from his inner coat pocket—which was odd, given he'd always used his nails—and slit open his palm. Blood pooled along his heartline and waited there, unmoving. After a moment, he reached around me with his free hand to grab a spare cloth next to a stack of bandages on the nightstand. Likely what'd been used to patch me up. He wiped away the blood, revealing healed skin, and I frowned.

"What are you showing me?" I held his hand and studied the reddish smear lingering there.

"I can't control it anymore. Which also means, I can't raise the dead."

I blinked. "What?"

He scrubbed at his palm a bit more until the smear was gone, then set the rag on the nightstand. "I think when I announced you as queen and we entered into Wilheim together, we reversed the curse that started with Zane and Mavis all those years ago. Here." He stood and offered his hand. Easing me up from the bed, he wrapped his arm around my waist so I could lean against him. Together, we shuffled toward the windows. He peeled back one of the curtains, displaying the courtyard outside of Wilheim's castle.

A giant chasm had split the statue of the First King in half. And out of its center, a beautiful tree had grown tall against the sky. Queen's Heart. I recognized the smooth white bark and full pink leaves. Its roots had crawled over the broken stone to drink from the water of the fountain. Noc pushed open the window, and a lukewarm spring breeze tickled my face.

He took a deep breath, savoring the sweet air that coursed around us. "Everything here feels lighter than I remember. More at ease."

"And your shadows?" I asked.

He smirked and summoned a single tendril that darted around me before disappearing. "I still have those. I just can't create any more undead. I don't think there will be new Sentinels in Wilheim's future, either."

I stared out over the quiet city. Fortunately, Ocnolog's fires hadn't reached the wondrous salmon, daffodil, and tangerine-colored buildings. Or the rooftop gardens dotted with blooming white rosebushes. The crystal waterways still flowed freely, cutting through the capital and running alongside the marble pathways. It was utterly tranquil.

Noc leaned forward and pressed his forearms against the windowsill. "Oslo had said we could rewrite history. When the descendant of the First King and a Charmer reconciled the wrongs of the First War."

Reconciled the wrongs. A bolt of lightning hit my spine, and I turned in place to grip Noc with both my hands. "What happened to the sedated Charmers? My parents?"

He smiled. "They're fine. Would you like to see them?"

"Please," I said, my answer barely a whisper.

"Can you walk? Or would you like me to have them sent up?"

"No. I–I want to go to them." For years now I'd had nothing

but memories of who they were. Stories my aunt had shared and that solitary, rose-gold ring I'd given to Onyx when I tamed him. Seeing both of them asleep in the bowels of Wilheim had made me realize how little I'd actually remembered. How much of them I'd suppressed to hide from the pain. I only hoped they'd forgive me for not seeking them out sooner.

With Noc's help, I dressed in a simple, loose gown and ran a comb through my hair. I'd spent several minutes in front of the mirror fussing about flyaways and frayed ends, leaving Noc to roll his eyes.

"They're your parents," he'd said. "They'll understand."

Even so, I felt like I should have at least dressed up a bit more. But my body was already protesting at the length of the walk, so anything more restrictive probably would've only caused more issues. Comfortable would have to do.

As we strolled hand in hand, I let my eyes wander to our surroundings. To the high ceilings adorned with crystal chandeliers, the endless stretch of windows overlooking the city. Being that we were several flights of stairs up, I could glimpse out over the diamond and marble walls surrounding our kingdom to the endless grasslands. Ocnolog's fires were extinguished, but there were still scorched patterns in the grass. A testament to what had happened.

But it was spring. New grass would bud and our world would keep turning. Peacefully, now, thanks to our efforts. My gaze drifted to the dark skyline on the horizon. The edge of Kitska Forest. And inevitably, what laid beyond.

My hand tightened in Noc's. "Does anyone know what happened to Hireath?"

He grimaced. "It's mostly gone. When Ocnolog rose out of the belly of the keep, he'd destroyed nearly everything. There are a few buildings that survived, but it will take time to rebuild it. Kaori and

Raven plan on returning there soon to further assess the damage and determine the best path forward."

A deep pang splintered through my heart. *Gone.* My first home, wiped clean off the map. The place where I'd tamed my first beast, where I'd lived happily with Mother, Father, and my aunt. Where I'd eventually risen to Crown of the Council. There were so many memories there. Not just for me, but for every Charmer who considered Hireath a sacred place. What would they do now? Where would they go?

"Fortunately, Cruor was unaffected, which means the Charmers who'd elected to stay there instead of participate in the war are unharmed." Noc glanced at me through the corner of his eye. "We will send aid. Hireath is part of Lendria, and our people won't be left to suffer."

A single tear slid down my cheek, and I nodded. "Of course."

We hit an ornate spiral staircase with a platinum railing, and together descended to the bottom floor of the castle. The receiving hall was empty, save a few attendants crossing from one side of the room to the other. Which took them a considerable amount of time, considering it was massive in size and could easily house at least two Cruor manors. All along the stone walls were polished, white oak tables, stalls, and vibrant canopies of every shade under the sun.

"The Royal Bazaar," Noc said. "It's only open in the mornings. We can go tomorrow if you'd like." He nodded to our right, where the wide-open archway of the castle led to a smooth landing and series of steps. Beyond, the courtyard with the now-split statue of the First King.

There, a small group of people lingered around the fountain, their light conversation carrying through the air. I recognized Oz, Kost, and Calem first. They were reclining on one of the benches, Kost and Calem obviously locked in one of their playful arguments, while Oz stood by with his arms folded across his chest. A few feet away, Kaori, Raven, and Gaige were also engaged in conversation, though far less animatedly.

But their beasts stole my focus and warmed my heart. Lounging on the edge of the fountain, Okean had one paw draped in the water and was batting at the trickling stream darting through the roots of the tree. Beside him, Felicks sat and licked at his fur, ears standing tall. A trilling birdcall sounded from above, and Effie, Calem's beast, soared over the tree. She darted between branches and showered the twigs with magic from her wings, encouraging more leaves to sprout. Even Noc's Gyss, Winnow, was there. Mischief glinting in her eyes, she floated across the surface of the fountain and splashed Felicks's freshly cleaned hide. And then there was Jax, sound asleep and baking in the sun.

The closer we got, the wider my smile grew. My family was alive. Safe. And so were our allies. Madeline and Isla were chatting with soldiers stationed near the exit of the castle, and they nodded politely as we passed. Rhyne had upheld their end of the alliance without fault, and soon we'd be expected to reopen trade routes with our once enemies, as well as employ Harlow as one of our principal captains. I wasn't sure Noc was overly keen on the idea, but working with her would be nothing compared to the challenges we'd already overcome.

When I stepped off the last stair, my stomach began to flutter. There, with their backs to me and faces upturned toward the magnificent tree, stood my parents. My father had his palm on the small of my mother's back, the ends of her long hair teasing his fingers. She'd leaned her head against his shoulder and was laughing about something. The sound rooted me in place. I *knew* that laugh. My heart pounded in my throat. Would they even recognize me? Would they remember me at all? What if their coma had wiped their minds?

Noc urged me forward. "Come on. They're eager to see you."

I swallowed thickly. "They are?"

"Of course." He frowned. "Why wouldn't they be?"

"I don't know, it's just been so long. What if—"

"Hey, Leena!" Calem shouted, million-bit grin on display. "Glad to see you're up and moving."

Both of my parents turned in place. My mother gasped, then covered her mouth with shaking fingers. Her wide eyes turned glassy. My father took a careful step forward. Then another. Then he was rushing toward me and wrapping me in a hug so tight my bones creaked. But I didn't care. I let out a sob and buried my head in the collar of his tunic. I heard my mother rush to our side and then felt the warmth of her arms around us. The splash of her hot tears against my neck. When I looked up at my father, I saw red-rimmed hazel eyes staring back at me. My eyes.

"Leena," he managed to choke out.

"Hey, Dad." I gave him another squeeze and then turned so I could see my mother. She cupped my face between her hands and trailed her thumbs over my cheeks. She studied every inch of my expression, as if she were committing it to memory. Gently, she placed a soft kiss on my forehead.

"You've grown so big."

I let out a laugh and wrapped her in a tight hug. "I missed you."

"We missed you, too," she said.

Sniffing, I took a step back and steadied myself with a long breath. I glanced around to see that we'd gained an audience. Everyone was grinning. Kaori even had a tear at the corner of her eye. My new family and my old, all in one place. Extending my hand to Noc, I pulled him over to us. His smile was kind, and he tipped his head in a polite hello.

"Mother, Father, this is Noc. He's my *anam-cara*."

They beamed at him, and my mother nodded. "So we've been told."

"I'm so happy for you, Leena." My dad looked between Noc and me. "All we ever wanted was for you to be happy."

"I am. And I always will be." Tipping my head upward, I stole a glance at my love. Noc grinned back down at me, a lightness to his expression that I'd hardly seen in our days together: Ease. Peace. We were finally *done*. Done fighting against curses, prophecies, and armies. We'd faced the impossible and somehow come out the other side still intact. Still together. Still in love. And even though there were things to take care of—rebuilding Hireath, maintaining an alliance with Rhyne, ruling over Lendria—I couldn't help but welcome it all. Because this new life we were embarking on, this new future of ours, was incredibly full. And as I looked at each one of my family members' beaming faces, I knew that even if life took an unexpected turn, we'd all be here for each other. Fighting curses, and prophecies, and armies, because we were a family.

And nothing could tear us apart.

EPILOGUE

LEENA

A re you sure I look okay? You think he'll like it?" I asked for at least the tenth time. Fiora, Wilheim's most skilled tailor, scoffed and placed her faintly scratched hands on her hips. Her fingers dug into the folds of her apron. She'd been making minor adjustments to my gown for hours and had finally deemed me perfect. But she still hadn't let me check the mirror, which left my stomach in knots.

"You're absolutely stunning. And if he does anything other than faint, I will take it as personal insult. 'Do I look okay?'" she muttered. "Please." Then, she turned to my mother, who'd been reclining on one of Fiora's overstuffed armchairs sipping tea from an ocean-blue cup. "Will you tell your daughter to stop fretting?"

She chuckled. "Let a girl fret. It's a big day, after all. Though she's right, Leena." She gave me a pointed stare, then set down her teacup on the low coffee table before her. "You look stunning."

"So do you. Dad's going to be speechless." I nodded to her flowy, butter-yellow gown trimmed in ivory lace. Fiora had insisted on crafting it as a gift for the queen mother.

Mother waved me off. "Today isn't about me. But thank you, sweetheart."

"Speaking of, the moon has already risen." Fiora nodded to one of the open windows on the far wall of her tailor shop. "He should be here any minute. It's my turn to get dressed, so I suppose you have permission to use a mirror now."

As she sauntered out of the room, I rushed across her shop, avoiding the rainbow-colored bolts of fabric and the antique sewing machine to stand before a floor-length mirror. My breath caught in my chest. The sleeveless gown hugged my figure through to my hips, where it flared out just slightly over my legs. Thousands of winking crystals dripped from my chest down to my waist. They were so densely packed that I couldn't even see the fabric beneath them until my gaze fell to the skirt. Feather-soft flowers had been hand-stitched into the charmeuse fabric, and rosewood-colored vines connected them all. The same crystals clustered across my chest were scattered about the folds, and when I spun in place, they glimmered like hidden stars.

Gently, I touched my fingers to the griffin tattoo on my chest. And beside it... I nudged my bestiary. Queen of Lendria and Crown of the Charmers Council. Never in my life did I expect to end up here. But I made a promise to myself right then and there that I would always do right by my people and my beasts—*all* of them.

My mother stood and came up behind me, wrapping one arm around my waist and pressing her chin against my shoulder. "I'm so glad I'm here to see this."

Throat tightening, I nodded and placed my hand over hers. "Me too."

A heavy knock sounded from the front door, and Fiora emerged in a sky-blue ball gown to wrench it open. Her autumn eyes lit up as she took in my father standing in the doorway. Apparently, Fiora had sent him an outfit to match my mother's, and he wore it well. The color of Ortega Key's beaches, the suit was tailored expertly to his form.

His gaze first fell to my mother, then to me. He swallowed twice before speaking. "I don't have words for how beautiful you are. Either of you."

Heat crawled up my neck, and I smiled. "Thanks."

"C'mon, you can compliment each other later. We're going to be late." Fiora practically shoved him out the door, dragging Mother and me with her. She quickly closed up shop behind us, then turned her back on her quaint brick cottage just outside Wilheim's gates.

I hadn't known quite what to expect when it came to my official coronation as queen. Noc had insinuated that it was like celebrating becoming a pair bond, but on a much grander scale. When I'd considered this, I'd asked him if we could make a few tweaks to accommodate some Charmer customs, given we'd never gotten the opportunity to celebrate choosing each other as *anam-cara*. He'd obliged without hesitation, so when I spied the paper lanterns hanging from every tree within sight, my heart nearly burst.

"Oh, Leena." My mother's words were full of emotion as she gazed at the lantern outside Fiora's home. A hand-sketched drawing of a Myad in rosewood ink stood out against the soft yellow paper. Each lantern would have a different beast, but something told me Noc had ensured that Onyx found his way to me.

"He's a good man," my father said. He wrapped me in a light hug, careful to mind my curled hair, and placed a soft kiss on my forehead. "I'm so proud of you."

"Now we know why you were told to be kept inside all day. He wanted to surprise you." My mom kissed my cheek. "Lead the way, sweetheart. We'll be right behind you."

I nodded, swallowing the rock in my throat, and started the procession that would end with me standing before Noc on the castle steps. My parents fell into line behind me, and Fiora rushed to the side of the marble path leading into the city. She joined some of her friends there and dabbed at her eyes with a handkerchief. I'd offered for her to walk with us, but she'd vehemently refused. Apparently, only family was supposed to partake in the procession.

Fortunately, Noc and I agreed that "family" was up to us. So when I passed through the gleaming gates marking the entrance to my newfound kingdom, I was thrilled to find Kost, Calem, and Oz waiting for me. Also dressed in stunning outfits provided by Fiora, they offered me wide grins before tipping their chins to their chests in respectful bows. One by one, they fell into line behind my parents.

At first, I hadn't understood why Noc was so insistent on the ceremony taking place during the first full moon of spring. Only a week had passed since our battle with Varek and Yazmin, and there was still so much to do. We'd made plans to travel to Hireath to oversee the rebuilding project and ensure the Charmers received whatever resources or funds they needed. And then there was Rhyne. Queen Elianna had been told of our victory and was awaiting our return to formalize trade routes. We'd promised to visit after our time in Hireath, but Noc had insisted everything could wait until after tonight.

And now I knew why. I stared at the sight before me. Tears stung at the backs of my eyes. He *remembered.* Touching my chin to my shoulder, I glanced back at Kost. His knowing smile was confirmation enough. I turned back around and stared at the splendor that was Wilheim under the light of the full moon. Specifically, the first full moon of spring.

For the first time in my life, I witnessed the Violet Castle. Wilheim's stronghold had been carved out of a lone mountain said to take on a purple sheen under the light of spring's first full moon. When I'd first learned of this phenomenon, I'd been standing near the train tracks outside Wilheim with Noc, Kost, Calem, and Oz. It'd been the beginning of our journey together, and I'd expressed how I'd never been lucky enough to see the white stone transform into this violet beauty.

"Leena?" my mother asked. "Everything okay?"

I sniffed and did my best to hold back tears. "Everything is perfect."

Starting up again, we walked down the marble pathways that made up Wilheim. The crystal waterways had been adorned with lily pads and lined with candles. The citizens had all dressed in fine attire and lined the streets, tossing pink petals gathered from Queen's Hearts throughout the city. The further in we walked, the more densely populated it became, and soon I lost sight of the stone beneath my feet and saw nothing but beautiful petals. About half-way through, we met Gaige, Kaori, and Raven at an intersection, and they too offered bows before joining our procession. They fell in line beside Kost, Calem, and Oz respectively, whispering their congratulations to me as they passed.

The moment I spotted the Queen's Heart growing out of the cracked fountain, my palms began to sweat. In a few minutes, I'd travel around its circular base and find myself at the foot of the castle. Right in front of Noc. Biting my lip, I tried to get a grip on my racing heartbeat. I couldn't explain the nerves. Couldn't fathom why now, after everything we'd been through, I was nervous for him to see me. Maybe because we hadn't celebrated any of this before. Maybe he'd think that I was wrong for him, now that our lives had calmed down. Maybe...

As I rounded the fountain and spied him waiting for me on the steps, all my doubts and fears fled with the breeze. Noc was a vision. His midnight-blue overcoat was trimmed in silver stitching and fell open to his thighs. His crisp, white dress tunic was unbuttoned just beneath the collarbone, a hint of his griffin tattoo on display. With tailored trousers and shined boots to round out the outfit, he looked ready to have his portrait done.

But it wasn't his clothes that assuaged my fears. Or the styled way his shock-white locks fell about his face. It was the way his ice-blue eyes lit up at the sight of me. How his lips parted ever so slightly before a magnificent grin took over his expression. I knew with utter certainty that this man loved me with everything he had.

Extending his hand toward me, he dipped his head in a bow. "My queen, you look absolutely ravishing."

"As do you." I took his hand, interlocking our fingers and giving them a squeeze. Behind us, the procession halted.

When he straightened, something peculiar caught my attention in his breast pocket. A mess of black curls dotted with tiny white flowers. As I peered closer, Winnow emerged with her hands tossed to the sky in mock surprise.

"Winnow?" I laughed. "What are you doing here?"

She hung over the edge of his pocket and grinned. *I'm here to pass along a message.*

"Honestly, I had no idea this is what she wanted." Noc gave her a bemused smile. "You're projecting your thoughts so she can hear you too, right?"

Of course. She batted his chest. *The message is for both of you.*

"Go ahead then, we won't interrupt," I said.

The gods wish to thank you for all that you've done. So they made these. She held out her hands, revealing two miniscule, teardrop gems that glittered like pure starlight. They floated off her hands and grew until they reached the size of cuff links.

"What are they?" Noc asked, eyeing the floating crystal.

Passage to the land of the gods. They can only be used once, though. And you can't return once you've crossed the bridge. Winnow shrugged.

Forever is a long time. When you're ready to leave this world, they'd like to welcome you to theirs. As equals.

With careful fingers, I retrieved my gem and held it in the palm of my hand. Forever *was* a long time, but we'd only just begun to live it. Maybe one day, way in our future, we'd consider embarking on a journey like that. But for now, I was happy with my slice of eternity. And one glance at Noc told me he was, too. He gently slipped the gem into one of the inner pockets of his coat, offering to do the same for me.

"Tell them they have our deepest gratitude," I said.

They know. Winnow winked before turning her mischievous grin toward her master. *Send me home. I don't want to be around for any additional...festivities between you two.*

Noc rolled his eyes but obliged, fishing her bronze key out of his trouser pocket and sending her back to the beast realm. He tucked it away and shook his head. "Honestly, that beast. Why did you ever gift her to me?"

I bit back a laugh. "Right. Because you were so against the idea."

Chuckling, he draped an arm over my shoulders and pulled me close, his lips just barely dusting the shelf of my ear. "Though honestly, I am rather looking forward to tonight's *festivities.*"

Heat ravaged my cheeks, and I turned to meet his devilish grin. "Me too."

Before we continued on, I took one last look at our family. They'd parted off to the side of the walkway, joining a group of Charmers and assassins. We'd been through so much—some more than others. My gaze softened as I spied Gaige with the assassins, just the hint of a shadow toying with his fingers. But he wasn't alone—far from it. He shared a quick glance with Kost, a glimmer of understanding in their eyes, and Kost turned away as a faint blush touched his ears. For the first time in weeks, Gaige's smile felt real. Hopeful.

"Ready?" Noc whispered into my ear.

I turned back to him and grinned. "Ready."

And together, we ascended the steps into the Violet Castle for all of Wilheim to see, with the promise of forever stretched out before us.

BESTIARY

Asura

Pronunciation: *ah-sur-ah*

Rank: B-Class

Description: An Asura is the size of a small child, with an upright humanlike torso, cow legs, and a cow head. Its body is covered in tan hide, and it sports six humanlike arms. It also has ten milky-white eyes, which correspond to the number of hits that can be absorbed by its shield. When activating its impenetrable defensive shield, the Asura holds two hands palm up toward the heavens, two flat and parallel to the earth, and two pressed firmly against the ground. The invisible, bubble-like dome this creates can withstand any attack for up to ten hits. The number of closed eyes indicates the number of hits sustained at any point during the battle. Asura are slow to move and incapable of physical attacks. Their shields will remain intact if they travel with their Charmer, but since movement requires them to remove their lower two hands from the earth, this weakens the shield.

Taming: Taming an Asura takes considerable time. The Charmer must sit cross-legged before the beast, with arms extended outward, and activate charm. This position must be held for several hours while the Asura chews on wheatgrass and evaluates the Charmer's power. If it finds the Charmer unsuitable, the Asura will walk away and become untamable for seven days.

Azad

Pronunciation: *a-zad*

Rank: C-Class

Description: Azad are small, mouse-like beasts with porcelain-colored fur and pearl-like eyes. They primarily reside in frozen landscapes, where food is scarce, and they will use their treasure-tracking powers to find their prize—grubs and grass. Their claws are incredibly sharp, and they can dig easily into frozen earth in search of food and to hibernate between feeds. Once tamed, Charmers can use their power to seek treasure of other types by communicating their desires to the beast.

Taming: Azads are incredibly hard to find, and only surface under the light of a full moon. While they're used to eating grubs and grass, they're particularly fond of fruit. Due to the frozen landscape in which they live, they rarely get to enjoy this treat. As such, if a Charmer wishes to tame an Azad, the easiest way to do so is to lure one out with fruit and wait under a full moon. Eventually, the scent will attract the beast. Initiate charm once it has started in on its meal.

Bockular

Pronunciation: *bock-u-lar*

Rank: D-Class

Description: The Bockular is a hedgehog beast the size of a teacup with glass-blue eyes and rainbow quills. It has abnormally large hands, and when they're pressed flush against an object, the Bockular can detect what's hidden on the other side. However, any barrier thicker than a few inches distorts the Bockular's magic, and the mental image it shares with its Charmer is either fuzzy or simply nonexistent.

Taming: No additional taming requirements are needed aside from standard charm.

Bone Katua

Pronunciation: *bone cat-ew-ah*

Rank: A-Class

Description: The Bone Katua is one of the ten legendary feline beasts and is russet-brown in color with bone spikes protruding along its spine. Its devil-red eyes have the potential to cause paralysis in prey, making it a supreme hunter. Since the Bone Katua can heal itself by rubbing its fur against trees, it's difficult to kill. Its yellow fangs stretch past its maw and can pierce thick hides with ease.

Taming: Bone Katua are difficult to locate, often living reclusive lives in mountains populated by dense forests. The Charmer must discover the Bone Katua's den and take up residence near it, demonstrating a willingness to live fully with nature by eating and drinking only enough to survive and maintaining no contact with the outside world. After several months, the Bone Katua will approach and paralyze the Charmer with its stare. It will then sniff and lick them from head to toe, determining whether they've truly dedicated themselves to nature. If it believes the Charmer has, it will sit before them until the paralysis wears off and then allow them to tame it. If it feels the Charmer does not value nature, or has contacted another human or indulged beyond what's necessary during those few months, it will kill them.

Boxismus

Pronunciation: *box-is-mus*

Rank: B-Class

Description: Nimble and fast, Boxismus swiftly move through jungle trees with ease. They're covered in orange fur with silver plates protruding from their shoulders and knees and along the backs of their hands and knuckles. They live in large groups together and are known to be extremely territorial, with the strongest Boxismus becoming the leader of the family and responsible for all members' safety. If a Boxismus considers a Charmer part of their family, it will go to any length to protect them.

Taming: To charm this beast, the Charmer must locate a family and challenge a Boxismus to fight in physical combat. However, entering directly into a fighting match with this beast will always result in serious injury or death, as the Boxismus has incredible power and stamina. To counteract this, set up a series of heavy sandbags and lure the Boxismus to them with fruit. The Boxismus will punch each one until they split. After five or so bags, they will have spent enough stamina for the Charmer to safely enter a fighting match without risking loss of life. Injuries will likely still happen, but once the Boxismus tires, initiate charm.

Canepine

Pronunciation: *cane-pine*

Rank: C-Class

Description: Canepine are wolf-like beasts with ivy-green fur and powder-blue eyes. Male Canepine have small white flowers that grow naturally along the undersides of their bellies, neck, and around their faces, while females have indigo flowers. They live in packs deep within the woods and are peaceful in nature. They have excellent tracking abilities, making them sought after by Charmers who frequent beast hunts. In addition, they can purify any water source, making it safe for consumption.

Taming: Taming a Canepine largely depends on whether or not the beast is attached to its pack. It is impossible to convince a Canepine to leave if it has already mated or birthed pups. Therefore, it's easier to tame youngsters than adults. Once a Charmer has caught the attention of a Canepine, they must play fetch for as long as the beast desires. Once the Canepine is satisfied, it will take an item off the Charmer and run away, returning sometime later. At that point, the Charmer must find the missing item. If they're able to track it down, the Canepine will allow itself to be tamed. If not, the Canepine will leave.

Cumulo Leo

Pronunciation: *cue-mew-low lee-oh*

Rank: A-Class

Description: One of the legendary feline beasts, the Cumulo Leo lives in high mountain ranges, specifically peaks hidden within cloud banks. They have four curling horns, long fangs, and golden fur. They only emerge under the high sun to hunt and are extremely difficult to track, given they can hide their presence by summoning clouds. When they attack and successfully draw blood, they immediately let out a misty, gold-flecked breath full of poison that kills once it comes into contact with the open wound.

Taming: In order to tame a Cumulo Leo, a Charmer must first set out a chest full of gold aurics in a cloud bank on a mountain peak during midday. Then, they must slice open their palms and dribble blood in a circle around the chest. After that, the Charmer must sit in silence without tending their wounds. If they apply any salve or bandages, the beast will view this as a sign of weakness and never approach. If a Cumulo Leo does approach, the beast will first inspect the chest to ensure there is an adequate amount of bits. If the beast is satisfied, it will consume the gold, giving its hide an even more lustrous shine. If the beast feels it has not been presented with enough bits, it will summon mist and kill the Charmer. There is no known amount of aurics to guarantee success, as it varies from beast to beast, but most Charmers willing to part with all their savings manage to live. After the Cumulo Leo finishes its meal, it will promptly fall into a deep slumber. Again, the Charmer must not move or tend to their wounds. Only when the beast has roused, sometimes several days later, will it allow itself to be tamed if the Charmer is still present and has not moved.

Devikara

Pronunciation: *de-vi-kar-a*

Rank: B-Class

Description: A Devikara feeds on emotion. This colorful beast is the size of a hawk and looks like a dragon. With crystal covered ears, colorful scales, and a tail that resembles flames, it's a beautiful beast. Its large wings can carry it high into the trees of the forest where they live. These very sensitive creatures eat berries and leaves, but love sweets. Devikaras cry crystals that can be used as weapons if they sense someone isn't kind or plans to do harm.

Taming: To charm this beast, a Charmer must set up a mirror with sweets and fruits surrounding it. Because Devikaras are so sensitive to what people are feeling, the Charmer must go with only happy and good thoughts in their mind. If not, the Devikara will be able to sense the Charmer's ulterior motive, causing them to cry crystal tears. These tears are dangerous weapons that disintegrate everything they come into direct contact with, causing harm to the Charmer and allowing the Devikara to flee. However, if the Charmer comes with pure intentions and successfully tames the Devikara, the beast's crystal tears can be used to heal the injured and bring joy to the sad.

Charmed by: Harlow Martin

Dosha

Pronunciation: *doh-sha*

Rank: D-Class

Description: Dosha are no bigger than teacups and have exceptionally long tails and large hands. They're generally tawny-colored, with slight coat variations between males and females. While all Dosha have three eyes, female eye color is blue and male eye color is green. The adhesive secreted from their palms is so strong that a single finger attached to a branch could keep them from falling. When they wish to unstick themselves, a secondary dissolvent secretion is released from their hands, granting just enough movement for them to dislodge themselves. They live high in the treetops to avoid predators and eat a variety of leaves and fruit to sustain themselves. Thanks to a special lining in their digestive system, they're immune to any poison they might consume. As such, they're useful for detecting whether or not food is safe for human consumption.

Taming: Dosha never leave their treetop homes. To tame one, the Charmer must climb as high as the tree will allow and present the beast with a ripe coconut. If the Dosha accepts, it will glue itself to the Charmer's body while consuming the fruit. Once the Dosha is finished eating, the Charmer should initiate charm.

Drakuar

Pronunciation: *drake-wahr*

Rank: B-Class

Description: The Drakuar is a steadfastly loyal beast with the body and shape of a jaguar, dragon-like wings, and blend of blue-black fur and iridescent scales. The creature's fur is dotted with spots, and the shimmering, turquoise scales cover potential weak points, such as the beast's ankles, chest, and underbelly. Once tamed, the beast is unflinchingly loyal, going to any and all lengths to protect its Charmer.

Taming: To tame a Drakuar, the Charmer must demonstrate unparalleled loyalty. After successfully finding the Drakuar's cave, the Charmer must first sit completely still and allow the beast to approach. Under no circumstances should the Charmer summon another beast or bring a weapon to the taming, as this will be seen as a threat. The Drakuar will then sniff the Charmer, determining if their intentions are kind, and then permit them to accompany the beast for several days. At this point, the Charmer must be willing to do anything the beast requires—hunt, seek shelter, protect the beast from threats. Once the beast feels like the Charmer has displayed true loyalty, it will kneel and allow itself to be tamed.

Charmed by: Jessica Pagac

Dreagle

Pronunciation: *dree-gul*

Rank: B-Class

Description: Dreagles live in flocks atop mountain peaks and form deep bonds with their family. As the seasons change, the coats of their deer-like bodies adapt to match the environment—dirt brown and black during the warmer months and snow-white during the winter. With powerful, eagle-like wings, they can fly for hours without tiring. They use their antlers and sharp talons to catch small game or unearth grubs. Their incredible eyesight cannot be fooled by magic, and they're able to detect threats from great distances.

Taming: Dreagles have a unique relationship with Charmers. So long as high peaks are provided for them to stand guard—as well as more secluded mountaintop perches to nest and birth young—they'll watch over a designated area without needing to be tamed. They can be tamed with standard charm, but it's generally not recommended to separate a Dreagle from its flock, due to their highly social natures.

Drevtok

Pronunciation: *drev-tock*

Rank: B-Class

Description: Drevtoks are no bigger than a toddler, with two spheres that make up their body. The bottom, larger sphere is hollow with branch-like bars that display an empty cage if the beast has not recently gathered food. The smaller, bulbous sphere is its head. Endless vines erupt from its center mass to snare its fruit and protect itself from potential threats. Drevtoks can open and close their lower sphere, and once tamed, store both people and belongings safely within their bodies.

Taming: Drevtoks are solitary creatures that live near orchards or locations with a large amount of fruit, which is their preferred food source. They only eat when hungry and the rest of the time protect their fruit from other threats by ensnaring them with vines. To tame a Drevtok, a Charmer has to successfully steal a piece of fruit. When the Drevtok attacks, the Charmer must bypass the endless vines without harming the beast in order to make it amicable to taming. If the beast is harmed, it will immediately flee.

Effreft

Pronunciation: *eff-reft*

Rank: B-Class

Description: Effrefts are roughly the size of small dogs, with falcon heads, long, feathered tails, and wings. Their mint-green coloring and pink eyes make them easy to spot during the day, so they typically hunt at night. They can shower the space beneath their wingspan with magic, encouraging plants to reach maturity in seconds, and the soil left behind is regarded as the most fertile in the world.

Taming: The Charmer should find an open field on a moonlit night and prepare a cornucopia. After overflowing it with a variety of food, they must initiate charm and wait. A successful taming may take several days, because Effrefts have unknown migratory patterns and might not be present. More sightings have occurred in the south, as they seem to prefer warmer wind currents.

Fabric Spinner

Pronunciation: *fabric spinner*

Rank: B-Class

Description: Fabric Spinners are reclusive beasts that live deep in caves far from civilization. While they're skittish in nature, they've been known to attack anything that strays into their territory. The wrap their prey in a web and slowly devour its organs over a period of time. They have humanoid heads with insect features, and human torsos that end in bulbous abdomens reminiscent of arachnids. With eight hairy legs, two pincers at the space where the torso transitions to abdomen, and two spiny, humanlike arms, they're exceptionally talented at snaring prey. The ducts on their inner wrists shoot an endless supply of near-unbreakable silken thread. Their fingers are coated in tiny, retractable barbs that allow them to slit their webs if need be. The spinner that protrudes from the beast's rear produces a single thread that tethers the Fabric Spinner to its lair. If it senses danger or wants to return after a successful hunt, it will retract that thread and be pulled at immense speed back to safety. Given they're solitary creatures and rarely mate—females often attempt to eat males after copulation—not many Charmers own this beast. Those who do own the beast are often tailors, using the silk threads to craft immensely sturdy clothing or other sought-after materials, such as fishing line.

Taming: After finding the lair of a Fabric Spinner, the Charmer must bring several buckets of fresh organs to present to the beast. It will examine each offering one by one, and if it finds the organ appealing, it will wrap them in webbing for later consumption. If one of the organs has gone foul, the Fabric Spinner will become enraged and attack. Assuming all organs are satisfactory, the beast will then weave an intricate web. The Charmer must willingly ensnare themselves and wait patiently while the Fabric Spinner eats the provided organs, symbolizing the patience the beast exudes while hunting. The Charmer must remain completely still for the entire duration of the meal, otherwise the Fabric Spinner will attack. Once the beast has finished eating, it will cut the Charmer down from the web and allow itself to be tamed.

Femsy

Pronunciation: *fem-zee*

Rank: D-Class

Description: Like the sparrow, the Femsy are small and flighty. They travel in flocks and rarely hold still, making it difficult to snag one's attention long enough to charm it. They're steel gray in color with violet breasts. When one is tamed, a yellow film slides over its three black eyes, marking it as owned. After a successful taming, the Charmer can tap into the bird's eyesight for short intervals by concentrating on the bond. Because there are no distance limitations to shared sight, the Femsy is often used for reconnaissance. However, the act is quite draining on the bird and can only be used three times before it must be sent back to the beast realm to recover.

Taming: No additional taming requirements are needed aside from standard charm.

Gigloam

Pronunciation: *gig-loam*

Rank: A-Class

Description: Gigloams are solitary, bear-like creatures that live in woodland areas and are the size of elephant bulls when fully grown. Their mossy green hides help them blend in with their surroundings, and they hibernate several months out of the year. They have stag-like antlers and a bone helm that grows over their skull, protecting their faces. In the center of their helm is the etching of a moon that changes to match the lunar cycle. When the Gigloam is ready to attack, it channels moonlight between its antlers and sends a beam at its prey. The closer the etching is to the full moon, the stronger the beast is and the more beams it can produce.

Taming: Gigloam are extremely territorial, and the only time a Charmer can tame a Gigloam is during a new moon when the beast has no ability to summon a beam of moonlight. The Charmer must bring a bag of moonstones that have been charged by the most recent full moon. Low on power, the Gigloam will be attracted to the stones, and, rather than attack the Charmer for entering its territory, will allow passage into its cave. Since the new moon is associated with new beginnings, the Charmer must share with the beast their goals and desires, as well as any barriers or hardships they wish to overcome. If the beast finds the Charmer's dreams suitable, they will bow their head to the earth and allow the Charmer to tame them. If not, the beast will attack.

Graveltot

Pronunciation: *grah-vul-tot*

Rank: D-Class

Description: The Graveltot is a small, spherical beast covered in slate and rocks. It moves by rolling across the ground, only popping out its head and feet when prompted to activate its power. When its hooves meet the earth, it manipulates the force of gravity in a perfect circle around it, making it impossible for anyone caught in its trap to move. It only lasts for fifteen minutes, and the Graveltot must rest for several hours before it can use its power again.

Taming: No additional taming requirements are needed aside from standard charm.

Groober

Pronunciation: *groo-ber*

Rank: E-Class

Description: Groobers are round, fluffy beasts with white fur softer than a rabbit's fluff. They have stubby arms and legs and circular eyes. When squeezed tightly, Groobers emit a mixture of lavender and valerian to aid with sleep.

Taming: No additional taming requirements are needed aside from standard charm.

Gulya

Pronunciation: *ghoul-ya*

Rank: B-Class

Description: The bat-like Gulya is the size of a child with leathery, paper-thin wings and circular, glass-blue eyes. Their ears are larger than their skull and can rotate in any direction to detect minute sounds. They use soundwaves to track prey, and when they activate their power, they become completely immobile, their gray hide turns ink-black, and their eyes burn red like fire. Black flames cover its body, and its ears stand at attention. When in this state, there is virtually nothing the Gulya can't detect within a five-mile radius. However, the Gulya uses a considerable amount of power while doing this, making their ability short-lived unless they're tamed by an exceptional Charmer.

Taming: Gulyas live in caves deep within forests to avoid contact with humans. They only way to tame this beast is to first locate a cave with suitable conditions for a Gulya, and then take up residence in a nearby, hidden location. Months might pass before a flock of Gulyas decide to make the cave their home. If the Charmer comes across an already full cave, the Gulyas will immediately flee, deem the area unsafe, and refuse to return for several years. If they successfully move in, the Charmer must then wait until high noon, when the Gulyas are sleeping, to enter the cave. They should then find the largest Gulya, which is the flock's leader, and announce themselves by emitting a sharp whistle. This will panic the Gulyas, but the leader will descend, allowing itself to be tamed, while the rest flee.

Gyss

Pronunciation: *giss*

Rank: C-Class

Description: Gyss are the size of coffee mugs, with human torsos and misty, wisp-like tails for the lower half of their bodies. They can only be found in sacred sites and often adorn their hair with flowers or leaves. Their sharp, pointed teeth are used to crack nuts, one of their preferred food sources. Exceptionally cunning and mischievous, they like to talk in riddles and are the only known beast with an active relationship with the gods. Male Gyss have been spotted but not tamed. Gyss have the ability to grant one wish every six months. There are no limitations, so long as payment is met. However, the breadth of their

ability is dependent on
the master's power and
intelligence. While Gyss
can use their relationship
with the gods to argue
for less severe payments,
they often don't, as they
take joy in using their
power to the fullest
extent of their abilities.
As such, they are rarely,

if ever, called upon. Many Charmers feel Gyss should be ranked
higher, but their restricted conditions for wish-granting caused
the Council to rank them as C-Class beasts.

Taming: Gyss can only be found at sacred sites and require utter
stillness to tame. Otherwise, standard charm is all that's needed.

Havra

Pronunciation: *hav-rah*

Rank: E-Class

Description: Havra are small and slender in stature with gangly
limbs and knobby fingers. They have long faces with four deer-
like eyes. They are solitary creatures who live in forests and
survive off berries. While holding their breath, they are able to
materialize through objects. Because of this and their bark-like
skin, they were initially thought to be tree spirits.

Taming: Havra can only be found in dense wood. The Charmer
should place a basket of fresh berries at the base of a tree and
wait. Once a Havra is spotted, the Charmer must hold their
breath and initiate charm.

Iksass

Pronunciation: *ik-sass*

Rank: B-Class

Description: The Iksass alters its constitution to suit its master's needs. Generally, though, they appear to be tall and slender and take human shape, but are faceless. Despite that, they have excellent senses. Limbs appear and disappear on a whim, and they prefer invisibility, making them difficult to locate. They lurk unseen and hunt small game or steal food from wandering travelers. Needing vast amounts of sleep to power their ability, they can only be called upon for one two-hour stint during a day once tamed. Many Charmers use Iksass for protection, as their shape-shifting abilities make them formidable opponents.

Taming: The key to taming an Iksass is locating it. Without a known preferred habitat, the only way to tame one is for the Charmer to catch it picking their pocket in search of food. When this happens, immediately activate charm to keep the beast from fleeing, and maintain it for two hours or until the beast tires.

Kaiku

Pronunciation: *keye-kew*

Rank: C-Class

Description: Kaiku are small, pale-blue beasts with jelly-like bodies and four stubby tentacles. They're found in shallow ocean waters (not on any Lendrian coast). Females have an aquamarine gem embedded in their centers, whereas males have a ruby. When its power is activated, the Kaiku can, without fault, guide the Charmer to any location they desire. Their gem glows as they determine the location, and then they direct accordingly with their limbs.

Taming: After discovering the Kaiku's habitat and noting its sex, the Charmer must acquire at least twenty matching gemstones and offer them to the beast. If the beast finds a stone that is shinier than the one embedded in its body, it will shed the old gem and replace it with the new one. Then, charm can be initiated. If the Kaiku does not find a suitable replacement, it will flee and taming will be unsuccessful.

Kestral

Pronunciation: *kes-tral*

Rank: Unknown

Description: The Kestral is an untamable beast that magically appeared when Wilheimians forced Charmers to flee after the First War. The Kestral emerged and created an unbreakable border around Hireath to keep the dark magic of the Kitska Forest out. The beast maintains the threshold at all times, only allowing Charmers and those it deems fit to cross. It has incredibly long tail feathers, a large wingspan, and a slender, paper-white body with blue eyes.

Taming: Not possible. Trying results in the beast casting the Charmer across the threshold, only allowing them to return after an undetermined length of time.

Krik

Pronunciation: *crick*

Rank: D-Class

Description: Krik are pear-shaped birds with tiny green feathers. They have small, trumpet-like beaks that emit a staticky, dissonant sound known to steadily drive those who hear it insane.

The Krik's lungs operate independently of each other, allowing the bird to inhale fresh air while still exhaling to maintain its call.

Taming: No additional taming requirements are needed aside from standard charm.

Laharock

Pronunciation: *la-ha-rock*

Rank: A-Class

Description: Larger than an elephant and built like a wingless dragon, the Laharock is one of the largest beasts in Lendria. It uses its thick claws to traverse the rough volcanic terrain of its preferred habitat and is surprisingly nimble. The bone mane around its crown acts as an extra layer of protection for the head, and large, pupil-less white eyes glow with the intensity of fire. Red scales rimmed in gold cover the Laharock's spine, neck, and legs, making the underbelly the only unprotected portion of its hide. These scales are easily corroded by salt water, which can cause damage to the Laharock. If the Laharock grows up in the

wild without threat or human interference, it will develop magic that allows it to summon scalding fires and intense heat. Offspring, on the other hand, are empathic metamorphs, susceptible to an outside trigger that could alter their power. Once the trigger event occurs, the power solidifies.

Taming: Laharock absorb minerals from the volcanoes on which they live. Charmers will need to seek out an active volcano and bring a freshly caught marlin. Once the Laharock spots the Charmer, they should leave the fish on a slab and take several steps back. While the Laharock is eating, the Charmer should insert ear plugs, then summon a Songbloom and use its lullaby to put the Laharock in a stupor. The Charmer must remember to approach slowly and find sure footing along the mountain, because one loose rock or loud noise can break the trance and enrage the Laharock. Regardless, the Laharock will produce an intense aura of heat as a means of protection. Being burned is unavoidable. To avoid severe damage, Charmers should immediately summon a Poi afterward to tend to their skin. Once upon the Laharock, Charmers must place a hand on its snout and initiate charm.

Alternative method (discovered by Leena Edenfrell): Find a Laharock with her recently birthed young. Separate the mother from the child. Carefully approach the offspring and tame it first (no additional requirements outside of standard charm). Be careful not to spook it, as that might cause a flood of unstable powers to occur. Once the offspring is tamed, the mother will call off her pursuit and willingly allow herself to be charmed in order to stay with her young.

Mistari

Pronunciation: *mis-tar-ee*

Rank: A-Class

Description: The Mistari is one of the ten legendary feline beasts and has a white coat and scaled crystal plates over its chest. Four wings sprout from each of its ankles, resembling jagged pieces of precious gems. They enable the Mistari to propel itself forward, even gliding over short distances. The crystal feathers are highly valuable and, when dropped, can be broken and embedded in the skin of two people, granting them the ability to share thoughts. Mistari live in small prides scattered throughout the plains. Due to their wings and speed, they are difficult to track.

Taming: Charmers should approach with caution and begin the following sequence: First, encircle the Mistari with a mixture of highly valuable gems and stones while half crouched and chuffing to symbolize deference. Then, lie facedown on the ground and remain completely still. If the Mistari does not approve of the Charmer's offering, the Charmer should run. Taming will not be successful and could result in death. If the beast does approve, it will pick the Charmer up by the scruff (Charmers should wear thick clothing to prevent injury) and bring them into the circle. Charmers should stay limp until the beast begins to lick them, then initiate charm.

Myad

Pronunciation: *my-ad*

Rank: A-Class

Description: The Myad is the largest of the ten legendary feline beasts, with a panther-like build, black fur, and a mane comprised of peacock feathers. The same vibrant teal and emerald feathers travel the length of its spine and tail, as well as onto its wings. Gold casings protect the weak points of its ankles and appear around the crown of its head. When the Myad is about to take flight, blue magic streams from its feet and eyes. The Myad has the unique ability to place its prey in a stupor while

prying into their deepest memories. The person in question is then forced to face the horrors of their past, which often results in insanity. If the Myad finds them unworthy, the person's mind is burned to ash, leaving them in a comatose state for the rest of their lives. Because Myads are carnivorous, they are likely to consume their helpless and unfeeling prey.

Taming: Taming a Myad is a dangerous three-step process. First, the Charmer must acquire the blood of a murderer, freely given, and present it to the beast. Second, they must offer a token of loyalty with high personal value. And finally, they must allow the beast to bite them, thus spurring a connection that enables the Myad to review memories and determine worth. Throughout the entire process, the Charmer must not scream, because that will break the Myad's concentration, causing it to either flee or attack. If the Charmer can survive the evaluation of their past, the Myad will grant permission to tame.

Nagakori

Pronunciation: *na-ga-kor-ee*

Rank: B-Class

Description: Nagakori mate for life at a young age and, as such, are always found in pairs. They are twin serpents that float in the air with dragon-like heads and whiskers that trail the length of their bodies. Females are electric-blue in coloring and can spew water from their unhinged jaws, while males are snow-white and shoot frost. When tamed, they must both be summoned at the same time, as they refuse to be separated.

Taming: Pairs can be found in cold areas near bodies of water. They're attracted to pleasant sounds, so Charmers should lure them out with a musical instrument or by singing. While maintaining the music, the Charmer must then perform a ribbon dance. The Nagakori will begin to mimic the flourishes of the ribbons, eventually surrounding the Charmer and allowing charm to be initiated. The Charmer cannot falter with the music, as this will cause the Nagakori to freeze them and flee.

Naughtbird

Pronunciation: *nawt-bird*

Rank: C-Class

Description: These small, sparrowlike creatures have hundreds of tiny iridescent feathers. When they're in flight, their wings move so fast they're hard to pinpoint, and their tail feathers resemble that of a boat's rudder, angling from left to right to help steer. They have long, needle-shaped beaks that can pierce nearly any hide. When that happens, their saliva infiltrates the target's system and places them in deep slumber.

Taming: Naughtbirds live in hives. To lure one out, create a trail of flower petals that lead to a small bowl of nectar. If interested, the Naughtbird will follow the trail and drink from the bowl. Once the nectar is gone, initiate charm.

Nezbit

Pronunciation: *nez-bit*

Rank: C-Class

Description: Nezbits are small, have rabbit-like builds with brown fur, and are coated with teal feathers. Exceptionally rare, they're near impossible to find because of their low numbers and their preference for living underground. They form small colonies and create large networks beneath the soil, only poking their wing-like ears up once every few days to absorb nutrients from the sun. Their ears can hear sounds from miles away, and they track reverberations in the earth to avoid danger. When tamed, they're used to listen to people's hearts and determine lies from truth. Their opal eyes flash green for truth and red for lies.

Taming: As they live underground, the Nezbits have no known preferred environment. Finding a colony involves luck and careful examination of the earth, because Nezbits leave behind small mounds after sticking their ears up from the ground. Once a possible mound has been sighted, the Charmer should remain still for several days until the ears appear. The Charmer should then quickly yank the beast up from the dirt and immediately initiate charm. It's important to note that the mounds in question are extremely similar to those left by prairie dogs, and because of that, reports of colonies are often inaccurate.

Nix Ikari

Pronunciation: *nix ih-car-ee*

Rank: A-Class

Description: One of the large legendary feline beasts, Nix Ikari are known as supreme hunters given their ability to completely mask their presence and teleport. They have snow-colored fur covered with dark, royal-blue spots with indigo inlays. When their power activates, glowing orchid light streams from their eyes and the spots, indicating they're about to teleport. They have elongated canines, twin curling horns behind their ears, and a thick, bushy tail twice the length of their bodies. They can travel great distances, though they normally only teleport in short bursts when hunting. The greater the distance required for teleporting, the longer it takes the Nix Ikari to recover.

Taming: Nix Ikari are fierce predators and will not be tamed without first deciding whether or not the Charmer in question is willing to fight. As such, very few Charmers have ever tamed this beast. After a Nix Ikari has marked a Charmer for a potential master, it will follow them unseen, judging their actions for an undetermined period of time. Once the decision has been made, the beast will appear and either kill the Charmer or allow itself to be tamed. Nix Ikari live in cold, near-inhospitable climates, and to start the taming process, the Charmer must provide prey, encircle it in the Charmer's blood, and decorate the area with fire opals.

Nyneve

Pronunciation: *nigh-neev*

Rank: C-Class

Description: A Nyneve is a medium-size aquatic lizard. It can be identified by its bright blue tongue, translucent body, and large luna moth–like wings. They are primarily found in large lakes. The Nyneve gains its energy from the sun, so during the day they can be found sunbathing. Under the sun, their skin hardens into scales for protection and turns a light-brown color. Their wings are fully formed but they are unable to fly. If attacked, the wings may be used to glide or propel an escape to the water. At night, the Nyneve glow a phosphorescent bright blue and travel in large groups to form beautifully intricate patterns in the water. The Nyneve's wings also glow, and they are used like fins to glide through the water. Finding a group of Nyneve is extremely rare and auspicious.

Taming: Once the Charmer has spotted the nighttime phenomenon of the Nyneve group, they must toss a shiny object—preferably something of great value to the Charmer—into the lake. If the Nyneve accept the offering, the Charmer must enter the water and follow the group, as they will lead the Charmer to the location of a long-forgotten sunken treasure. If the Charmer is unable to secure the treasure before sunrise, they must try again the following night. Once the Charmer has successfully retrieved the treasure, the leader of the Nyneve pack will present itself for taming. Once tamed, the Nyneve can successfully locate a new hidden treasure once every few months, which the Charmer can sell or keep, making taming this beast a lucrative path.

Charmed by: Anna Hampton

Ocnolog

Pronunciation: *ock-no-log*

Rank: Unknown

Description: Ocnolog was the first beast ever to be tamed by the goddess Celeste. He is the only dragon beast known to Charmers, and his immense power nearly turned all of Lendria to ash. Larger than Hireath's mountain, he can fly at incredible speeds and destroy entire cities with his endless fire. He has gleaming, alabaster scales and ruby-red eyes, and until former Crown Yazmin awakened him, slumbered beneath the keep in Hireath.

Taming: Yazmin awakened Ocnolog by performing a forbidden dark magic ritual involving bones of a tainted Charmer, blood of an undead prince—recognized by the gods—and her heart. While this resulted in Ocnolog rising from his crypt, Yazmin couldn't fully control him. It was not until Leena Edenfrell, current Queen of Lendria and Crown of the Charmers Council, used her ability to break taming bonds and sacrifice her heart that Ocnolog found peace in the beast realm at Celeste's side.

Ossilix

Pronunciation: *oss-eh-lix*

Rank: A-Class

Description: While Ossilix are the smallest of the legendary feline beasts, they exude a calm fury and are lethal, using size to their advantage to outmaneuver prey. Slightly larger than an ocelot, they have lithe bodies coated in metal, giving the appearance of silver and making their hide near impenetrable. They're known to be incredibly intelligent, displaying exceptional tactical thinking and striking only when they see the possibility of a killing blow. Ossilix saliva is a potent healing balm with the capability of bringing someone back from the brink of death. However, accepting this gift requires the recipient to sacrifice a sliver of humanity in exchange. The effects vary from person to person, but largely involve a physical transformation to that of a beast.

Taming: After finding an Ossilix, the Charmer must allow it to inflict a life-threatening injury and then accept its healing balm. If the Charmer does not accept, it will kill them quickly. If they do accept, the Ossilix will retreat and watch from a distance as their humanity slips away and they transform into a beast. This transformation represents the constant fury the Ossilix feels and, as such, is incredibly difficult to control. The Ossilix will study the Charmer's behavior, killing them if they're unable to withstand the burning rage, or accepting them as its master if they're able to revert back to human form.

Poi

Pronunciation: *poy*

Rank: B-Class

Description: Poi are solitary creatures that often establish territories over small clearings in the woods. They have fox-like bodies with white fur and a single black stripe running the length of their spines. Their most identifiable feature is the jewel-like amethyst orb nestled between their ears, which turns cloudy when a prediction is brewing and clears once the future has been set. Poi bites are venomous and will slowly kill, but the poison can be removed by the beast if tamed. Their saliva can close minor wounds and alleviate burns, though their true power lies in their ability to predict outcomes two minutes into the future. When tamed, the Poi can share its visions with its master.

Taming: No additional requirements are needed outside of standard charm, but the Charmer must hold their charm for several minutes while making no sudden movements, allowing the Poi to perform a series of predictions and determine the outcome of being tamed.

Prentiss

Pronunciation: *pren-tiss*

Rank: S-Class

Description: The Prentiss is a ferocious, serpentine beast with an arrow-tipped tail, bat-like wings, and monstrous claws at its first wing joint. Its fangs are longer than elephant trunks and twice as thick, but its most devastating attack involves its normally deflated belly. When it inhales, it creates a vortex that disrupts magic and devours anything. Once the creature's belly is full, it releases violent tornadoes from its maw. The beast lives in the Gaping Wound and only stirs when someone other than the royal family crosses to Tyrus's Ruins. It will attack intruders and feed on them, only returning to hibernate in the canyon's depths once it deems the area safe again.

Taming: Unknown.

Quolint

Pronunciation: *qoh-lint*

Rank: D-Class

Description: These small, frog-like beasts are the size of one's finger, with bright-green skin and red spots. They have tiny, see-through wings, allowing them to glide short distances while hunting for flies. Their skin secretes a viscous poison that has memory-altering powers. In the wild, this acts as a defense mechanism, causing a predator to pause and forget its actions if the poison touches its mouth. When tamed, Charmers can wear gloves to safely siphon some of the secretion and brew memory-altering concoctions that are tasteless.

Taming: No additional requirements are needed for taming other than to initiate charm, but it's important to note that the

Charmer must not touch the Quolint during the process. While ingesting the poison will cause more lasting memory loss, touch can still cause temporary amnesia. Thus, if the Charmer grazes the Quolint while taming, they will forget why they're there, and the beast will escape.

Revmandra

Pronunciation: *rev-man-dra*

Rank: A-Class

Description: One of the most formidable water beasts, the Revmandra is a solitary creature that travels the ocean in search of treasure, which it affixes to its hide via a sticky secretion from its skin. It has a salamander-like body and three moose antlers that grow from the base of its skull. The Revmandra is the size of a whale and remarkably fast, and because of its ability to produce air bubbles which can be caught on its antlers, Charmers often seek out this beast as a means for safe underwater travel.

Taming: Taming and locating a Revmandra is exceedingly difficult, though sunken ships and areas with invaluable treasures are generally considered the best place to start. Once a Charmer has spotted a Revmandra, they must prepare some bait: fish, seashells, a pirate's treasure, and a pearl. After acquiring the needed ingredients, the Charmer should carry the bait into the ocean, drop beneath the surface, and initiate their charm. As Revmandra are called to treasure, it is highly likely that multiple beasts will appear. They will then battle for the right to claim the treasure. If for any reason someone interferes with the taming, the Revmandra will view the new person as a competing beast and attack. If the person survives, the Revmandra will consider the bait claimed and disperse. If the person dies, the Revmandra will continue to fight to claim the treasure. Once there is only one remaining beast, it will approach the Charmer. After the Revmandra inspects the bait and deems it worthy, the Charmer can then tame the beast.

Scorpex

Pronunciation: *scor-pex*

Rank: B-Class

Description: The Scorpex is a dangerous beast that can grow to roughly thirty feet in length. Its wormlike body is plated in thick orange scales and coated with a shimmery mucus. It has four legs, each ending in hooked fingers, and a barbed tail with a stinger like that of a scorpion. Its poison is painful but not incurable. With six eyes, three on either side of its mandibles, the Scorpex is difficult to catch off guard. It is carnivorous and uses its eight tongues to strip carcasses down to the bones in a matter of minutes.

Taming: Scorpex are rarely owned, because taming one requires collecting carcasses for weeks to accumulate enough food to entice the beast. The smell alone dissuades most Charmers, not to mention the danger of the Scorpex itself. After presenting the pile of carcasses, the Charmer should wait until the beast has finished eating to initiate charm. If the Charmer has not provided enough to satiate the Scorpex's hunger, it will strike. A relatively "safe" number of carcasses to present is somewhere in the high twenties.

Songbloom

Pronunciation: *song-bloom*

Rank: D-Class

Description: The Songbloom is a relatively harmless beast found in rosebushes in remote parts of Lendria. The lower half of their bodies mimic the petals of a flower, and their humanlike torsos bloom out of the center of the bulb. They can detach and float from plant to plant, reattaching via miniscule roots at the base of the petals that allow them to pull nutrients from the plant. Male Songbloom are ivy-colored and camouflage with the leaves, whereas females take after the actual roses. Both male and female Songbloom spend their days singing in an unknown language. There are a variety of tunes, and each one has a unique effect on the listener, ranging from feelings of elation to causing temporary slumber. Charmers frequently use Songbloom to elicit feelings of joy and love during ceremonies between mates.

Taming: Find a Songbloom colony by listening for their voices while searching through rosebushes. Once found, the Charmer must seat themselves before the beast and listen to a song of the Songbloom's choosing. Once the tune is complete, they should offer applause and then initiate charm. If the Songbloom elects to perform a sleeping tune, the Charmer will fall into slumber and be unable to offer applause, and the taming will fail. As the effects should only last a few minutes, the Charmer is free to try again once waking, assuming the Songbloom has not fled.

Sparklainha

Pronunciation: *sparkle-ayn-uh*

Rank: C-Class

Description: A ferocious-looking, but ultimately amiable, marine predator, the Sparklainha has glittering pink skin and makes quick work of its prey (smaller marine creatures and ill-prepared Charmer) with its seemingly infinite rows of razor-sharp teeth. This shark-like beast has the ability to swallow its enemies whole when threatened, though as it lives far out in remote depths of the ocean, this is a rare occurrence.

Taming: Finding a Sparklainha can take a great deal of time, as they have no singular home and are constantly on the move. The best thing to do is wait for weeks on end in the deepest part of the ocean and hopefully spot one. To tame a Sparklainha, the Charmer must source the Sparklainha's favorite snack— namely, tacos, cheesy crackers, and the flesh of its enemies— and then present it calmly. Once the Sparklainha has eaten its fill, the Charmer can initiate standard charm to tame the beast.

Charmed by: Lindsay Landgraf Hess

Sunnari

Pronunciation: *sun-are-ee*

Rank: A-Class

Description: One of the larger feline beasts, the Sunnari looks like a tiger that glows, its fur filled with light. It has pure white wings that are tipped in sunlight. It is said to live above the clouds, and gets its glow from the sun. As such, it has the ability to summon and control pure light.

Taming: To tame the Sunnari, a Charmer must first find a place with very thick clouds of the purest white. Then they must lay down a circle of gold and wait for the Sunnari to appear, which can take minutes to hours. If the beast appears, it will sit outside the golden circle and wait as the Charmer summons their strongest or most-prized beast within the circle. The Sunnari will examine it, mentally and physically. If it finds it to be in a strong and healthy condition, then the Charmer must also summon their weakest beast. The Sunnari will once again assess the beast, ensuring the Charmer cares for all beasts fairly, regardless of strength, shape, or size. If so, it will allow itself to be tamed. If the Sunnari determines the Charmer's beasts have been mistreated, it will attack.

Charmed by: Sophia Pyper

Telesávra

Pronunciation: *tell-eh-sav-rah*

Rank: D-Class

Description: The Telesávra is a lizard the size of a small boulder and has a rocky hide. It can detach its jaw to suck in air and summon a flickering white portal that will transport any beast or person with Charmer's blood to a designated location, referred to as a hearth point. The Telesávra can only remember one hearth point at a time. Many Charmers set Hireath as their hearth point for efficient and safe travel home.

Taming: No additional taming requirements are needed aside from standard charm.

Uloox

Pronunciation: *oo-locks*

Rank: C-Class

Description: The Uloox is a black snake with yellow eyes and three
fangs found in caves. It can eat prey up to five times larger than
its body size, thanks to its unhinging jaw and fast-acting digestive system. Tiny ducts are found along the roof of its mouth,
just behind its fangs. Uloox venom is dangerous, and is known
to cloud the mind and cause hallucinations, as well as weaken
the body. Muscles will seize and become nearly immobile until
the venom fades. Very few Charmers own one, as they're known
to be temperamental and find little joy in being summoned from
the beast realm.

Taming: To tame an Uloox, a Charmer must allow themselves to
be bitten as many times as the beast deems fit. This is highly
dangerous, as multiple bites can result in death. Once the Uloox
is satisfied that the Charmer has become immobile, it will wait
until its venom has cycled out of the Charmer's system. Only then
will it allow itself to be tamed. However, if the beast becomes
hungry during the taming process, it will slowly devour parts of
the Charmer, such as fingers or toes, until it is either full or the
Charmer is able to move. It's recommend that several field mice
are brought along to the taming to prevent this.

Visavem

Pronunciation: *vee-sah-vem*

Rank: E-Class

Description: A Visavem is a small, flightless, spherical bird the size
of a yarn ball with one spiral-shaped leg. They live in grassy
plains and travel in herds by bouncing on their oversized foot.

When they bounce, they produce a dust that can be collected and used as a preserving agent.

Taming: No additional taming requirements are needed aside from standard charm.

Vissirena

Pronunciation: *vis-sy-reen-ah*

Rank: B-Class

Description: Vissirena have human torsos and fishlike lower bodies that end in long, colorful tails. Iridescent scales varying in color cover the entirety of their figure, and their hair is a mixture of seaweed and tentacles. Their faces also share similar structures to those of fish, and additional fins often develop along the forearms. Vissirena live in schools in the waters to the west of Hireath. The fleshy voids on their palms can open and close, altering currents to bring prey in their direction. When tamed, they can channel powerful streams of water with immense force. Vissirena can only be summoned in bodies of water.

Taming: Do not attempt to charm a Vissirena underwater. At the first hint of danger, they will send the threat to the bottom of the ocean via an unforgiving current until drowning has occurred. Likewise, do not attempt to catch from a boat, as they'll simply destroy the ship. Instead, a Charmer should fish for one from the shore. Only a magically reinforced pole, coupled with fishing line made from Fabric Spinner silk, will hold the

Vissirena's weight. Preferred bait is tuna wrapped in orange peel. Once the Vissirena is hooked, the Charmer should prepare for a fight that could last several days. After the Charmer has reeled one in, they should initiate charm.

$\mathcal{V}$rees

Pronunciation: *vrees*

Rank: S-Class

Description: As one of the five known S-Class beasts, the Vrees's power exceeds that of all A-Class beasts. Normally, the beast is massive in size with burning, white eyes. It has a fox-like head with the body of a wolf and three foxtails. Its form is more like a sieve with cutouts and negative space that mist passes through. In its center, a ball of blue electricity sparks and summons lightning. Weapons cannot scathe its hide, and only the right type of magic can harm this beast. When summoning a bolt of lightning, it takes a few minutes to charge prior to striking. When there are no threats around, the Vrees will shrink in size, reaching about midthigh in height.

Taming: The exact number of Vrees in the wild and their breeding habits are entirely unknown, as they are thought to live in storm clouds. Tracking this creature takes years and can span many continents, as they have no set home. To start, the Charmer must first find a lightning storm and look for a storm cloud in the shape of a wolf. Then, they must follow the storm until the clouds reach a sandy area. If it strikes, the lightning will petrify, creating an object that looks similar to a tree branch. Once cooled, collect the petrified lightning. If the bolt came from a cloud other than the wolf-shaped one, it won't work. If the Charmer is lucky enough to collect petrified lightning from the wolf-shaped cloud, they must then wait again for the storm to reappear, sometimes years later in an entirely different location. When this happens, the Charmer must present the petrified lightning. The Vrees will sense the offering and strike it, shattering the object and manifesting before the Charmer. It will then strike the Charmer with a bolt of lightning, and if they survive, allow itself to be tamed.

Vyprale

Pronunciation: *vie-pray-elle*

Rank: A-Class

Description: With a snakelike body and the head of a falcon, the Vyprale is a stunning flying beast covered in shimmery, reflective feathers. Its lion's mane trails the length of its extensive form, and its wingspan can cast several houses in shadow. The creature is so bright it's often mistaken for the rising sun or a shooting star, and it never lands. It pulls power from the sun's rays and can shoot blasts of pure light in the shape of arrows from its wings.

Taming: Vyprale are migratory and near impossible to track, as they never touch the earth and instead hover in the clouds to recharge when they're not flying across the globe. If a Charmer is lucky enough to discover a Vyprale, it is solely because one has descended from the clouds in search of mate. They do not wish to compete with the sun's brilliance, and in fact, if the Vyprale finds a mate while high in the sky, they often do not couple, as they're both distracted by the beauty of the sun. In order to grab the Vyprale's attention, the Charmer must adorn themselves in bright feathers and gold paint to rival the beast's luminous coat. Then, the Charmer must shimmy and move in a jerking, circular pattern, paying mind to angle their body toward the sun to reflect the most light. When the Charmer glimpses the beast, they must emit a suitable birdcall to lure it down. If the Vyprale is pleased, it will attempt to snare the Charmer with its teeth in a display of affection. This often ends in injury due to the size difference, but if the Charmer is able to withstand the pain, they can initiate charm and the Vyprale will accept.

Whet

Pronunciation: *wet*

Rank: B-Class

Description: Whets are owl beasts that lead solitary lives and can only be found in high treetops at night. They have three gleaming ocher eyes, bark-colored feathers, and twin branch-like horns that stretch outward on either side of their head. In the wild, these horns embed themselves into trees and telegraph information to the Whet about where their prey are, making them expert hunters. Once tamed, they can be used to record information into tomes based off what they hear.

Taming: Whets are extremely difficult to locate, as they can sense when another being is in their territory and will flee. However, if they have recently eaten and are sated, they're less likely to fly away and will instead survey the approaching Charmer. The Charmer must then sit on the forest floor and read to the Whet for hours. As the Whet will likely get hungry during this process, it's necessary to bring small game to keep them in place. Once the Charmer has finished reading at least a minimum of three hundred pages, the Whet will be open to taming. Initiate charm.

Xifos

Pronunciation: *zy-fos*

Rank: A-Class

Description: Because of its replication magic, the Xifos is regarded as one of the most difficult legendary feline beasts to tame. It has a slender, slate-gray body with twin tails that form sharp arrowheads. When the Xifos is activating its power, all the hair on its body stands on end, solidifying into fine needles, and then it shudders, creating an exact replica of itself. The number of copies one Xifos can maintain varies, though the recorded high is two hundred and three. Each copy can attack with the full strength and force of the original. If a copy is injured or otherwise incapacitated, it will dissolve into smoke. Xifos are solitary, yet they usually have a pack of copies flanking them for protection.

Taming: A Xifos will only bond with a master cunning enough to separate the original from the copies. Simply approaching the beast and initiating charm will cause the beast to activate its power, surrounding the Charmer with copies. After the copies have shuffled, the Xifos will wait until the Charmer touches the one they believe is real. If they're wrong, the copy disappears, and all remaining forms attack. No one has ever guessed correctly via this method. Instead, after locating a Xifos, the Charmer should study it for several months to ensure they have the original version pegged. Charmers should find a cavern that can be used as a den, and construct an elaborate display of mirrors. They should then lure the Xifos to the cavern with the mating call of a pheasant, their preferred prey. If arranged correctly, the mirrors will trick the Xifos into thinking it has already summoned copies of itself. While it's searching for the pheasant, the Charmer should slowly approach. Thinking the Charmer is already surrounded by copies, the beast will sit and wait for them to choose. Touch the original Xifos, and initiate charm.

Yimlet

Pronunciation: *yim-lit*

Rank: B-Class

Description: Yimlets are beetle beasts with iridescent orange hides, barbed horns, and pincers larger than their heads. The size of a small dog, these beasts are surprisingly fast and can fly short distances, making it easy to snare their prey. When they bite their target, a toxin secretes from their mouths, deteriorating the skin of their prey immediately upon impact. The toxin will spread, eventually killing the target and allowing for the Yimlet to eat in peace. They can ingest up to five times their body weight in one sitting.

Taming: The only way to tame a Yimlet is to capture it with a net made of Fabric Spinner thread. Any other material will dissolve with the Yimlet's venom, and they will attack the Charmer in a rage. Because Yimlets eat so frequently, they will soon become hungry after capture and allow for the Charmer to tame them, simply so they can be sent to the beast realm to hunt.

Zavalluna

Pronunciation: *zah-val-loo-nah*

Rank: A-Class

Description: Zavallunas are incredibly rare horselike beasts found only in foreign lands near places of highly concentrated magic. Auroras of varying colors, ranging from emerald to fuchsia to turquoise appear across their ink-black hides as they move. They have large feathered wings and a single bladelike horn that glows white. When their power is activated, they produce a dome of magic in a small radius that amplifies the abilities of any beast. This can only be done for a short amount of time, though, as extended use may cause permanent damage to the Zavallunas' horns.

Taming: Zavallunas are extremely selective when it comes to choosing a Charmer. As such, many become family beasts that are passed down from one generation to the next. To tame a wild Zavalluna, the Charmer must first travel to mage lands and partner with a mage in order to summon the beast. Once the beast has appeared, the mage must make a case on behalf of the Charmer, attesting to their magical prowess and kindness. Zavallunas will only agree to a taming if the mage and Charmer have been true friends for several years. The stronger their relationship, the more likely the taming will be a success.

Zystream

Pronunciation: *zy-stream*

Rank: A-Class

Description: The Zystream is the only legendary feline beast that prefers water to land, though it's capable of breathing in both environments. Liquid-blue, its coat is a mixture of water-resistant fur and scales. It has a long tail that ends in fins, as well as finned whiskers lining its jaw and throat. Fluid in nature, it's nearly impossible to pin and can shoot immensely powerful jet streams from its mouth. It's stronger in water and can summon small rain clouds to follow it when on land.

Taming: The Zystream can be found in fresh or salt water during the warmest month of summer. A Charmer must approach while the beast is swimming, where it will assess the Charmer by circling them several times. At some point, it will dive beneath the surface and snare the Charmer's foot, dragging them into deep water. It's imperative that a Charmer does not resist. If they do, the beast will become irritated and either kill them or release them and flee. If the Charmer remains calm, it will continue to swim until it senses the Charmer's lungs giving out. At that point, it will leap out of the water and place the Charmer on the bank. Then, it will press its snout to their chest and use magic to coax any water from their lungs and encourage them to breathe. Now that the Charmer has become one with the water in its eyes, the Zystream is ready to be tamed.

A Note on Honorary Bestiary Entries

While these beasts do not appear in the main plot of the Beast Charmer series, these wonderful creations were dreamt up by fans of the books, and I wanted to share their ingenious ideas with all my readers. All honorary beast entries have a Charmer's name included at the bottom.

BONUS CHAPTER

CALEM

The ship never really slept. There was always someone moving, someone doing something, to keep the *Sea Mare* on track. But after a few days of watching from the shadows and keeping tabs on the crew's routine, I'd found my opportunity for stealing Harlow's most prized treasure: Queen Jessamine's Conch. And not a moment too soon, since we were scheduled to pass Kings Isle in a few hours' time.

Slipping out of my cot, I glanced around the dark cabin and found my boots. Thick curtains hung over the only window, and faint dawn light ghosted around the edges. Ozias snored away on the folding bed next to mine, a giant, unmoving mound curled beneath a thin blanket. Across the room, Leena and Noc slept on a bed meant for one. Or rather, Leena slept. Noc must've heard me move, because he'd propped himself up on one arm and was eyeing the exit. Listening to the skeleton crew move about on deck, likely. There was no doubt he could hear them, too, senses heightened by death and all.

Noc whispered just loud enough for me to pick up over the perpetual creak and groan of the ship. "Don't get caught."

"Super helpful tip. Thanks for that." I flashed him a grin. "I'll be fine. I did this for how many years before you found my sorry ass?"

"It only takes one mistake."

"Yeah, yeah," I mumbled as I moved toward the door. Leave it to Noc to focus on the one mishap I'd encountered during my days as a thief. Of course, that mishap had resulted in my death and eventual raising, but semantics. I'd been reckless, stolen from the wrong person, and found myself at the end of a blade.

Lesson learned. Shaking my head, I steadied myself with a breath and focused only on the task at hand. The last thing I needed was to lose control. To shift into a monster on a ship full of innocent people. That would've been just peachy.

Slipping out of our cabin, I paused on the other side and trailed my fingers along the gilded frame of a massive portrait obscuring the hidden door. I let it shut behind me, the quiet click an inevitable sound that was near-deafening under the current circumstances. Flinching, I quickly scanned the room. The captain's quarters were still, as I'd expected. Bookshelves littered with trinkets—glass-blown vases, glittering figurines, jewel-encrusted bookends—and aging tomes dominated most of the walls. And Harlow's monstrous oil-rubbed desk sat in the middle of it all. Maps and charts were stretched out across it, and a freestanding copper globe stood tall beside her cushioned chair. The locked draws had a certain appeal, and while picking them had been easy, I'd suspected all along Harlow wouldn't store her conch there.

My eyes cut to the door across the room. Her sleeping chambers. Ozias had joked about me spending the night with her to gain access to her quarters. And while that would've been easier—and Ozias wasn't wrong to suggest such a tactic, given my history—something about that idea had given me pause.

It wasn't that Harlow wasn't striking. She was. Possibly even more so than the first time we'd worked together. But every time I caught her gaze, had the opportunity to answer her flirtatious grin with a smirk of my own, an image of Kaori had flashed in my mind. Her dark, intriguing stare hid so much. Occasionally I'd eke a hard-won smile out of her.

None of it made sense. She'd saved my life and become a close friend in that short time we'd spent together training in Hireath. And for whatever reason, every time I thought of doing something dubious, all I could picture was her disdainful glare. I'd spent years enduring Kost's similar looks, but they had nothing on Kaori.

So annoying. Once this war was over, things would return to normal. At least as normal as they could be with this damned beast lying in wait in my veins. Without any immediate threats, control would be easier. Maybe then I wouldn't have to suffer from the mental image of Kaori's disappointed expression.

Quietly, I moved across the room. A row of windows stretched along the back wall, displaying the ink-black waters and faded purple hue of the sky. I needed to get into Harlow's quarters and snag the conch before the sun fully rose. Otherwise, she'd be awake and ready to take me down with her cutlass.

Once at the door, I crouched before the handle and studied the bolt. I used to enjoy the subtle art of lock picking, the quiet scratch of metal on metal as I coaxed open doors and treasure boxes. The shadows eliminated the need for that particular skill, though. I didn't even carry my tools anymore. The ink-black tendrils I wielded were more than enough.

Eyeing the keyhole, I called forth a shadow and solidified it to match the opening, creating a key that would grant me access to Harlow's room. The resounding click was both satisfying and, again, entirely too loud. I held my breath as the door swung inward, and I waited at the threshold.

Harlow slept soundly beneath maroon silk sheets, a brightly colored headscarf wrapped around her hair. Leaning against the nightstand beside her large four-poster bed rested her sheathed cutlass. A threat in and of itself. My gaze bounced from place to place as I tried to determine where she'd hidden her most valuable treasure. I'd turned over her main cabin the night before just to make sure she didn't have a hidden safe stowed away somewhere. She hadn't, which meant the conch was in here.

Calling on the shadows, I blanketed my footsteps and moved about her room. Pushed aside trinkets, searched for trapdoors, hidden safes. All the while she slept, unperturbed by my presence. Still, I kept the shadows ready in case I needed to disappear quickly. In the days I'd been following her, she'd never checked on her treasures once. I'd found a trunk of gold aurics and some other valuables of my own volition, but she'd never given away any hints about their whereabouts. The mark of a thief. A *smart* thief. Normal people always subtly gave things away. Which meant she was being cautious. Careful. The last thing she wanted was for me to go snooping based off a cue she hadn't meant to give.

Especially since Noc was onboard and Queen Jessamine's Conch was his by birthright.

The light outside grew stronger, shifting from pale pink to buttery yellow, and I cursed the rays that snuck between the curtains. It wouldn't be long before her duties as captain forced her out of bed. After I'd perused her shelves a third time, I dropped to the floor and peered beneath her bed. There was nothing but mothballs and a forgotten stray garment collecting dust. As I moved away from the frame, my fingers grazed the edge of a handwoven wool rug. Large and circular, it obscured most of the worn floorboards. It was thick, too. Dense enough to dampen the sound of creaking wooden planks overlaying hidden hollow spaces.

I peeled back the edge of the carpet. The flooring was slightly cleaner, thanks to the rug's protection, but one plank was just higher than the rest. As if it'd been pried open and shoved back into place time and time again, eliminating a perfect seal. A grin stole over my lips, and I wrenched my fingers beneath the board. I gave it a forceful yank. The board answered with a quiet groan, and I stiffened. Harlow's snoring stopped. Every sound thundered in my ears as I waited for her to move. The waves crashing against the side of the ship. The scuttle of feet across the deck. Muffled conversations passed between crew members. Shadows formed in a pool beneath my body, ready to engulf me and hide me from view. The sheets rustled, and I glanced back at the open floorboard. A small leather pouch tied off with a red cord teased me with every passing second. Just waiting to be snatched.

Finally, Harlow let out a contented sigh, and her rhythmic snoring picked up again. Adrenaline left me in a rush, and a cool, sweeping sensation raced over my skin. I snatched the sack and replaced the floorboard in record time, tugging the rug back into place. Now, with the prize safely in my grasp, I stepped into the shadows and winked out of existence.

Queen Jessamine's Conch was mine.

ACKNOWLEDGMENTS

Writing Noc and Leena's story was a journey for me, and I couldn't have done it without the love and support of so many people. I have to give a giant shout-out to Lindsay Landgraf Hess, Alexa Martin, Katie Golding, and Tricia Lynne, as they've all been with me every step of the way, from the beginning of the Beast Charmer series until now. Their continued support and investment in my series have been a blessing.

I want to thank all my readers who've gone on this journey with me. And to those of you who reached out, thank you tenfold. Hearing your experience with my work and how much you love the world I created kept me going when I could hardly find the energy to type. My stories are for you, always.

I can't have an acknowledgments section without thanking my agent, Cate Hart, and my editor, Mary Altman. These rock stars are the reason *The Shattered Crown* and the entire Beast Charmer series exists today. They've supported me unflinchingly through the publication process, and they've never questioned my undying love for Noc. And Kost. Okay, Calem and Oz, too. (Though perhaps they've tried to fight me for the assassins' affections.)

And last, but certainly not least, I want to thank my family. My parents, my brother, my husband, my children—you're all integral parts of my life, and I'm so fortunate to have a solid foundation and support system like you all. I love you more than I can put into words.

Their story is far from over...

Coming soon,

SHADOWS OF THE LOST

Gaige is a Charmer. At least, he used to be a Charmer...until he died and was brought back as something different, something darker. He knows he shouldn't blame Kost for raising him from death, but he's not sure he can ever forgive him for having even a small hand in his rebirth. But when Gaige is lost to the shadow realm, Kost is the only one with any chance of bringing him back: if they can learn to trust (and perhaps love) each other again.

ONE

KOST

I couldn't bear to look at him. Not for more than a few moments. It had nothing to do with physical appearance—of course not. Pretending that Gaige was anything other than devastating was a lie. It was impossible not to acknowledge the pleasing curve of his lips, or the intricate, steel-blue shade of his eyes, so much like the polished blade of a sword dipped in ocean water. Textured, hickory-colored hair curled about his ears, and he let out a visible sigh as he stared out at the Kitska Forest lining Cruor's back lawns. Sitting alone bathed in the light of the moon, he was truly…something else.

It all just hurt too much to see.

Shadows writhed around him, slithering between blades of grass like wild snakes. He had no desire to control them. To harness his newfound power and form weapons out of the darkness. Instead, he let them run wild as if they were beasts he didn't have the power to charm. Absently, he dragged his fingers along faint stubble clinging to his jawline. Gloved fingers.

My shoulders tensed. Those leather gloves hid a sight *Gaige* couldn't stomach—his faded Charmer's symbol. Before, the inked marking had been a vibrant, citrine tree full of life. Now… It was nothing more than a smeared, charcoal etching. A permanent reminder of the beast realm, and all the creatures, he could no longer access.

All because of me.

I turned my back on the window from my study overlooking the lawns, both reluctant and relieved to tear my gaze away. Sinking into the ornate stuffed chair behind the desk, I nudged a few pieces of parchment to the side. Bounties. More people for the assassins of Cruor to kill. A dull ache simmered behind my eyes, and I rubbed my temples. Becoming Cruor's new guild master after Noc was crowned king was a wonderful distraction, but even now, with jobs and responsibilities laid out before me, I couldn't keep my mind off Gaige. The back of my neck prickled, as if he were staring at me through the window. It was absurd to think that he was—that he might want to look my way at all—but still, I itched to push away from the desk and see for myself.

A whisper of shadows swirled in the corner, snagging my focus. Tendrils pulled from every hidden crevice in the office, and they interwove in indistinct patterns until knitting together in the shape of a man. Noc. He craned his neck from side to side before tucking his hands in the pockets of his fitted trousers. He didn't wear a crown, but the royal insignia, a griffin, was embroidered on the chest of his tunic. It should have been a bold silver, but the shadows washed out all color—even the crystalline-blue shade of his eyes.

"Your majesty," I said, a slight smirk toying at my lips. Shadow walking meant we could visit each other whenever we desired, despite the distance between Cruor and Wilheim, Lendria's capital city. It was a small boon in an otherwise unfortunate predicament. I'd never expected the guild to feel so empty without the man who had somehow, over the years, become my closest friend.

He scoffed, and the shadows about his jaw fluttered in response. "Not you, too. Calem already says it every chance he can."

"He does it precisely because it elicits a rise out of you." I leaned back in the chair, allowing my muscles to mold into the worn fabric. It'd only been a week since Noc and Leena's wedding and subsequent crowning ceremony. And Calem, who was undoubtedly causing a ruckus somewhere within the guild, made it a point to refer to Noc as "king" whenever the opportunity arose. Calem's relentless antics were often tiresome, but at least for the moment they weren't directed at me.

"Yeah, well," he glanced about the room, as if taking in the familiar surroundings of his former office, "I'll have to come up with something equally irritating to call him."

"Good luck with that." I braced my elbows on the desk and straightened a stack of bounties. "How's everything going?"

"We're making progress. Trade has officially reopened with Rhyne, so we should see an increased shipment in goods in the coming weeks."

"And Captain Harlow?" I raised a careful brow. We'd struck a deal with the scheming pirate during our fight against the former king Varek, granting Harlow the sole right to command a fleet of transport ships between Lendria and Rhyne. While Noc likely could've reneged on his promise, he remained true to his word and hoped the profits from such work would entice her to stay in line.

Noc grimaced. "About as pleasant as expected, but I have people in place to make sure she doesn't turn to marauding along our new ally's coast."

"I'm sure we can afford to send a few members down that way if necessary." I shuffled the parchment before me, eyeing a few requests and the details of the hits.

"Not necessary." Noc ghosted his hand along the bookshelves lining the wall as he moved toward the desk. Shadows dissipated and appeared with every subtle shift, and his fingers turned to wisps as they grazed the bindings. "If anything, we need the help in Hireath."

Hireath. When the legendary dragon Ocnolog rose from his underground tomb, he'd destroyed the peaceful city. Gone were the elaborate houses built high in the trees. The breathtaking keep that'd been carved out of an alabaster mountain near the falls had been reduced to rubble. The gargantuan tree housing the library—burned to ash. Ocnolog had leveled it all. Set it ablaze and never looked back. There was nothing left but debris, charred trees, and scorched grass. Fortunately, we'd evacuated everyone before he'd awoken. While many used the newfound peace between Wilheim and the Charmers to find homes elsewhere, Hireath was still a sacred site, and the Charmer's Council would not rest until it was restored to its former glory.

Most of the Charmer's Council. I pursed my lips. "Gaige hasn't been back yet."

"I know." Noc came to a halt across from me, eyes cast downward. "Kaori and Raven have been asking about him. They're handling the rebuilding effort just fine, but they worry. We all do."

"Ozias has tried to get him to train with the others. But..." I stood and began to pace. The study walls seemed to close in as I strode from one end of the room to the other. Ozias, my second-in-command and personal friend, was an expert at teaching members of Cruor to control the shadows. Even so, he couldn't coax Gaige to learn.

And that was a dangerous thing.

"I don't know what to do," I said.

"How close is he?" Noc's question was barely audible, but it rang through my mind with the force of a gong.

"Too close." I stopped and removed my glasses, pinching the bridge of my nose. Then, I extracted a small, mulberry cloth from my breast pocket and polished the lenses. "I don't think he has much time life."

Noc strode toward me and placed his hands on my shoulders. The lack of true contact was apparent, but the icy familiarity of those dark tendrils soothed my frayed nerves. "He'll come around. He has to."

Or he won't, and we'll lose him to the shadows. The unspoken truth of Gaige's future hung heavy in the air, and I swallowed thickly. Learning to wield the shadows was a necessity. If they grew with abandon, unconstrained and ravenous, they'd devour their host and pull them deep into the shadow realm, never to be seen from again. I'd only witnessed such a fate once before, and even then, Talmage, the guild master before Noc, killed the assassin before the darkness could swallow him whole. The power behind those virulent ink-black tendrils had been otherworldly.

And Gaige's shadows were nearly just as disastrous.

Noc let his hands fall to his sides. "Leena and I leave tomorrow for Rhyne. When we return, we'll stop through Cruor on our way to Hireath. If he hasn't figured it out by then, she'll knock some sense into him."

With a quiet sigh, I replaced my glasses. "I hope she's successful."

"She will be." Noc tipped his chin ever so slightly, peering at me for a long moment before frowning. "I hate to leave to abruptly but..."

"Go." I waved him off as I returned to the desk. I slid into the chair and grabbed the nearest quill and inkwell. "I need to evaluate these contracts and determine who would be best suited for the jobs."

"Maybe Gaige needs an assignment. Purpose will help." Shadows gathered around him in a flurry, temporarily darkening the room and obscuring the candlelit chandelier. He hesitated for a breath, half his body already lost to the shadow realm and other still firmly planted in my study. "We won't lose him, Kost."

But as I nodded in answer and Noc disappeared, I couldn't help but feel like we'd lost Gaige already. The man we knew before had died. This new person was shrouded in a darkness I couldn't control, and no matter how much I wanted to try and pierce that veil, I wasn't sure he'd let me. For what must have been the fifth time that evening, I pushed aside the bounties and returned to the window. But when my eyes scoured the quiet, manicured lawns, Gaige was nowhere to be found. While I knew the shadows hadn't claimed him yet, there was something sinister about the way the darkness cast by the Kitska Forest seemed to pulse with power.

One way or another, the shadows would come calling. And the only person who could stop them was Gaige.